Billionaire BACHELOR

LAURA LEE

Editing: Ellie McLove at My Brother's Editor

Cover Design: Y'All That Graphic

This one's for my fellow smut-loving neurospicy babes.

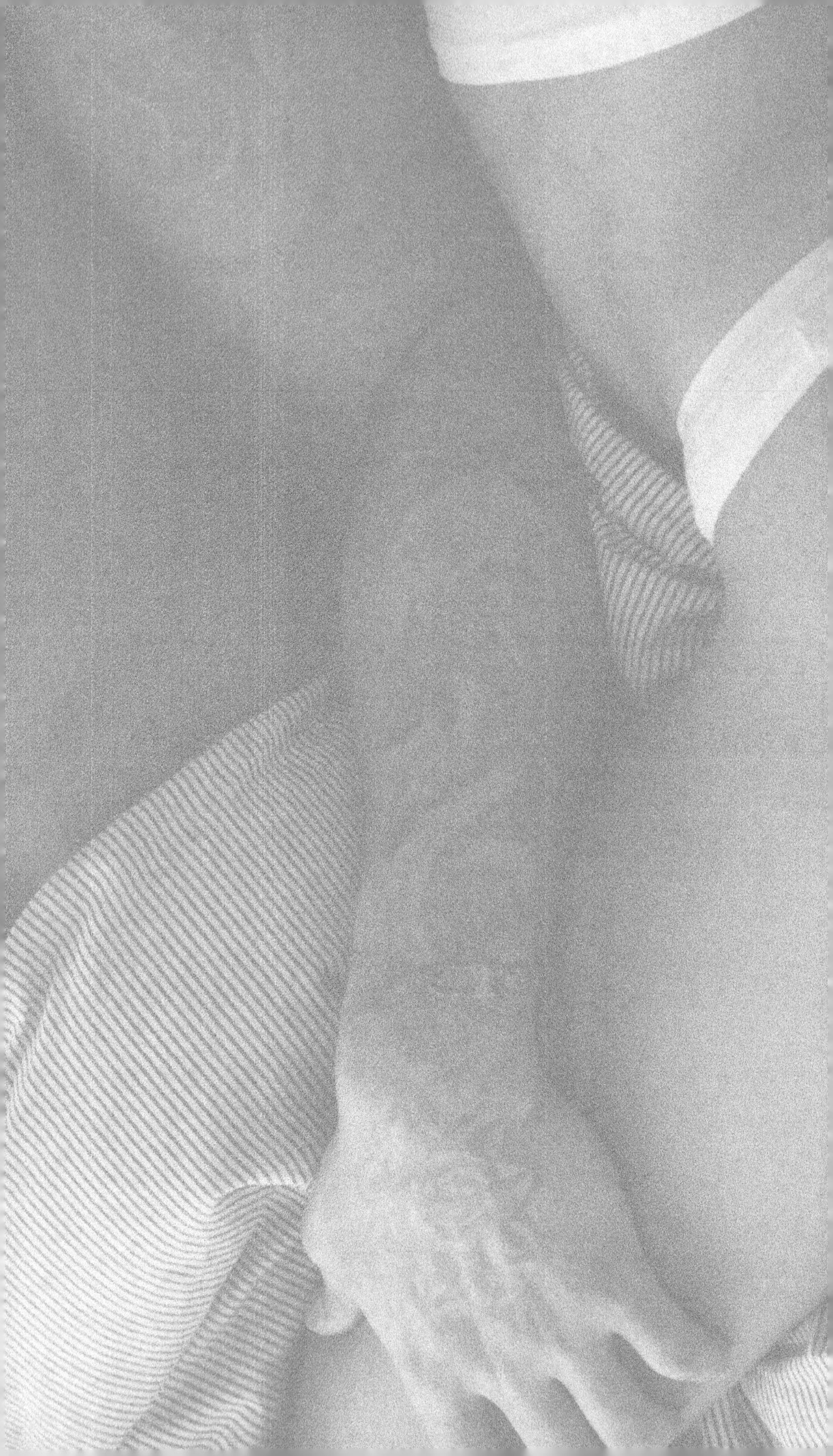

CHAPTER ONE
ROSALIE

If Valentine's Day were a man, I'd punch that bastard in the nuts faster than I'd swipe left on the guy whose job is listed as *Health and Wellness Coach*.

Fool me once, shame on you. Fool me twice, and suddenly I'm drowning in enough protein powder to outlast Armageddon. You'd think I'd learn after the first fiasco, but apparently, my optimism knows no bounds—much like my talent for dating douchebags. Case in point. Julian, my boyfriend of two years, got down on one knee last Valentine's and promised me forever. Too bad *forever* only lasted until he got caught banging the neighbor. So instead of walking down the aisle today in a pretty white dress—*gah, I want to puke just thinking about how cliché that is*—I'm escaping to my family's cabin in Tahoe.

Thank god I had the foresight to plan this trip so I could get the hell out of LA and its sea of red and pink everywhere I turned. The reminders of my failed engagement were suffocating, and I couldn't take it for another second. Julian despises the cold, so spending what would've been our wedding day in a winter wonderland is sweet, sweet irony. I'm actually looking forward to having three whole days of solitude, copious amounts of wine, and not a stupid cupid in sight.

As I drive south from the airport, the scenery gradually shifts from the urban sprawl of Reno to towering pines, and as the miles tick by, I can almost feel the weight lifting off my shoulders. On the tail end of my journey, an incoming call rings through the vehicle's Bluetooth connection. I came here to get away from civilization, but I happily accept it when I see one of my favorite people's names on the display.

Hitting the green phone button, I say, "Miss me already, huh?"

"Bitch, I'm too busy and sleep deprived to miss you," Sylvie replies. "You're lucky I'm even taking the time to grace you with this conversation."

"Well, I'm honored you decided to be so magnanimous. To what do I owe the pleasure?" I glance at the clock. "It's been less than twelve hours since we last spoke."

Sylvie is technically my cousin, but we're the same age and grew up together, so we're more like sisters. We haven't gone more than a few days without talking to each other our entire lives.

Don't let the sarcasm fool you—it's our love language.

"I know reception can be spotty at the cabin, so I wanted to check in one last time before you get there. I'm also driving back from my postpartum checkup—where I got the all-clear to screw Hudson's brains out. Go me! And I had to tell you what happened this morning."

"What?"

"Well...you know how I told you that whenever Olivia cries my boobs leak?"

One of my favorite things about Sylvie is she rarely

censors herself. What you see is what you get, and over-sharing is her jam. Since she recently pushed a human out of her vagina, she's had all sorts of gross, yet incredibly amusing, stories.

"I believe the exact words you used were, 'My giant milk jugs turn into Niagara freaking Falls,'" I deadpan.

"Yeah, *that*." She laughs. "Anyway...since my vag has been out of commission, Hud's been spending *a lot* of extra time playing with my boobs. He's kind of obsessed with them, really, since they're enormous right now. Not that I mind because I've learned nipple orgasms are *not* a myth, but that's neither here nor there."

"Lucky bitch," I tease.

"Maybe you'll get to experience it for yourself one day if you ever date someone who isn't a selfish prick."

"Harsh," I complain.

"But not untrue," she insists.

She's not wrong. I haven't had the best luck with men.

"Was there a point to this story?"

"I'm getting to that," Sylvie huffs. "Pay attention, Rosalie. So, this morning, we were fooling around, and we were pressed for time because, you know, kids. Well, Hud was *really* going to town sucking on my nipples, shooting for the aforementioned nipplegasm. Anyway, right before I was about to get off—seriously, I was *so* freaking close—Olivia started wailing. Since the monitor is right by our bed, my body thought it was baby breakfast time.

"Without warning, the dam broke, flooding Hudson's mouth so fast, it flew down the wrong tube. He was coughing and gagging, and drooling, and his face was so red, I was legit concerned he wasn't getting enough oxygen."

I press my lips together, trying my best to contain my laughter.

"Rosa, are you listening to me?! *I deep throated my husband with breastmilk!*"

Aaaaand just like that, I lose it, laughing so hard I snort. Leave it to Sylvie to make me laugh on a day like this. Between a newborn and her young stepdaughter, she should be exhausted, but Syl always finds time to make me feel like less of a disaster.

"Wow. That's quite the visual."

"I know, right? I mean, a little leakage is totally normal when having sexy times with a nursing woman, but I never thought I could drown the poor man with my tits. I usually have *some* kind of warning before they go into full let-down mode, and even then, it's never been *that* powerful before."

"Speaking of your husband...how did he handle his near-death-by-boob experience?"

"That's the best part!" she shouts. "As soon as he stopped gasping for air, he wiped up the saliva hanging from his chin, then it was as if it never happened! He was totally *Mr. Cool-as-a-Cucumber-I-Totally-Didn't-Almost-Die-Choking-On-Breastmilk.* He felt bad that I was robbed of an orgasm though, so he promised to make it up to me tonight."

"Man, he's a keeper, that's for sure."

Sylvie's sigh is audible over the phone line. "That he is."

A grin stretches across my face, as I think about how happy my cousin has been since reconnecting with her soulmate. They give me hope I might find that one day, too. Our conversation has taken the edge off my moodiness, which I suspect may have been her intent. Sylvie knows how much I've been dreading this day and exactly why I've chosen to become a recluse for the weekend.

"Anyway," Sylvie says, "I'll let you go. Remember, if

you need to vent or anything, call me anytime, day or night. I mean it, Rosa."

"Thanks, Syl. I love you. And tell Hudson he's a trooper."

"Will do. Love you, cuz. Don't do anything I wouldn't do!"

"Which leaves very few things off the table," I tease, disconnecting the call after saying our goodbyes.

The last bend before I reach my destination reveals the vast expanse of Lake Tahoe, its mirror surface reflecting the morning sky, framed by white-capped pines and distant mountains. The snow is falling steadily, leaving a fresh coat on the ground, making it even more breathtaking. The snow crunches beneath my tires as I turn down the private road that leads to our cabin. As I catch my first glimpse of the familiar log dwelling, I spot a bright blue BMW SUV parked on the slab off to the side of the front deck.

What the hell?

My parents and brother are the only other people who have access to this place, and I know for a fact all three of them are back in LA. I didn't tell my family I was coming here because I didn't want their pity. Not that I thought I had to—this cabin has been in my family for three generations, and they're fiercely protective of it. Renting it out is completely off the table. We have a local management company that checks on the cabin once a month to make sure everything's in order, but they usually handle that at the beginning of the month.

Still, someone is definitely inside. The thick smoke puffing out of the stone chimney leaves no doubt. My pulse kicks up as I pull in right beside the Beemer and shift my rental into park.

Who could be here? It's gotta be the management company, right?

I grab my phone to call my brother, Ryan, to see if he knows anything, but the screen taunts me with *SOS Only*.

"Dammit," I mutter, pulling the keys from the ignition.

I summon all the courage I can muster and step into the crisp air. I decide to knock rather than use my keycode—I don't want to startle whoever's inside. Plus, my odds of fleeing if there's an axe murderer in there are much better if I stay outside. I climb the front steps, hand raised to knock, when the door swings open, scaring the crap out of me.

"Stay back!" I shout. "I know karate!"

"Rosie?" The man's voice is deep, rumbling, like maybe he just woke up.

It takes a moment for my brain to process, but when I notice who's standing in the doorway, framed by the warm glow of the cabin, my heart drops to my feet. The mystery guest is none other than Logan Edwards—my brother's best friend and the star of every teenage fantasy I've ever had. Okay, and maybe a few of my grownup fantasies, too. It's not like it's my fault, though. The man is ridiculously attractive, *all the damn time.*

Even now, standing before me with his messy dark blond hair and annoyingly sharp hazel eyes, wearing simple jeans and a fisherman's sweater that shouldn't look good on *anyone*—but somehow, he makes it work. And then you have the bare feet—strong and masculine, with clean lines and well-groomed nails—just casually gripping the hardwood floor, completely unaware they could make a fortune on OnlyFans. My god, since when are feet so cliteriffic? The man doesn't even have an oddly long toe, for shit's sake. Only Logan Edwards could make feet sexy, I swear. Of course, he had to be the one who witnessed my moment of supreme idiocy. *I know karate.* Where did that even come from?

"Logan?" My voice waffles between shock and...something else I'd rather not name because acknowledging it feels way too dangerous, given the circumstances. "What are you doing here?"

He looks as surprised as I am. "I could ask you the same. Ryan said the cabin would be free."

A thousand emotions whirl through me—embarrassment, annoyance, the old ache of unrequited love, and the unshakable rush that always surfaces when he's near me. Am I intruding on a romantic Valentine's weekend? I try looking behind him for any evidence of Logan's latest lady friend, but his stupid body is so big it's like trying to see through a wall.

Logan's eyes narrow as they look me over, landing on my bare arms. "Why aren't you wearing a coat? Get in here. It's below freezing." His gruff tone leaves no room for argument. I legit have to bite my tongue before I blurt out an enthusiastic, *Yes, sir.*

I blink as a large snowflake lands on the tip of my nose. "Um..." I jerk my thumb over my shoulder. "It's in the car. I should, um...probably get it. My bag is in there, too."

His jaw clenches. "Get inside before you turn into a popsicle," he demands, stepping aside to make room for me. "I'll get your stuff."

Sheesh. When did he get so bossy? And seriously, why is that so freaking hot?! As I pass by him, a hint of cologne fills my senses, stirring memories and desires I thought I'd packed away long ago.

Sure, keep lying to yourself, Rosa.

Logan's fingers flex as he holds out his hand, palm up, his stance solid and unwavering. "Keys?"

I drop the car keys into his hand as I kick off my Uggs. Call me a basic bitch all you want. If you want me to stop wearing my comfy-cozy sweater boots, you're going to have to pry them off my cold, dead feet.

"You really don't need to do that. I can get it."

"Rosie," he growls, stepping into a pair of shoes sitting by the door. "Park your ass in front of the fire. I'll be right back."

The authority in his voice sends a shiver down my spine, though I'll totally blame it on the cold if anyone calls me out. I shuffle toward the fire, grateful for the blast of heat as I rub my hands together. My gaze flickers around the room, scanning for signs of a feminine presence. Logan's coat was the only one on the hook, and there aren't any shoes by the door that aren't sized for ogres. But this cabin is tiny—most of the living space is visible from the front door —so if Logan does have a *friend* with him, she's probably in the bedroom or bathroom. It's Valentine's Day, for shit's sake. *Of course*, he brought a woman here.

Logan's relationships are fairly short-lived, but he never lacks female companionship for very long. I wouldn't be surprised if there was a literal line of women waiting for their turn to pounce. Not that I'm keeping track or anything.

Oh, god, what if they were in bed, and I interrupted them?

I do my best to stuff my mortification aside as I stand by the fire, rubbing my hands together some more. I take deep breaths, inhaling the comforting scent. You don't encounter wood-burning fireplaces too often anymore, which is a damn shame if you ask me. In no time at all, Logan is back, shaking the light dusting of snow off his head, and hanging my coat on a hook.

"I think I got everything." He sets my weekender bag on the entryway bench.

"I'm sorry for interrupting...whatever," I blurt out.

"Why are you apologizing?" He frowns. "You have every right to be here."

I shake my head. "But you were here first, and I don't want to intrude. I'll call around and see if any of the lodges have a room available." I cringe when I remember I don't have any reception. "Shit. My phone doesn't have any bars. Is yours working? If not, I can drive a bit until I get service, and then I'll call. I'll be out of your hair in no time, so you can get back to...whatever."

Logan leans against a post, crossing his arms over his broad chest. "That's the second time you've said that."

"Said what?"

"*Whatever*," he answers, tilting his head to the side. "What exactly do you think is going on here, Rosie?"

I can feel my face flushing, making this even more awkward. "It's Valentine's Day. You're hundreds of miles from home, in a cozy cabin overlooking picturesque scenery. Some might say it's the perfect setting for a romantic holiday weekend."

His brows lift. "And?"

"*And* I assumed you had *company*."

Logan's full lips curve into a smirk when I practically whisper that last word. "Why would you assume that?"

Oh, god, he's really going to make me say it, isn't he?

I gesture toward him. "Uh...because you're you."

"What does that mean?" His brows lift, his tone infuriatingly calm, like he's daring me to explain.

I roll my eyes. "Logan, let's cut the bullshit. You know *exactly* why I assumed you'd have someone here with you."

"Fair enough," he concedes, his smirk widening. "But

for your information, I've been here all week by myself." His gaze holds mine, unflinching, and I swear the green in his eyes just got brighter. "But I'm not alone anymore, am I? So, why don't you tell me what *you're* doing here, Pip? I get the feeling Ryan wasn't expecting you to show up."

Oh, how true that is. My older brother has made it crystal clear over the years that his best friend is off-limits. There's no way he would've knowingly put me and Logan in the same place at the same time. Which is complete bull-shit, if you ask me. Logan's shown no sign he'd want to date me, so I don't know why Ryan's panties are always in such a twist.

I give Logan a sad smile. "No, he wasn't."

The silence that follows is heavy, crackling with tension. Logan's hazel eyes travel over me slowly, pausing on my breasts, lingering just long enough to make my pulse skip. Heat floods my cheeks some more as I fight the urge to cross my arms over my chest.

When our gazes finally meet again, something unspoken passes between us—an undeniable charge, like the calm before a storm. And then Logan speaks, his voice low and full of intent, making my toes curl.

"Well, what your brother doesn't know won't hurt him, right?"

CHAPTER TWO
LOGAN

The expression on Pip's face is priceless. Her chocolate brown eyes widen in surprise as her pouty lips form into an O.

"What's the matter? Cat got your tongue?" I tease.

I bite back a groan when that tongue peeks out and wets her lips. Damn, she has no idea what that does to me.

"How long are you staying?" she asks, carefully ignoring my loaded question.

"Trying to get rid of me already?" Just for the hell of it, I wink.

I'll be the first to admit I'm a flirty guy. You'd think Rosie would be used to it by now, but it never fails to make her cheeks flush. One of my favorite things about her, if I'm honest.

"No." Pip coughs out a nervous laugh. "I'm just curious if you're going to be here the whole weekend."

"That's the plan," I reply. "Why? Do you have a hot date coming?"

My fists clench as I think about some random dude

showing up here. There'd only be one reason he'd do that, and it doesn't sit well with me, irrational as that may be.

"No." She frowns. "Do *you?*"

And just like that, the tension in my shoulders melts away.

"Nope." I grin. "Looks like it's just the two of us."

Rosie swallows as her eyes shift toward the hallway. "Well, since there's only one bed, and you've been using it all week, I guess I'll sleep on the couch."

Oh, hell no.

"Not going to happen, Pip. *I'll* sleep on the couch."

She rolls her eyes again. "Don't be ridiculous, Logan. You're, like, a foot taller than me, and your legs would hang off the edge."

"So?" I challenge. "Do you really think that matters to me?"

"Well, it matters to *me,*" Rosie huffs, propping a hand on her hip. "I know you're trying to be chivalrous or whatever because that's how you roll, but you can't deny it makes a lot more sense for the shorter person to take the couch."

"As obstinate as ever," I mutter. "Look. How about we table this argument for now? We have the whole day ahead of us. We can figure out our sleeping arrangements when it's actually time for bed."

Great, now I'm imagining Rosie in bed. Or me *with* Rosie in bed. I will my dick to drop that line of thinking, but it's much easier said than done.

"Fine."

The air feels thick with tension, like a rubber band on the verge of snapping.

I walk into the kitchen and grab a bottle of prosecco out of the wine fridge, hoping to lighten the mood. "You want a drink?"

"It's eleven in the morning," she points out.

I open the main fridge and grab some orange juice. "Mimosa, then?"

Her laughter echoes softly around the cabin, chasing away some of the heaviness between us. "I mean, I am technically on vacation, so why the hell not?"

"That's my girl." I wink again just to see her cheeks pinken some more. "Have you eaten yet? I don't have much to offer, but if you're hungry, I can do eggs and toast."

She crosses the room and takes a seat at the kitchen island. "Eggs and toast would be great."

"Consider it done."

As I crack eggs into the sizzling skillet, I let my gaze linger on her face. The cabin feels smaller with Rosie here, though not in a bad way. There's an undercurrent of awareness in the air, I think. It's subtle, but impossible to ignore.

I can't remember the last time I was alone with this woman, but one thing I know for sure. I won't waste the opportunity. I did enough of that when we were kids.

Rosie leans her elbows on the granite countertop, sipping her mimosa. "When are you heading home?"

"Next Saturday," I reply, flipping the eggs with a practiced flick of the wrist.

"And you came here for a quiet vacay?"

I nod. "Things are about to get really crazy at work, so this is my attempt to ward off the inevitable burnout I feel during an acquisition. I figured a change of pace would be good, and you can't really find peace and quiet in LA. Or snow," I add, gesturing toward the wall of windows where large flakes are steadily falling. "What about you? Long weekend?"

She nods. "Yeah. My flight leaves Tuesday morning."

"So, you're stuck with me for three whole days then."

Rosie's teeth press into her lower lip. "And nights."

"And nights," I repeat with a smile, thinking about our one-bed situation.

I don't care how stubborn she is. There's no way I'm letting Rosie sleep on the couch. And knowing her, there's no way she'll let *me* sleep on it either. She wasn't kidding when she said I'd hang off of the damn thing. This is a one-bedroom cabin, which leaves us with only one option. I'll be hard as a rock all night, dying to touch her, but I can be a gentleman if that's what she wants.

But I really fucking hope that's *not* what she wants. The universe has handed me the perfect chance, and I'd be a fool not to grab onto it.

I slide the golden, flawlessly cooked eggs onto two plates and add a couple slices of toasted sourdough. Placing the dish in front of her, I join her at the island with my breakfast and freshly topped-off mimosa.

"Thanks, this looks amazing," she says, her eyes lighting up as she takes her first bite. "I was planning to hit the grocery store on the way here," she continues. "But then Sylvie called, and I got distracted."

"We should go into town after we eat," I suggest. "I was planning on it anyway. The weather forecast calls for heavy snow this weekend, so it's better to be prepared."

Rosie nods in agreement, sipping her drink. "Sounds like a plan."

"How's Sylvie doing, anyway? She recently got married and had a baby, right?"

"She's disgustingly happy." Rosie laughs, her eyes sparkling with genuine affection for her cousin. "Living in oversexed wedded bliss—her words, not mine."

"Oversexed wedded bliss, huh?" I grin. "Sounds like my kind of marriage."

The laughter fades as we share a prolonged look until Rosie sets her glass down with a soft clink. "Do you ever see yourself settling down and getting married? You know, in the future?"

Her question is heavy with implications, so I take a moment, considering my answer carefully.

"I'm definitely not opposed to it," I finally say, meeting her gaze squarely. "With the right woman. If I ever get to that point in life, I want it to be a onetime deal. You know?" I clear my throat. "What about you? One minute I'm getting an invitation to your wedding, and the next, you're no longer engaged. What happened there?"

I can't say I wasn't relieved when Rosie called off her engagement. There's no way I would've skipped the wedding, given how close I am to her family, but the thought of watching her marry a guy who clearly didn't deserve her had been eating me alive. Hell, if I'm being honest with myself, I can't stand the thought of her marrying *anyone* else, no matter how awesome the guy might be. I don't normally believe in woo-woo stuff, but the fact that Rosie's here with *me* on the day she was supposed to marry that douchebag, makes me wonder if there are cosmic forces at play, finally working *with* me instead of against me.

What I don't know is *why* Rosie left him. The only time I get to see her these days are during Morales family get-togethers. They're a tight-knit group, so that happens on a fairly regular basis, but I can't exactly get her alone under her brother's watchful eye. I've thought about asking Ry more than a few times, but I didn't want him to get suspicious about the reason behind my curiosity.

Rosie sighs, the lightness in her eyes dimming. "Well, it's about as cliché as it gets. He proposed last Valentine's

Day, and as you know, we planned to get married this Valentine's Day. But right before Christmas, I caught him in bed with our neighbor. I'd left to do some last-minute shopping, but when I got to my car and realized I'd forgotten my phone, I went back upstairs to grab it. I was gone less than ten minutes, Logan. They must've been waiting for me to leave the apartment and jumped into bed the second I walked out the door."

I curse under my breath, gut clenching at the thought of someone hurting her like that.

"Afterward...Julian admitted they'd been having an affair since last June. The asshole begged me to stay. Said she meant nothing to him and promised it would never happen again. But I was done the moment I caught them. He was screwing her in *our* bed. The cheating was bad enough, but that felt like an extra level of betrayal. You know? So, I packed my shit and stayed with my parents for a couple of weeks until I could find a new place. Sylvie saw them at Starbucks just last week, and she was sporting a shiny new rock on her left hand, so clearly she means *something* to him."

"He's a dumbass."

And so am I, apparently. I spent Christmas Day at her parents' place, but I had no idea she'd been living there at the time. How in the hell did I miss that?

"Thanks, Logan." She gives me a dejected smile. "But really, it's fine. I dodged a major bullet. Better to find out before the I dos, right?"

"Definitely." I nod, then decide to change the subject to something lighter, because I can't bear the sadness in her eyes. "But hey, on the bright side, at least you didn't end up as fodder for *StarBuzz*."

I feel ten feet tall when her eyes brighten, and her

laughter fills the room again. "Oh, the poor billionaire bachelor. Must be tough, your tragic life of luxury surrounded by a bevy of babes."

"First of all, I think *bevy* is a bit of an exaggeration." I shoot her a mock glare. "Second, I never asked for this pseudo-fame I've somehow acquired, and I certainly don't understand why the paparazzi give a single shit about me. Got any professional insight?"

Rosie works for a PR firm that manages A-list celebrities, so she's no stranger to those vultures.

"Well...you can't exactly stumble out of nightclubs with actresses and supermodels in Los Angeles and *not* get noticed by the paps. Not when you look like you could be a leading man yourself."

"Okay, I get that," I grumble, combing a hand through my hair. "But why are they *still* interested? I haven't been to a club in over six months, which is like six *years* in Hollywood."

"It could be a lot worse." She shrugs. "At least they don't camp outside your building or chase you wherever you go. You're more of an opportunistic photo grab."

"Could you break that down for me in non-PR terms?" I deadpan.

Her lips quirk. "Basically, if a pap is out and about and they spot you, they'll take the shot. But they're not going to actively seek you out. You need to watch your back in public, but they're not disrupting your daily life."

"Still...I can understand if I'm *out and about* with a celebrity, which barely even happens anymore. But when I'm alone? I really don't get it. I'm just a computer nerd, trying my best to fly under the radar."

She chuckles. "Except you're the *worst* kind of nerd. I don't think you're capable of flying under the radar."

"What's that supposed to mean?"

Rosie twirls her index finger in my direction. "Well, physically speaking, you're the opposite of the computer nerd stereotype. You've got the whole sexy, bad boy thing going on, with your leather jackets, the tats, and the Ducati. The fact that you're also smart, successful, kind, and funny? *Of course*, they're going to be interested in you, Logan. You can't possibly be that naïve after growing up in LA. Paparazzi love the pretty people, and you, my friend, are definitely a member of that club."

"Was that a compliment?" I ask, feigning confusion, but I'm strutting around like a peacock in my mind.

I'm not usually an arrogant shit, but a compliment from Rosie Morales is the best kind of high.

"Maybe," she teases, tucking a strand of hair behind her ear. "Depends on whether you use your powers for good or evil."

I lean into Rosie's ear. "In my experience, the people sporting halos aren't having nearly as much fun as those who aren't."

She playfully swats me away, but I don't miss the goose bumps scattering up her arms. "You're an idiot."

My mouth gapes in mock offense. "I'm wounded, Pip. Really."

She lets out an adorable little snort-laugh. "I'm sure your ego is as big as ever, Logan." Her gaze wanders down my torso. "Among other things."

Well, well, well.

Is Rosie Morales actually flirting back?

My brain short-circuits for a second, caught somewhere between smug satisfaction and pure, unfiltered need.

I lean in closer. "Careful, Pip. You keep looking at me like that, and I might forget how to behave."

She doesn't back down. Instead, she tilts her head, lips curving into a slow, teasing smile that makes me wonder if she knows just how much power she holds. "Who said I wanted you to behave?"

Well, okay then.

Blood rushes straight to my cock, and if I stay here a second longer while she's giving me those eyes, I'm going to do something reckless—like kiss the hell out of her and never want to stop. The stool scrapes loudly against the floor as I bolt to my feet, grabbing my keys from the counter like they might save me from myself. "Let's head into town."

Her brows shoot up. "What?"

"The grocery store," I clarify, quickly snuffing out the fire.

She's staring at me like I've lost my mind. "But...the food."

I glance at her half-eaten eggs. "I'll buy you a muffin. There's a new drive-thru coffee stand on the way. C'mon, you know you can't stop thinking about it now."

The girl never turns down an offer for baked goods.

The excitement in her eyes tells me she has no plans on starting now. "Fine, let's go, Mr. Impatient. But for the record, you're acting like a crazy person. And I want *two* muffins."

"Crazy about you," I mumble under my breath.

She freezes for a beat, her cheeks flushing a deep shade of pink. "What did you say?"

I clear my throat. "I said, *deal*. Two muffins it is."

Her brows pull together in mild suspicion, but she doesn't press me on it. Instead, she grabs her coat from the hook by the door and slips it over her shoulders. "Are we going, or what?"

"Now who's the impatient one?" I chuckle as I watch

her hopping on one foot, trying to put her boots on. "Having trouble there?" I pull on the socks that were stuffed in my shoes, and slide into my Air Jordans, giving her a look that says, *See how easy that was?*

Her brown eyes narrow as she continues the little hop-shuffle-hop thing she has going until both feet are covered. "Ass," she grumbles. Rosie gasps as we step outside into the crisp winter air, the cold biting at our faces as snowflakes tumble from the sky. "You can't just dangle a muffin in my face and expect me not to bite. Sheesh, it's like you don't know me at all."

My lips kick up in the corner. "I probably know you better than most, Morales."

She bumps her shoulder into my arm. "If that were true, we'd be on the road already. Because someone who knows me as well as you think you do, would know I turn into a beast when I'm hungry."

Her quippy response makes me grin. God, I've missed this. Her quick wit, the way she's always ready to spar with me.

"Oh, trust me, I am *well* aware of that fact."

Rosie skips ahead a little, flipping me the bird along the way. "Get a move on, Edwards."

I take a second to appreciate the view—of her and everything around us. Freshly fallen snow, the quiet woods, the crunch of her boots on the icy gravel as we approach my rental.

I open the passenger door, and Rosie pauses before sliding in, eyes locking with mine. "Thanks," she murmurs softly, her cheeks still a little pink from earlier.

I wink. "Anytime, Pip."

I climb into the driver's seat and press the ignition button, the heater humming softly as we make our way down the long driveway. Rosie flips through the radio stations, landing on some pop song that fades into the background of my racing thoughts.

Out of the corner of my eye, I see her staring out the window, seemingly deep in thought. But there's a restlessness to her...her knee bouncing slightly, her fingers absently toying with the zipper of her coat. Rosie's always had trouble sitting still, but she's learned how to hide it pretty well over the years. Right now, though? She's downright twitchy.

The more she fidgets, the tighter her lips press together, like she's trying to stifle the impulse to blurt something out. Sometimes, Rosie will start a sentence inside her head but finish it out loud—which is what I suspect she's trying to avoid right now. She calls it one of her many ADHD quirks. I call it cute as hell. I love those brief glimpses into her mind, unfiltered and real, even in small doses.

I wish she'd let it spill because I need to know if she feels the same buzz I'm feeling. That undercurrent of energy between us has always been there, humming in the background. But when I opened the door earlier and saw her standing on the porch, it surged to life, impossible to ignore.

I grip the steering wheel tighter, forcing myself to focus on the road ahead. I've got three days, I remind myself. Three whole days with Rosie Morales. No distractions. No interruptions. And most importantly, no big brothers throwing death glares my way every time I look at her.

For the first time in years, I feel like maybe, just maybe, I have a chance to shoot my shot.

And I can't fucking wait to see if I score.

CHAPTER THREE
ROSALIE

Stepping out of the warm cocoon of Logan's rented BMW into the crisp winter air is a jolt to the senses. The snowflakes are falling thick and fast now, and the wind is blowing lightly.

"Gah!" I shout as a fat flake lands in my eye. "Right in the eyeball!"

Logan laughs beside me, his breath a cloud in the chilled air. "That's what she said."

I give him the side-eye. "Real mature, Edwards."

His brows lift. "Don't pretend you weren't laughing on the inside."

"I admit nothing." I stick my tongue out, making him laugh harder. A sudden gust of wind blows right up my puffer coat, causing my teeth to chatter slightly. "Damn, it's nipple-y out here."

Logan steps closer as we approach the store, shielding me from the wind. "I'll have to take your word for it." He gives me a playful grin. "But if you're in the mood for a little show and tell later, you just let me know, Pip."

"Haha," I mutter, thankful I have the cold to blame for my rosy cheeks.

Fucking hell, I've blushed more in the last few hours than I have in the last few years.

I don't know what it is about this man, but the slightest innuendo makes my cheeks flame like a nun caught red-handed in the smut section.

Inside the grocery store, Logan grabs a cart and gestures for me to lead the way. We start in the produce section, where a vibrant array of vegetables gleam under fluorescent lights.

"You good with a big salad for lunch tomorrow?" I pick up a bag of mixed greens and place it in the cart. "We can grab some grilled chicken from the deli for yours, if you'd like."

"Sure," Logan replies, carefully inspecting some bell peppers. "You're still avoiding meat, right?"

"Yo ho! Yo ho! A vegetarian's life for me," I singsong to the melody from *Pirates of the Caribbean.*

He shakes his head, eyes twinkling with amusement. "Now who's the geek?"

"A." I point to him. "I called you a *nerd*, not a geek. And B, we've already established you make a *terrible* nerd."

"Oh, that's right." Logan rubs his chin in mock contemplation. "Why was that again? I can't quite remember."

"Yeah, right." I snort. "You can keep on fishin' for those compliments, buddy, but I'm not biting."

"Noted. You're not a biter." I startle when his lips suddenly touch my ear as he adds, "But what's your stance on being bitten?"

An image of Logan's sandy hair between my thighs as he's nibbling on my sensitive skin flashes through my head.

Dear god.

I give him a little shove, trying my best not to look as aroused as I suddenly feel. What is with him today? Logan's naturally flirtatious, but he's never been so bold with me.

Except that one time we both like to pretend never happened.

"Pip, did you hear me?"

"Huh?" I blink a few times as I realize I was spacing out.

Logan gives my ear a little flick. "I asked if vegetarian chili and cornbread sounds good for dinner tonight. I have a kickass recipe in my arsenal."

"That sounds amazing," I tell him. "Since when do you have *any* recipes in your arsenal?"

"I'm full of many surprises." He grins shamelessly.

Oh, I bet you are, big guy.

We weave through the aisles, Logan steering the cart with a practiced ease. It feels odd, doing something so domestic with him, but at the same time, it feels perfectly natural. I guess it's not so strange when I consider how much time we've spent together growing up. I've always felt comfortable just hanging out with him.

When we cruise through the bakery section, which is loaded with Valentine's treats, my inner Bitter Betty is nowhere to be found. I think talking about what happened with Julian earlier made me realize how much I *don't* miss what we had. Considering it's been only two months since we ended our relationship, that's a real eye-opener for me. Sure, I'm pissed about his betrayal, and I feel like an idiot for not seeing the signs that were *definitely* present. But I don't actually miss *him*. Hell, I'm *glad* I'm not getting married today.

I spot freshly-baked heart-shaped doughnuts and rub my hands together in glee. "Oh, come to Mommy, you beautiful things."

Logan chuckles. "The muffins you inhaled in the car weren't enough?"

I gasp. "I did not *inhale* them! I nibbled them like the delicate lady I am."

"Whatever you say, Pip." He shakes his head, giving me a *"You're delusional"* look.

I glare, but let it drop, because we both know I hoovered those muffin tops down in less than five minutes. There was nothing delicate or ladylike about it, but I have no regrets. They were freaking delicious.

I set a four-pack of doughnuts in the cart. "Besides, there's no such thing as too many baked goods. You're just jealous I'm not a weirdo who doesn't appreciate them. You know that's not natural, right?"

"I like *some* baked goods," he argues. "I've just never had much of a sweet tooth."

"You like *one*." I hold up my index finger. "And if you ask me, cheesecake barely counts, unless it's the triple chocolate from Sweet Temptations."

Logan smirks. "Agree to disagree, Pip."

I smile in victory. "Agree to disagree" is Logan speak for "I know you're right, but I don't want to admit it."

We continue our shopping adventure, and when we get to the spice aisle, Logan reaches over to grab some cumin, sending a jolt through my veins when his arm accidentally brushes against my chest. I catch my breath, hoping he doesn't notice the effect he has on me.

Play it cool, chica.

"Don't think I didn't notice you sneaking chocolate," I tease, nodding toward the Cadbury bar he's tucked halfway beneath the bread.

"I'm using that to make hot chocolate. If you ask nicely, I might even be willing to share."

"Or I can just get my own," I say, laughter bubbling up between us.

God, I feel so much lighter than I did when I got off the plane this morning, and I know the man beside me is partially responsible for that. Maybe I was supposed to run into Logan this weekend. Maybe the powers that be knew spending time with him would help bring this sudden epiphany of mine to the surface.

As we approach the checkout, the narrow lane nudges us to stand even closer. Logan's cologne—a combination of cedar and cinnamon—makes me want to bury my nose in his neck, maybe even nibble his ear near that tiny silver hoop he wears. I never knew a grocery store could be so damn erotic, but this one sure is.

Time for a distraction, Rosa.

"So, after we get back to the cabin, what's next? Are we doing it like Anna and building a snowman or maybe a snowball fight? I promised myself some snowy fun while I'm here, which means you are obligated to join in on said fun, since you're here, too."

Logan's smile turns mischievous. "A snowball fight could be fun. Fair warning, though, I've got a pretty good arm."

"We'll see about that," I counter, bumping him playfully as we load the groceries onto the conveyor belt.

Logan insists on paying for the groceries, despite my protests. "Make me breakfast in the morning, and we'll call it even. I have a feeling we'll both be famished by then."

The words are innocent enough, but his tone is loaded with suggestion. My cheeks heat, and I can't help wondering if that was intentional. The cashier's knowing smile only adds to my embarrassment.

"Have a happy Valentine's Day, you two," she says as we wrap up.

Logan flashes her a grin while I duck my head, busying myself by zipping my coat. Damn him and his effortless charm.

We gather up the bags, arms full as we head out into the cold. After the last bag is stowed in the SUV, I take a moment to check my phone—habitual, really—wondering if the patchy mountain service has graced me with a bar or two. Surprisingly, I have full reception again, so I quickly type out a message to my cousin, my fingers numb from the cold.

> Me: So…the cabin was unexpectedly occupied when I arrived. By LOGAN. And he's being EXTRA flirty which is making me feel a certain kind of way. I don't know how to stop myself from wanting to climb him like a tree.

I hit send before I can second-guess sharing that bit of juicy news.

Sylvie's response is almost instantaneous.

> Sylvie: Why would you want to stop it? The big guy upstairs has handed you a golden ticket, Rosa. Jump his bones! Hard, fast, and REPEATEDLY. I expect a detailed report afterward, including measurements.

> Sylvie: *Austin Powers "Yeah, baby!" GIF*

> Sylvie: *Magic Mike floor humping GIF*

Heat rushes to my cheeks at Sylvie's not-so-subtle suggestion, and I can't help but chuckle softly to myself.

The thrill of it lingers, whirling in my chest, when I sense Logan close behind me.

Glancing up, I catch him leaning over my shoulder. His eyebrow arches, a teasing smirk tugging at his lips, but there's a question in his eyes, a curiosity that suggests he might have seen more than I'd hoped.

"Who are you texting, Pip?"

Flustered, I shove my phone back into my pocket with more force than necessary. "Just checking in with Sylvie while I have reception." God, I hope my voice doesn't betray the sudden spike in my pulse.

"Figured." Logan's smirk widens. "She's always had a way with words. And GIF selection, apparently."

Now, I *know* he read at least part of the conversation. Fuck my life.

Logan shuts the back hatch. "Do you want to stop anywhere else while we're in town? It looks like there's definitely a storm rolling in, so this might be our last chance."

I glance around, noting the fresh blanket of snow that has accumulated while we were in the store. In just thirty minutes, at least a couple more inches have piled up, turning the parking lot into a glistening sea of white.

"Wow. It's really coming down now. I'm good to go back if you are."

He walks over to the passenger side and opens my door, acting like it's no big deal he just caught me talking about possibly banging him. Well, fine. If he can pretend, so can I. "I'm good, too."

After I'm tucked inside, he rounds the hood and climbs behind the wheel. As Logan starts the engine, the warmth from the heater washes over me, melting away the chill. I snuggle deeper into my seat, pulling the edges of my coat closer. My phone vibrates quietly in my pocket, no doubt a string of innuendos and GIFs from my cousin, but I don't dare check it right now.

Logan's presence is both comforting and unsettling. Glancing over at him, I notice the focused way he navigates the snowy road, his hands steady on the wheel. A slice of sunlight cuts through the gray sky, highlighting the rugged contours of his face and his closely cropped beard. In this quiet moment, with Logan beside me, it's too easy to imagine what Sylvie suggested. Too easy to want it. I tear my gaze away, but it does nothing to derail my train of thought.

Could I have a no-strings-attached fling, just this once, to get him out of my system? Here, away from the real world, could Logan and I share something temporary that wouldn't make things awkward between us afterward? I could swear he's feeling the same sparks, the same curious tension that's been tugging at me since I arrived. The flirty banter, the way he's been looking at me, those fleeting glances laden with desire—am I imagining them? Would he be open to a weekend of being more than just my brother's best friend?

These thoughts run through my mind as Logan pulls into the cabin's driveway. He kills the engine, and the sudden silence feels heavy with potential.

"You okay?" he asks, his voice soft in the car's quiet.

"Yeah, just thinking about how much snow we'll need to shovel tomorrow." I offer him an airy grin that hopefully masks my inner musings.

Logan chuckles, reaching over to squeeze my hand briefly. "We'll manage."

We head inside, and as I put the groceries away, Logan starts a fire in the hearth with skillful hands, the glow of the flames dancing across his chiseled jawline. I can't help but admire his toned back and broad shoulders as they strain against his sweater. My heart races when he pulls that sweater over his head, setting it aside. The white T-shirt he has on underneath clings to his torso, showcasing the beautiful ink wrapped around each one of his arms. I imagine those strong limbs banding around me as I writhe in pleasure. His fingertips brushing over my skin, teasing me relentlessly until I'm begging him to put them inside of me.

"See something you like, Pip?" His voice is casual, but the heat in Logan's gaze tells me he's reading me like a book right now.

"Still on your fishing expedition, Edwards?" I sass, trying to throw him off the scent of my internal-quandary-slash-X-rated-daydream.

"Always," he replies with a wink.

When I catch myself practically drooling over a fantasy of the man sitting right in front of me, a sudden resolve settles in. I need to know if there's a chance for something real between us, even if it's temporary. I know Logan's no stranger to casual sex, but I'm not naïve. Nothing between us could ever be *just* casual. Logan's an undeniable part of my inner circle, a constant presence during the holidays and family barbecues.

I try to imagine Logan smiling across from me at our annual Fourth of July celebration, as if nothing had happened. Would we still joke and tease, or would the memory of us tangled in the sheets hang between us, forever changing the way we interact with one another? Or worse, what if I was the only one who couldn't stop thinking about it? My chest tightens at the possibility of him treating me like just another one of his fleeting hookups. I don't think that would happen, but it is something to consider.

I'm not sure if I'm ready for this, but the thought of

never knowing kills me. For once, I want to stop holding back and see what happens. I nearly married a man who never made my heart race, not even close to the way Logan does with a single glance. There's just something about him that makes me feel *alive* like no one else ever has. Thirty years from now, I don't want to look back on this moment, constantly wondering what could've been. The risk of crossing this line with him is enormous, but as I continue watching Logan move about the cabin with an ease that feels like home, I realize that the bigger risk might be never knowing at all.

CHAPTER FOUR
LOGAN

Pip's been acting weird since dinner, but I can't quite figure out why. I know she was impressed with my culinary skills because she wolfed down her bowl of chili like she hadn't eaten in days. She had *three* servings of my homemade cornbread, moaning with each bite she took. I love it when a woman has a healthy relationship with food, but listening to her making sex noises as she ate became painful. Literally. I don't think I've ever been so hard in my life, and denim isn't exactly an erection-friendly material.

"You want a refill?" I ask, placing a tab in the dishwasher and pressing start.

Rosie stretches her arm across the counter, holding out her wineglass. "Yes, please."

I grab the bottle of Pinot Noir and pour the last few ounces into the glass. "Damn, we finished this whole thing already. Want to open another?"

"Sure." Rosie nods, then tilts her head. "Total subject change, but did you happen to fill the hot tub and switch on the heat before I got here?"

I nod. "I did. It's nice and toasty with a perfectly balanced pH. Why?"

She gives me a coy smile. "I was thinking we should take that wine out to the hot tub. Interested?"

Hell yes, I'm interested.

Especially after seeing those text messages earlier. I know reading over her shoulder was a dick move, but when I saw the unmistakable look of arousal on her face, I couldn't resist. I had to know if she was sexting some dude. When I saw what she and her cousin were talking about, it took everything in me not to pin her against the car and let my instincts take over. I had to remind myself that Rosie Morales is not some random girl, therefore, I had to think this through. I'm not a moron. I know she's attracted to me. But I did *not* know she was considering acting on it before this afternoon.

I couldn't hold back my cheesy grin if I tried. "Absolutely. I'll grab my trunks and change in the bathroom. You can use the bedroom."

"'Kay," Rosie agrees, hopping off the stool she was perched on.

I change into my swim trunks as fast as humanly possible, grabbing a couple of bath towels from the linen closet before heading into the main living space. A minute later, Rosie is strolling into the room, wrapped in a fluffy white robe.

Damn, I can't wait to see what she has on underneath.

"Can you hold these for a sec?" I gesture to the towels.

"Sure." She extends her terrycloth-covered arms, grabbing the towels.

A bolt of static electricity shoots up my arm the second our fingertips brush against each other, and I swear to fuck, there's a visible spark between us.

Symbolism at its finest, ladies and gentlemen.

I reach into the wine fridge and retrieve the bottle of prosecco we opened earlier. "Does this work for you? I think there's enough left for two glasses."

"Is that a real question?" she sasses.

"Smartass." I make a gimme motion, waiting for the *better than being a dumbass* retort I know is coming. "C'mon, you know you're dying to say it."

She laughs. "Dying to say *what?* Did you suddenly develop mind-reading skills?"

I wish.

I remove the stopper from the bottle. "We've already established I know you better than most people. That's what happens when you spend nearly every day of your adolescence together."

"That's true," she concedes. "But we barely hang out anymore. Not like we used to."

That's because I couldn't stand seeing you with that douchebag, so I purposely kept my distance whenever he was around. Which was way too often, if you ask me.

My jaw clenches as I recall what that fucknut did to her. "What's your point?"

"*My point* is that I think you know Teenage Rosalie a lot better than Grownup Rosalie. Sometimes it feels like you still think I'm that starry-eyed girl who's always following her brother and his friend around."

My eyes slowly wander from her pink-tipped toes up to her beautiful brown eyes. The shapeless robe she's wearing does nothing to deter my cock from springing to life at the thought of watching her take it off.

"Trust me, Pip. I am *well* aware of how grown up you are."

She points to me. "The fact that you still call me Pip says otherwise."

I frown in confusion. "What does that have to do with anything?"

Rosie props a hand on her hip. "Logan, you gave me that stupid nickname on the day we met, when I was *eleven*."

"Yeah, because you were *tiny*, as in *pipsqueak*." I wave my hand toward her. "You still are. You're what? Five-two? That's fun-sized."

"Is not," she huffs. "Did you ever think maybe you're just a giant?"

I'm six-three and just over two hundred pounds. I'm certainly not a small guy, but I'm definitely not a giant either.

"You're ridiculous," I tell her. "Look, *Rosalie*. If anything, I call you Pip out of habit or affection, nothing more. I sure as shit do *not* think you're still some starry-eyed kid. I had no idea it bothered you so much. Now that I do, I'll try to eliminate it from my vocabulary."

She exhales. "It doesn't *bother* me, exactly. If I'm being honest, I kinda like the familiarity it implies. Don't stop using it, Logan."

I pinch the bridge of my nose. "Women are so confusing."

Rosie grins. "Oh, whatever. You'd be bored out of your mind if we didn't keep you on your toes."

I laugh, knowing she's right. "You've got me there, Morales."

"Exactly. Now shut up and thank me." She winks, nodding toward the back door. "C'mon, there's a hot tub calling our names."

I follow her, mesmerized by the sway of her hips. Rosie

flips on the exterior lights, brightly illuminating our path. She squeals as she opens the door, a blast of cold air rushing in.

I'm pretty sure my balls shrivel up as it hits me. "Holy shit, that's cold!"

We both start hauling ass across the snow-covered deck in our bare feet, racing toward the gazebo where the hot tub is. I barely have time to appreciate the view as Rosie tosses her robe onto the built-in bench and flips the lid open. In true Rosie fashion, she wastes no time, submerging herself into the bubbly water within seconds.

Dammit.

"Ah, that's good stuff," she groans, resting her head against the lip of the tub as the water lifts her legs when she stretches them out.

"I wouldn't know." I hop from side to side, trying to ward off the chill. "Think you could make a little room?"

She opens her eyes and spots me literally freezing my balls off while she hogs the whole thing. "Oops."

"Oops, my ass," I grumble, knowing damn well she did that on purpose.

The top of Rosie's breasts are exposed as she slides to the other side of the two-person tub. My eyes are instantly drawn to them like a beacon through the fog. I shake it off as I climb in, feeling like a creeper. I don't know what it is about this girl, but I can never seem to keep my eyes off her. Maybe it's the forbidden aspect—her being my best friend's little sister—but that thought fades as I reflect on the invisible tether that's always been between us. Normally, I'm much more discreet than this, though. Over the years, I've practically mastered the art of sneaking glances without getting caught.

"Shit," I say as I realize I didn't bring the wineglasses.

The thought of getting out of this warm tub so soon makes me cringe. "I forgot glasses."

Rosie smiles, taking the bottle of wine from my hand. "I don't mind drinking straight from the bottle if you don't." She takes a healthy swig. "I'm classy like that."

I grab the bottle back from her and take a small sip. "I'll swap bodily fluids with you any day of the week, babe. Just say the word."

Her eyes widen, and mine do, too, when I realize what I just said. Fuck. It was off the cuff, but the tension between us just went nuclear in this tiny Jacuzzi, the bubbly water doing nothing to suffuse it. We lock eyes, silently acknowledging just how slippery this slope has become. How obviously tempted we both are to lean into it. If she were anyone else, I'd have closed the distance and kissed her by now.

I should make some lame excuse and head back inside, but I'm frozen, wondering—waiting to see—what Rosie will do next. I'm leaving the ball in her court, letting her decide whether she wants to cross this line. We've danced around this for years, but her brother was always a barrier. And then Julian...that prick. But now we're both single, and Ryan's back in LA. There's nothing in our way if she gives me the green light.

Please, for the love of God, give me the green light.

Her gaze flickers to my mouth, and for a split second, I'm sure she's about to lean forward, but then she bites her lip instead.

Okay, I need to lighten this up before things go downhill. The last thing I want is for her to feel pressured.

I smirk, letting my shoulders relax a bit. "You know I was—"

"You know what we should do?" Rosie interrupts. Her

voice is softer now, almost as if she's testing the waters herself.

"What's that?" I ask, half expecting her to suggest we head back inside, but hoping like hell she doesn't.

Her gaze flickers downward, as if she's trying to see beneath the water. My pulse thrums in my ears as the moment stretches, the tension between us palpable.

After what feels like an eternity, she looks back up at me, a small, almost teasing, smile playing at her lips. "We should play, *Never Have I Ever*."

I blink a few times, processing her words. It wasn't a direct invitation to ravage her body, but I don't exactly hate the idea.

"Standard rules?"

"Yep." She nods.

"All right, Pip, I'll play." I sit up straighter, catching Rosie's gaze lingering on my chest. "Ladies first."

She taps her index finger on her lips, her eyes sparkling with mischief as she contemplates for a moment before kicking the game off. "Never have I ever...gotten a tattoo."

"Trying to get me drunk, I see. We might need more wine if you keep this up." I grin, taking a drink and passing the bottle. "Okay, let me think. Never have I ever...worn a dress."

Her eyes narrow as she lifts the bottle to her lips. "Never have I ever designed a dating app and sold it for one-point-three billion dollars."

"That was awfully specific." I give her a wry look before taking a big swig. "Never have I ever graduated from USC, majoring in public relations."

Rosie takes another sip. She stares at me for a few seconds, seeming to have some kind of internal debate. "Never have I ever gone down on a girl."

Well, that escalated quickly.

"Shame. I highly recommend it." I wink before taking a few gulps. "Never have I ever had a dick in my mouth."

"Shame. I highly recommend it," she mocks, right before grabbing the bottle from me and taking a drink.

I'm equal parts aroused and enraged at the thought of her giving head. The latter mostly because I know I wasn't the lucky recipient. Although, with the direction this game is heading—pun definitely intended—maybe my luck is changing.

"Never have I ever..." Rosie hesitates for a moment before continuing, "Had an orgasm during sex."

"Oh, shut the fuck up."

She glares. "Rude, much?"

"I didn't mean for it to come out like that." I shake my head. "But you have to admit, you aren't playing by the rules."

"How do you figure?" She stares me straight in the eye as her next words shock the shit out of me. "*I've never had an orgasm during sex.* Seems to follow the rules just fine."

My jaw drops when I realize she's not joking. "Wait... seriously? How is that possible?!"

"It's not from lack of trying." Her shoulders lift in a shrug. "I think maybe I'm just...broken or something."

I blink rapidly, absolutely flabbergasted. "Okay, I'm sorry, but you cannot tell me something like that without more detail. You've *really* never had an orgasm? You're twenty-seven."

"Thanks, Logan. I almost forgot how old I am. What would I ever do without you?" She gives me a look that screams, *jackass.* "And I didn't say I've never had an orgasm. I've had plenty of them using my own hand. Or toys."

Do not get sidetracked wondering about her toy collection, dude.

"Something isn't adding up. Break this down for me." I set the nearly empty bottle on the ledge that curves around the tub and rake a hand through my hair. "So, you haven't had an orgasm during penetration, right? I mean, that's not unheard of, I guess."

"Right," she replies, licking her lips. "Or during the foreplay that precedes it. And since this game's turned into *'Let's talk about how pathetic Rosa is,'* I've technically only had one partner-induced orgasm *ever*, back in college during some third-base action. And quite frankly, we were both so drunk, it's possible I imagined the whole thing."

"Shit."

If anyone is pathetic in this situation, it's the idiots she's been with—especially that asshole who was about to trap her into a marriage filled with mediocre sex. Why would she settle for that?

Rosie's shoulders lift. "For whatever reason, I just *can't* get there when someone else is doing the work. I can't turn my mind off—which, as you know, is totally normal for me— but it's pretty extreme during sex. I get so hyper-focused on trying to relax that I wind up stressing out about how I *can't* relax. And if I can't relax, I won't be able to come. And if I don't come, then I have to figure out if I'm going to fake it and just move on or be honest with my partner about my problem. And if I choose the latter, then I worry about how to break it to them, so their ego isn't smushed. And then I wonder about all the possible outcomes of *that* conversation. It's neurospicy self-sabotage at its finest. Like I said... broken."

Challenge fucking accepted, Pip.

If this isn't a sign that I need to get this woman naked as

soon as possible, I don't know what is. I mean, what kind of friend would I be if I let her go through life any longer thinking she's the reason the chumps she's been with couldn't get her off?

I spread my arms along the top of the tub. "I'm going to say something, and I need you to hear me out entirely before you say a word. Do you think you can do that?"

She eyes me warily. "I suppose."

"There's absolutely nothing wrong with you, Rosie." I hold my hand up when her mouth pops open to argue. "Seriously. Hear me out. If the guy is doing his job right, you wouldn't even have time to overthink it. You'd be too far gone, lost in the moment. Trust me—*he's* the problem, not you."

"I disagree." She shakes her head, her lips pressing into a frustrated line. "Look. I'll admit *some* guys I've been with didn't even try. But a few really did, Logan. They gave it their best shot."

I take a deep breath, tamping down the urge to growl like a damn caveman. Then, I look her directly in the eye, knowing what I'm about to say is going to make things really fucking awkward between us, or really fucking awesome.

"Well, then, if you're willing...I'd be honored if you'd allow me to prove you wrong."

CHAPTER FIVE
ROSALIE

When I suggested we take a dip in the hot tub, I thought we'd have some wine, a heavy dose of flirting, and maybe a side of banter. If things went especially well, we'd make out a little and then see where it goes from there. But never in a million years, did I think I'd share something so embarrassing, and in turn, Logan would offer to give me an orgasm.

Logan Edwards wants to give me an orgasm!

Me! An orgasm!

Am I hallucinating? Perhaps I drank more than I thought, blacked out, and now I'm dreaming. That makes a helluva lot more sense than all of my teenage dreams suddenly coming to life.

"Rosie? Did you hear what I said?"

I'd be honored if you'd allow me to prove you wrong.

"Oh, I heard you all right." I wave my hand breezily. "I'm just trying to figure out if you're real or a figment of my imagination."

Logan's deep chuckle reverberates through my veins. "I

can assure you, I am *very* real, sweetheart. If you come over here and sit on my lap, you'd have no doubt."

His hazel eyes burn through me, silently begging me to call his bluff.

"Are you screwing with me? Is this because of the texts you saw earlier?"

He takes a moment to answer. "I've never been more serious about anything in my life. Those texts were *awesome*. I would never give you—or any woman, for that matter—shit for being sex-positive. But I don't want to fuck this up, Rosie. You're too important to me."

His words slam into me, obliterating any lingering doubts about seeing this through.

"If you want this," he continues, his voice deep and rough, each word tinged with a gravelly edge, "I need you to make it crystal clear because once we cross that line, there's no going back. If you're not interested, that's cool, too. I promise I'll fully respect your decision, and we can pretend this entire conversation never happened."

I take a moment to steady myself, my pulse thrumming in my ears as my mind races. Logan's sincerity is undeniable, his raw emotion laid bare in the way he looks at me—open, honest, and unwavering. My decision is already made but acknowledging it—saying it out loud—will make it real, and that's what has my nerves buzzing like live wires.

Here we go.

The steaming hot water cascades down my body as I rise, sending shivers over my skin. My nipples harden in response to the cold air, drawing Logan's mesmerizing greenish-gold gaze. I close the short distance between us, straddling his lap with a confident grace. I can feel the undeniable evidence of his arousal beneath me, and without hesitation, I sink down.

"Fuck," he says under his breath, swallowing hard.

"I know." I moan as the outline of his shaft rubs against me, igniting sparks of desire throughout my body. "Is this clear enough for you?"

He wraps a hand around each one of my hips. "And then some."

"Good," I whisper as he tilts his chin up. "So, what are you going to do about it?"

His grip tightens, his thumbs pressing just enough to make my pulse hitch. "So many things."

The steam rises around us like a curtain, clinging to my skin. The hot water bubbles and hums beneath me, but it's nothing compared to the heat pooling low in my belly. Logan's eyes lock on mine—steady, unyielding, and blazing with intent—as the entire world around us seems to fade away.

When our mouths finally collide, an explosive rush of emotions and desire course through my veins. My lips part, and our tongues dance as I continue to grind on his lap. An inferno blazes between us, a fire that neither of us are in any hurry to extinguish. I can feel Logan's eager anticipation in every touch, every kiss, every thrust, and I return it with equal fervor.

"I never thought I'd have the chance to feel your lips again," he murmurs. "It's even better than I remember."

My breath catches as memories of that night flicker through my mind. They're soft and fleeting, his lips on mine, the faint taste of champagne on his tongue, and the bittersweet ache of something we both wanted but were too afraid to claim. But it ended before we ever really had a chance to begin. After that night, we seemed to have an unspoken agreement to pretend it hadn't meant *everything*.

God, why did we wait nine long years to do this again? We were such fools.

I nod in agreement, not trusting my voice to get the words out.

Logan's hands move to my jaw, fingers tracing the contours of my face. I run my hands through his hair, feeling its softness under my touch.

"You feel so fucking good, Pip. So fucking *right*."

"You, too," I pant.

There's a wild hunger in his eyes—a raw, burning desire I'm sure is reflected in mine. But Logan's carries a gentleness within, a promise that I'll always be safe with him.

"If you want to hit the brakes, or if I do anything you don't like, you tell me right away, okay? I mean it, Rosie. You're in the driver's seat here. Always."

"Okay," I agree, although in this moment, I can't imagine anything he could do that would be unwanted, unless it was stopping altogether.

My hands roam his body, feeling the hard muscles he's worked so hard to achieve. I trace the ink trailing down his right arm, dipping beneath the water until I reach his hand. Never breaking eye contact, I bring that hand over to my needy core, pressing it against me. Logan groans while I gasp, his cock jerking in response as the tip of his middle finger dips inside of me, the thin Lycra still between us.

Logan's hips buck upward, grinding his erection against me. "You have no idea how many times I've thought about this." His lips find my neck, trailing kisses over to the sensitive spot behind my ear, causing me to tremble in his arms. "How many times I've jerked off, imagining your hands, your mouth, your pretty, wet cunt gripping me instead."

"Sweet baby Jesus, that's hot," I pant.

He gives me a crooked grin. "You like it when I talk dirty, Rosie?"

I nod enthusiastically, adding a totally unnecessary "Uh-huh. A lot. Like, *a lot*, a lot."

His grin widens as he slowly reaches behind my neck with his free hand, pulling the tie of my bikini loose. Before releasing the strings, Logan's eyes meet mine, silently asking for permission. When I give him a subtle nod, the black triangles that were covering my breasts fall.

His eyes widen when he notices my piercings. "So fucking sexy." Logan's finger traces a circle around my right nipple, lightly brushing against the small barbell. "When did you do this?"

I gasp as he rolls the jewelry between his thumb and forefinger before sealing his mouth around my other nipple, grazing his teeth over that barbell.

"On my twenty-first birthday. You could say I had a little too much to drink, and I was feeling adventurous."

He releases me with a pop, simultaneously pulling the second tie free. My bikini top floats along the bubbly surface as he says, "You want me to tell you what I plan on doing with these beautiful tits?"

"Yes, please," I beg.

His eyes darken with desire as they drop back down to my chest. My piercings have been a confidence booster from day one, but I've never been happier to have them than I am now. There's no doubt Logan appreciates them, which makes me preen with satisfaction.

"I'm going to wrap my lips around these perky nipples and suck until they're swollen. And then, I'm going to pinch them between my fingers until you squirm, straddling the line between pleasure and pain." His fingers graze my nipple right before he palms my breast, bringing it to his mouth again. His tongue darts out in a torturous tease, tracing circles around the pointed tip, flicking the barbell.

I arch my back, moaning in delight as Logan delivers on his promise. I don't know what kind of voodoo he's wielding right now, but there's no denying the pressure building inside of me, and he's barely touched me.

Logan pulls away from my breasts, licking a trail up the side of my neck as he pulls the ties at my hips free. As the jets carry away the flimsy material, he palms my ass. "God, this ass, Rosie. I've been waiting a lifetime to get my hands on it."

"Oh, yeah?" I moan as he slides a finger down my crack, pressing against the tight hole.

"Has anyone ever fucked you here, baby?" Logan pulls my cheeks apart slightly, waiting for my answer.

"No," I answer.

Swear to god, the man growls. "I can't wait to be the first."

"So presumptuous," I tease because I just can't help myself. This jealous, possessive vibe he's giving off? Yeah, I'm *so* into it. But I'm still me, and needling him is practically a reflex. "What makes you think I'll let you?"

Logan shifts back, looking me directly in the eye. "Because once I make you come so many times you've lost count, you'll be *begging me* to take your ass, too. You'll want me *everywhere*, Pip. I guaran-fucking-tee it."

Holy hell, I could get used to this. I never knew I could be so aroused by filthy words, but apparently, I've just never heard anyone do it right before.

"Speaking of *feeling you...*" I reach below the water, but Logan clamps a hand on my wrist before I can reach my target.

"As much as I'd love to have your hands all over me, I made a promise that I intend on keeping first."

In the next blink, he's hopping out of the Jacuzzi and scooping me up, bridal style. The sudden exposure to the cold is so shocking it takes my breath away, but only a few seconds later, we're inside the house, dripping all over the hardwood floors as he carries me toward the hearth. Logan lays me down gently on the soft rug, the fireplace immediately chasing away the chill. His gorgeous face is alight with an orange glow as he stands, removing his swim trunks and kicking them away.

Well, hot damn.

I'm awestruck by his sheer physicality as Logan looms over me. His naked body is a sight to behold—powerful muscles that seem to ripple under his skin, tattooed arms glistening with droplets of water, and a long, thick cock jutting upward, hitting right below his belly button. I wet my lips, staring at the thick veins going up his shaft, as he gives himself one long stroke.

His eyes are intense as they lock onto mine, a look of possession and hunger in their depths. "You still good?"

I love how careful he's being with me, ensuring I want this as much as he does. But the time for that is long gone, because I've been wanting this for over a damn decade of my life.

"Logan," I whimper, my voice barely audible. "I need you."

He smiles softly, telling me he understands. "You've got me, Pip."

The moment he crawls on top of me, effectively pinning me down with his muscular legs, I'm consumed by passion. By the significance of this moment. His gaze never leaving mine, Logan lowers his head, taking my right nipple into his mouth, drawing the taut peak deep inside before releasing it, and repeating the process on the other side. His hands roam my body as he carves a wet path down my torso with his lips, igniting a fierce need within me.

He nuzzles his face against the curve of my hip, inhaling deeply as if committing my scent to memory. My hands clutch at the rug beneath me, nails digging in as I arch my back, yearning for more. Logan moves lower, teasing the sensitive skin around my thighs. I whimper as he slides two fingers through my slick flesh, groaning when he finds my entrance. His fingers glide inside me, but only for a moment before he withdraws them and props himself up.

He paints my lips with those same fingers. "Taste how much you want me, Rosie."

I lick my lips, savoring the salty sweetness of my arousal, moaning as he does it again before slamming our mouths together. As our tongues tangle, his fingers slip back inside of me, pumping in and out, curling just right to hit that elusive spot, making me squirm in delight.

I whine when Logan pulls away but quickly forgive him as he trails kisses down my torso again. This time, he takes a much more direct path, his deft fingers never breaking the rhythm. When he finally—*finally*—puts his mouth where I need him the most, my toes curl. Logan seals his mouth over my clit, perfectly in sync with his fingers. The pleasure is overwhelming, inundating every nerve ending. My cries echo throughout the cabin, the firelight dancing in Logan's eyes as he devours me.

It happens so suddenly, *so fiercely*, it takes me a moment to process what's happening. My lips part in a silent scream, back bowing off the floor and stars exploding behind my eyelids as I writhe in pure ecstasy. I'm shocked, shaken, and I've never been happier to be wrong about something in my entire life. The relief washes over me like a tidal wave, the realization that I'm not broken after all filling me with a sense of reassurance I never knew I needed. I want to hold on to this moment forever, burn every detail into my brain. Unbidden tears roll down my face as Logan softens his tongue, licking me slowly through the final tremors of my release.

His eyes are filled with a mix of smug satisfaction and tenderness. He inherently knows these are tears of happiness. There's no worry in his gaze, only vicarious joy. Logan crawls back up my body, stroking my cheeks tenderly with his thumbs, kissing the tears away.

"See? Not a damn thing wrong with you," he whispers.

I choke back a sob. "Guess not."

I reach up and cup Logan's face in my hands, my fingers tracing the taut lines of his cheeks, the sharp angles of his stubbled jaw. He leans into my touch, closing his eyes as if savoring the intimacy of the moment. When he opens them again, they're filled with something I can't decipher.

"What are you thinking?" I ask.

The firelight brings out the gold flecks in his eyes as he contemplates his answer. "You're so fucking beautiful, Rosie. I don't think I've ever told you that before. At least not so directly."

"Thank you." I stretch my neck, brushing a tender kiss across his lips. "You're not so bad yourself. Especially when you do that swirly thing with your tongue."

A deep chuckle rumbles from his chest as he draws me closer. "Give me that smart mouth of yours."

I eagerly comply, my lips parting on a sigh. As our kiss deepens, I trace the lines of his back, the ridges on his abdomen. I wrap my legs around his hips, pulling him into me.

Logan freezes when the tip of his erection presses against my entrance. "Please tell me you're on birth control."

I smile. "I am."

There's nothing else that needs to be said. I know the pill doesn't protect against STIs, but the trust we've built over the years tells me neither of us would take a risk if there was any reason to worry.

"Thank fuck," he exhales. "But this is not happening for the first time on the floor."

Before I have the chance to say a word, he's scooping me up yet again, carrying me toward the bedroom.

I laugh. "I can walk, you know."

"Don't care," he says, depositing me on the king-size bed. "I don't want to stop touching you."

Logan punctuates his statement by planting wet kisses down my throat, across my collarbones, and over to my left breast. He takes my nipple into his mouth again while playfully twisting the barbell in the other one with his fingers. His hands are gentle yet authoritative as he continues to explore every curve and contour of my body. His lips are soft yet teasing as they trace my flesh, leaving a trail of fire in their wake. And when his mouth brings me to orgasm for a second time, I finally understand the phrase *la petite mort,* because I swear I leave this earth for a few seconds.

My god, if foreplay with Logan is this life-altering, I might not survive a full night in his arms.

But, man, what a way to go.

CHAPTER SIX

LOGAN

I'm a generous lover. I'm not saying that out of arrogance —it's just a fact. Two of my favorite things in life are eating pussy and watching a woman come, knowing I'm the one who brought her there. But eating *Rosie's* pussy and watching *Rosie* come?

Fucking transcendent.

I don't know what kind of sexually inept asshats she's been with, but I'm more than happy to prove she's not broken. Plus, my inner teenage boy is losing his shit that I get to lay claim to one of her firsts. There was a time when I thought she'd be the girl to take my virginity. I had romanticized the hell out of it—as much as a gangly sixteen-year-old could—thinking we'd be each other's first *everything*.

But I was a late bloomer. All height and no muscle, braces, acne, and a fascination with computers. Basically, I had as much game as a cardboard box. Pip didn't seem to mind, though. Sometimes, I swear she'd look at me like I was that British pop star all the girls were obsessed with. I wanted to make a move on her so many times, but I'd always get in my own damn way, and never actually go through with it.

By my senior year, the jocks had noticed her—how could they not? She'd made varsity cheer, grew into her confidence, and started hanging out with *them* more than me and Ryan. Watching Rosie spread her wings and take flight was mesmerizing, and I was genuinely happy for her, but her rise in social status made her even more out of my league. When she started dating one of those jocks, any hope I'd had left was gone. I figured it was better to remain friends than make a fool out of myself and lose her entirely.

But now?

As I look down at her, smooth skin slick with sweat, a lazy, satisfied grin playing on her lips, and eyes burning with the same longing I've felt for her all these years...I know I'm going to do whatever it takes to hold on to her. There's no way in hell I'm losing her again.

"Logan, please don't make me wait any longer," Rosie begs.

I groan as the little minx grabs my cock, lining it up. I take the hint and slowly ease myself inside her, savoring the feeling of her tight, warm cunt. She gasps as I bottom out, her walls clenching around me, sending a jolt of pleasure straight to my balls. I lean down, kissing her deeply while holding still, ensuring she has time to adjust to my size.

Rosie breaks our kiss. "What are you waiting for? You need to take a minute, so you don't embarrass yourself *prematurely?*"

I laugh, but that quickly turns into another groan when she squeezes me tighter. "Of course, you're still giving me hell, even when I'm *inside of you*," I grumble, biting her bottom lip. "Sounds like you're asking me to wear you out until you forget how to form words."

Her eyes dance with amusement. "Bring it, Edwards."

After that saucy little challenge, I'm even more determined to give her the best dicking of her life.

"So, it's like that, huh?" I grab her ankles, propping them on my shoulders and leaning forward, folding her in half. "Don't say you didn't ask for it, Morales."

"Don't hold back, Logan. I want all of you." Rosie reaches up, her fingers threading through my hair, pulling me into a kiss.

Her wanton moans and the delicious heat of her pussy stoke the fire within me, driving me onward as I thrust harder, hellbent on claiming every single inch of her before the weekend is over.

"God, you feel so, so *good*," she whimpers, stretching out the last word. "Why didn't we do this a long time ago?"

"Fuck if I know," I grunt. "But we're sure as hell going to make up for it now."

As I establish a punishing rhythm, a chorus of yeses fly out of Rosie's mouth, while a string of dirty talk shoots from mine.

"Look at you taking my dick like a good girl." Her eyes flutter shut, and her breath hitches. "Eyes on me, Pip." She instantly complies, making my inner Neanderthal pound his chest. "You're going to look at me as you come around my cock." I grab a pillow, propping it beneath her ass, giving me just the right angle to make that happen. "And after you do that, you're going to flip over and show me that pretty ass of yours while I pull your hair and take you from behind."

She moans. "Oh, holy hell!"

I grab her left ankle, crossing it over the right one that's still on my shoulder. Shit, she's so much tighter like this. I need to make her come fast, so I can change positions and make this last.

I wrap my free hand over her hip and continue thrusting. "Think of all those wasted years spent with fuckwads who couldn't get you off when you could've been getting railed properly this whole time. I ought to spank your ass for withholding this gorgeous body from me all these years."

"Logan," she pants, fisting the bedspread. "I...I think I'm going to come again. How is that possible?"

"*Of course*, you're going to come again," I promise. "When I'm done with you, you're never going to want any dick but mine. Because you're going to know that nobody else can light your body on fire like I do."

The tendons in my neck strain as I maintain a brutal pace, but I don't let up. I can feel how close she is to exploding. Her pussy is gripping me like a goddamn vise.

"Oh, Logan, yes! Just like that!" Rosie's voice is ragged and desperate as she adds, "Please don't stop."

"Never, baby. I'm never going to stop."

I lean down, capturing her lips, our tongues dueling with the same passion as our bodies. Rosie's nails dig into my back, urging me on. The sound of skin slapping skin echoes throughout the room. The musky scent of arousal with a hint of chlorine floats through the air.

Rosie's hips buck, matching my rhythm with each glorious thrust. Her breath hitches as she breaks away from my mouth. Her dark chocolate gaze never strays from mine as her pussy contracts around me. and her limbs begin to shake. She screams as her whole body convulses with the force of her release. I slow my pace, her skin flushing as she moans my name over and over. My balls tap against her ass as her orgasm wanes, and I barely give her a moment to recover before I pull out and flip her over.

The urge to climax consumes me, turning me damn near feral at this point. With Rosie's luscious ass in the air, I line myself up and drive into her like a man possessed. I wrap her silky-soft hair around my fist, pulling on it viciously as I lose myself in the lust and passion that's taken root within me.

"Fuck, Pip," I pant. "You're so goddamn perfect. I never knew it could be like this. I'm so pissed I've gone all these years without knowing how well this pretty pussy can take me."

I spank her ass, *hard,* and she moans. "You like that, Rosie?"

"God, yes!" she says. "Do it again!"

Jesus. This woman was made for me.

I spank the other cheek, feeling a primal surge when I see my handprints on her ass. "I need you to come one more time before I can let go, Pip."

She shakes her head. "Logan, I don't think that's possible."

I spank her ass again. "That's for doubting me."

I pull her closer, slamming our bodies together as one. With one hand on the middle of her back, holding her chest against the mattress, I use my other hand to spread her cheeks and spit directly on her asshole. Rosie's writhing beneath me, muttering nonsensically as I play with her, spreading my saliva around, testing and teasing her tight hole. A guttural moan rips from her mouth as I dip my thumb inside, my fingertips resting on her lower back. I thrust harder, my mind focused solely on bringing her to the edge once more before I blow my load.

Her moans become more frantic, urging me to push harder, to take her higher. I feel it then, the ripple of her orgasm building deep within. Rosie's pussy tightens around my cock, her asshole clenching around my thumb.

"Good girl," I praise. "That's my fucking girl. Come for me, Pip. C'mon, baby. I need it."

A low groan escapes my lips as she hits her peak, triggering my release. Her cunt milks me for all it's worth, drawing out every drop as she bucks wildly beneath me. When the rush subsides, I pull out and collapse beside her, my heart pounding like a freight train flying down the tracks.

"Wow," Rosie breathes, "who knew you were so dirty? That was..."

"Only the beginning," I finish for her. "I may never let you leave this room. Just give me a few minutes, and I'll be ready to go again. I don't care if my dick breaks. It'll be worth it."

She laughs softly, her eyes dancing with affection, as she reaches over and strokes my spent cock. "I've got plans for this thing, so if you need to pace yourself, that's exactly what you're going to do, mister. No broken boners allowed."

I grin, brushing the damp hair away from her face. "Is that so?"

"Yep. If you've got a problem with that, keep it to yourself." Rosie giggles as she leans into me, placing a chaste kiss on my lips.

I chase her mouth, deepening the kiss as she attempts to retreat. Cuffing my hand around the back of her neck, I break away and rest my forehead against hers. "As long as you're here with me, I'll have no problems at all."

CHAPTER SEVEN

ROSALIE

Soft morning light filters through the curtains, casting a glow across the room. I stretch languidly, every delightful ache reminding me of the mind-blowing night Logan and I shared. I smile to myself, recalling the way his touch had electrified every nerve ending. How his kisses ignited an insatiable fire within me. And then there was the dirty talk. Sweet Jesus, the filth that flew out of his mouth really got me going. The fact that Logan could back it up made it even better.

I suspected Logan would be good in bed, but I truly did not know how amazing sex could be with *anyone* until last night. Every experience from my past pales in comparison. Logan is a giver—and then some—and it's obvious he enjoys doing it. I lost count of how many orgasms I had last night.

And the wildest part? My brain—the same organ that usually won't shut up, that overthinks and analyzes everything into oblivion—actually quieted. For once, I wasn't stuck inside my head, spiraling about my fear of failure and the resulting fallout. Last night, I stayed in the moment and just *felt*. Cherished, aroused, and satisfied in a way I never thought possible.

Beside me, Logan stirs. I turn to face him, propping myself up on one elbow to watch him wake up. His hair is disheveled, and the neatly trimmed beard on his jaw gives him an irresistibly rugged look. Those hazel eyes, more green than brown today, blink open and focus on me, a lazy smile spreading across his lips.

"Morning," he murmurs, his voice still husky from sleep.

"Morning," I echo. "Sleep well?"

"Like a rock. How about you?" Logan stretches, muscles rippling under the covers.

"Same." I'm sure my smile is dopey as hell, but I couldn't care less.

The blankets fall to his waist as he turns toward me. I have to make a concerted effort to keep my eyes above his shoulders.

"How are you feeling?"

"Sore," I admit, a mischievous grin tugging at my lips. "But it was totally worth it."

"Oh?" His grin matches mine. "So, I take it you enjoyed yourself?"

"Major understatement." My gaze travels over his broad shoulders and trim waist, down to the obvious bulge beneath the sheets. "It was incredible, Logan."

He stretches to place a soft kiss on my lips. "I aim to please. You were pretty damn incredible yourself, Pip."

We share a look filled with unspoken longing and mutual admiration. The connection between us feels even stronger now, a blend of familiarity and newfound intimacy.

"So, you don't have any regrets?" I hold my breath, waiting for his answer.

Logan frowns. "No way in hell. Do *you?*"

I sigh dreamily. "Not one bit."

"Good." He wets his lower lip. "But I do have one question."

"What's that?"

Logan leans in like he's about to share a juicy secret. "Do you really know karate?"

It takes a moment to connect the dots, but when I realize he's referring to my moment of supreme idiocy on the porch, I bury my head under a pillow and groan.

"I'm never going to live that down, am I?"

He knows damn well I am not trained in *any* of the martial arts.

He yanks the pillow off my face and tosses it to the floor. "Not a chance. But I think we can work with it. You'd look hot wearing a white gi and nothing else. I'm up for a little role play, if you are. I'll be the sensei, and you can be the new student at my dojo."

An embarrassingly loud snort-laugh flies from my mouth right before an equally loud grumble comes from my stomach.

Logan throws his head back in laughter and climbs out of bed. Offering a hand, he says, "C'mon, Daniel-san. Let's get you some breakfast."

He pulls on a pair of sweats while I grab one of his T-shirts. Since Logan's so much taller than me, it hits me mid-thigh and covers up all my naughty bits. As we make our way to the great room, I'm acutely aware of the way his eyes linger on me, and I may or may not swing my hips with a little extra flair.

"Wow," I say, taking in the breathtaking sight outside the wall of windows. "It's a good thing we stocked up yesterday."

Snow is piled high against the glass, a pristine white blanket covering everything in sight. It's clear that a massive amount of snowfall occurred overnight, and flakes are still falling, so it'll be even deeper soon enough.

"Agreed," he replies. "I chopped plenty of wood a few days ago, so I'll grab it out of the shed after breakfast. I haven't seen a generator though. Did I miss one?"

"Unfortunately not." I walk over to the hallway closet. "But as you know, my dad likes to be prepared." I open the door, scanning the shelves. "If the power goes out, we have flashlights, batteries, an old radio, bottled water, and a battery-powered lantern. There should be a camping stove and coolers in the shed and then the stone oven out back." I lift on my toes to pull a box down. I hold it up, showing him everyone's favorite top-hat-wearing tycoon. "If we get bored, we have plenty of games."

Logan's long legs cross the room in a matter of seconds. Before I know it, his hands are bracketing my hips, and his lips are pressed against my ear. "I can guarantee boredom will *not* be an issue."

I bite my lip. "Is that so?"

His fingers creep under the hem of my borrowed tee. "I'd be happy to give you a reminder." My stupid stomach growls again. "*After* we eat."

I yelp as he smacks my ass. "Hey!"

Logan grabs my hand, pulling me toward the kitchen. "C'mon, woman. I'm starving. You promised to make me breakfast, remember?"

I smile. "That I did."

Logan brews some coffee while I whip up some banana chocolate chip pancakes. We fall into an easy rhythm, exchanging playful banter and flirtatious glances. The casual domesticity feels natural, almost like we're a married couple who've been doing this for years. As we sit down to eat, I can't help but think about how quickly things have changed between us. Less than twenty-four hours ago, I was facing a lonely, bitter weekend, and now here I am, sharing breakfast with Logan after a night of mind-blowing sex. Life has a funny way of surprising you.

"Whatcha thinking about?" Logan asks, a knowing smile on his lips. "You're awfully flushed all of a sudden."

I laugh, caught off guard by his perceptiveness. "Fishing for an ego boost again?"

"Nah, I know what I bring to the table." He winks playfully, but there's a stark vulnerability lingering in his gaze, reminding me of his teenage self.

I smile softly. "You're the total package, Logan. You know that, right? Honestly, I do not know how some woman hasn't nailed you down by now. Any girl would be lucky to have you by her side."

He shrugs. "Maybe I've been waiting."

I scrunch my brows. "For what?"

"For the timing to be right with the right girl." He gives me a pointed look as if he's encouraging me to read between the lines.

Could he possibly be referring to me?

I've spent half my life hiding or ignoring my feelings for this man, and if I'm reading him correctly, he's been doing the same with me, for part of that time at least. I've known Logan is attracted to me—he hasn't exactly made a secret out of it—but, at some point, I'd become complacent, thinking we'd never move beyond the flirty friend zone. I had convinced myself that the moment we shared all those years ago was nothing more than a drunken blip.

But I think last night may have been our *game-changer*.

My mind desperately wants to dissect and discuss every

single moment, asking what last night meant to him. I want to shake him and scream, "Were you referring to me just now? Am I the girl you've been waiting for?!" But I stifle the urge, reminding myself there's a time and a place for that, and the afterglow period isn't it.

"Oh." I gulp. "Yeah, timing *is* important."

Logan chuckles, pulling me into a quick side hug, letting me go as he stands and plops a kiss on the top of my head.

"Not that I'm complaining," I begin, "but what was that for?"

He strides over to the fireplace, crouching low to the ground. "Stop worrying, Rosie. We'll figure it out when the time comes."

"*Worry?*" I laugh awkwardly. "You think *I'm* worrying? Pfft." I wave my hand dismissively. "I'm totally calm over here. Practically in a meditative state, in fact."

Logan gives me his, *You're a hot mess, but you're an adorable hot mess*, headshake before looking over his shoulder. "Rosie, we don't have to have all the answers right now. Let's just enjoy this—*us*—for what it is, one moment at a time. I promise, no matter what, *I've got you.*"

I stare at him for a beat, worrying my lip. "You make it sound so easy," I say softly, more to myself than to him.

Logan stacks the logs with practiced ease, his broad shoulders shifting as the muscles in his back flex enticingly. Once satisfied, he strikes a match, the slight flare flickering briefly before the flames crackle to life. The firelight dances across his profile, highlighting the sharp line of his jaw and the focused curve of his brow. Even with the daylight pouring through the windows, the golden glow of the fire adds warmth to his rugged features, drawing my gaze like a magnet. The faint scent of pine smoke mingles with the lingering aroma of pancakes and coffee, wrapping the cabin in a cozy, heady mix that eases the edges of my anxiety, if only for a moment.

"Maybe because it is."

I roll my eyes as I pick up my coffee mug and take a slow sip, letting the steam rise around my face. *Easy.* God, wouldn't that be nice?

"Well, if you're so determined to keep me from spiraling, you'd better make sure I'm well fed." I stab another bite of pancake, the melted chocolate still warm and gooey, trying to ignore the flutter in my chest. "I'm talking three meals a day, snacks at the ready..." I hold up my mug before taking another sip. "Coffee on demand...the works. Keeping Hangry Rosalie in her pen is a full-time job. Not for the faint of heart, mind you. Your Average Joe wouldn't last an hour."

Logan chuckles, his voice low and indulgent. "Good thing there's nothing *average* about me, as I think I proved last night. Besides, you're worth the effort, Pip. Even when you're narrating your life in the third person."

I stick my tongue out, wielding my fork like a royal scepter. "Well, someone's gotta make sure that brilliant brain of yours stays in peak condition," I quip. "Think of it as a fun exercise—'How to Prevent Rosalie from Becoming Hangry: A Survival Guide.' Step one: Snacks. Step two: Coffee. Step three: Repeat until I'm no longer a threat to society."

His lips twist as if he's biting back a smile. "Noted. Avoid Hangry Rosalie at all costs. Emergency chocolate will be kept on standby at all times."

"Smart." I nod, satisfied he's taking this important task seriously. "Now, get back here and finish your food before I do."

"Lemme finish this really quick."

Logan grabs the fire-poker-thingy and nudges the logs, his movements deliberate as the flames curl higher. I swear to god, the man makes tending a fire look downright indecent. Leave it to him to turn something so simple into a whole damn thirst trap.

He stands, putting the iron thingy back in its place, and strides toward me with a calm confidence that makes my heart do a little happy dance. As he reaches the breakfast bar, he leans down, placing a soft kiss on my forehead, lips lingering just long enough to make me forget how to breathe.

"Consider me your official snack distributor and barista," he murmurs against my skin, voice low and teasing. "Say the word, and I'm at your beck and call twenty-four seven. And don't worry—I take my job seriously."

Before I can muster a coherent reply, he straightens and strolls back to his stool, snagging a fork and taking a big bite of pancake like he didn't just turn me into a puddle of goo.

Swoony bastard.

We finish our breakfast, then after, Logan goes out back to gather extra firewood from the shed while I tidy up the kitchen. The snowfall continues steadily, creating a serene and almost magical atmosphere. Once we're sure our emergency supplies are in order, we settle on the couch, snuggling under a warm blanket.

"So, what do we do now?"

Logan wraps an arm around me, pulling me closer. "We enjoy being snowed in. No distractions, no interruptions. Just you and me, Pip."

His words send a thrill through me. The idea of spending the next forty-eight hours alone with Logan, exploring this new facet of our relationship, is incredibly appealing.

Despite the suffocating sexual tension, there's a comfortable familiarity between us. Every little touch is laced with a new awareness, but neither one of us seems to be in any hurry to move things beyond the occasional stolen kiss. We spend most of the day just hanging out like we used to do as kids. We talk, watch a few movies, and play several rounds of Uno, laughing and teasing each other as we keep score. Logan wins most of the games, but I kick his ass a few times, ensuring to rub it in as much as possible when I do. I may even tack on a touchdown dance or two, much to his delight.

The hours slip by, and before we know it, it's time for dinner. We decide on grilled cheese and tomato soup, which complements the comfy-cozy vibe we've crafted. Logan insists on making the sandwiches, using a mix of cheeses that melt perfectly between slices of golden, crispy bread. He tops each one with a smidge of garlic salt and toasts a sprinkle of extra cheese on top. The end result is part cheesy garlic bread, part childhood favorite, and all freaking delicious.

"This is the best grilled cheese I've ever had," I say around a mouthful of cheesy, garlicky goodness. "Seriously, how did I not know you can cook?"

"Glad you approve," Logan replies, his eyes twinkling with satisfaction. "I enjoy watching you eat."

"Well, as we established earlier, I like eating, so we're a perfect match." I pop the last bite into my mouth, licking the salty goodness off the tips of my fingers.

"Definitely," Logan rasps.

It was a lame joke, but the heated way Logan is staring at my mouth makes me gulp. My heart races as he rises from his chair and rounds the table until he's standing before me, keeping his gaze locked on mine the entire time. My breath hitches when Logan's inked hand brushes a strand of hair behind my ear before he gently cups my chin. He leans down until our lips meet, softly at first, but the intensity quickly rises. I wrap my arms around his neck, pulling him closer as our tongues dance. Logan's strong arms cradle me, his hands gliding down my back, and I can't help but moan softly into his mouth.

This isn't just a kiss, I realize. It's a complete surrender to the connection between us, the truth we've been avoiding for so long finally taking root.

Time slows as we savor each breath, every touch, etching this moment into our souls. The swirling storm outside rivals the emotions stirring within me. Logan groans, effortlessly lifting me from my seated position onto the table. Dishes slide down the wooden surface as he sweeps an arm out, not once breaking our kiss. When we finally part, we're both breathless and flushed.

He presses his forehead against mine. "Fuck, Pip. Do you have any idea how many dinners I've sat through, across the table from you, imagining this very thing?"

"How many?" I ask.

"Hundreds."

I pull back just enough to meet his gaze. "Show me, Logan."

His lips curve into a sexy smirk as he takes a seat in front of me, bracing his hands on my thighs. "Open up, baby. It's time for me to eat my dessert."

Anticipation skitters down my spine while I spread my legs. I took a shower earlier, so I'm wearing panties and another one of Logan's shirts, but I didn't bother with pants since it's just the two of us. Logan traces a finger over my center, teasing me with feathery touches through the lace. When he looks up, his eyes are glinting with hunger.

"Watch me, Pip."

I lock eyes with him, my heart pounding in my chest. He gently slides a finger into my panties, first dipping just at the entrance and then deeper, curling the tip just so. I moan quietly, my breath hitching as he finds a spot that makes me squirm with delight.

"So responsive," he praises, drawing small circles around my clit with his thumb. "I love that about you, Rosie. So fucking much."

He adds a second finger, quickly driving me into a frenzy as he pumps them in and out. Logan somehow knows exactly where to touch me for maximum impact. His pacing is precise. His deft fingers craft magic, sending a shockwave of pleasure through my veins. He has me so worked up that by the time his tongue joins the party, I instantly detonate.

My hips buck, and my back arches as I explode, crying out his name and grabbing on to his hair with both hands. As I shatter into a thousand shards of bliss, Logan flattens his tongue, softly lapping at me. I expect him to pull away as my orgasm wanes, but he surprises me by doing the exact opposite. Logan's mouth dives back into my pussy, while his wicked fingers plunge deeper and faster, taking me right back to the edge of that cliff. He groans as he eats me like I'm the finest meal he's ever had, and I'm all too willing to offer myself up to the ravenous beast inside of him.

"So fucking beautiful," Logan murmurs against my heated flesh, lifting his gaze to meet mine.

"So fucking *good*," I moan in reply.

"So fucking *mine*," he counters.

The wind howls beyond the windows, a reflection of

the passion surging between us. I whimper as he swirls his tongue some more, our intense eye contact heightening the sensation.

I rock against Logan's mouth as another climax approaches. "Oh, god, Logan! I'm going to come again."

Before I can even finish my sentence, my entire body is flooded with toe-curling tingles, and I'm screaming his name so loudly, the houses on the other side of the lake can probably hear me. I fall back, my back flat on the table as I catch my breath.

Logan softly kisses my inner thigh before pulling away. "Who needs baked goods when I can eat your sweet pussy for breakfast, lunch, and dinner?"

His joke draws a shocked laugh out of me, so forceful, he can't help but join in. And as he helps me down from the table, and kisses me oh, so sweetly, all I can think is, I'd happily let him.

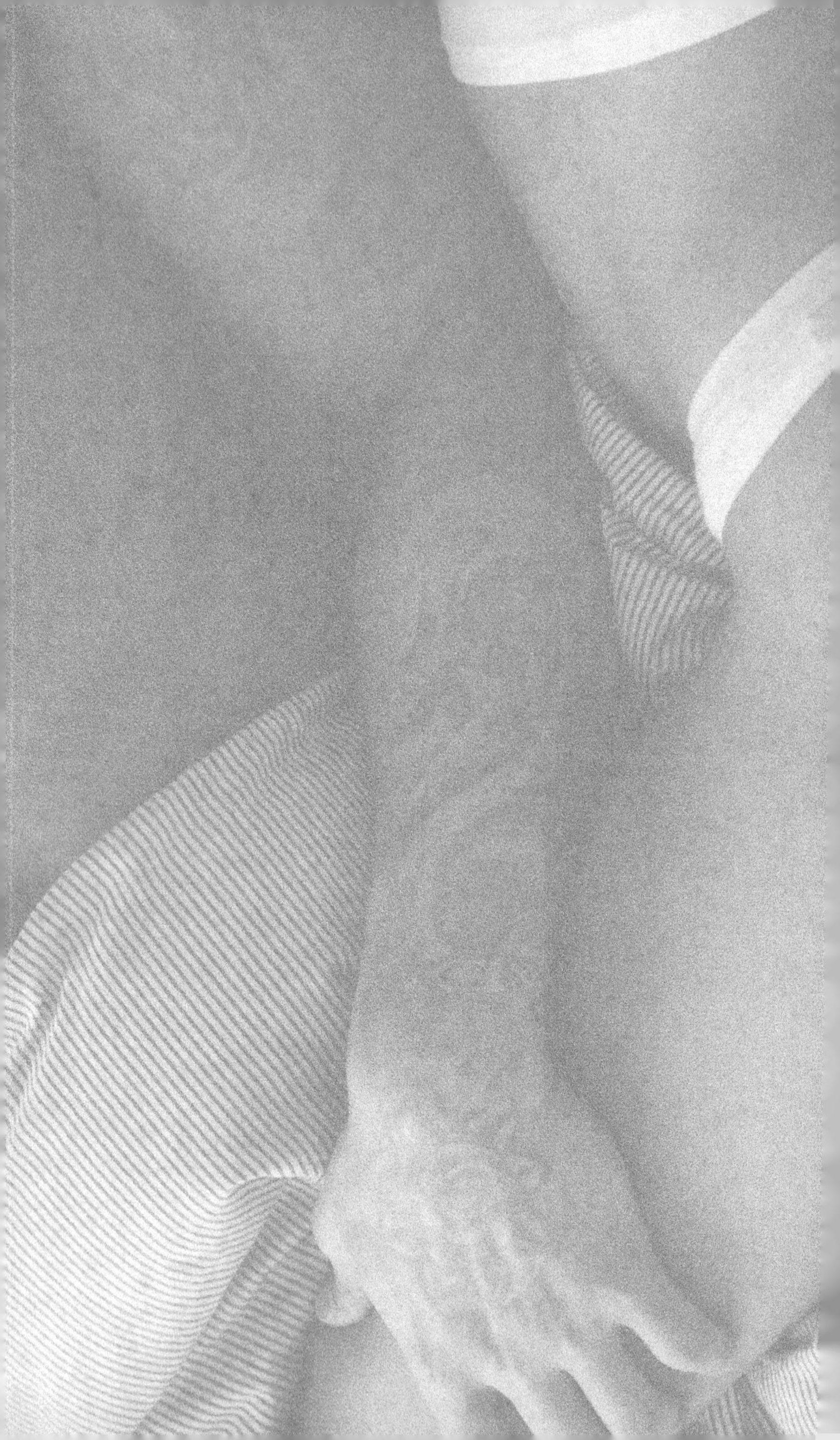

CHAPTER EIGHT
LOGAN

The fire crackles softly in the hearth, its steady warmth a stark contrast to the frozen world outside. The snow continues to fall, but the whistling wind has finally quieted. The world feels hushed, as if the storm has settled into a peaceful slumber, leaving just Rosie and me, wrapped in this moment of tranquility.

She's sitting on the other end of the couch facing me, a glass of wine in her hand. The dim light from the fire dances across her face, highlighting the delicate curves of her cheekbones and the softness in her eyes. She stretches her legs out beside mine, wiggling her knee-high-fuzzy-sock-covered toes.

I grab her left foot and start rubbing the arch.

"Oh, mama," she gasps.

I smirk, bringing her other foot to my lap, rubbing that one with my other hand. "Feel good?"

A dreamy smile plays on her lips. "If you keep spoiling me like this, I may never let you out of my sight."

"I see no problem with that." I wink.

Rosie chuckles. "Careful what you wish for, Edwards."

"Right back atcha, Morales."

Except for an occasional moan from Rosie's lips as I rub her feet, we sit in comfortable silence for a while longer. I study her face, the sight of her looking so relaxed and at ease triggers a memory I haven't thought about in years.

"Remember the old treehouse in your backyard?" I ask, my voice a little rough around the edges.

Rosie's eyes light up with recognition. "Of course I do. I was bummed when my dad tore it down. Stupid wood rot."

"Me too," I say. "We had some good times up there."

She smiles, sipping her wine before speaking again. "You mean our secret dirty rendezvous?"

"I *wish* they were dirty." I laugh. "How did that become our thing, anyway? I can't remember."

"Neither can I." Rosie shrugs.

"Our conversations up there were the best part of my day most days."

"Same." She nods, her expression turning wistful. "It always felt like we were in our own little cocoon. Nothing in the world could touch us."

"I didn't care how cramped it was. I could've stayed up there with you all night."

Her full lips curve into a smile. "I know the feeling."

"Remember the time I stole a bottle of whiskey from my dad's liquor cabinet?"

Rosie laughs, nodding her head. "God, yes. The summer before my junior year. That was the very first time I ever tasted alcohol. I didn't even like it, but I wanted to seem cool in front of you."

"Yeah, I kinda figured that out when you took a monster swig and couldn't stop coughing afterward." I chuckle at the memory. "We were so convinced we were being grown-ups."

She laughs again. "We were such dorks."

"Yeah, but we had fun," I say, my tone turning more serious. "I have a confession."

"What's that?"

"I was planning to kiss you that night after I downed a little liquid courage."

Her brown eyes widen. "Seriously? Why didn't you?"

"I chickened out," I answer with a shrug. "And then we both got a little too shitfaced. Christ, that treehouse was the setting for most of my teenage fantasies."

"I bet." Rosie snorts. "It was the perfect hideaway. I'm pretty sure my brother lost his virginity in it."

"He did," I confirm. "To Chelsea Caldwell. Then he continued using that treehouse to hook up with your fellow cheerleaders and half the dance team. He went really wild during our graduation party and brought a cheerleader *and* a girl from the dance squad up there. Now that I think about it, it was quite the den of iniquity during our senior year, thanks to him."

"Ew." Rosie crinkles her nose, like she's sucking on something sour. "I really didn't need to know that. Why do *you* know that?"

I laugh. "Ryan was a cocky little shit with a big mouth. Thankfully, he's grown up, and no longer regales me with stories of his conquests. But let's just say I know *far* too many details about his sex life back then."

Ryan was one of those dudes who got along with everybody—still is, really. And unlike me, he was not an ugly duckling in high school. Far from it, and the fucker knew it. He didn't need to play sports or join a clique. People were naturally drawn to his charming ass, so they sought him out.

Most days, we hung out at his house after school because he preferred to just chill, but on weekends, if one of our classmates was throwing a party, he'd be there, looking for weed or girls. He dragged me to a beach party once, and I felt so out of my element, I avoided them at all costs after that. But no matter how popular Ryan was, it never impeded our friendship. He's always been more than a best friend to me—he's like the brother I never had. And growing up, I spent more time with him than with anyone else, including Rosie.

Back then, it was easier to bury my feelings for her because I didn't want to betray him. But now? Hell, now I'm *actively* crossing the line. And I can't stop thinking about what might happen if this doesn't work out. It's not just my relationship with Rosie on the line—it's my bond with Ryan, too.

But then I look at her, radiant and so damn sure, and I know I'd regret not trying more than anything Ryan could throw my way. If there's one thing I've learned this weekend, it's that Rosie is worth the risk. She always has been.

Rosie jabs my arm with her finger, snapping me out of my thoughts. "So, how many girls did *you* hook up with in high school?"

"You mean besides Palmela?" I wiggle the fingers on my right hand, making her laugh. "None."

Rosie's laughter fades, replaced by a curious look. "Seriously?"

I nod. "Dead ass."

"Why not?"

I look her straight in the eye. "Because right before I had the balls to finally make a move on the only girl I wanted, she started dating Cody Warren. And she didn't stop dating him until I was already at Stanford."

A crease forms between her brows. "But *I* was dating Cody Warren right before you left for Stanford."

"Bingo." I fire off quick finger guns with a playful wink.

Rosie's face falls. "Logan, if I had known...I never would have...I was only with Cody because I thought...God, I lost my..."

I lean forward and press my index finger to her lips, silencing that train of thought. "It's in the past, Pip. We could ponder all the what-ifs for days. Trust me, I've been there, done that. But you know what I've learned over the years?"

Rosie sets her wineglass on the table and crawls onto my lap, legs hanging off to the side. "What?"

I trace the delicate curve of her jaw. "Hindsight has a way of putting things into perspective. Remember what I said about timing?"

She nods.

"Well...as ecstatic as I would've been if we'd been together in high school—or hell, even college—the timing would've been awful. I may be a so-called genius, but I was an absolute dumb fuck when it came to interpersonal relations back then. And honestly? My self-confidence was shit, which only made it worse. I needed the time to mature into the man I am today."

"Why was your self-confidence shit?" Rosie waves a hand toward me. "Have you seen you?"

I laugh, planting a kiss on the top of her head. "My self-confidence is *just fine*, now."

"I'll say," she snorts.

I clear my throat. "But back then, not so much."

"Why not? You were adorable back in high school."

I groan. "*Adorable*? Just what every teenage boy wants to hear from the girl he's been crushing on for years."

She blushes, a small, self-conscious smile playing on her

lips. "But you *were* adorable. And smart. And funny. And sweet."

"And scrawny. And awkward," I add. "You were so out of my fucking league, Pip. You *still* are, but I'm cocky enough now to go for it, anyway."

"Well...I disagree. If you would've made a move on me back in high school, I *definitely* would've been into it." She stretches her neck to kiss me. "You were, hands down, my favorite person."

"*Were?*" I smile against her lips. "How high do I rank on your list of favorites now?"

"You're pretty high up there, Logan. That's never changed." The warmth in her voice, the sincerity in her dark chocolate eyes—hits me like a punch to the gut.

I look at her, really look at her, and I see the same girl I used to sit with in that tree house, but I also see the woman she's become. One who's had her heart broken, who's carved her own path in the world, who's still a big part of my life after all these years. Without thinking, I lean in, my lips finding hers. Rosie responds immediately, her hand grasping the back of my neck, pulling me closer. The fire pops in the hearth, its warmth wrapping around us as we kiss, a quiet exchange of unspoken promises.

"What happens when we get back to LA?" she asks softly, pulling back slightly to look at me. "Does what happens in Tahoe stay in Tahoe?"

"That's up to you," I reply, searching her eyes, trying to read her emotions. "But just so you're clear on where *I* stand, I don't want to give this up when we get home. The location doesn't matter, Rosie. Tahoe, LA, Abu Dhabi— wherever we are, it doesn't change the fact that I want this. I want *you*. But I understand if you're not ready. If you're not looking for anything serious being so fresh out of a relationship. Whatever you're comfortable with, I'm good."

Unless she tells me she wants to call it quits. That would really fucking suck. I can't predict the future, but one thing I'm certain of is that I don't want to go back to a life without this woman in my arms. Now that I know what being with Rosie feels like, no other woman will *ever* compare. I know that in my gut. She filled a void I didn't even know existed before this weekend. But if she needs time, I'll give her time. I've already waited half a lifetime for this opportunity. A little while longer is nothing in the grand scheme of things.

Rosie glances at our intertwined hands, her thumb gently tracing circles on my skin. "Being here with you...it's made me realize how much I *don't* miss Julian. If anything, it's made me reflect on everything that was wrong with our relationship. I'm *glad* we're not together anymore, Logan. Relieved."

Her words calm the worries that have been gnawing at my insides. "You're sure about that?"

"I'm positive. Julian and I...we were comfortable, but that was it. There was no fire, no genuine passion. Being here with you...it's shown me what I was missing all along. And I don't want to give that up either."

Halle-fucking-lujah.

"How are we going to break it to Ryan?"

Rosie lets out a small laugh, shaking her head. "We're both grown adults, Logan. We don't need my brother's permission to date."

"I know," I agree. "But you know how Ry can be. He's going to have a lot of questions and even more opinions about why he thinks us being together is a bad idea."

"I think Ryan is more bluster than bite." She pauses to

take a deep breath. "But maybe we keep it a secret for now, just until we know for sure where this is heading. I kinda like the idea of not having to worry about outside influences while we're figuring this out."

I admire how practical she's being, even though the thought of keeping this hidden doesn't sit well with me. I want to shout it from the rooftops that I've finally got the girl I've been wanting for years. But I know that's a dangerous thought to vocalize, especially so soon.

"You're probably right. But for the record, I don't like the idea of hiding."

Rosie gives me a small, understanding smile. "Me neither. But I think it's the best way to avoid any awkwardness, at least for now." She adjusts herself until she's straddling my lap. "Plus, I like the idea of keeping you all to myself for a while. The forbidden thing is kinda hot. We should milk that for all it's worth."

I groan as she presses down, gliding over my dick through my sweats. "How hot are we talking?"

She nips my jaw before pressing her lips against my ear. "Scorching."

My fingers curl into her shapely hips. "I'm a little unclear on how the scale works. Maybe you should give me a demonstration."

Rosie smirks, her eyes filled with mischief. "Maybe I need a little incentive." She fists my T-shirt. "Take this off."

"Yes, ma'am." I reach behind me, grabbing the neckline with one hand and pulling it over my head. "Satisfied?"

I fold my hands behind my head as her big, brown eyes blatantly check me out.

"Mmm." She trails a finger over my bicep. "Not yet. But as you've proven many times this weekend, I will be. But there's something I need to do first."

I groan as she plants a series of tantalizing kisses on my chest, working her way down until she meets the thin trail of hair that points straight to my dick. Said dick is eagerly reaching for her, twitching beneath my sweats as she kisses right above the waistband of my joggers. As Rosie pointed out, we've had sex several times now, in all sorts of fun ways, but I have not yet had the pleasure of feeling her plump lips wrapped around my cock. But I think that's about to change, and I couldn't possibly be more excited about it.

She runs her index finger beneath the elastic band. "You want me to keep going?"

God, I want her mouth on me so badly, she could get me to agree to anything right now to make it happen.

"*Fuck, yes* I want you to keep going," I blurt out.

Rosie lets out a small, seductive laugh before reaching down and pulling my sweatpants and boxer briefs down to my knees. My erection springs free, standing tall and proud against my stomach.

My eyes are fixed on her every move as she lowers her head, tracing the vein on the underside of my cock with her tongue before taking the tip into her heavenly mouth and gently applying suction.

"Fuuuuuuuuuck," I groan, my hand automatically gripping the back of her head.

Rosie moans around my shaft as my fingers wrap around her long hair.

"You like it when I pull your hair, baby?"

Another moan as she sucks me in deeper.

Fuck.

The room is filled with slurping noises as Rosie sucks my dick like a pro. Her right hand works in tandem with her hot mouth, while the left cradles my balls, giving them a little tug to match every suck. Tension builds in my balls, signaling my impending release all too soon. I can't even summon any embarrassment about how quickly this is happening, because I'm too fucking consumed by bliss.

My hips buck involuntarily. "Baby, I'm going to come any second. If you don't want to swallow, you need to back off."

Her eyes flicker up, meeting my gaze, right before she takes me so deep, she gags. Saliva pools out of the sides of her mouth as she keeps going, communicating her intention to stay right where she's at. When she swallows, sucking the tip into her throat, I swear I see stars.

"Goddamn, Rosie. Your mouth is heaven. You want me to come down that pretty throat of yours?"

She hums in response.

I brace both hands on her head. "Then hold on, baby."

I thrust upward, triggering her gag reflex once, twice, three times before an electric charge radiates in my balls, shooting through the rest of my body as I explode into her waiting mouth. The sight of her beautiful face, flushed with arousal, my dick between her pouty lips, I swear I've never seen anything hotter. Rosie flattens her tongue one last time before releasing my dick with a deliciously obscene pop. I amend my previous thought when she swallows, her gaze never leaving mine.

I smirk as I spot a dab of cum leaking from the corner of her mouth.

I reach my hand out, swiping it up with my thumb. "Don't want this to go to waste."

Rosie's eyes dance with a mixture of amusement and arousal as I paint her lips. We both know exactly what I'm doing. I'm marking her in the most primitive way a man can, and I'm not ashamed in the least. My chest inflates as I marvel over the sight of her glossy, swollen lips. I can't help but lean in for a kiss, tasting both of us on her mouth. Part salty from my release, and part sugary sweetness from the wine she was drinking.

I groan as her tongue glides against mine, deepening the kiss. We set a leisurely pace, Rosie's fingernails scraping through my scalp, my hands cradling her jaw. When we part, her eyes are full of desire, and something much... bigger. I've no doubt I have a similar look in my eyes, but I remind myself that now is not the time to have that discussion. Rosie wants to take it slow, give us time to adjust to this new dynamic between us, so that's what I'm going to do.

In desperate need of a distraction so I don't beg her to have my babies or something equally disastrous, I use surprise as my advantage to tackle her until she's flat on her back.

"Logan!" Rosie laughs, playfully smacking my flank. "What are you doing?"

"What does it look like I'm doing?" I give her a cocky grin. "I'm returning the favor, baby."

And because I'm a man with incredible work ethic, I return that favor with unbridled enthusiasm.

Five times.

CHAPTER NINE
ROSALIE

I pull the covers tighter around me, snuggling deeper into the warmth of Logan's body, reluctant to start the day. His soft breaths against my neck are calming, and for a moment, I close my eyes, willing time to slow down, just for a little while longer. I'm scheduled to fly home tomorrow morning, but I'd much rather stay hidden in this cabin, away from reality. Here, no explanations are necessary. We don't have to define our relationship or worry about what other people think. There are no brothers warning Logan away from me. No stunning, sophisticated women chasing after him.

As much as I'd like to say the latter doesn't bother me...it does. Most days, my self-confidence holds its own, but it's hard to ignore that Logan's usual type is Hollywood-perfect women, while I'm more girl-next-door. If we went public and the gossip rags got wind of it, I'm sure they'd jump at the chance to point that out. Ever since *Celeb Insider* named him *Sexiest Billionaire Bachelor* a few years ago, he's gained millions of followers, many of whom, I'm guessing, don't care about tech updates or sports betting apps.

Logan likes to downplay it. Because despite the cockiness, he really is humble at heart. But there's no denying it. The man has a massive female fanbase, and they are *thirsty*.

As I lie in his arms, I can't help but wonder what will happen when we get back to LA. The thought of bringing what we've found here back home terrifies me. We're both busy people. What if we can't find time for one another? What if it all falls apart, and I lose Logan completely? And hell, what if my brother doesn't accept our relationship, and Logan is forced to make a choice?

Despite my earlier bravado about not giving Ryan another option, that's not realistic. The brotherhood he and Logan share is irreplaceable. They have a lifetime of loyalty and history between them, and I couldn't live with myself if that bond was compromised because of me. But at the same time...the thought of giving this up, of going back to being just friends with Logan, is unbearable.

Now that I know what it feels like to be held in his strong arms...to be looked at like I'm the most precious thing in his world...to be *seen* in a way no one else ever has seen me—I can't imagine walking away from that. This weekend has given me a taste of something I've never dared to hope for before—*real, terrifying, beautiful hope* that he could be my forever. How could I possibly let that go?

I was kidding myself when I thought Logan and I could have some sort of weekend fling. My heart has been fully invested for much longer than I'd like to admit—especially considering I was recently engaged to another man.

Logan shifts behind me, his fingers skimming across my skin. "You're thinking too hard," he murmurs, his voice husky with sleep.

I smile, even though he can't see it. "How do you know?"

"Because I know *you*. Overthinking is what you do."

I sigh, rolling over to face him. God, he looks so damn good in the mornings—mussed-up hair, the faint scruff shadowing his jawline, and that sleepy, satisfied grin.

"I'm trying *not* to overthink everything," I assure him. "But this is our last day together before reality sets in. How can I not?"

He brushes some hair away from my face, fingers lingering against my cheek. "Then stay the week with me."

I wish.

I shake my head. "I can't. I have a high-profile image campaign starting this week. There's too much to do."

He thinks about that for a moment. "Then I'll change my flight plan and go home early."

"I don't want you to do that, Logan." I wrap my leg around his. "You work so hard. You deserve the break."

He pulls me closer, groaning when my quad brushes against his inner thigh. "At the risk of sounding like a stage-five clinger, I'd rather be wherever you are. I know you need to work, Pip, but I'd love to spend more time with you at the end of the day." He trails a row of kisses along my collarbone. "I even promise to let you sleep after...let's say...only three orgasms."

I laugh. "How generous of you."

"Baby, I think I've already proven how *generous* I can be." He lowers the sheet, nipping the top of my right breast, making me yelp. "But if you need a reminder..."

I playfully swat him, squirming out of his hold. "Hold that thought. Nature calls."

Logan groans, flopping onto his back as I get out of bed.

I toss a wink over my shoulder, shimmying as I catch

him blatantly check out my ass. Goose bumps prickle my skin as I make my way to the bathroom down the hall. After taking care of business and washing my hands, I grab the fluffy robe off the hook, tying it securely. The cabin's insulation isn't terrible, but when the outside temps are in the teens, the absence of a roaring fire is definitely noticeable.

I pad back into the bedroom, the cool air nipping at my bare legs beneath the robe. Logan's sprawled out on the mattress, one arm bent behind his head, and the other idly draped over his abs.

God, those abs are ridiculous.

"Well, aren't you comfy?" I tease, crawling back onto the bed, straddling his thighs.

He hums low in his throat, unties the belt on my robe, and pulls me into a wide-leg child's pose. "But this is much better."

I nuzzle into him, my head resting on his chest. "Agreed."

Logan's heart thumps beneath my ear, lulling me into a contented daze.

"We should get up," I murmur, but make no effort whatsoever to move out of my sexy yoga pose. "You know...make breakfast...do all the things."

My fuzzy robe is still fully draped over my back, but every part of my front is touching *his* front. The skin-to-skin contact is making me all kinds of needy.

His hands slip beneath my robe until they're each filled with one of my ass cheeks. "I have a better idea."

"I'm sure you do." I snort.

"Just trying to make the most of our final day." Logan's fingers climb upward, lightly massaging the muscles on each side of my spine as he goes.

"Damn, that feels good," I mumble against his chest.

His hips rise off the mattress. "I can make it feel even better."

I chuckle. "You're impossible."

If I don't get out of this bed right now, we're never going to leave it. And as much as I like the idea—because seriously, I'm insatiable with this man—I'd like to spend *some* non-naked quality time with him, too, while we have the chance.

Logan grunts as I extricate myself from his arms and hop off the bed, quickly tying my robe closed.

"C'mon, Lazy Bones, I need food in my belly. And afterward, I think we should go for a nice, long walk in this beautiful winter wonderland. There should be some snow-shoes in the shed."

"Seriously?" His brows lift. "You'd rather brave the below-freezing weather than stay in this nice, warm bed with me? Who are you, and what have you done with Rosalie Morales?"

I give him a wry look. "I know, I know, I'm more outside-y than outdoorsy, but we're surrounded by a gorgeous landscape, and I haven't really had a chance to appreciate it."

Logan sits up, muscles flexing as he stretches. "The things I do for you. Fine. Let's go."

I smile. "I knew you'd see it my way eventually."

"Uh-huh." He sticks out his lower lip. "Just keep blatantly abusing your position of power, and I'll keep taking it up the ass."

I prop a hand on my hip. "Is that your way of telling me you're into pegging?"

Logan bolts out of bed, stark naked, and grabs me around the waist. As he nuzzles his nose into my neck, he murmurs, "Sweetheart, whatever *you're* into, I'm game. Just make sure to use plenty of lube if you're sticking a dildo up my ass."

I giggle, pushing him away as my cheeks flush. "Put some clothes on, perv." I flick my hand toward his stupidly perfect, beautifully inked body. "I can only take so much of your grotesque muscles."

He barks in laughter. "Damn, Pip. You're brutal on the ego."

"Nah," I deny. "You know you love it. Somebody's gotta keep you in check." I dig through the dresser, grabbing a pair of thermal leggings and a sweater.

"You volunteering for the job?" Logan's full lips quirk up in the corners.

"Oh, honey, I've already reported for duty and signed all the HR forms." I give him one of those winks he's so fond of.

"Is that so?" He retrieves his own set of clothing, his bare ass leading me out of the room. "C'mon, baby. I'll show you how much I appreciate your *professional dedication* in the shower."

I sigh, feigning exasperation. "Fine. If you must."

I know I just told him I wasn't getting sucked into this, but I follow him into the bathroom anyway. I blame the ass. Seriously, you could bounce quarters off the damn thing.

And when he pulls me into the tub, caging my body against the tiles, the hot water isn't the only thing steaming up the room.

CHAPTER TEN
ROSALIE

By the time we're showered, fed, and bundled in several layers of winterwear, the snow has finally stopped. With his gloved hand firmly clasped in mine, Logan pulls me through the back door. The snow, still pristine and untouched, blankets the entire area and sparkles in the sunlight. Cold, crisp air nips at my cheeks as I take a deep breath, inhaling the earthy aroma of wet pine and soil. I breathe in and out a few more times, immersing myself in the peacefulness of it all.

"It's pretty incredible, right?"

Logan's eyes roam over the white-capped pines and cobalt water, its glass-like surface reflecting the fluffy white clouds up above.

"It really is," he agrees.

Our feet sink into the fresh powder as we make our way over to the shed to retrieve the snowshoeing gear. Once we find the right sizes, we head to the wooden picnic table that sits right beside it.

Logan releases my hand to clear the snow off the bench, gesturing for me to sit.

"Let me help you with these, milady." He kneels in front of me with a grin, grabbing one of the smaller snowshoes.

"Such a gentleman," I tease as he tightens the first strap over my boot.

"Pip, I'm currently at eye level with your delectable pussy. The *last* thing I'm thinking about right now is being a gentleman."

I belt out a shocked laugh. "Too bad it's buried under three thick layers of clothing, huh?"

"Is that a challenge?" His lips kick up in the corner as he straps me into the second snowshoe. "Because I can assure you, I'd have no trouble divesting you of those layers in record time."

I gasp mockingly, pressing a hand to my parka-covered chest. "That is the last place I'd ever want frostbite. I can't believe you'd risk my poor kitty like that. Have you no shame, sir?"

I flex my feet experimentally, adjusting to the bulk of the aluminum deck.

Now he laughs. "Don't worry, baby. My mouth would keep your *kitty* plenty warm. Keep calling me 'sir,' and you'll find out real quick."

An image of me kneeling on the ground completely naked, while anxiously awaiting Logan's next command pops into my head.

Dear god.

I am not submissive by nature, but Logan bossing me around in the bedroom seems to be the exception to that.

I use the clunky contraption on my foot to gently push him away, sending a silent apology to my vagina. "Slow your roll, bucko. This is my only chance to enjoy the snow before I have to leave. You can ravage me later."

"Fine." Logan pouts dramatically, taking the spot next to me on the bench.

He slips his boots into the bindings with ease, adjusting the straps before grabbing his trekking poles. Rising to his feet, he extends a gloved hand toward me, a soft smile playing on his lips, silently offering his help.

"Ready to do this?" he asks, gripping the poles lightly.

I rise up and nod toward the tree line. "Lead the way."

Logan squeezes my hand for a moment before releasing it and plants his poles firmly in the snow.

The trees stand tall and proud around us, though a bit sparser this close to the water compared to the higher elevations. The rhythmic crunch of our snowshoes and the light taps of our trekking poles echo softly around us. We've walked maybe a thousand feet under the cover of the trees when Logan gestures toward a massive sugar pine towering above the rest.

"Does that tree bring back any memories?"

I tilt my head, studying it for a moment before realization hits. "Wait, are you talking about that year you came up with us for winter break?"

Logan grins and nods. "Yep."

A rush of nostalgia floods through me as the memory surfaces. "God, that was a good week, minus the sleeping arrangements."

My parents have since refurnished the cabin, but back then, we had an old pull-out couch with a thin, worn mattress, and an oversized chair that doubled as an equally uncomfortable twin-size sleeper.

He cringes. "That mattress was terrible. My feet hung off the end and one of its coils dug into my back. Not to mention the fact that Ryan wouldn't stop trying to spoon me in my sleep."

I chuckle, bumping his shoulder. "Aw, but you guys were so cute, all cuddled up."

Logan gives me the side-eye. "Well, I'm glad you got some entertainment out of it. It's really fucking awkward waking up with your best friend's morning wood nestled against your ass."

I snort. "Hence the wall of pillows you insisted on building the second night."

"Exactly." His lips twitch into a teasing smile. "But the joint the three of us shared behind that tree made it marginally more tolerable."

I smile, remembering that night in vivid detail. "Dude. You were *so* stoned. You would not shut up about coding, despite the fact that Ryan and I didn't understand the first thing about it. You were so cute, rambling on and on about that Tetris-y game you developed and how great it was going to look on your college applications."

"Hey! You were just as blitzed, and that game was a masterpiece! It got me into my number-one school, so I think my excitement was warranted, thank you very much."

I roll my eyes playfully. "But here's my question. How did you go from developing arcade games to the most popular hookup app known to man?"

Logan's smile dims for a moment, a thoughtful look crossing his face as he contemplates my question. I hold my breath as his expression softens, the weight of something unspoken suddenly hanging between us. "Do you remember my freshman year, when I came home from Stanford for winter break? That party we went to with Ry?"

"Of course, I remember." I nod, my heart giving a little flutter, because that night's been living rent-free in my head ever since.

It was the first time Logan had kissed me. We were two

of the only singles at mutual friend's New Year's Eve party. When the clock struck midnight, couples began making out all around us. What started as a chaste peck on the cheek quickly led to Logan dry-humping me against a wall. I'm not sure how long we'd been going at it before my brother spotted us and absolutely lost his shit, but it was long enough to make my lips feel bruised.

After that night, there seemed to be an invisible wall between us. Logan was always friendly, oftentimes even flirty, but we never spoke of it again. Just went on with our lives, as if it never happened. I shared a lot of drunken kisses with guys in college, trying to replicate the euphoria of Logan's lips on mine, but not one of those kisses came close to igniting the same spark.

Eventually, I had convinced myself I was blowing it way out of proportion. That I was romanticizing it, making it so much better than it actually was, and I needed to stop being so critical of every guy I dated. But as I've learned this weekend, my memory was perfectly fine this whole time.

Logan's eyes meet mine. "Yeah...well, let's just say I felt inspired after that night."

My breath catches slightly, but I keep my voice steady. "How so?"

Logan stops walking, prompting me to do the same. "You really don't know?"

My eyes bounce between his, the gold flecks on his irises shining in the bright light. "I don't think I do." My fingers curl in my gloves and my pulse quickens as I wait for his answer.

Logan pauses, his gaze dropping to the snow. "I didn't intend for things to go that far that night. I mean...I would've loved to take things further if you were up for it, just not in front of an audience. That kiss had been years in the making, Pip, and when it finally happened, it felt... fucking perfect. I didn't want it to stop."

"Me either," I agree softly. "But then Ryan came out of nowhere and took you down like a linebacker."

He nods, a distant look in his eyes. "I'd never seen him so mad. He tore into me, throwing out the whole 'bro code' bullshit like it was gospel. Ryan was my best friend, Rosie. *Is* my best friend. I convinced myself I had to forget about that kiss—the hottest fucking night of my life—because I couldn't lose him. And because...I wasn't ready to be the guy you needed. I had too much to figure out in my head."

My chest tightens at the sadness in his voice. "But how is that night related to the app?"

Logan shrugs. "I needed a distraction after I got back to Stanford. I figured if I couldn't have you, maybe I could help myself—and a bunch of other awkward nerds like me— figure out how to meet girls. It's not my proudest moment, but my hormones were definitely a big factor. I was a nine-teen-year-old virgin, and after feeling up a pair of tits for the first time, creating a campus dating app felt like the most logical solution to getting another shot at it."

My eyes widen. "*My* boobs were the first boobs you've ever touched?!"

"Yep," he says, lips tugging back into a smile.

"Wow...just...wow. I'm honored, I think?" I laugh, the sound echoing through the quiet forest. "So Flingr was born and the rest is history?"

"Pretty much," Logan confirms. "It was meant to be a small thing, just for Stanford students. But then it blew up way faster than I ever expected."

"I'll say." I shake my head in amazement.

"It's been a whirlwind, for sure. BetMasters's fifth anniversary is coming up next month, and I have no idea how that happened. Seems like just yesterday we were a tiny startup."

Logan became a baby billionaire shortly after his twenty-third birthday, when he sold Flingr to the parent company of several other dating apps. He used the money from that sale to launch his current company, which grew even bigger and faster than Flingr, making him a key player in the tech industry.

We walk in silence for a few moments, the memory of that night, and everything that's happened since hanging between us. It's funny how a moment that felt so right to both of us could cause such a mess but also turned out to be such a blessing.

"You know...what I'm hearing is that my boobs are partially responsible for your fortune. Maybe I should consult an attorney about getting a cut of that." I wink in jest.

Logan leans his trekking poles against a tree trunk and turns toward me. His big hands cup each side of my jaw as he says, "Rosie, you could ask for the fucking world, and I'd find a way to get it for you."

God, this man. Could he be any swoonier?

It's tricky wrapping my head around how we got here, with so much history between us, all these years later, but I know one thing for certain: Whatever this is, no matter the challenges we're going to face, it's worth exploring.

CHAPTER ELEVEN
ROSALIE

The cabin feels impossibly quiet as I pull on my coat and set my bag by the front door. It's early; the sun is barely peeking over the snow-covered pines, lighting up the room in a soft glow. I sigh, feeling the weight of my impending departure. This weekend was everything I never expected—everything I never knew I needed—but now it's over, and it's time to jump back into reality. I rub at the ache over my sternum, not ready to say goodbye. Unfortunately, I don't have much of a choice because my flight takes off in a few hours, and I need time to return my car to the rental agency.

Logan wanted to drive with me to the airport, insisting he could take an Uber back to the cabin, but I knew saying goodbye would be easier if we didn't make a big deal out of it. It's not like this is the end for us. Logan and I are both on the same page. We want to explore this new dynamic we've established, even if we have to keep it between us for now. I'm sure the next five days will fly by because I'll be so busy at work. It really *isn't* a big deal. So why am I being so damn emotional?

I close my eyelids and take a deep breath, tuning into my senses. The fireplace crackling softly, the smell of charred wood mixing with the pine-scented air. God, it's already starting to feel like a distant memory.

My misty eyes pop open when Logan's footsteps pull me from my thoughts. He takes one look at me, and I know —*I just know*—he's reading my mind right now.

He crosses the room in a few long strides, pulling me into a hug. "You're killing me, Pip. Are you sure I can't drive with you? It'll give us an extra hour before we have to say goodbye."

"I'm sure." I squeeze him back, burying my face in his chest for just a moment longer. "I'll be fine, Logan. I'll see you as soon as you get back home."

"I'm holding you to that," he promises, crouching down to cup my face in both hands. Today his everchanging irises are more of a burnished bronze, barely a hint of green exists. "Don't overthink it, Rosie. We'll figure out how to make this work. As far as I'm concerned, there's no other option. You hear me?"

I nod, holding back a sob as his lips meet mine in the sweetest kiss. I reluctantly pull away, already missing the comfort of being in his strong arms, but I need to hit the road if I'm going to make my flight. I straighten my shoulders and take a steadying breath. With one last look at Logan, I grab my bag and step outside into the cold morning air.

The snow crunches under my boots as I walk toward my rented SUV, the icy chill a stark contrast to the heat I felt in Logan's arms moments before. I throw my bag into the back, slide into the driver's seat, and start the engine. As I pull the car around, my eyes flicker to my rearview mirror. Logan is standing on the front porch, watching me drive away, a solemn look on his face. I raise my hand in a small wave, but I don't trust myself not to go back if I linger too long, so I hit the gas and head for the main road.

I don't bother turning any music on or even calling my cousin to make the miles go by faster. My mind is too preoccupied wandering back to the cabin, to the memory of Logan's hands on my skin, simultaneously heating me up and sending chills down my spine. His lips tasting and teasing, yet bringing me the greatest relief I'd ever known. The way we moved together, so exhilarating, yet so comfortable, as if we'd been intimate a thousand times before. It's all so confusing, but at the same time, it makes so much damn sense.

But right along the edges of those warm memories, reality tugs at me, persistent and impossible to ignore. No matter how effortless this weekend felt, the situation is complicated, and it's bound to get messy at some point. Our jobs alone are demanding enough. Throwing my family, our shared history, and a secret relationship into the mix is just asking for trouble. But the thought of walking away? I can't picture myself doing that.

A text notification dings from my phone, but a distracted driver I am not, so I let it go unanswered for now. Before I know it, I'm pulling into the rental car return and heading into the airport. I'm not checking a bag, so I decide to use my phone app to check in rather than waiting for a kiosk. When I retrieve my cell from my purse, I smile, my heart beating wildly as I see the incoming text from earlier.

Logan: Miss you already, Pip.

My grin widens as my thumbs fly across the screen.

> Me: I miss you, too. Just got to the airport.

He replies almost instantly.

> Logan: I'm counting the minutes until I get to kiss your pretty lips. BOTH sets. But in the meantime, if you'd like to send some sexy pics to tide me over, I wouldn't complain. 😏

A deranged snort-laugh flies out of me, so loudly it draws the attention of several people in the bustling terminal. I tuck my chin in embarrassment, shaking my head as I type out my reply.

> Me: I'll see what I can do when I get home. 😏

> Me: But for now, I need to get to my gate. They should be boarding any minute. I'll text you as soon as I land.

> Logan: Have a good flight, baby.

I'm grinning like a loon as I weave through the crowd toward security. Luckily, I have priority screening, so I'm through in under five minutes; no hour-long shuffle behind grumbling passengers required. Honestly, the eighty bucks I threw down for the Homeland Security background check was some of the best money I've ever spent. Five out of five stars, for sure.

By the time I reach my gate, they've just started boarding, so I don't bother sitting down. Once I'm settled in my window seat, I take out my phone to send a quick message to Sylvie.

Me: On the plane, about to head home. Can you sneak away for brunch? We need to chat ASAP.

Sylvie doesn't keep me waiting long.

Sylvie: Um, DUH. You know damn well I've been waiting for all the spicy tea. Hudson's here, so it shouldn't be a problem. Noon at our usual spot?

I mentally calculate how long it'll take me to get to the parking garage once the plane lands. Our favorite brunch spot is a café in Manhattan Beach, so it's a quick drive from LAX.

Me: I should be able to make it by then. I'll text you when I get to my car.

My thoughts won't stop wandering during the flight. Memories from the weekend play on a loop in vivid detail. Logan's laugh, the way his fingers laced with mine as we talked late into the night. Logan's touch. His absurdly talented tongue. I can't stop grinning like an idiot, and my cheeks feel like they're on fire. If the expression on my seat neighbor's face is anything to go by, I'm guessing I look a little crazed.

I try reading for a while, but considering I'm working through a brother's best friend romance, it's not exactly helping keep my mind off Logan. Its trope is a pure coincidence considering I started it on the plane ride *to* Reno, but I'm sure Freud would have a field day with the fact that at least a third of the books in my library have the same theme. I'm getting antsy, anxious to get everything off my chest with Sylvie, so when the city below comes into view, I breathe a sigh of relief.

Once we land, I flip off Airplane Mode and find another message from Logan already waiting.

> Logan: You just spent the last two hours imagining me naked, didn't you?

I roll my eyes, even though he can't see me and send a quick reply.

> Me: Nice try, but this little fishy still isn't biting… (Just landed btw. We're taxiing to the gate now.)

> Logan: Glad you made it safely. (I'll get you to admit it one of these days. 😏)

> Me: Meeting Sylvie for brunch on the way home. Do you want me to text you when I'm done?

> Logan: You'd better.

I chuckle, unable to resist the urge to mess with him.

> Me: And if I forget?

> Logan: Oh, Pip. You really wanna go there?

> Me: I'm sorry, I'm not following. I'll need you to rephrase the question, please.

Logan: Sure. I can do that. Enjoy your brunch, Rosie. I know you're dying to unload on your cousin, so have at it. But when you get home afterward, if you don't text me, or better yet, FaceTime me, I'm going to hop on the next flight to LA, drive over to your place, strip you naked, and spank your ass until you're dripping wet and begging me to fuck you. That clear enough for you?

Dear god.

Why is it so damn hot in this plane all of a sudden? I fan my flaming cheeks before typing my reply.

Me: Well, now you're just tempting me to go radio silent.

Logan: Good to know.

I blink rapidly when I realize he's texting me from the cabin.

Me: How are you texting me from a dead zone anyway?

Logan: Who said it was a dead zone?

Me: Uh…the zero bars on our phones said so.

Logan: YOUR phone may have had no reception. We must have different carriers because mine's been fine this whole time.

My jaw drops.

Me: What?!

Logan: You didn't put it together when I used my phone as a hotspot so we could watch Netflix?

Oh, for fuck's sake. No, I *didn't*, probably because I was too distracted by all the sex. And thinking about the sex.

Logan: I'll take your silence as a no.

Me: I hate you.

Logan: No, you don't.

Me: Fine. I don't. But I AM annoyed with you for letting me think I had no means of communication all weekend.

Logan: Oh, baby, I think we communicated just fine.

My toes curl when a memory of how well we *communicated* flashes through my mind.

Me: And on that note, I'm going to shove my phone in my purse before I spontaneously orgasm in the middle of a crowded plane. Talk soon.

Logan: Can't wait.

CHAPTER TWELVE
ROSALIE

I arrive at the café a few minutes before noon and spot Sylvie seated at a corner table, already sipping a mimosa. She raises her glass, grinning, as I slide into the chair across from her.

"You're allowed to drink now?" I raise a teasing brow, taking a sip from the glass she had the courtesy of ordering for me.

"Yes..." My cousin rolls her eyes. "I pumped right before I left the house, and I'll pump and dump as soon as I get home. There's plenty of milk in the fridge to last all day if need be. The girls were both napping during my last pumping sesh, so Hudson ate me out while I was doing it. Orgasms really get the milk flowing."

"Jesus," I sputter, practically spraying champagne and OJ all over the table. "Warn a girl, will ya?"

"Have you met me?" Sylvie gives me a wry look.

I raise my champagne flute. "Touché."

I've truly never met someone with less of a filter, at least around adults. Nothing is off-limits with Syl. Her husband's newfound lactation kink, what it was like to take her first poop after giving birth, the exact length and girth of said husband's penis, you name it. She's an open book and completely shameless about it. But Hudson takes it all in stride, smiling at his new bride like she's the best thing since cavemen learned how to make fire.

"All right, spill it, bitch," she says with a mischievous glint in her eye. "I've got about ninety minutes before my tits turn into bowling balls, so let's make it count."

Of course, that's the exact moment our waiter shows up to take our order. His gaze keeps drifting to Sylvie's newly enhanced chest, like he actually believes her boobs are about to morph into sporting equipment. I laugh, flipping through the menu even though I already know I'm getting the same thing as always. Once the poor guy scurries off to the kitchen, I dive into explaining my dilemma.

"I'm still wrapping my head around it. *A lot's* happened in the last few days."

"Okay, lemme start." Sylvie's hazel eyes assess me carefully. "You're definitely rocking a post-coital glow, so I think it's safe to assume you and Logan banged like bunnies."

Despite my best efforts to stay composed, I can feel my face flushing again. "Maybe."

"There's no *maybe* about it, Rosa." Sylvie twirls her index finger in my direction. "You don't get *that* kind of glow unless you've been burning up the sheets with someone who knows what they're doing. Did you measure his cock like I asked you to?"

"Shh!" I mouth a silent apology to the woman sitting at the table next to us, literally clutching her string of pearls. "Keep it down. And no, I did *not* measure anything this weekend. Speaking of...Logan saw your horndog texts, so thanks for that."

She smirks. "You're welcome."

I scratch the bridge of my nose with my middle finger. "I wasn't *really* thanking you. I was mortified when I realized he was reading over my shoulder."

"Eh, you'll get over it." Sylvie shrugs. "But back to the important stuff. Are we talking little smokies, bratwursts, or a cucumber?"

My lips twitch. "Oh, cucumber, for sure. One of the longer, fatter ones."

"Good for you," she says, clapping her hands excitedly. "It's about damn time. God can you imagine if you actually went through with the wedding? You would've been stuck with Julian's limp dick for life, or at least until you came to your senses."

"Julian's dick isn't limp," I argue, keeping my volume at a *much* lower level than she is. "It's just not that long. Or... thick."

Sure, having sex with someone who's anatomically blessed is nice. But I'd never fault a man for something he couldn't control, like penis size. There are plenty of ways he could compensate if he had any interest in satisfying his partner. But since Julian doesn't care about anyone's orgasms but his own, and the asshole cheated on me, fuck him. Or *don't* fuck him, rather.

She laughs. "At least now you can finally say you know what it's like to have your pussy eaten properly."

My eyes widen. "Sylvie! Seriously, dial down the volume."

She waves me off. "Pfft."

"Besides, how do *you* know, *I* know, what that's like now?"

"Puh-leez." Sylvie scoffs. "Logan's pretty, no doubt, but that's not the only reason he was given the top spot on the sexy billionaire list."

I cross my arms. "I'm fairly certain physical attributes are a *big* factor when *Celeb Insider* decides who makes that stupid list."

"I'm not saying it's *not* a factor. But it's not the *only* factor. Sex appeal is just as important, and Logan Edwards has sex oozing out of his pores." She jerks her thumb to the red-faced woman beside us. "Even Prudence McPrudester could take one look at Logan and gather that he eats pussy like a champ, fucks like a demon, and doles out orgasms like the world is ending, and he's planning to go out as a legend."

Good ol' Prudence gasps.

"I can't take you anywhere," I mutter.

"Rosa," Sylvie continues, completely ignoring the woman glaring at us, "you work with beautiful people for a living. You know damn well looks aren't everything. Think of all the douche-nuggets who've hit on you at work. If the guy's an asshole, or selfish in bed, his sex appeal goes down the shitter. But Logan is neither of those things, so, again, *good for you*. I'm...so...proud. My baby is all grown up." She wipes an imaginary tear from her eye for dramatic effect.

I take another sip of my mimosa. "You're ridiculous."

Sylvie's brows lift. "But I'm not wrong."

I try holding back my grin because I don't want to encourage her, but it's a losing battle. "No, Syl. You're not wrong."

Logan definitely belongs on that list.

"So...why am I sensing hesitation?"

I sigh. "It's...complicated."

"Then *un*complicate it," Sylvie suggests matter-of-factly.

"Trust me, I would if I could. But I can't, so we've decided to keep it a secret for now—except you, obviously, because I needed someone to talk this through with me, and I know you're a vault."

"Why the secrecy? Because of your stupidly overprotective brother and all his 'bro code' bullshit?"

"That's part of it," I confirm. "But also because I don't want to ruin *my* friendship with Logan, nor do I want to compromise his relationship with my parents. If they knew we were...dating, or whatever, they'd be over the moon. Hell, knowing my mom, the minute I told her, she'd probably shove one of her signature *fun kits* in my arms and encourage us to go upstairs and try it out. Meanwhile, she'd be planning our wedding and drawing a diagram of all the best Kama Sutra positions for our honeymoon."

If someone ever tells you having a mother who's a sex therapist is anything but awkward, they're lying their ass off.

Sylvie chuckles, knowing firsthand how outrageous Dr. Tatum Morales can be. "That does sound like something she'd do. So, if your parents would be thrilled about the two of you dating, why are you worried about them?"

I take a moment to think about my answer. "I know Logan would never hurt me on purpose, but if for some reason this doesn't work out, it's going to *hurt,* and I don't think I could mask my feelings around the people who know me best. They'd see right through me, and I'm afraid they'll perceive Logan differently if I'm hurting because of him. For all intents and purposes, Logan and Ryan are brothers, and my parents love him like one of their own. I can't take that sense of belonging away from him. You know he doesn't get that from his actual family."

She gives me a sad smile. "Yeah, I know. His parents suck."

I nod. "They do."

Logan hated being home when we were younger because his parents are two of the coldest, most selfish people I've ever met. Harold and Caroline Edwards excelled in making their son feel invisible. Logan acted like their indifference didn't bother him, but I knew the truth after spending so many nights together in the treehouse talking about it.

He was starved for affection the first twelve years of his life, so when Logan and Ryan became friends, and our entire family immediately welcomed him with open arms, he soaked up every morsel he could get. I could never rob him of that. He should've had it from the day he was born, and it breaks my heart every time I think about how he didn't. I don't think he's even spoken with them since they moved to Miami while we were in college.

"Logan's a good man—*a great man*—and he deserves my family's love no matter what happens between the two of us."

"Hence, why you're proceeding with caution," Sylvie surmises.

I point to her. "Exactly."

Sylvie sips her mimosa thoughtfully, nodding. "Okay, here's my unsolicited two cents. Whether you realized it or not, you and Logan have always had this 'will-they-won't-they' thing going on. I *know* Ryan picked up on it long before your New Year's Eve make-out sesh, which is why he was so loud about the bro code nonsense. But regardless of Ryan's misguided warnings, have you ever considered that maybe you and Logan are inevitable? Why fight it?

"Look at me and Hudson. I knew from the moment we met something was different about him. About the way he made me feel. That's why it hurt so badly when I thought he didn't want me. When I moved back to LA, I had no intention of ever seeing him again. But then all these years later, he was thrown back into my life. And as hard as I fought it, as many mistakes as we've both made along the way, I know this is how it was meant to happen. If I hadn't left, we wouldn't have Lily in our life. That's not a reality I'd ever want to live in, and I can guarantee Hudson would say the same.

"So, I'm going to give you the same advice my brilliant cousin gave me in the not-so-distant past. You don't have to make all the decisions right now, Rosa. Don't worry about what's at stake. Don't worry about all the hypothetical what-ifs. You're allowed to enjoy this experience, wherever it may lead you. Just focus on what you're feeling in the moment, every time you're with Logan. Focus on how inexplicably bereft you feel when you're not together."

"Man, this cousin of yours sounds pretty smart," I sass, considering *I'm* the one who gave her that advice. "But how do you kn—"

Sylvie holds a hand up. "Girl, don't even try telling me you're not missing him like crazy right now, because it's written all over your face."

"But that's weird, don't you think?" I ask. "We've only been exploring this new facet of our relationship for three days, Syl. Three. Days."

She gives me a *'Don't give me that bullshit'* look. "Rosalie, this has been coming for fifteen *years*. You two have been carrying a torch for each other since day one. You've been suppressing these feelings for so long, *of course* it's going to be super-intense once you finally give into it."

I think about that for a moment, tracing my finger on the rim of my glass. "There's just so much on the line."

"Nuh-uh," Sylvie says, shaking her head. "We're not doing that, remember? Look. If you want to keep it a secret for now, fine. That part doesn't matter. What *does* matter is how being with Logan makes you *feel*. If you focus on that, the rest will work itself out."

I nod, feeling the weight in my chest lift, just a little. Sylvie's right. I've spent too much time worrying about what might go wrong instead of appreciating what's already gone right. Logan's promise echoes in my mind. *Let's just enjoy this—us—for what it is, one moment at a time. I promise, no matter what, I've got you.*

If he's willing to take this risk, I owe it to both of us to do the same. There's no guarantee things will be easy, but the thought of walking away now—before we've even had a chance to see where this could lead—is infinitely worse.

By the time our food arrives, I've made up my mind. For the first time in a long time, I'll stop overthinking and let myself feel. Logan deserves that. *We* deserve that.

As we finish our meal, Sylvie raises her glass one last time. "To orgasms and big dicks. May we always be blessed with both."

I chuckle, clinking my glass to hers. "*Salud.*"

CHAPTER THIRTEEN
ROSALIE

The sleek downtown office of Maxwell and Company buzzes with energy as I step through the doors. My heels clack along the polished marble flooring in a steady staccato, mixed with the ever-present hum of conversation and keyboard clicks. Trish, aka our chaos coordinator extraordinaire, gives me a quick smile as I approach the reception area.

"Welcome back, Rosalie!" Trish says. "Did you have a nice mini vacay?"

Only if you consider countless orgasms with the sexiest man you've ever met "nice."

Since I can't say that without giving her all the tea, I go with, "Morning. I did. But I suspect you're about to tell me I'm going to pay for having Monday and Tuesday off."

Trish winces dramatically as she hands me a stack of messages. "I sent quite a few people to your voicemail and gave another few your email address, too."

"Great," I reply, stretching the word out.

"But the good news is, you only have one appointment

today. Avery wants you to sit in on her Zoom call with Gabbie and Ethan Baldwin at two o'clock."

"Damn, now I want a cupcake."

"I know, right?" Trish laughs. "I could go for one of their piña colada tarts."

Gabbie and Ethan are celebrity chefs who own Baldwin's Sweet Temptations, my favorite bakery franchise. Every time I'm in Santa Monica, I have to stop by their original location for a cannoli cupcake, or if I'm lucky and it's not sold out for the day, a slice of their triple chocolate cheesecake.

"Well..." I shake the stack of messages. "I suppose I'd better get to it. Thanks, Trish."

"Anytime, Rosa. By the way, you had a delivery about half an hour ago. I put it on your desk. Be prepared for my inquisition once you get caught up."

I tilt my head in question, trying to figure out what she meant by that. "Thanks, Trish."

She chuckles. "It'll make sense once you see what it is."

I head toward my lovely corner pod, passing a series of other workstations tucked behind frosted glass partitions. When I duck into mine, I'm greeted by a stunning sight—a large crystal vase filled with two dozen lilac roses. My breath catches, and I step closer, fingertips grazing the soft petals. Lilac roses have been my favorite for as long as I can remember, a preference very few people know about. Roses might be a common flower, but to me, the lilac shade is an understated beauty, so subtle and unique. It has an inexplicable calming effect, reminding me to take a deep breath and literally smell the roses.

Curious, I pick up the small card nestled among the blooms. A huge smile stretches across my face as I read the inscription.

Miss you already, Pip.

There's no signature, but only one person calls me Pip, so there's no question who sent them.

I retrieve my phone out of my purse as I'm taking a seat, intending to text Logan, but my boss, Avery, strides into my workspace before my ass even hits the chair.

"Welcome back, Rosalie. Nice flowers," Avery says in the no-nonsense tone she's known for. "Let's talk about Jett's image strategy."

Some people may think her abrupt arrival and instant demand is rude, but Avery Jacobs-Maxwell is one of the kindest, most understanding people I know, with a wicked sense of humor. She's a badass in the public relations world —one of the top in the industry—but it didn't come easily. In this business, no matter how hard you work or how much you contribute to the bottom line, when you're a woman— especially one as stunningly beautiful as Avery—you have to be tough on the surface to be taken seriously. Even though the majority of publicists in this country are women, most of the PR executives those women report to are men.

Avery's husband, Liam, may have founded Maxwell and Company with his New York counterpart, but she was promoted to partner after single-handedly bringing in so many large-scale clients during her first year as a publicist with our Entertainment Division that Maxwell's already impressive profits grew astronomically. Not only that, but she somehow managed to tame the bossman, ridding him of his infamous playboy ways. If the rumors are true, Avery and Liam used to hate each other's guts, but professionally, they meshed so well that they begrudgingly tolerated working together. It's honestly hard to imagine, though, because that man worships the ground she walks on and makes no attempt to hide it. I always joke with Sylvie that I want to be Avery when I grow up, and I don't think it's difficult to see why.

I turn my computer monitor on and say, "Of course. Let me just get signed on."

"No need," she says. "Take a walk with me. I need coffee, *pronto*."

I barely have time to grab my iPad and stylus pen before Avery's out the door, walking down the hall at a brisk pace.

"As you know," Avery begins, "*Of Blood and Honor* can be a game-changing film for Jett's career, if we do our jobs right. This is our opportunity to show his evolution from teen drama heartthrob to serious Oscar contender. *We* know Jett is an incredibly talented actor, but his past transgressions on and off set are working against him right now. The early squawking has made the studio nervous, but I assured them we had a plan to turn it around."

She pauses to blow a kiss to her husband as we pass his open office door. I swear to god, he looks like he's two seconds away from bending her over his desk and fucking the daylights out of her. Jesus, it's making *me* blush.

Avery's breathing pattern momentarily changes, before she shakes herself out of it. "Where was I?"

I clear my throat. "The studio is concerned, but we have a plan."

"Right." She points to me. "So, as I was saying, the *plan* is to really focus on his personal growth. He's no longer the douchey, drama-stirring, party-going guy of the past. All of his posts over the next six months should paint a pretty picture proving he's a full-fledged, responsible adult now. Not the wild teenager he portrayed on TV. Leverage his close relationship with his mother...people eat that shit up. Show his volunteer work with the children's hospital, but don't lean on it so heavily, it looks like he's only doing it for the photo op. Throw in *lots* of photos of Jett with his rescue pitbulls—animals always get social engagement. Really work the 'adopt, not shop' angle there.

"Sprinkle in some sexy pictures of him at home. Maybe some shots lounging beside the pool reading a book. Or cooking shirtless, looking irresistibly disheveled, implying he's preparing breakfast in bed for someone special. You get the gist. We all know that sex sells in this business, but you need to be careful his entire feed doesn't turn into a thirst trap. Every post needs to be intentional, peeling back layers of his character so by the time the press junkets begin, people will be champing at the bit for the movie's premier."

I jot down a few notes on my tablet and say, "Understood."

She gives me a determined nod, her eyes flashing with the intensity she brings to every campaign. "I trust you to set the tone. Let's make it impossible for audiences to imagine anyone else in that role."

I nod, absorbing her vision and already imagining the posts that will shape Jett's new image.

"Make sure Erin is synced in on this. She's my number two on this one."

"Got it." I nod, noting to forward all copy to one of our more seasoned junior publicists for approval.

Avery stops to pop her head into another publicist's office. "Trevor, I need that press release on my desk in thirty."

"It'll be there in twenty," he replies. "I'm just finishing up."

She turns back to me and resumes walking. "While you were away, Hans Van Sant got arrested for DUI and solicitation. Now his wife's filing for divorce, and he's checking into rehab for alcohol and sex addiction. What a mess."

My eyes widen. "Oh, shit."

Hans Van Sant is a renowned director and producer. Every actor worth their salt dreams of starring in one of his films. Hollywood relationships are known for being short-lived, but Mr. and Mrs. Van Sant have been publicly flaunting their self-proclaimed 'Romance of the Century' for the last twenty years.

"You can say that again." Avery laughs as she steps into the employee break room, with me hot on her heels. "I have a feeling I'm going to need quite a few of these today."

I watch as she places a mug under the spout of our fancy drink machine, selecting the caffè latte button. As perfectly frothed milk and freshly ground espresso fills her cup, she takes a deep breath and turns toward me.

"Now that we got that out of the way... how was your weekend?" she asks, her tone softening.

Avery is one of the few people who knows why I went to Lake Tahoe.

"It was...good. *Great*, actually." Dammit, I can feel my face flushing.

Her dark, sculpted brows rise as her gaze shifts to my undoubtedly pinkened cheeks. "You don't say. Does the reason it was so great have anything to do with that gorgeous bouquet sitting on your desk?"

I bite my lip. "Possibly."

"Interesting." Her signature red lips curve into a smile. "If you need to talk about it, let me know. Although, I have a feeling Trish will be grilling you before lunchtime until you crack and spill all the details. Sometimes, I think that woman missed her calling as an interrogator for the CIA."

I snort-laugh. "No doubt."

Avery's expression turns serious. "But really, Rosa, if

you need to talk, I'm here. I know things are hopping this morning, but I'll find the time if need be."

I smile. "Thanks, Ave. I appreciate that."

See? Badass boss bitch, kind, and funny. Have I mentioned she's my hero?

She picks up her mug, moaning as she takes the first sip. "All right then. Back to work we go."

"I'll get Jett's proposed timeline and narrative to Erin by end of day."

"I know you will, Rosalie. And I'm sure it'll be *great*." She emphasizes the last word, clearly tying it into my comment about the weekend. With a wink she adds, "Maybe not multiple-orgasm great, as your weekend clearly was, but fantastic nonetheless."

And with that, she pivots and heads down the hall, her attention already shifting to the next task. I shake my head, laughing to myself as I pick my jaw up off the floor and return to my desk.

After sifting through all my messages and scheduling follow-ups, I start a rough draft of Jett's posting timeline. Hours feel like minutes as I work through his monthly, weekly, and daily content calendars, ensuring all the key events are loaded first, properly organized and beautifully color coded. My fingers are tap, tap, tapping away when my phone buzzes on my desk with an incoming text notification.

> Logan: How's my favorite social media strategist? Get any unexpected deliveries today?

A smile breaks through the professional mask I wear, lighting up my face.

> Me: I did, in fact. Some smokin' hot guy sent me a beautiful arrangement of my favorite flowers. He's going to get a BIG thank you the next time I see him. 😜🥒

> Logan: This guy sounds like he's pretty into you. (And he can't wait 😌)

My smile widens.

> Me: I'm pretty into him, too.

> Logan: I bet he'd love to be IN you right about now.

I shake my head, biting my lip as I type.

> Me: Considering he's hundreds of miles away, I suppose he'll have to settle for another FaceTime sesh when I get home.

A rush of heat and longing runs straight to my core as I think about the phone sex we had via FaceTime last night. Watching Logan stroke himself while he was issuing dirty commands, telling me exactly how to fuck myself with my trusty vibe, was one of the hottest experiences of my life. Second only to every minute I spent with Logan last weekend.

> Logan: *Groan* You're killing me, Pip. My poor dick is raw from jerking off too many times, remembering how fucking sexy you were last night.

I squeeze my thighs together, trying to stifle the sudden throbbing happening between them.

Me: Send video or it didn't happen.

Logan: Way ahead of you, babe.

Logan: *incoming video

I gasp when I see his big hand wrapped around his perfect cock in the thumbnail image. I quickly save the video, then delete it from our text thread so it doesn't tempt me.

Dear God, how am I supposed to get any work done now, knowing that's sitting on my phone just waiting for me?

Logan: What's the matter, baby? Cat got your tongue?

Logan: You're dying to watch it, aren't you? Maybe lock yourself in the office bathroom to rub one out while you do? Make sure you turn the volume up.

For fuck's sake. I need to end this conversation before I wind up doing exactly that.

Me: I hate you.

Logan: No you don't. You just hate the fact that you'll be painfully aroused for the rest of your workday.

Me: Not helping, asshole.

Logan: All right, all right. I'll be good.

Logan: Seriously though, I miss you, Pip.

Me: I miss you, too.

Logan: Now get your ass back to work.

I smirk as I think of a way to get him back for making me so randy at work.

Me: Yes, sir. Permission to change my horribly damp panties first, sir?

Logan: *Groans AGAIN* Anyone ever tell you that you play dirty?

Me: Anyone ever tell you that you talk dirty?

Logan:

I laugh.

Me: BTW I was just kidding earlier. I'm not wearing any panties.

Me: Gotta go now. *Byyyyyyyyeeeeee GIF*

Logan: You're evil. You're also getting a spanking the next time I see you.

I bite my lip, my heart quickening as anticipation swirls in my chest. God, it's only been a day since we last had sex, but my body is acting like it's been a damn month. What is this man doing to me? I've never been this ridiculously horny before.

My eyes widen when I glance at the clock and see that I only have an hour to go. I really do have to get my ass in gear if I want to get out of here in time. But before I do, I add a note on my running to-do list:

Charge ALL the toys

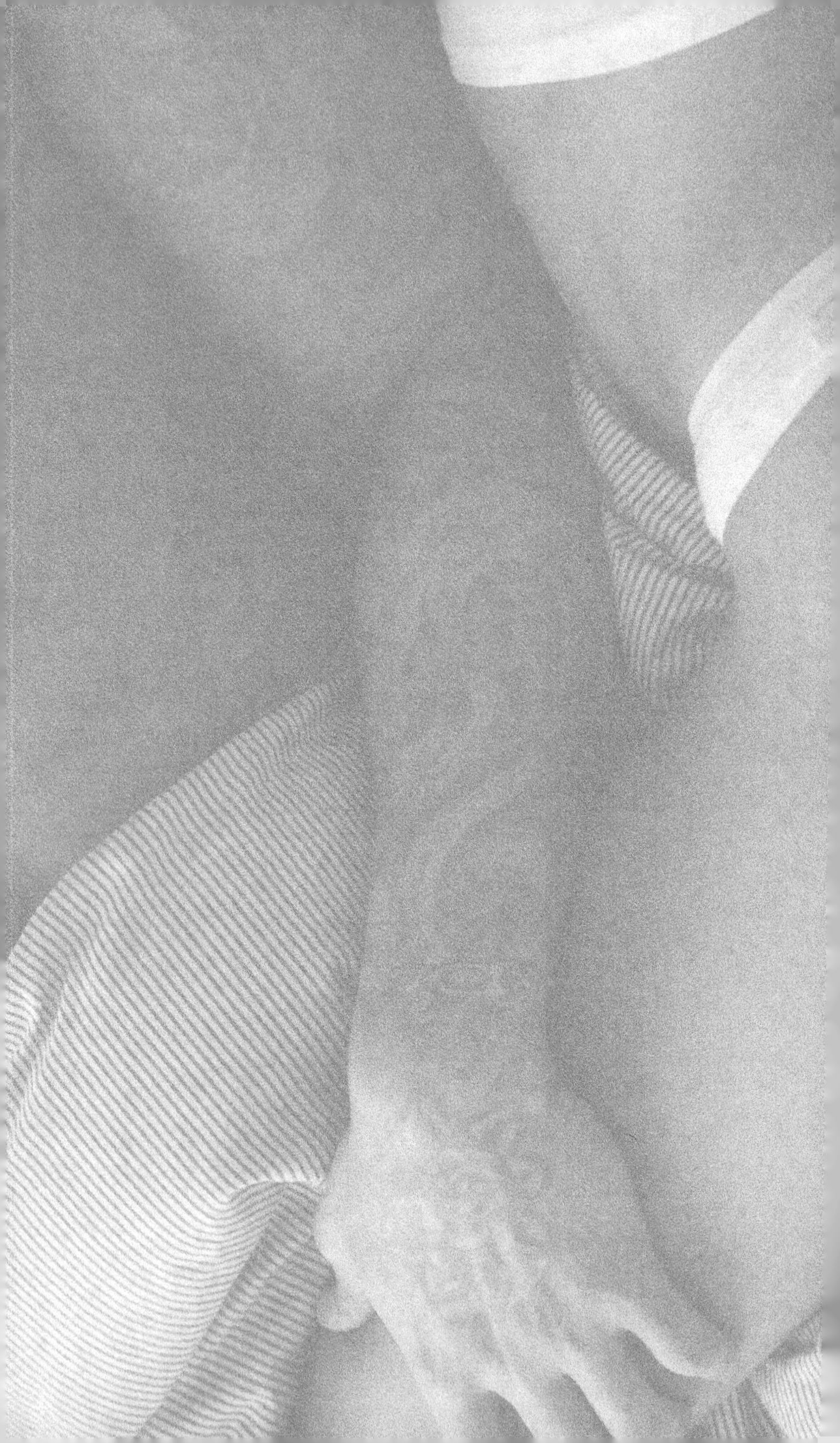

CHAPTER FOURTEEN
LOGAN

The sharp ding of the elevator's arrival pulls my focus from the scuff on my new biker boots. It took me one night—*just one*—before I couldn't stand being in that cabin anymore. I told myself I could use the time in Tahoe to clear my head, to plan the next steps for the company without the distractions of LA. But everywhere I turned, I found traces of Rosie—her vanilla perfume lingering in the air, the faint scent of her coconut shampoo on the sheets, and the fuzzy socks she'd left behind—each one a stark reminder of how much I missed her. There was no way I would've been able to concentrate.

Leaning against the wall outside her apartment, my pulse kicks up as the elevator doors slide open, hoping she's finally back from work. A jolt of electricity races through me as Rosie steps out, her head bowed slightly while she rummages through her oversized handbag. I'm already at half-staff as I shamelessly give her a once-over. I don't think I've seen her in business attire before, and I'm realizing what a shame that is.

The sleek black pencil skirt she's wearing hugs her

curves in all the right places, and the silk of her sleeveless pink blouse showcases her full breasts, the color a perfect contrast to her golden skin. Her long, dark hair sways as she moves, curling softly over her shoulders, while what appears to be a blazer is folded neatly over her arm. And those heels —black, sky-high, and utterly devastating—click against the tile with a rhythm that demands attention.

I bite down on my knuckles, barely holding back a groan.

Work Rosie is sexy, yet professional, all no-nonsense confidence and effortless grace. I wonder if she'd be into a little office role play. I'd bet those heels would look even better perched on my shoulders.

Damn, that's a nice visual.

"Logan?" Rosie says, startling me out of my X-rated daydream.

I grin, stepping forward. "Surprise."

She tilts her head to the side. "What are you doing here?"

I reach into my pocket and pull out a pair of fuzzy socks, holding them up for her to see. "You left these at the cabin. I thought you might need them."

Rosie's lips part, but she seems to be at a loss for words. Her dark eyes meet mine, softening as she realizes why I'm really here. "You couldn't take being away from me any longer, huh?"

I wrap a hand around her hip, pulling her closer. "Exactly." I lean into her ear and whisper, "And I bet you missed being woken up by my tongue this morning, didn't you?"

I can't resist brushing my lips against hers when Rosie's cheeks flush the prettiest shade of pink. It's just a taste, not nearly enough to satisfy the growing need inside of me, but the hallway of her apartment building isn't the best place to do all the dirty things I've been imagining.

She swats my chest, a teasing glint in her eyes and a soft smile playing on her lips. "Wow. You really are a stage-five clinger, aren't you?"

"Only when it's something, or should I say some*one*, I really want." I grin, watching her blush deepen.

Her brows lift. "You're awfully sure of yourself, Mr. Edwards."

"You're awfully cute when you're pretending to be so disinterested." My gaze falls to her lips. They're painted a dusty shade of pink today, perfectly accentuating her cupid's bow. "Open the door, Pip."

Rosie punches in a code on the keypad and pushes the door open. I'm right behind her, nudging it closed with a soft thud. Her subtle scent drifts through the air, mingling with a warm hint of jasmine, likely lingering from the jarred candle on the coffee table. Her new place is small, but the high ceilings and exposed ductwork give it an open, airy feel. The wall of windows showcasing LA's skyline adds a sense of grandeur, making the space feel far more expansive than its modest size suggests.

It's an open floor plan with a neutral base, but Rosie's personality shines through in the details. The first thing you notice is an exposed brick wall with a huge canvas of Frida Kahlo wearing a crown of marigolds. The painting is bold, like its subject. Unapologetic. Maybe even a little rebellious. I smile to myself, thinking how much it reminds me of Rosie. Wouldn't surprise me if she picked it to anchor herself...to remember who the hell she is every damn day.

Just beneath the painting, nestled into the gallery wall, is a framed photo from Rosie's graduation trip to Ireland. The Cliffs of Moher stretch out behind her, mist curling at the edges, while she and Sylvie beam at the camera with frizzy, wind-swept hair. Their moms stand beside them, equally disheveled and just as fierce. Four women, locked arm in arm, laughing like they owned the damn world.

"God, I remember how excited you were while on that trip like it was yesterday."

She smiles softly. "It was a pretty magical week."

Rosie and I communicated often while she was gone. I was constantly on alert because she flooded my phone with daily photos while I was hanging out with her brother. I didn't want to explain to Ry why I was talking to his sister so much, but I also didn't want her to stop, so I encouraged her to send as many pictures as she could.

I spent more hours than I'd care to admit scrolling through those snapshots of her trip while I was at Stanford. If I was feeling particularly homesick, they were guaranteed to make me feel a little less so. Rosie and Sylvie standing in front of castles or houses with oddly short colorful doors. The numerous traffic jams—aka sheep walking along the road—they encountered while driving through the countryside. Celtic cross headstones, beautiful cathedrals, rolling green hills, random ruins, jagged cliffs, you name it. I even got the occasional dirty souvenir item she found hilarious. I felt like I was right there with her sometimes.

I desperately wished I *was* there with her the *entire* time.

Shaking out of the memory, my eyes continue to scan the room, catching on a turquoise coffee cart with hand-painted mugs hanging from a rack, then a Talavera plate brightening the corner of the white kitchen counter. Next to the plate is a small silver dish I swear I've seen before, but I can't quite place it. I step closer, narrowing my eyes as the overhead light catches on four faint etchings around the rim.

"Why does this seem familiar?" I ask.

Rosie glances over and smiles. "It sat on my dresser when we were kids. You probably saw it a million times without realizing."

I nod slowly. "Okay, now I remember. You used to keep your lip balm and loose change in it."

"And hair ties. *So many* hair ties."

I chuckle, running my thumb along the worn edge. "What do the symbols represent?"

"They're the four treasures of the Tuatha Dé. The sword, the spear, the cauldron, and the stone. My Nana Mór was *very* into ancestral magic. Her stories about the Irish warrior gods are what spawned my obsession with romantasy, so can't say I'm mad about it."

I laugh. "Any excuse to read fairy smut with you."

Rosie's eyes roll. "Nobody *needs* an excuse to read fairy smut. They just do it because it's *awesome*."

She snort-laughs, coaxing me to grin like a fool. I give the dish one last glance before continuing my slow sweep of the apartment.

Velvety eggplant-colored drapes frame the windows, their rich hue softened by the glow of retro brass lamps. The dark gray couch is understated, but the lime green crocheted blanket tossed over the back adds just the right hit of playful contrast.

"This place really suits you, Rosie."

She glances around, as if she's trying to see it through my eyes. "You think so?"

"I do," I say with a nod. "It's warm. Feminine." My eyes are drawn back to the eclectic gallery wall. The varying sizes and styles of art create a perfect balance of whimsy and charm. Grinning, I hold my thumb and forefinger an inch apart and add, "A little chaotic."

Rosie's eyes glimmer with amusement. "That tracks."

A pile of paperbacks sits on the side table. They're stacked on top of one another like a game of Tetris gone wrong, each with a bookmark protruding from the pages. I cross the room, inspecting the covers, confirming my suspicions.

"Ooh, what do we have here?" I flip to the marked page in one of the books, landing on a particularly spicy scene between a woman and two...no, wait, *three* men. "You dirty, dirty girl. I knew you liked reading romance, but I had no idea you were into the *extra* smutty stuff."

"Don't judge me," Rosie huffs, swiping the book from my hand and smacking my arm with it.

"I'm *not* judging," I say with a chuckle, catching her wrist and pulling her toward me. "I like it." I brush some hair away from her face and add, "I like *you*, Rosie. I don't think there's a damn thing about you that I don't like."

She lifts her chin, meeting my eyes. "Yeah?"

"Yeah," I confirm.

Rosie smiles bashfully, and her cheeks flush.

"So fucking beautiful," I murmur, pressing a soft kiss to her temple and breathing in her sweet, familiar scent before pulling back slightly. My hands cradle her face, my thumbs tracing the delicate curve of her jaw. Rosie's pupils darken, her breaths quicken, and I know she feels the same fevered energy crackling between us.

I'd love nothing more than to get lost in her curves all night, but I don't want her thinking I flew back early just for sex. Don't get me wrong—the sex is incredible, and I wouldn't say no if she's game—but honestly, I'd be just as happy cuddling on the couch while she reads one of her dirty books. I just want to be in her orbit.

With a deep breath, I let my hands fall to my sides and take a step back, giving us both a moment to clear the lust-infused haze.

"So, are you going to give me the grand tour?" I ask, flashing her a grin.

Rosie shoots me a wry look. "You've pretty much seen it. It's a one-bedroom loft in the Arts District, not a mansion up in the hills."

"Humor me, smartass," I deadpan.

She sighs, kicking off her heels and leading me down a short hallway, that opens into a bedroom dominated by a queen-sized bed with a padded white headboard. The duvet is soft gray, accented by a cluster of brightly patterned throw pillows, and a boho macramé wall hanging above the bed. In the corner, a round fuchsia chair is barely visible beneath a precarious pile of clothes, at least two feet high.

"Short on closet space around here?" I tease, smirking.

"Haha," she mutters, flipping me off. "I've been busy, okay?"

"Uh-huh." I arch a brow, clearly unconvinced. Rosie's always been allergic to putting away clean laundry.

She huffs and rolls her eyes. "At least I didn't let the load sit in the washer for three days like I normally do. I call that a win, thank you very much." She props a hand on her hip, narrowing her eyes. "May we move on?"

Grinning, I grab her hips, pulling her into me. I kiss the spot just beneath her ear, feeling her soften under my touch. "Aw, Pip, don't be mad. I was just giving you shit."

Rosie sighs dramatically but smirks, taking my hand and leading me back into the hallway. She shows me a small, but modern bathroom followed by a laundry room—aka closet—before we reached the end of our tour.

"And we've hit a dead end," she announces, leading me back into the main area.

"Man, you weren't kidding. This entire apartment can't be more than six or seven hundred square feet."

She shrugs. "Seven twenty-three, actually, but I love it."

I know I'm getting ahead of myself, but that comment demonstrates yet another reason why she's the perfect woman for me. Rosie may appreciate her designer shoes and purses, but she's not materialistic. Never has been, and that's so fucking refreshing.

All those nights partying with Hollywood's so-called elite, I felt like an impostor in my own skin. I won't lie and say I didn't have some fun, but the constant shallowness and toxicity gutted me after a while. No matter how great my life seemed on the surface, the emptiness only grew, clawing at me from the inside out.

But I haven't felt that darkness since the moment I saw Rosie standing on a frozen Nevadan porch, looking like my greatest dream come true. Unsurprising, considering she's one of the most authentic people I've ever met. She's always had a way of grounding me like no one else, brightening my world by merely existing.

"I really like it, Pip."

She takes a seat on the couch, folding her legs beneath her. "Thanks. It's funny because my last apartment was three times this size, but I *hated* it. It never felt like home to me. Julian had lived there first, and he was such a minimalist neat freak, I didn't feel comfortable trying to add my own touches."

I frown as I join her. "The more you tell me about this guy, the more I want to throttle him."

God, what a prick. Rosie's lived in this place for maybe six weeks, and it already has that lived-in feel. It's homey, a place you'd look forward to coming home to at the end of the day. I know that's one hundred percent her doing, and it kills me to think of that pompous ass making her feel uncomfortable in her own home. I don't understand why she'd put up with that. The Rosie I know would never allow someone to stifle her fire like he so clearly did.

I rest my head on the cushion, turning to the side to meet her gaze. "Why did you agree to marry him, Rosie? Did you really see yourself growing old together?"

She looks down for a moment, and when she lifts her chin, her eyes glisten with unshed tears. "When I imagined a future with him, I didn't see *anything*...good or bad. It was just...blank. Maybe I should've taken that as a warning. I'm always planning ahead, always pondering 'what ifs,' but with Julian, there was this...void. I guess I convinced myself that *no brain chatter meant no impending disasters.*" She scoffs, shaking her head. "I learned my lesson the hard way on that one, huh?"

I reach out, brushing my fingers against hers where they rest on the couch cushion. "Don't beat yourself up about it, Pip. Humans make mistakes. It's one of the few guarantees in life."

Her lips twitch into a faint, humorless smile. "Yeah, but even without the cheating, there were *a lot* of clues he wasn't as committed to our relationship as he should've been if we were getting married."

I tilt my head, studying her. "Like what?"

"Stupid things, really, but things that make me *me*. Like...even in the beginning, he never really made an effort to know me. Didn't bother asking questions, unless the topic involved him. To this day, he has no clue how I take my coffee. Or what my favorite food is. You know how some-times I need to step away to find a quiet place? Julian had no clue that meant I was overstimulated and needed a few minutes to regroup. I told him directly what I was doing *and* why, but it must've gone in one ear, and out the other. The very next time I tried slipping away, he'd follow me, demanding I come back before my supposed rudeness embarrassed him.

"He'd regularly have an excuse to avoid my family gath-erings, even though I was quite vocal about how important they are to me. I'd happily hang out with him and his friends, but he'd never do the same with mine. I could go on and on, Logan. When I look back on the entirety of our rela-tionship, it was very one-sided. But I was so lost at the time, I didn't see the obvious." Her gaze is raw. Searching. "Why did I let it get that far?"

"Because you give people the benefit of the doubt," I say matter-of-factly. "There's nothing wrong with that."

She shrugs. "I still feel like an idiot sometimes."

"Rosie, *he's* the idiot for not appreciating what he had."

"That's what Sylvie says. Although, she usually adds a string of expletives afterward." She chuckles lightly, but she still seems dejected.

I pull her into a side hug, kissing the crown of her head. "The important thing is you got out, and that took guts, Rosie. You should be proud of yourself for that. I sure as hell am."

Her breath catches, and she laughs shakily as she wipes at the lone tear rolling down her face. "Why do you always know the perfect thing to say?"

"It's a gift." I lean back into the couch and wink.

Rosie rolls her eyes but grins, the melancholy in her

expression lifting just a little. "And then you go and ruin it by being an arrogant ass," she teases.

I laugh. "It's not arrogance if I can back it up, baby."

She shakes her head, fighting a smile, then nudges my thigh with her own. "Hey, Logan?"

"Yeah?"

"Thanks for always being my safe space. I don't know if I've ever said that before."

I smile softly, squeezing her hand. "Anytime, Pip. Always."

Her stomach growls, making us both laugh.

"You hungry?"

"Starving," she replies. "What are we ordering?"

"Pizza work for you?"

"Pizza *always* works for me."

"Pizza it is," I say, opening the DoorDash app. Once our order is placed, I add, "Done. It'll be here in about forty-five minutes."

Rosie slowly inches her lips toward mine. "Feel like fooling around while we wait? You kinda owe me."

"*Owe you?*" My brows lift. "For what?"

She shifts her body toward me, lifting her skirt just enough to straddle my legs. "I watched the video you sent me earlier, but I never actually got the chance to do anything about it."

I grin. "You need some relief, Rosie?"

"I mean, if you think you can accomplish that, I wouldn't say no." She shrugs, feigning nonchalance, but her eyes sparkle with mischief.

"I can *always* accomplish that, baby," I tell her.

There's no doubt I want her, but I refuse to be another person in Rosie's life who fails her. I need to make sure she has no doubt how much I value her mind and her heart, not just her body.

"For the record, Pip, I flew back early for *you*, not your body." I kiss her gently.

"I know that, Logan." She kisses me back, fingertips tightening on my shoulders as she pulls away. "The hot sex is just a bonus."

Her words awaken something deep and primal inside of me, and I slide my hands up her silky thighs, feeling the tension in her muscles relax beneath my grip.

"Well, in that case...consider me at your service."

The smile she hits me with is blinding. I don't know what I've done to get so lucky, but I'm sure as hell not taking it for granted. Without a doubt, Rosie is what I've been waiting for all these years. Being with her on this new level makes me feel whole in a way I never have before. I know she's not there yet, but if I play my cards right, I'm hopeful I can do the same for her.

CHAPTER FIFTEEN

LOGAN

I don't think there's a better way to start my day than with Rosie Morales in my arms. Her back molded to my front, messy hair tickling my nose, soft curves filling my hands. Even her too-small mattress can't dampen the euphoria, although if sleeping at Rosie's is going to become a regular thing, I might have to buy her a new bed. I love having her pressed up against me, but I also like feeling like I'm not about to roll onto the floor at any moment.

I groan as she playfully wiggles her ass against my dick. "Don't start something you're not willing to finish, Rosie."

She giggles. "Who says I'm not willing to finish?"

Her mouth opens on a gasp as I lightly tug on her nipple rings. "I like the way you think."

Rosie moans, arching into my palms.

I relish in the current that zings through my veins with each caress. How her breath hitches as she writhes beneath my touch. I grind my length against her, driving us both crazy with anticipation. Goose bumps blossom across her shoulder as my lips brush against her nape. I pull Rosie closer, not an inch separating us as I inhale her sweet skin.

"Logan," she breathes, telling me she's feeling this, too.

I've never been so consumed by another person. Every pulse, every glide of skin on skin, is amplified a million times over.

"I know, baby."

My wandering hands reach the apex of her thighs, confirming what I already knew. She's more than ready for me.

Rosie whimpers, hips lifting, begging for more. I spread her thighs, resting one leg over my knee, giving me just the right angle to enter her tight body.

"Fuck," I grunt. "Nothing feels better than this. Your sweet pussy was made for me, Rosie. Tell me you know that."

Being inside of this woman is like coming home after years of aimless wandering. Every thrust is filled with promise. Every kiss laced with possibility.

"God, yes," she agrees.

Rosie cranes her neck backward, seeking my mouth. I kiss her passionately, our tongues dueling as our bodies work together in perfect harmony. The outside world fades away, we're just two people lost in each other's touch, driven by a dance as old as time. I never want to stop feeling this close to her. Never want to stop making her feel this kind of pleasure.

I never want her to be anyone else's but mine.

I reach down and rub her clit, feeling her body tremble beneath mine. She's right on the edge, hips bucking, trying to pull me deeper inside. I press my body impossibly closer, working her over until she's so tightly wound, she has no choice but to let go.

"That's it, sweetheart," I murmur into her ear. "Be a

good girl and come on my cock. Let me feel you come undone, Rosie."

She clenches around me, crying out as she reaches the peak. I drive deeper, prolonging her orgasm as long as possible before I feel a familiar tingle in my balls. I pound into her hard and fast, the air filling with the sounds of bodies slapping. Moaning and gasping. When I can no longer resist, I come with a roar, her name a prayer on my lips.

As the high wanes, I pull out and gently turn her body toward mine. I probably have the stupidest grin on my face when I see the dick-drunk look in her eyes, proud as hell I'm responsible for it.

I lean down and brush a kiss against her forehead. "That is officially my new favorite way to start the day."

She hums, nuzzling her face into the crook of my neck. "Same."

I wrap my arms around her and squeeze. "What time do you need to be at work?"

"Eight," she answers with a yawn. When her phone starts buzzing on the nightstand she adds, "And there's my alarm, telling me I need to get my ass out of bed."

I reach over to silence it, seeing it's a quarter past six. "Hop in the shower, Pip. I'll have breakfast and coffee waiting when you're ready."

"I wish we could stay in bed all day." She nips the underside of my jaw. "But I like being able to pay my rent, so work it is."

I playfully smack her ass as she climbs over me to get out of bed.

Rosie gives me a mock glare. "Rude."

I fold my arms behind my head, giving her a thorough—and appreciative—once-over. We never closed the blinds last night, so the room is bathed in the soft, bluish hues of early dawn, tinged with the faintest blush of pink. My eyes trace every line and contour of Rosie's gloriously nude body, captivated by the beauty before me. Thankfully, the windows in here are clerestory, so we don't need to worry about anyone else enjoying the view.

"You love it." I wink.

Her lips twitch. "Maybe."

She squeals when I make a grab for her, and darts out of the bedroom.

A short while later, Rosie steps into the main room dressed in a sleek black blouse with some flowery thing near the collar and tailored gray pants. The look is understated and classy, yet on her, there's somehow a suggestive edge to it as well. Or maybe that's just my dirty mind.

"Sit," I say, setting a plate on the breakfast bar.

She smiles as she glances at the steaming omelet and fresh fruit. "I could get used to having a personal chef."

I finish sweetening her coffee, placing the mug before her. "Didn't we already cover this? I'll do anything to keep Hangry Rosalie at bay."

She laughs. "That was in Tahoe. Here, you have an empire to run."

I wave her off. "Meh, I have help doing that."

Rosie snorts. "You do, but I also happen to know you make a habit of leading by example with work ethic and drive, so I'm sure you have your hands in all the pots."

I raise my brows. "Who've you been talking to about my office habits?"

Her shoulders lift in a slight shrug. "Ryan's mentioned it once or twice."

"Ah."

I should've known. The guy loves roasting me to my

face, but he's always been one of my biggest cheerleaders, singing my praises to anyone who'll listen.

And yet, here I am, thanking him for that unwavering support by sneaking around with his sister behind his back.

Christ, I'm an asshole.

Rosie sips her coffee, humming in approval. For a moment, we just look at each other, the silence stretching between us with everything we're not saying.

Ryan.

Her brother.

My best friend.

The guy who's trusted me with *everything*—his friendship, his secrets, his career, *his family*, who means more to him than anything. There's no way he won't see this as a betrayal when he finds out.

Rosie's fingers tap lightly against the rim of her mug, seemingly lost in thought. When our eyes meet, I'm pretty sure she's thinking the same thing I am.

This is dangerous.

We're toeing a line I don't think either of us ever expected to cross, but neither of us wants to stop.

She breaks the tension with a soft smile. "What's on the agenda today, Mr. CEO?"

I open my mouth to answer at the same time my phone chimes with a text alert. Rosie and I both glance down and see Ryan's name on the screen.

"Speak of the devil," she mumbles.

I exhale sharply, opening the message.

> Ryan: Dude. When are you back from Tahoe? Shit's hitting the fan with PPA. We need to talk ASAP.

"Fuck."

Rosie frowns. "What's wrong?"

"I don't know exactly," I reply. "But it sounds like we've run into a snag with the acquisition."

PPA, or Peak Performance Analytics, is the firm that created an industry-leading algorithm capable of predicting gaming outcomes with freakish accuracy. If BetMasters acquires its IP, I can move forward with my plan to pitch an exclusive partnership with Olympus Resorts & Gaming, the biggest player in Vegas. Ryan has a contact there, so we've already made it past the gatekeeper. I just need the technology.

Which is why I *need* this fucking deal to go through.

I hit the call button, holding my index finger up to my lips in a universal 'be quiet' gesture.

Rosie nods once, her expression unreadable.

Ryan picks up on the first ring. "Hey. Sorry to pull you away from whichever rando you've got in your bed, but I knew you'd want to hear about this right away."

I ignore his assumption about me hooking up with random women.

"What's going on?"

"We've got a problem with PPA."

I pinch the bridge of my nose. "What kind of problem?"

Ryan is my VP of Acquisitions. BetMasters wouldn't have grown nearly as much as it has if he wasn't on my team.

"I'm hearing buzz they might be thinking of backing out," he tells me. "I should have more information in the next few hours. You're back this weekend, right?"

"I...uh, I'm back now actually. I came home last night." I take a sip of my coffee to stifle my guilt. "I was planning to check in with you after I woke up a bit."

Or, you know, after I left your sister's apartment.

I feel Rosie's eyes on me as I rub a hand over my jaw, exhaling through my nose. She knows me well enough to pick up on my distress—my clenched jaw, the tight set of my shoulders, the way my fingers drum restlessly against the counter. She doesn't interrupt, doesn't press, but her quiet presence grounds me even as my mind races.

"Why would they back out? I thought everything was pretty much a go."

"That's what I'm working on now," he answers. "Why don't we meet for lunch? I should have enough intel by then. Say Lou's at one?"

"Yeah, that works. I'll see you then."

I end the call, raking a hand through my hair.

"You okay?" Rosie asks.

She rounds the counter, wrapping her arms around my waist and resting her head against my chest.

"Better now." I squeeze her back. "As for work, I don't know all the details yet. Ry's looking into it, and we're meeting for lunch at one."

Rosie's chin lifts. "Are you worried about seeing him? Having to hide...this?" She gestures between us.

I tuck a piece of hair behind her ear. "Of course, I am. I don't like lying. You know that. And it's not like I have any chance of avoiding him. Now is not the time to work remotely."

She sighs. "I feel like I'm being unfair, asking you to do this."

I crouch down to meet her at eye level. "I will do whatever I need to do to protect this." I mimic her gesture from earlier. "I know this is new, and intense, and you're scared, but I'm not going anywhere. Take as much time as you need. When you're ready, I'll fucking tell anyone who'll listen that you're mine."

She smiles shyly. "I'm yours, huh? Does that mean I get to call you mine?"

"Rosie, I've been yours since the day we met." I grin. "I've just been waiting for you to catch up."

She lets out a soft laugh, shaking her head as if I'm ridiculous, but the pink tint on her cheeks gives her away. With a glance at the clock on the microwave, she groans. "I have to go," she says reluctantly. I watch as she pulls away and grabs her bag, slipping her shoes on before turning back to me. "Lock up when you leave?"

I nod. "Have a good day at work, Pip."

"Good luck at lunch, Mr. CEO." She smirks, then heads for the door, pausing just long enough to look back at me.

I step forward, pressing one last kiss to her forehead. "Drive safe." I add another to her lips because once isn't enough. As I watch her walk down the hallway toward the elevator, I realize I'll likely never get my fill of kisses from that woman.

Now I just need to figure how to make her feel the same way about me.

CHAPTER SIXTEEN

LOGAN

I spot Ryan the moment I step inside our favorite diner, tucked into a booth near the back, scrolling through his phone. This place hasn't changed much since the '50s, with its chrome fixtures, checkerboard floors, and faded red vinyl booths. It's kind of a dive, to be honest, and the smell of bacon grease and coffee is permanently embedded into every surface, but the place is clean, and they make the best burgers in town, so we come here often.

Ryan looks up as I approach, locking his phone and tossing it onto the table. His brown eyes, a near match to Rosie's, sharpen as they take me in.

"You look like shit." His dark brows lift.

I snort as I take a seat across from him. "Good to see you too, asshole."

He smirks. "What's the matter, pumpkin? Haven't had much sleep lately? Too busy sinking balls-deep into hot ski bunnies? How many were there? Be honest. Two? Three? Twenty-Five?"

Nope. Just your sister, dude.

"Jesus." I roll my eyes, shaking my head. "You really

think I spent the entire time I was in Tahoe hooking up with strangers? *And twenty-five?!* I was gone ten days. What the hell, man?"

"Okay, maybe twenty-five was a bit of an exaggeration." Ryan shrugs.

"Ya think?" I deadpan.

"But a few wouldn't be all that unreasonable."

"Hi, Pot. The name's Kettle." I flip him off and flag down a waitress.

When I told Rosie her brother no longer blabbed about his exploits, that didn't mean he wasn't interested in hearing about mine. Not that I've shared—I've never been one to kiss and tell—but since I've taken a break from dating, he's been awfully invested in getting me back on the horse, so to speak. I'd say maybe he wanted to live vicariously through my adventures, but Ryan always has a beautiful woman on call, so that can't possibly be it. I think he misses going out to clubs more than anything. I'm certainly not stopping him from going, but he says it isn't the same without me.

"But seriously. Why'd you come back early?" He reaches for his water, taking a sip. "I thought for sure I'd have to fly up there and drag you away from some blonde with big tits."

"Nope, no blondes." Technically true. "Talk to me about PPA. What'd you find out?" I keep my voice casual, hoping he doesn't notice my obvious deflection.

Ryan leans back, draping one arm over the booth. "Rumor is, they're considering licensing the algorithm instead of selling it outright."

My jaw tightens. "Since when?"

Our waitress, Beverly, shows up before he can answer. "Two bacon cheeseburgers, extra fries, and a Coke?"

We both nod, confirming we'd like our usual order. As

soon as she walks away, I cross my arms over my chest. "Go on…"

"I got wind of it this morning, so I think it's fairly recent. If it's true, we're hosed, dude." He rubs his jaw. "If they license instead of selling, we lose all leverage." He shakes his head. "Olympus would be dead in the water before we even had a chance to formally pitch. They made it clear they'd only be interested in exclusivity. No proprietary rights to the algorithm, no deal."

Fuck.

Partnering with Olympus would be a game-changer for our profits, and we're so fucking close to making it happen. If we owned PPA's algorithm outright, and subsequently closed the deal with Olympus, BetMasters would dominate sports betting *and* sports data analytics.

But if PPA changes course? We're fucked. Back to square one, with zero options on the table.

"What's their angle?" I ask. "Why switch to licensing at the last minute? I thought Simon wanted to take the company in a different direction and focus on that."

Ryan exhales, shifting forward. "I don't know yet, but I'm working on it. My gut says someone's gotten in his ear."

I frown. "A competing firm?"

He shrugs. "Maybe. Or maybe an investor convinced him he'll make more long-term money by licensing instead of selling outright." He taps a finger against the table, deep in thought. "Simon was all in on selling a few weeks ago. Something changed his mind."

I rake a hand through my hair, already running through ways to counter this. "We need to shut that shit down. If he wants more money, we offer more money."

Ryan nods. "That's exactly what I was thinking. I have a call lined up with him later this afternoon. I'm going to try getting a read on him, and if I'm lucky, ferret a confession out of him."

"Good." I nod. "Call me as soon as you're done. And see if you can schedule an in-person meeting for Monday. I'd like a few days to gather as much information as we can."

"Already done." Ryan smiles.

I arch a brow. "That was fast."

"I'm a man of action."

Beverly swings by with our drinks, refilling Ryan's water and setting my Coke on the table. "Your food will be out in just a few more minutes."

"Thank you," we say in unison.

Ryan takes a sip, then shifts gears. "Now that we've got that out of the way, what do you have planned on Friday?"

I narrow my eyes. "Why?"

"You know Penelope, the hot barista from the lobby?"

"The blonde with the nose ring?"

He points to me. "That's the one."

"What about her?"

"Well...I have a date with her on Friday. But her friend just came into town unexpectedly, so now she can't go unless *I* have a friend to set her friend up with. She doesn't want to ditch her."

"Oh, hell no." I laugh.

Ryan gives me a ridiculous pout. "C'mon, man. It's not a pity date. I swear this girl is a smoke show. Penny showed me a picture. When's the last time you went on an actual date? It'll be real chill. She wants to hit up a food truck then we're going to see a movie at the rooftop cinema."

The last thing I want to do is cozy up on a bean bag for two hours with someone who isn't Rosie.

I shake my head. "Sorry, man. Not gonna happen."

"Why not? You got your eye on someone?"

I hesitate, making *his* eyes narrow.

Shit.

I shrug. "I'm just not in the mood for a setup, man. Work's a mess right now, and I don't need the added distraction."

Ryan scoffs. "I call bullshit. You haven't been in the mood for a *distraction* for several months now, which is weird as hell for you, dude. You say you weren't fucking your brains out in Tahoe. You claim you're not interested in anyone. So, what's the harm in spending a few hours with a beautiful woman? She lives in Sonoma, so it's not like she's looking for anything beyond one night. It's a win-win situation, Logan."

I reach for my drink, buying myself a second to think. I don't trust myself to sit here and outright lie to his face. But if I don't come up with a solid reason, he's going to keep digging. And if he keeps digging, it won't be long before he realizes that all signs point to Rosie.

Fuck, fuck, fuck.

"Okay, fine. There *is* someone I'm interested in." I hold a hand up when he opens his mouth to speak. "No, I'm *not* giving you any details, because it's new, and she's asked me to keep it between us for now. I'm going to respect her wishes."

Well, look at that. One-hundred-percent honesty, no fists to my face. How's that for a win-win situation, buddy?

Ryan studies me, a little too intently for my comfort, as he swirls the ice around his glass. "Where'd you meet her? Is she an actress? Model? Oh, maybe an influencer? She must have some level of fame if she asked you to keep it quiet."

I shake my head, shutting him down. "*No details* means you don't get to ask questions."

He leans forward, resting his arms on the table. "Fine. I'll let you have your little secret for now. I'll get it out of you eventually." His lips curve into a smirk. "Or maybe I'll have my mom grill you for answers. You're still coming to her birthday party, right?"

I nearly groan.

There's no way I can flake on this party. But the thought of me and Rosie being in the same house as her brother, their parents, and half their extended family feels like a live grenade, waiting to blow. It'll be hard enough keeping my hands off of her, but I honestly don't know if I'll be able to keep my eyes off of her, too. And I'm scared shitless I'll give something away the second one of her family members catches me doing it, especially their mom. Tatum Morales is nothing if not tenacious when she senses one of her children is interested in someone. And even though I'm not blood, she's almost as invested in my love life as Ryan is.

Dammit. I need to veer this conversation into safer territory.

"Of course, I'll be there. I'd never miss an opportunity to make you look like a chump when it's time to open gifts."

"Real funny, dick." He flips me off.

I laugh. "You're worried now, aren't you?"

Ryan glares. "No."

"Sure, buddy. You keep telling yourself that."

"Fuck off," he mutters.

Beverly's back with our food, and after that, thankfully, our conversation remains in neutral waters. But my brain is still running calculations. If PPA is playing us, I need to figure out a way to get ahead of it. Because I really can't afford to gamble on this deal.

CHAPTER SEVENTEEN
ROSALIE

I'm just getting home from work when my phone buzzes. I grin like a fool as I open the text message, seeing Logan's name on the screen.

> Logan: Let me take you out tonight.

I'm not sure if I should be giddy or anxious in this situation. I decide maybe a little of both as I text him back.

> Me: That depends. Where are you trying to take me?

His response is almost immediate.

> Logan: Somewhere dark and intimate. Trust me, you'll love it.

> Me: Cocky, much?

> Logan: What's that, you say? You'd like me to send you a dick pic?

I snort but can't say I hate the idea.

> Me: Define dark. Are we talking literal darkness, as in we won't be able to see five feet in front of us? Or are you trying to lure me into some kind of freaky sex dungeon?

> Logan: Do you WANT me to lure you into some kind of freaky sex dungeon? 😏

I laugh.

> Me: You wish, Edwards.

> Logan: Hey, I'm not kink-shaming. We both know you're into spanking, Rosie. I can't say dungeons have ever appealed to me before, but if that's how you want to play, I'm definitely interested.

Deliciously filthy man.

I jokingly bring up pegging and now, BDSM torture chambers—two things that have never been on my personal radar before—and he just rolls with the punches, saying if *I'm* into it, he's into it. Which then makes me think about doing those dirty things with him, wondering if that's something I *would* be into. Which then makes me think about all the other sexy things I've never really considered doing before.

I wouldn't say my sex life has been entirely vanilla, but it certainly wasn't adventurous either. Or, you know...*satisfying*, considering the lack of orgasms. But if I'm going to explore my curiosities, there's no one I trust more than Logan to do that with me. And I know that whatever we do —even if it's something I might not be interested in repeating—he'll ensure I'm satisfied during the experience itself. Man, I need to start making a list. Okay, first there's butt stuff. I definitely want to try that. Then, maybe some—

My phone buzzes again, jolting me out of my mental hopscotch.

Logan: Did I scare you off just now?

I smile softly, easily imagining the concerned look on his face, and how he's probably berating himself, thinking he made me feel uncomfortable.

Deliciously filthy and *respectfully sweet man,* I amend.

Knowing I need to alleviate his anxiety, I hit the dial button on my phone so he can hear the sincerity in my voice.

"Hey," he says, picking up right away. "You okay?"

"I'm *fine,* Logan," I assure him, walking down the hallway toward my bathroom. "I just got sidetracked, imagining what being in a sex dungeon with you might look like. Which made me curious about other sexy things..."

"Oh yeah?" I can hear the smile in his deep voice. "Tell me more about these sexy curiosities."

I switch my phone to speaker and set it on the vanity. "Maybe if you're a good boy, I'll tell you in person later."

"Is that a yes to our date?" he asks.

I pull my blouse over my head and unclasp my bra, sighing in relief as my breasts are freed. "Of course, it is. But I'd like a little more information on where we're going. What if we run into someone we know?"

"Rosie, I've got it covered. I was being literal when I said this place is dark. It's also exclusive. None of the mutual people in our lives have access to it, as far as I know."

"What time should I be ready? And what kind of dress code are we looking at?"

"Can you be ready by eight? And cocktail attire."

"That works." I unzip my pants, sliding them down my legs.

"Did I just hear a zipper? What are you doing right now?"

My panties follow. "Getting naked. I'm about to hop in the shower."

A FaceTime notification instantly pops up, making my lips twitch.

"Accept the video request, Rosie," Logan demands, making my toes curl.

"No can do," I say cheekily, despite my vagina's protest. "I have a hot date to get ready for. Gotta-go-byyeeeee!"

I end the call, laughing as I cut Logan off mid-curse. Was that a little mean? Maybe. Am I looking forward to the retribution I know he'll deliver?

Hell, yes.

I TOLD Logan I'd meet him in the lobby of my building, so fifteen minutes before he's scheduled to arrive, I open my apartment door, only to jump when I see him right there, propped against the opposite wall, waiting for me.

He gives me an infuriatingly sexy smirk. "Well, at least you didn't threaten to karate-chop my balls off this time."

I roll my eyes, closing the door behind me. "The man thinks he's a comedian," I mutter.

Logan chuckles, but when I look up, the hunger in his eyes robs me of breath. "Christ, Pip. Look at you." His voice is deeper now. Rougher. "You trying to kill me tonight?"

His golden-green gaze blazes a slow path over me, starting at my Ruby Woo red lips, drifting to my bare shoulders, then lingering for a moment over my breasts. His teeth graze his knuckles, like he's physically restraining himself, as my nipples pebble, making it painfully obvious I'm not wearing a bra.

Once he sees the low back of the dress, he'll understand why.

His gaze slides down my bare legs, tracing every inch until it lands on my bright red heels, then slowly makes its way back up. With the unseasonably warm weather, I figured it was the perfect excuse to wear my favorite mini. Judging by the way Logan looks one strong breeze away from combustion, I'd say I made the right call.

A little edging never hurt anyone, right?

I take a moment for my own perusal, and heat floods through me, pooling low in my stomach. Logan is a thirst trap on any given day, but this is something else entirely. His dusty lavender button-up clings in all the right places, the top two buttons undone just enough to tease at the sculpted ridges of his chest. The sleeves are rolled up, exposing the dark, intricate designs winding over his forearms, each line and shadow adding to the quiet confidence he wears like a second skin. A flat silver chain glints on his wrist, subtle yet intentional, in direct contrast to the bold edges of his ink.

His black slacks are tailored to perfection, hugging his strong thighs and long legs in a way that should be criminal. They end in polished black boots, sleek and expensive, with just the slightest scuff marks, probably from riding his motorcycle. The whole look is sophisticated and sexy, but with an edge. It's so quintessentially Logan that it causes a fluttering sensation deep in my belly.

Looks like I'm not the only one who'll be hanging from a cliff all night.

"Rosie, if you keep looking at me like that, we're never leaving your apartment."

I bite my lip as our eyes meet, silently telling him I'd be more than okay with that.

He groans, then tugs on my hand. "C'mon, woman. I'm taking you on a proper date. Lock the door."

"Party pooper," I say, sticking my tongue out as I hit the lock button on the keypad.

We take the crowded elevator down to the street level, and as we all spill out, Logan laces our fingers together, his grip warm and steady as he leads me outside.

I expect us to head toward his Range Rover parked along the street, but instead, he veers deeper into the neighborhood.

"We're hoofing it?" I ask.

"Yup."

I glance down at my strappy sandals and cringe. "But..."

Logan chuckles, already anticipating my complaint. "Don't worry, Rosie. It's not far."

I sigh, pretending to be put out, but the truth is, I'll walk as far as I need to, blisters be damned. I want this—a night out, where we can just be two people out on a date, not Logan and his best friend's little sister, doing something they shouldn't. I know I should be worried about holding his hand in public. Someone could see us. Word could get back to Ryan. But there are a lot of people in LA, and the odds of blending in are in our favor. Besides, Logan doesn't seem concerned. And I like holding his hand.

"Any updates on your work thing?" I ask him.

Logan ran into some major problems with a business deal, and he's been really stressed about it. If he can't turn it around, it'll be a *massive* loss for BetMasters.

He shakes his head. "Not since I told you about it. But

we're still a go for our meeting on Monday, so that's a good sign."

I squeeze his hand. "Well, I'm keeping all my fingers and toes crossed for you."

With our hands still clasped, he pulls my arm closer, kissing the underside of my wrist. "Thanks, Pip."

I can't help it. The moment his lips touch my skin, my eyes dart around nervously, expecting my brother—or even my parents—to pop out of the crowd like a whack-a-mole.

The side street we're walking down pulses with life, like a secret world tucked inside the city. Overhead, strands of warm Edison bulbs crisscross between buildings, casting a golden glow that makes everything feel a little more alive, a little more intimate, a little more romantic. The sidewalks are packed with couples giving each other heart eyes while stealing kisses, and groups of friends clustering around outdoor pub tables under flickering heat lamps. Voices rise and fall with easy-going conversation. Cocktail glasses clink while carefree laughter rings through the air. With the distant sounds of traffic, it's an urban symphony, one that normally makes me feel at home. Tonight, though, my nerves won't let me settle into it.

I breathe in deeply, hoping the familiar scents will ground me. Smoky carne asada sizzling from the taco place, the bold aroma of espresso wafting from my favorite coffee shop, the unmistakable scent of burgers and fries drifting from a crowded gastropub.

This is exactly why I chose to live in the Arts District— the energy, the vibrancy, the overflowing sense of community—but tonight, my mind is too restless to enjoy it.

Logan follows my gaze, his eyes scanning the crowd. "What are you looking for?"

"Oh, you know, just scanning for one of my family members."

His lips twitch. "You're acting like we're committing a felony."

I huff. "If Ryan finds out, we might as well be."

He slides a hand down my bare back, his palm resting just above my ass, warm and possessive. I shiver as he briefly dips his pinky beneath the fabric of my dress. "Relax, Pip. Your brother has a date on the other side of town. I'm pretty sure he'll be tied up all night."

My brows lift. "The same date he tried to rope you into? I thought that girl wouldn't go out with him unless she could double with her friend who's in town."

He clears his throat. "Yeah...well...evidently, Ryan convinced *both* of them to be his date tonight."

It takes me a second to do the math.

"Oh." I scrunch my face. "God, he's such a fuckboy."

Logan shakes his head. "Ryan isn't afraid to settle down, Rosie."

"Yeah, right," I snort.

"I'm serious," he insists. "Your parents set a pretty great example. You've never talked about this stuff with him before?"

Now it's my turn to shake my head. "Not really. We kind of have an unspoken agreement not to discuss our love lives with each other. I honestly don't think he'd care if I screwed half of LA, as long as he didn't have to hear about it." I bump my hip into him. "Except when it comes to you. *Then* he feels compelled to preemptively cockblock. Obviously."

"Obviously," he echoes with a sigh.

"Are you sure he's not trying to keep you for himself?" I joke, trying to bring some levity back into the conversation.

"Maybe he's been pining for you ever since that morning he woke up with his dick nestled against your butt cheeks."

"Wiseass." He pinches *my* butt cheek, making me squeal. "I'm *positive* Ryan is into pussy and *only* pussy. As am I, so it wouldn't matter, even if he *was* into me. But back to the fuckboy comment, I don't think Ryan jumps from girl to girl on purpose. I guess you could say he approaches dating as if it's an ongoing search for *the one*."

"And he thinks he'll find her by having threesomes with randos from out of town?"

Logan shrugs. "You never know. Throuples are all the rage these days. At least according to the current book on your nightstand."

I laugh. "You've been reading my book?"

"I read *some* of it before I met Ry for lunch yesterday." Logan grins. "I was really getting frustrated with the married dude, though, so I had to take a break. It's *so* obvious he wants to fuck his best friend, but he keeps fighting it, and he's hurting everyone by holding back. I don't get it. He loves watching his buddy fuck his wife, they're all in love with each other, and his wife's totally okay with his bisexual awakening. Just get over your hangups and do it already, man!"

"Wow," I muse. "It sounds like you read *a lot* more than just *some* of it." I laugh. "Who would've thought Logan Edwards would be into MMF romance?"

He shrugs. "It was hot. I don't have to like dick to see that."

"I suppose not," I agree.

Logan puts slight pressure on my back, guiding me around a corner down an alley. "And on that note, we're here."

We stop in front of the same brick building where my

favorite coffee shop is located, but instead of a cozy café entrance, we're at the back end of it, at the opposite corner.

No signage. No storefronts.

Just a single iron door, matte black and imposing, the surface worn from years of use. It's the kind of door that makes you hesitate, wondering if you're about to stumble into something nefarious.

"This really *is* a sex dungeon, isn't it?" I whisper-shout.

"I told you it was exclusive. This is how they keep it that way." Logan smirks.

He presses a round button off to the side, barely noticeable in the shadows. A second later, a tiny platform pops out of the door at waist level.

It's a scanner.

Logan pulls up a QR code on his phone, places it over the sensor, and waits. The red light turns green, and the scanner retracts. A moment later, I hear the distinctive sound of a latch disengaging, right before the door swings open on its own, revealing the interior of an elevator.

"Holy secret lair, Batman," I mumble. "What the hell am I about to walk into, Logan? Will you just freaking tell me?!"

"See for yourself," he replies with a grin.

My jaw drops. "Oh, come on. You're not going to even give me a hint?"

"Nope." He gestures for me to step inside. "After you, Pip."

I hesitate. "If you're leading me to a murder chamber, I'm going to haunt you for the rest of your life."

Logan chuckles under his breath, pressing softly on my lower back. "Trust me, Pip. If I wanted to off you, I'd hire someone to make it look like an accident."

"Not funny." I glare.

He counters with a grin. "Get your ass in the elevator, Rosie, before you draw attention to us."

"Ugh, fine." With a reluctant sigh, I move closer to Logan, feeling the warmth radiating from his body as we step inside the elevator. The doors glide shut behind us, sealing us into the dim, metal box. There are no floor selection buttons, just a soft chime before we begin our descent.

I shift on my feet, as the confined space seems to amplify the faint brush of his arm against mine.

Logan gives me a smug grin, his gaze lingering on me. "Am I making you nervous?"

"No," I deny. "I'm just trying to figure out when you became so James Bond-y."

"I'll take that as a compliment." He winks, a playful glint in his eyes.

I roll my eyes. "You would."

A second later, the elevator glides to a stop, and the doors slide open with another chime.

I gasp when I see the stunning reception area before us.

The shift from the bustling thoroughfare up top to the quiet, sultry interior is almost jarring, like stepping through a portal into another dimension. My heels click against the polished dark wooden floor as I glance around, my eyes adjusting to the ambient glow dripping from an antique chandelier overhead. The walls are covered in black damask wallpaper, its intricate pattern threaded with gold, and barely visible in the low lighting. This room reminds me of some kind of Gothic boudoir, minus the bed. It's elegant, mysterious, and so far from what I was expecting that I find myself momentarily speechless.

A small podium sits to the side, sleek and minimalist, its surface uncluttered aside from a tablet. A woman stands beside it, wearing a black tuxedo blazer, a matching skirt, and a pair of bejeweled Louboutins that probably cost more than my rent. Her white-blonde hair is slicked back into a ponytail, and her lips are painted the exact shade of my favorite Bordeaux.

Her expression is cool and indecipherable, but when her gaze flicks to Logan, her lips curve in the barest hint of a smile. "Welcome to the Gilded Dagger, Mr. Edwards," she purrs. "I'm Claudia, and I'll be your concierge tonight. I see here you'd like to begin the evening with a table for two?"

He nods. "Yes, that's correct."

Her grin is in full effect now. "Right this way."

I glance at Logan, arching a brow. "Come here often?"

"Not exactly," he murmurs.

I narrow my eyes, but before I can question him further, Claudia's swaying hips are leading us down a long, dim hallway, the rich scent of aged liquor and leather growing stronger with each step. The hall funnels into a dark and intimate bar, with vaulted ceilings and gold-plated moldings. It's a magnificent blend of modern luxury and Gatsby-era charm. The patterned wallpaper carries into this space, barely lit by golden candelabras hung in equal intervals on the wall.

The bar itself is a work of art. Long and polished to perfection, its marble top gleaming beneath the dim glow of amber pendant lights. The front is lined with plush barstools, each spaced just enough to give patrons an impression of intimacy without losing the social energy of the room. Behind the counter, rows of meticulously arranged bottles sparkle like jewels. I can't read any of the labels under this moody lighting, but something tells me you won't find any Jim Beam on those shelves.

A bartender, dressed in a tailored white shirt and crisp bowtie, moves with practiced precision, pouring the contents from a shaker into a martini glass, and garnishing it with something fancy.

Our hostess stops beside a curved leather booth tucked into a secluded corner. The seating in this place is unlike any bar I've ever been to. There are only about ten tables in total, and each one is spaced so far from another, it's clear privacy was a key consideration in the design.

"Here we are," Claudia says smoothly, handing Logan a leather-bound pad after he slides in beside me. Rather than a traditional menu, a single sheet of linen paper is attached, bearing a QR code.

"If you scan the code," she continues, "you can view the menu and place your orders directly. Should you need any additional services arranged, you can send a request to me by pressing the 'Concierge' button in the upper right corner." She smiles, showing off her perfectly straight teeth. "Enjoy yourselves."

"Thank you," Logan says, already pulling out his phone.

Low conversation hums all around us, with soft jazz playing in the background. This entire places oozes elegance, but oddly enough, it doesn't feel pretentious.

As Claudia disappears into the shadows, I pick up our conversation where we left off. "Explain 'Not exactly.'"

His lips curve as he uses his phone to scan the code. "I promise I'll do that in a bit. But I think we could both use a drink right now, so pick your poison, Pip." He slides the phone over to me so I can peruse the menu.

The specialty cocktails are decadent blends of high-end liquor, house-made infusions, and unexpected additions like milky oolong, smoked rosemary, or honeycomb. Their names—like Velvet Sin, Scarlett Kiss, and Midnight Rendezvous—are as sexy as the atmosphere.

My fingers hover over the screen as I narrow it down to

two different drinks. "Should I choose posh and mysterious? Or wicked and dangerous?"

"Why not both?" Logan's expression is definitely leaning toward the latter.

Well, okay then. I guess it's going to be one of those nights. My toes curl in excitement.

I return his smile. "Both it is."

CHAPTER EIGHTEEN

LOGAN

"I can't believe this place is right around the corner from my apartment, and I had no idea it existed." Rosie is halfway through her second cocktail when she starts the interrogation. "Spill, Edwards. If you haven't been here before, how did you find it? And why did *Claudia the Concierge* act like she knows you?"

I have to refrain from laughing when she says our concierge's name like a curse.

"My, my, is that jealousy I detect?"

"You wish." She glares.

Oh, Rosie, you can get possessive over me anytime.

I lean into her, placing a hand over her bare knee and rubbing the silky-smooth skin with my thumb. "Don't worry, Pip. I've never seen Claudia before. I assume she knew how to address me because every access code is personalized. My name was probably on her tablet."

Rosie thinks about that as she sips from her glass—some cherry, blood orange, and bourbon concoction. "I had no idea *any* businesses existed below street level around here."

"That's the point," I tell her.

"To maintain the exclusivity?"

I nod. "In part, yes."

Her brows draw together. "What's the other part?"

I take a sip of whiskey, then ask, "What do you know about the original purpose of this building?"

Rosie shrugs. "I assume it was used for manufacturing, like most buildings in the neighborhood."

"Right." I confirm. "Textiles, specifically. But in the 1920s and early 30s, that was just a front for the *real business* beneath the surface."

Her delicate brows lift. "Bootlegging?"

"Bingo." I take another sip. "This place was modeled after the original speakeasy that sat in this very spot during prohibition. What makes it so special nowadays, is the same reason it was so special back then. It's connected to a section of the old tunnels that wasn't sealed off. But the Gilded Dagger isn't the only exclusive establishment down here. There are two other places, and they're all connected by the tunnels, so you can go between each one while staying underground and protecting your anonymity."

Her eyes widen, fingers tightening around her glass. "Seriously? What else is there?"

"Well, there's a steakhouse with a Michelin-starred chef..." I chuckle when Rosie scrunches her nose. "Yeah, didn't think you'd care too much about that one. It's not the most vegetarian-friendly place in town."

"What else?" Her breasts lift as she leans on the table, drawing my eyes to the abundance of cleavage now on display.

Christ. I've been dying to touch Rosie since I first laid eyes on her tonight, but after discovering her dress is backless, I've been going crazy. It wouldn't take much for me to access my favorite ladies.

"Logan," she whisper-shouts. "Stop staring at my boobs and finish what you were saying."

I blink rapidly. "Shit. What *was* I saying?"

Her husky laughter makes my dick perk up. "We've got a speakeasy and a steakhouse. What's the third? And how do you know about them?"

I give her a salacious grin, not at all ashamed she caught me checking her out. Now that I can finally be open with Rosie about how much I desire her, I'm going to make damn sure she never has any doubt.

"The third is sort of like a nightclub, but one where *every* table is a VIP table. But there's also...*live enter-tainment.*"

"You mean like concerts?" she asks.

I clear my throat. "Less musical, more...exhibitionists on stage."

It takes her a few seconds, but the moment she decodes my statement, her lips form into an O. "There really *is* a sex dungeon down here?"

I shake my head. "From what I understand, patrons go there to watch, not participate. They have themed nights on occasion, but overall, it's not a BDSM club." It's fairly dark in here, but that doesn't stop me from noticing the flush rising on Rosie's chest. "I guess you could say it's the same concept as a strip club, but instead of pole dancers, this place has actual sex on display."

"Is that..." Rosie takes another sip of her drink, pausing whatever she was about to say. I use the time to appreciate the flickering candlelight reflected in her dark eyes, and the way her luscious red lips wrap around the rim of the glass. "Is that why you brought me here? You wanted to watch a live sex show?"

I try not to get distracted by the thought of being with

Rosie in a place filled with people fucking. "Do you really think I'd ambush you with something like that?"

"No," she replies, stretching the word out.

"Good to know you don't think I'm a total schmuck." I laugh. "We're just here for drinks and appetizers, Rosie."

"Um...sure. Okay."

What the...? Is she pouting?

I think about our earlier conversation over the phone, specifically those sexy curiosities she mentioned.

"Did *you* want to check out the club, Rosie?"

"Maybe?" She shivers as my fingers skate down her arm.

Fuck. I can't get over how responsive she is. If I wasn't already obsessed with this woman, that would be the clincher.

"Maybe?" I repeat. "Care to elaborate?"

She nibbles her lip for a moment before replying. "Dear god, I can't believe I'm about to admit this, but it's you, so here I go." Rosie takes a breath and blows it out. "Back in college...I was invited to a few parties that got pretty wild. People would start going at it, not caring who was watching them. It honestly seemed like they were extra enthusiastic *because* they had an audience. I couldn't imagine putting myself on display like that or sharing partners for that matter. I don't think there's anything wrong with either, provided everyone consents, it's just not for me. But...um, I really enjoyed *the watching* part of it. I think I might *still* enjoy that. You know, assuming the people involved wanted to *be* watched. I mean...I'm a big fan of internet porn, so what's the differ-ence, right?"

Rosie's cheeks are even more flushed now, and her eyes are filled with an electric curiosity. Even in this dim light-ing, I can clearly see her excitement. Fuck me, I'm in trouble. Never in a million years would I have guessed that Rosie's had a voyeurism kink.

And quite conveniently, so do I.

This could be *fun*.

The thought of taking her to a club...holding her and teasing her as we watched *other* people get off...yeah, I could easily get onboard with that. My god, the sex would be out of this world once I whisked her away to somewhere more private.

My lips curve into a crooked grin. "Interesting."

"Interesting?" she repeats mockingly. "I share something with you that I've never told anyone—not even Sylvie—and all you have to say is *interesting*?!" Rosie licks her lips, drawing my gaze to them.

"No, that's not *all* I have to say." I shake my head. "First, I appreciate you trusting me with that. Second, we're definitely circling back to the internet porn topic later. And third, I'll give you *two* things I've never told anyone—not even Ryan."

Her brows lift in an '*I'm waiting*' gesture.

"Wow. Tough audience." I laugh. "Okay, here goes. This place—the Gilded Dagger—I'm a silent investor, which is how I knew about it in the first place. Killian—a friend of mine from Stanford—was a little short on capital, so he came to me with a proposal. With their target clientele, it had the potential to earn big returns, so it didn't take much to convince me, despite the fact that I've never had any interest in business outside of tech or real estate. The steakhouse and club owners are Killian's best friends, so as a perk, I have unlimited access to all three establishments, and I get to bring along a guest. Usually, their members have to go through an intense vetting process and pay exorbitant fees, so it's a rather nice incentive. Ironically, I've never taken advantage of it before tonight. I've met Killian down here a few times outside of business hours, but I've never been while they were open."

"How come?"

"That's secret number two." I wink, motioning for her to come closer before leaning into her ear. "You see, Pip, I *also* enjoy watching." I smile as she sucks in a breath. "It's not a driving need, mind you. I wouldn't go to a place like that by myself just to watch. But...if *you* ever wanted to check it out, I'd be more than happy to take you. You see, I haven't told any of my friends about the Gilded Dagger because I didn't want to tell them about the club connected to it. I guess I wanted to keep the option open to bring *a special guest* along if I ever decided to cash in on my free membership."

She pulls back just enough to look me in the eye. "I feel like I'm missing some key information. I know for a fact you used to hang out with people who are into the club lifestyle, because my agency has had to cover some of their asses on a few incidents that went viral. Why wouldn't you want your friends to know about the club?"

Oh, Rosie, I *still* hang with people who are into kink clubs—namely, your brother—but I'm not about to bring him into this conversation.

"That doesn't mean I have any interest in frequenting sex clubs with them." I rub a hand over my beard. "In fact, that's something I've *never* done and have zero intention of *ever* doing."

She appears to be mulling that over. "Huh."

I narrow my eyes. "Rosie, why do I feel like you have some preconceived notion of what my sex life looked like before you came along?"

"Maybe I do." She takes a sip of her drink. "I'd say it's

more of an educated guess considering you've spent several years living your best Hollywood life, never dating the same person for more than a few months. Part of my job is to know all the dark and dirty details of what *really* goes on in VIP sections, or at wrap parties and whatnot. But I'm certainly not judging you for it, Logan. Quite frankly, I'm reaping the benefits. You're very good at all the sexing."

"I'm glad you think so." I chuckle. "But your job also tells you reality isn't necessarily as scandalous as a strategically angled photo might suggest, right?"

"Right," she concedes.

"There you go." I point at her. "I haven't always been a saint, Pip, but I don't fuck for sport. Before Tahoe, I hadn't slept with anyone in over seven months. People might assume certain things, but I've *never* shared details about my sex life, not even with my best friend. And whenever I *was* dating a woman, I made damn sure we were on the same page from day one. Those relationships were so brief because that's all they were ever meant to be."

"And me?" she asks. "You said in Tahoe that you're all-in with this. What exactly does that mean?"

"Oh, Rosie, I don't think you're ready to hear exactly what that means."

"Try me."

She's throwing down the gauntlet, which is sexy as fuck. But as bold as she's being right now, I also know she's vulnerable because of what that prick Julian did to her. The truth is I want *every-fucking-thing* from Rosie, but until she's ready to tell her family about us, I know she doesn't fully trust I won't break her heart. Which means I need to work harder to *show her* that her heart is safest with me, and *then* I'll be happy to give her the words along with it.

"How about this?" I brush a piece of hair behind her

ear. "Why don't *you* tell *me* where you'd like our evening to go from here? Whatever you want to do, I'm in. You just need to say the words."

Rosie's big brown eyes bounce between mine. I can practically see the thoughts racing through her mind, ping-ponging off each other, weighing all the options and possible conclusions. I remain silent, slowly rubbing my thumb against her thigh as she deliberates. I know the moment she makes a decision because those beautiful eyes of hers are filled with curiosity, but also a heavy dose of excitement.

"Question." Her tongue darts out to wet her lips as she leans into me until our mouths are a hairsbreadth apart. She smells like cherries and bourbon, and I'm having a really difficult time keeping my mouth to myself. "You said you get to bring a guest to this club? Anyone you choose?"

"Anyone I choose." I suck her lower lip into my mouth, groaning when I get a taste.

She returns the favor with *my* lower lip. "Take me to the club, Logan. *That's* what I want to do next."

I graze my lips along her jaw, grip tightening on her thigh. "I'll have Claudia make the arrangements."

CHAPTER NINETEEN
ROSALIE

The moment we step through the doors of Eros, it's obvious this is no ordinary nightclub.

Sure, it has the usual club fare: curved booths hugging low-lit tables, a polished bar lined with people vying for the bartender's attention, beautiful bodies packed onto a dance floor, the rhythmic pulse of bass vibrating beneath my feet. But there's an understated opulence. An undercurrent of sex in the air. A whisper of primal indulgence.

"Wow," I say.

Logan's hand rests low on the bare skin of my back as he guides me forward. "Yeah, it's pretty impressive."

You could say that again.

I tilt my chin upward. "That's quite the disco ball."

Hanging from the impossibly high ceiling is the largest chandelier I've ever seen, dripping with crystal pendants. Light bounces off its faceted teardrops, scattering prisms across the glossy black floors.

"Probably the most expensive one in existence." Logan's lips curve into a grin.

"Why do you say that?"

He gestures toward the ceiling. "These tunnels were originally built for function, so the ceilings were eight, maybe twelve feet high at best. But if you have enough money and the right connections to speed up permits, you can excavate downward to create more vertical space. So that's what they did."

I nod absently. "Makes sense."

He leans in, his voice low and smooth. "You okay? If you want to leave at any time, just say the word. I mean it, Rosie. No questions asked. Your comfort's the most important thing to me, okay?"

"I don't think that'll be happening on my end." I give him a reassuring smile. "But the same rule applies to you."

Logan smiles with a glint in his eye. "I've got a surprise lined up for you."

My brows rise. "What kind of surprise?"

So many possible answers flood my brain at once, I go into system overload and immediately forget every single one of them.

He chuckles, like he can sense the static inside my brain.

"Relax, Rosie. It's a good surprise. Promise."

I take a steadying breath. "Where is this surprise of yours located?"

He jerks his chin toward the nearby metal staircase. "I'm guessing right there, since it's the only staircase I can see."

I follow his gaze.

The stairs lead to an apparent mezzanine overlooking the dance floor. It's hard to know for sure, thanks to the half-wall stretching across the front, blocking most of the view.

"What's up there?"

"The owner's lounge," he replies. "And we're in luck,

because it happens to be empty tonight. I texted Donovan, the owner of this place, asking if there were any spaces that would give us a little more privacy, and he hooked us up."

My face heats. "Oh."

His lips curve, and the way his eyes darken sends my stomach into a free fall. "You wanna check it out?"

I exhale a quiet laugh and nod. "Sure."

"He said the shows begin at the top of every even hour." He pulls his phone out of pocket, checking the time. "Which gives us less than five minutes."

Holy hell.

I'm about to watch a live sex show in public. Even if Logan secured a semi-private space for us, there are still hundreds of people just below. My senses are suddenly heightened in anticipation. The low hum of conversations surrounding us, meaningful glances exchanged in the dim glow of a booth, the faint smell of sweat from bodies grinding.

"Shall we?" Logan's voice cuts through my thoughts.

I arch a brow. "Huh?"

His eyes flick toward the metal staircase. "Upstairs."

"Oh. Yeah."

Logan's mouth tips up in the corner as he takes my hand, effortlessly weaving us through the crowd toward the staircase. A broad-chested bouncer stands guard, arms crossed, his gaze aloof yet somehow also hyperaware.

The man's dark eyes flick to us as we approach. "I'm sorry, but this level is reserved."

Logan tilts his phone screen toward the bouncer, showing him a QR code. "Yes, for us."

The man watches him for a beat, then pulls a small device from his back pocket and opens an app. He holds it up, scans the code on Logan's phone. After a brief pause, the device emits a soft chime.

"Enjoy your evening, Mr. Edwards," he says, stepping aside. "If you need anything, scan the code on any table, and a staff member will bring it right up."

Logan nods. "Appreciate it."

"Thanks," I add, offering a small smile as we step past him and ascend the stairs.

"So, this place has personalized entry codes and digital ordering too. Fancy."

"The steakhouse does as well." Logan's hand never leaves my back as we climb the stairs. "I designed the software for them."

I pause mid-step. "Excuse me?"

His eyes twinkle with amusement. "They needed a system that was universal across all three establishments. Customized access points, concierge services, food and beverage orders, encrypted communication for privacy..." He shrugs. "Pretty basic. A middle schooler probably could've done it."

"Yeah, maybe *you* in middle school," I say. "*Me* in middle school? Or the general population for that matter? Not so much."

He laughs. "Get a move on, smartass."

We reach the top of the stairs, stepping into a small, dark room. It's intimate...only three booths, spaced far apart for privacy, two plush couches facing each other, and a few pub tables near the half-wall overlooking the crowd below.

Golden track lighting casts a soft glow along the floor, guiding us toward a sleek black table at the center of the room. A silver bucket of ice cradles a bottle, its glass chilled with condensation. Beside it, two delicate flutes wait, untouched.

Logan releases me just long enough to pluck the bottle from the ice and twist the cork free with practiced ease. The soft pop is barely audible over the music pulsing from the dance floor below.

He pours us each a glass, handing one to me before taking a sip of his own.

I taste the bubbly wine, pulling back with a smile. "They actually had this on the menu?"

Blackberry prosecco is my favorite, but I don't come across it out in the wild too often. Logan likes regular prosecco just fine, but he's not a big fan of sweetened drinks. The fact that he's drinking one without complaint right now is extra swoony.

"If they didn't, they managed to get it when I placed the request." He lifts a cocky brow.

I take another sip, the crisp, fruity bubbles dancing on my tongue. "You're pulling out all the stops tonight. You do know I'm a sure thing, right?"

Logan leans in, his voice warm with amusement. "Oh, *I know*, Rosie."

I roll my eyes but can't fight my grin. "Ass."

"You knew what you were signing up for," he teases.

I give him another dry look as I drift toward the half-wall, where the crowd below moves in a hypnotic rhythm. Even with the bass thumping through the floor, I feel like we're in our own little world. A private oasis in the middle of chaos.

"Damn," I murmur, setting my glass on a table.

"Donovan said it's the best seat in the house."

It really is. I can see the entire floor from up here. Although, I don't see a stage, so I wonder where the show will take place.

Logan steps behind me, his chest a solid wall of warmth

against my back. His hands cage me in on either side, gripping the ledge. He doesn't say anything, just lets his presence wrap around me like a second skin, thick with heat and tension.

Below us, the club pulses with energy. Couples sway together in a slow, seductive rhythm, moving in time with the beat. My pulse picks up, the space between my thighs warming as I think about what's to come.

I tip my head slightly, my cheek brushing against Logan's shoulder. "This place is insane," I murmur.

His lips are close to my ear when he replies, his voice a low rumble. "Just wait. I'm sure it'll get even better in a minute."

As if on cue, the lights flicker. The couples dancing below pause mid-step before scattering to the tables along the perimeter of the room. The energy shifts, a new kind of anticipation crackling in the air.

The music changes, slowing to something sinfully seductive. The volume is lower than before but still commands attention.

"Here we go," Logan says.

I inhale sharply as the club darkens significantly, fingers gripping the ledge a little tighter. A single spotlight pierces the void, illuminating the dance floor. The empty space ripples with movement, and I blink in disbelief as the very center of it begins to split open.

A hidden platform rises from the floor, smooth and controlled, until a sleek, velvet-covered bed takes its place. On the bed lies a beautiful naked woman, her small breasts and pointed pink nipples exposed. Her arms are stretched above her, cuffed to the metal headboard. Her legs are spread wide, inviting any and all who dare to take advantage of her vulnerable position to see. The sight is both erotic and powerful, a display of female dominance that leaves me breathless. The crowd below gasps in unison, their eyes glued to the unfolding spectacle. Logan's arms wind around my waist, pulling my backside into the very noticeable bulge in his pants.

"You look so fucking sexy right now, Rosie," he says in my ear, his voice low and husky.

I don't have a mirror handy, but I imagine my eyes are glazed over, fixated on all the naked flesh below. My nipples are painfully hard, the stretchy material of my dress feeling damn near abrasive against them.

The woman on stage is joined by two men. The tall and muscular man with dark hair starts to kiss the woman's neck while his hands slide down her body to cup her breasts, slowly twisting her nipples between his fingers. The other man, a younger, leaner figure with short blond hair, kneels between her legs, running his hands up and down her thighs before dipping a finger into her noticeably wet slit.

When she moans, I startle. There must be a microphone near the stage because it sounded like she was right beside me.

The sight is intoxicating as she arches her back, and the men continue their advances. A thrill of desire ripples through me at the sight of their intimate connection.

Logan presses his erection against my side, his arm tightening around my middle.

My heart hammers in my chest as the man on stage begins licking the woman's pussy. The second man climbs onto the bed, kneeling near her head. He takes her shoulders, pushing gently as she leans up, the cuffs preventing her from fully turning to face him. He licks along the side of her neck, then kisses it before whispering something in her ear that makes her moan again. He suckles on her breasts, alternating between them as she reaches her hips toward the man between her legs.

The man by her face strokes his erection, presenting it to her. She starts sucking with great enthusiasm, her head bobbing up and down in a rhythm that's in perfect sync with the pulsing bass of the music.

Logan's breath is hot against my neck as we watch the scene unfold.

My body trembles with arousal, the sights and sounds all too enticing to resist.

The two men on the bed continue their passionate dance, their bodies moving in perfect harmony as they pleasure the woman before them. Her moans grow louder, her hips bucking against the bed as she takes the man's cock deeper into her throat.

The one below continues feasting on her, his tongue darting in and out of her wet folds, causing her to quiver with pleasure. Her hands grip the metal headboard, knuckles turning white as she tries to hold back her orgasm.

Logan's fingers trail along my waistline as we watch the tantalizing display, teasing me with a gentle caress.

"You like what you see, Rosie?" he whispers into my ear.

I nod. "God, yes."

He smiles against my cheek. "Nobody can see us below this wall. If you need more, I'll give you more, and not a single person down there will have a clue. Or if you want to leave, we'll leave immediately. You're in control here, Rosie. You just need to tell me what you want. Understand?"

My mind is racing, my heart pounding in my chest. The woman moaning below us has me on the edge of desire, and I know that if Logan were to touch me intimately, I would be putty in his hands.

I turn my chin up to him, our eyes locking. "Logan," I whimper.

I don't even know what I'm asking for. I feel like I'm having an out-of-body experience. I'm standing in a hedonistic playground with the man I've wanted for so long, but never thought I'd have. I don't think I've ever been so aroused, the throbbing between my legs becoming more demanding by the second.

His eyes flare with desire. "Do. You. Understand?"

I nod. "Yes."

"You sure?" His gaze is searching, trying to find any hints of discomfort, I'm guessing.

"Positive." I reach back, rubbing his erection through his pants.

"Fuck, Pip," he groans, his head falling forward.

The woman below suddenly lets out a loud mewl, distracting us. Her body tenses as she reaches her climax, while the man by her head groans, eyes rolling back as he strokes himself, decorating her breasts with long ropes of cum.

Logan's hands move deftly down my waist, tracing the curve of my hips before moving lower, tickling the edges of my thighs. Goose bumps rise on my skin as he continues to tease me, his touch feather-light yet undeniably electric. I can feel myself growing wetter by the second, my desire spiking with each little touch.

I glance at Logan, expecting to find his attention glued to the stage, but it's not. He's watching *me*. Like *I'm* the show he came here to see.

The fingers on his left hand trace lightly down my spine before dipping beneath the stretchy fabric and cupping my breast. He teases my nipple as a moan escapes me. The sounds coming from the trio below grow louder, fueling the intensity of the moment.

"Goddamn, Rosie. Seeing you like this is driving me insane. I need to taste you."

"Do it," I pant.

Logan doesn't hesitate, instantly dropping to his knees behind me. His firm hands grab my hips, shifting me back until I'm bent nearly in half, my forearms resting on the ledge.

"Don't take your eyes off the stage, Rosie. If you do, I'll stop. You got it?"

"Got it," I answer, whimpering again when he pushes my dress over my ass, sliding my thong to the side.

Logan's tongue darts out, licking my pussy from behind. It's raw. Animalistic. My body responds immediately to his touch, my hips bucking involuntarily as he continues to tease my clit with his flickering tongue.

"Fuck," I mutter, my hands gripping tightly onto the wall for support.

On the stage, the man kisses her passionately after his climax ends. His lips are rough against hers, a proud display of lust and triumph.

My mind is spinning with pleasure, my entire world reduced to the sensations coursing through me. The music pulses in time with my heartbeat, every note driving me further into a state of pure ecstasy.

Logan continues working his magic, devouring me from behind as the woman below us climaxes once more. My body trembles under his expert touch, the ability to stifle my moans becoming more precarious by the second.

The sounds of our own passion and the trio below us combine into one symphony of lust, pushing me closer to the edge. The blond man on stage is now thrusting with reckless abandon, his dick glistening with arousal as he continues to bury himself deep inside the woman. Her cries become more pronounced, each surge of his hips causing her to shout in pleasure.

Logan's hands move from my hips to my inner thighs, gripping me tightly. His tongue darts out again, this time plunging deeply into my core, making me gasp. My body trembles as he sucks on my clit, his fingers teasing my entrance.

The dark-haired man spreads his cum over her breasts, paying extra attention to her nipples as she's being fucked by the other one. The blond man starts to groan, his movements becoming jerky and erratic. His rhythm falters for a moment as he reaches his own peak, his eyes rolling back in ecstasy. He lets out a long, lusty moan before finally collapsing on top of her.

"Oh, fuck, Logan. I'm going to come," I gasp, my voice barely above a whisper.

Logan doesn't falter. He increases his pace, fingers plunging deep inside of me. My walls clench around him, pulling his fingers in deeper with every thrust. He continues licking and sucking on me with fervor as sparks of pleasure race through my body. I'm a ball of whimpering, panting need as I climb closer and closer to the edge.

"That's it, baby." Logan pulls back, lightly biting one of my ass cheeks as I teeter on the brink of ecstasy. "Come all over my tongue, Rosie."

It's futile to do anything other than obey because in the next moment, I'm freefalling off a cliff, my entire body quaking with the force of my orgasm. A tidal wave of pleasure crashes over me until I'm practically boneless. Logan's talented tongue continues to lick and suck at me until my knees buckle, panting heavily as he pulls my ragdoll body into his lap.

"You're incredible, you know that?" he whispers, kissing me deeply as our breaths mingle.

I'm incapable of words, my mind still reeling from the experience.

Logan brushes some hair away from my eyes. "You wanna head back to your place and continue this?"

I nod, still incapable of speech.

My god, that was probably the most erotic experience of my life. I feel like I say that a lot these days, but it's true every time until a new one surpasses it. But what I loved most about this particular one is that he gave me a safe space to explore my desires, without judgment, without shame. Even better, he was getting off on it just as much as I was. And the best part is knowing that this was only the beginning. I can't wait to see where our journey takes us next.

CHAPTER TWENTY

LOGAN

I'm sitting in my office, its floor-to-ceiling windows framing the million-dollar view that convinced me to buy this building. The California sun glimmers off the neighboring high-rises, casting brilliant rays of light across the pavement. The 110 cuts through the sprawl, traffic thick with commuters cutting each other off and likely cursing up a storm. Behind the mirrored skyline, the Hollywood Hills rise in the distance, a rugged contrast to the madness below. And beyond it all, the Pacific peeks through the haze, a reminder that no matter how relentless this city gets, there's always something bigger and badder waiting on the horizon.

The entire floor is buzzing, analysts buried in screens poring over betting patterns, designers fine-tuning the interface, developers pushing out updates to keep us ahead of the competition. This kind of energy is usually my crack, the fuel that keeps me sharp.

But none of it registers the way it usually does.

No matter how hard I try, I can't stop thinking about Rosie. The way she felt pressed against me at Eros. Her breath hitching as the club went dark, anticipating what was coming next. The way she watched the trio on stage, her body strung tighter than a bowstring. The way my name sounded on her lips every time I've had her since. I don't know what that woman is doing to me. I've always had what I've considered a healthy sex drive, but with Rosie, I'm insatiable. It's an inconvenient distraction considering I'm trying to close the biggest deal of my career, but I can't find the will to care.

I need to get a grip. Instead, I'm picturing how Rosie would look bent over this desk.

"You're thinking about her, aren't you?"

I glance up to find Ryan standing just inside the doorway, smirking as he watches me fantasize about his sister.

Oh, if only he knew, that look would be wiped off his face in an instant.

"Jesus, do you ever knock?" I mutter.

Ryan ignores me, dropping into the black leather chair across from my desk. "Don't even try to deny it." His shit-eating grin deepens. "That look on your face could only be about one thing."

I sigh, pinching the bridge of my nose. "Not this again."

Ryan leans forward, resting his forearms on his knees. "I know, I know, you're not ready to tell me about her yet. But I've gotta say, this is a good look for you."

I arch a brow. "Distracted CEO?"

He laughs. "No, lovestruck. Though it's probably too early for that. Maybe it's more of a *lust drunk* situation?"

Eh, you were probably right on the mark with the first one, dude.

Fuck.

I didn't realize I was being so transparent. If I'm not careful, Ryan's going to keep pressing until he figures out exactly who's responsible for putting that look on my face.

Time to shift the focus.

"I take it you had a good weekend?" he asks.

"How about we talk about *your* weekend instead?" I counter. "How was your big night out with Penelope and her friend from Sonoma?"

Ryan groans, dragging a hand down his face. "Jesus. Don't remind me."

"That bad?"

He leans back in the chair, shaking his head. "It started out really well. Good conversation, good energy. It was going *exactly* how I'd envisioned. Penny's awesome. I wouldn't mind getting to know her better. But Mercedes..."

"The friend?"

Ryan nods. "The *ex-girlfriend*."

I arch a brow. "Well, there's a plot twist I didn't see coming."

"I know!" Ryan scoffs. "Penny swears they were more like friends-with-benefits, but I don't think Mercedes agrees. I'm pretty sure the only reason she agreed to the whole *three's company* vibe, was because she wanted to prevent Penny from hooking up with me."

I chuckle. "What'd she do that gave you that impression?"

He rubs the back of his neck. "At first, it was small little digs, like implying I wasn't Penny's type, or talking about all the reasons why *they* were perfect for each other. I let it slide because whatever, I get it. Penny's hot and she seems like a fun girl. So when her first plan failed, Mercedes claimed she felt a migraine coming on and wanted to head back to Penny's place. But when Penny invited *me* over to hang out while her friend rested, Mercedes's headache miraculously disappeared."

I laugh. "Of course it did."

"Right? And when *that* didn't work, she switched tactics and started hitting on me. I got the impression she was trying to make Penny jealous, except Penny was too busy flirting with me herself to notice."

"So, let me get this straight. The one you *really* liked seemed to dig you as well. But you spent the evening trapped in some weird pissing match with her ex while said ex also used you as a pawn in her jealousy ploy?"

Ryan groans. "Pretty much."

"How did you manage to extricate yourself from that awkward situation?"

"I didn't want to be straight-up rude, but Mercedes was really pushing it, so I just called it a night. It's not like I won't have plenty of opportunities to see Penny again."

"True."

Ryan's disastrous date runs the coffee shop in our lobby. We see her nearly every morning on our way up, sometimes multiple times a day.

He shrugs. "I figured it was better to wait until Mercedes leaves town."

"Seems like a smart move," I agree.

"*Women*," he groans, scrubbing a hand down his face. "But man, at first, that date had so much potential. A Penelope-Mercedes sandwich seemed like a solid investment."

I shake my head. "But instead, you ended up in the middle of some unresolved ex drama and went to bed with your right hand."

"Asshole." Ryan flips me off.

I snort. "You really know how to pick 'em, Ry."

"Yeah, yeah. Lesson learned." Ryan groans and stands, stretching. "Well, I should let you get back to *pretending* you're focused on work. But don't think you're off the hook about this mystery woman, bro."

I pointedly glance at my watch. "We've got twenty minutes until the meeting. Why don't you duck downstairs, grab us some coffee, and see if you can get Penelope to commit to a solo date with you."

He smiles. "I like the way you think."

I exhale sharply as he darts out, relieved my distraction worked.

At least for now.

Thankfully, all it took was a slight increase on our offer, and we officially acquired the IP rights to PPA's algorithm. We're about to have our first team meeting to discuss logistics. I have just enough time to skim through my inbox and review the final integration plan before it starts.

I'm the last to arrive just as Jared, our Head of Product and Innovation, pulls up a presentation deck on the screen. All the executives are here today because we have to pull this off without a hitch. If everything isn't perfect when we walk into that meeting with Olympus, we're fucked. Failure isn't an option, but there's only so much I can control. Precision is paramount, so if anyone on my team has a question or concern about the project, now is the time to discuss it.

I quietly take a seat at the head of the conference table. "Jared, the floor is yours." I take a sip of the coffee that was waiting for me, nodding to Ryan in thanks.

"Thanks, Logan." The Peak Performance Analytics logo flashes across the top as Jared clicks to the first slide. "Now that our algorithm is locked and loaded, we're moving into Phase One of the integration." Jared advances to the next slide which shows the project's timeline. "Over the next four weeks, we'll be integrating PPA's predictive model into our platform and running internal tests to make sure it performs accurately before launch. If everything stays on track, we'll be ready to demo the enhanced system and begin external testing by the end of next month." He clicks to the next slide, which lists each milestone along the way: stress testing the algorithm against historical data, running live simulations without glitches, and proving it can adjust odds in real-time without tanking our risk models.

Li, our Chief Technology Officer, lifts a finger to get Jared's attention. "And this will give us hard proof our platform can predict betting patterns better than anything else on the market?"

Jared nods. "That's the goal."

"Any concerns from Simon's team on feasibility?" Brandon, our Head of Data Science, asks.

"Not yet," Jared replies, clicking to the next slide, which maps out PPA's availability. "As you can see here, Simon will remain on retainer as a consultant for the next three months, per our agreement. If we need to make changes on the backend, or fine-tune the connection, he's on call for an additional three."

Jared glances around the room, scanning for any last concerns. "Assuming we stay on schedule, we should have enough real-world data for our pitch to prove our platform's accuracy and demonstrate why Olympus should lock in an exclusive deal with us." He advances to the next slide, a financial breakdown of the project. "Gretchen, I'll hand it over to you for the financials."

Gretchen, our CFO, makes her way to the front of the room as Jared takes a seat. "Thanks, Jared. From a budget standpoint, we've..."

I'm only half-listening as she dives into cost projections, revenue expectations, and the financial risks tied to the roll-out. None of it is news to me—I could recite these figures in my sleep—but it's a necessary formality for everyone else in the room.

Next, Brandon walks us through what we're doing to keep our risk models from imploding, Li reassures everyone that our infrastructure can handle the load, and Carlos, our Head of Risk & Compliance, breaks down all the red tape we'll need to cut through before launch. It's a lot of back and forth, mostly fine-tuning details we've already discussed in smaller meetings.

By the time we wrap, the consensus is clear. We have one shot to sell Olympus on this deal. And if we don't, someone else eventually will.

I hang back as the room clears, stretching my arms above my head as Ryan rolls his neck. Jared collects his laptop, giving us both a nod before stepping out of the room.

"That went well," Ryan muses, closing his leather notebook with a flick of his wrist. "Don't you think?"

"Yeah, but I'm not celebrating anything until we have Olympus locked in. Those bastards are playing hard to get."

Ryan smirks. "That's rich coming from you."

I arch a brow. "What's that supposed to mean?"

"What do you think it means?" he counters. "You're no stranger to making people work for your attention, Logan."

I snort, shaking my head. "Jeez, dude, way to make me sound like an arrogant douche."

He rolls his eyes. "I just meant you're...extraordinarily selective about who you spend your time with."

I shrug. "I don't see a problem with that."

Ryan tilts his head, studying me. "Hey, totally off topic, but when's the last time you talked to Rosalie?"

Not as off topic as you think, bud. As a matter of fact, I talked to her just this morning, when I left her naked and supremely satisfied from our morning fuckfest.

My pulse jumps, but I keep my expression neutral,

taking a slow sip of my coffee to cover my reaction. "I dunno. Why?"

Ryan exhales, rubbing the back of his neck. "I'm kinda worried about her. I tried making plans with her over Valentine's weekend, thought she could use a distraction from, you know...everything."

"What'd she say?" I ask, working to keep my tone casual.

Ryan frowns. "That's the thing. She was cagey as hell. Just said she already had plans but wouldn't tell me what they were."

A muscle tightens in my jaw. If Ryan somehow finds out she went to Tahoe, there's no way he won't do the math.

He blows out a breath. "Maybe I'll swing by her place tonight with dinner and try to feel her out. Pump her for information."

"Yeah, sure. Good idea."

I make a mental note to text Rosie, giving her a heads-up. I'm pretty sure I left my jacket hanging on the hook by her front door.

Damn. We need to be more careful.

It'll be a disaster if Ryan finds out before Rosie's ready. Hell, who am I kidding? It'll be a disaster either way. He'll know we were sneaking around behind his back. But I'd rather break it to him on our terms, not his. But besides that, I don't want Ryan to blow this up before it's even had a chance to *become* something.

As much as I hate hiding what she means to me, over the last week, I've come to understand why Rosie wanted to wait to tell her family about our new dynamic. It's been really fucking great having time together—just us—without anyone second-guessing what we are to each other. We're learning each other in a whole new way, and I don't just mean sexually. I don't think it would've happened this easily with outside noise getting in the way. This thing between us, it has endgame potential. I know it. She knows it.

But she's guarding her heart, and I won't push her before she's ready. Rosie is an overthinker, and when that happens, sometimes she's plagued with intrusive thoughts. She's told me before that she needs time to process—to sort facts from bullshit, as she puts it—or she risks spiraling. The last thing I want to do is trigger her fight-or-flight response, which is why I've been making a conscious effort to stay steady, to *show* her I'll be as patient as she needs me to be. When she's ready to move on to the next stage—and I'm confident she *will* be at some point in the near future—then I'll be right by her side.

Ryan taps his pen on the table, dragging me back to the present. "You good?"

"Yeah," I say, forcing a smirk. "Just wondering how long it'll take before your sister turns the tables on you and gets you to spill all the details about your twisted love triangle."

Ryan laughs. "Oh, fuck off."

I roll my shoulders, pushing aside the unease creeping through me. I fucking *hate* lying to him. But Rosie's worth the temporary discomfort it's causing. I knew she was mine the second she let me pull her into my arms that first night in Tahoe. I knew it every time she's looked at me since. And I know it now, as I sit here, pretending I don't care that my best friend is one step away from figuring it all out. But I'll do whatever it takes to protect this until Rosie gives me the green light to tell him.

Ryan studies me, his expression unreadable. "You sure you're okay?"

I give him a cocky grin because it's a lot easier than admitting the truth. "Absolutely."

CHAPTER TWENTY-ONE
ROSALIE

Feature photoshoots are my prime opportunity to capture behind-the-scenes content. In Jett Ashford's case, they're also my chance to make sure the photographer's vision doesn't derail our image campaign. Everything was going swimmingly until Thorne Wolfe—yes, that's his real name, or so he claims—declared every single shot he'd taken was worthless. *A crime against aesthetics*, he called it. The man easily had over a thousand photos to choose from. *Hundreds* of them were perfect, in my opinion. But Thorne refused to attach his name to any of them, insisting we had to reshoot immediately.

I'm cutting it way too close for comfort, so I text my cousin as soon as I get to my car, begging for help.

Me: 911. Ryan's bringing over dinner at 7. Pleeeeaaase tell me you can come over to assist, so he doesn't figure out I'm a Liar McLiarpants.

Sylvie: Is this about the thing I don't know about ,but I do totally know about, but HE doesn't know I know about?

> Me: Sylvie! Now is not the time for sitcom references! Logan's jacket is hanging behind my front door, and I know there's more stuff scattered around the apartment. My client's photoshoot ran over 2 hours late, so I'm freaking out. I'm leaving now, but I won't be home until 6:45 or so. Can you please head over and hide anything you think may be his?

> Sylvie: I've got you covered, bitch. But I need to pump first, so I probably won't get there until right before you.

I breathe out a sigh of relief.

> Me: Thank you. I OWE you.

> Sylvie: You can pay me in food.

The traffic lights were out to get me, so by the time I park my Bronco, I have less than ten minutes before Ryan's due with dinner. The boy is annoyingly punctual, but if I'm lucky, he'll have trouble finding a parking spot, which will grant me a few extra minutes. Normally I wouldn't care what my apartment looked like when Ryan came over, but when Logan texted me with a warning about his jacket, I couldn't stop thinking about all the little things I knew he had lying around. Sylvie should be clearing my apartment now—because she's the best cousin ever—but my anxiety won't ease until I see for myself that all traces of Logan have been erased.

I ride the elevator—which stops at the lobby, collects a bunch of people, and literally stops *at every level along the way* to let them out—so I'm practically bolting out of it when it finally reaches my floor. In my haste, I stumble through the front door of my apartment, barely catching myself on the counter before I faceplant.

Sylvie, casually perched on one of the barstools, chuckles. "Smooth."

I give her a dirty look, shoving the door closed behind me. "Are we in the clear?"

She gestures toward the chair beside her where Logan's leather jacket is hanging like a goddamn neon sign. A bottle of cologne sits next to his black signet ring on the breakfast bar. "This is all I could find that was super obvious. Well, plus a black electric toothbrush I'm assuming is his. I shoved that in your nightstand."

I frown. "Why would you put a toothbrush in my nightstand?"

"I dunno," she says. "In case you wanted to diddle yourself with it later. I'm sure Logan wouldn't mind. It's not like he hasn't slurped up all your pussy juices before."

I gag. "Please never say something like that again."

She lowers her voice a few octaves. "Not even if I talk like a sexy manly man?"

"Not even then." I glare.

I grab Logan's ring and toss it into the junk drawer, slamming it shut like I'm sealing Pandora's box. Before I can reach for the cologne, Logan's signature scent—warm spice, cedar, and pure sex appeal—fills the air.

I whip around, finding my cousin pointing the bottle toward the sky. "Sylvie! What are you doing?!"

Her eyes go wide. "Oh, shit!" She waves a hand around, as if that'll make the scent magically disappear. "I'm sorry! I wasn't thinking! I just wanted to know what it smelled like, and you can't get the true effect while it's in the bottle!"

"Well, now anyone walking into my apartment *will get the true effect of walking into Logan's chest!*" I shriek.

"I can see why you want to bang him all the time if he smells like that up close," she muses.

"Sylvie!" I throw my hands up. "Ryan's going to know that's Logan's cologne!"

"Will he?" She cringes. "Maybe Ryan has a cold? We can hope his nose is plugged, right?"

I groan. "We have to light a candle! Now!"

"Ooh! Good idea!" Sylvie jumps off the stool and heads toward the coffee table where a three-wick candle is sitting. "Wait. Where's the lighter?"

I frantically spin around in my kitchen. "I don't know!"

"Well, we have to find it!" she insists.

"No shit, Sherlock! Look around!"

We both take off in opposite directions, rifling through drawers and cabinets. I yank open the junk drawer again—pens, receipts, a pack of gum, seventy bajillion packets of hot sauce—but no lighter.

"Where the hell is it?" I shout. "It's a long candle lighter. Finding it should not be this difficult!"

Sylvie squats down on the floor, looking under the TV stand. "Damn, Rosa, when's the last time you vacuumed down here?"

"Why would it be under the TV stand?!" I yell.

She gets back up, brushing off her knees. "I'm just trying to be thorough. No need to bite my head off."

I spin in another circle, eyes narrowing on the refrigerator as a memory surfaces. "The fridge! It's on top of the fridge!" I stretch my toes, blindly patting the top until my hand lands on the prize. "Yes! I got it!"

Why in the hell did I put it up there in the first place?

"Catch." I launch the lighter across the room, where it bounces off Sylvie's chest and clatters onto the floor.

"Ow!" She rubs her boob, bending over to pick it up. "You don't need to be so violent!"

"I wasn't trying to be! I said, *catch!*"

Sheesh. It's like the universal sign for, '*Heads up, I'm about to throw something at you.*'

"Well, excuse me for not having catlike reflexes!" she huffs.

I point to the candle. "Light the damn candle, Sylvie!"

The butane must be low because it takes a few tries before the flame ignites.

"Hurry!" I shout.

"Bitch, I'm trying!" Sylvie leans over the candle after all three wicks are lit, waving a hand toward the front door. "There. Problem solved!"

"I'm pretty sure it needs to burn for more than *two seconds* before the scent actually spreads," I deadpan, hands on my hips.

"How long could it possibly take?" she asks. "This loft is tiny."

I narrow my eyes. "The rent on this *tiny loft* is three thousand dollars a month! LA is expensive. We can't all be married to billionaires, you know."

"Oh, bite me. You know I don't give a crap about the money." She rolls her eyes. "Also, never say never, Rosa. I'd say you have a damn good shot at marrying a billionaire one day in the near future."

My jaw drops. "Wha—"

A sharp knock on the door makes us freeze.

"Fuck," we mutter in unison.

My stomach knots as I check the peephole.

"It's him," I whisper-shout.

I open the door, stepping aside to let my brother in. "Hey."

"Hey." His eyes dart between us as he steps over the threshold and hands me a bag of delicious smelling food. "What's with all the yelling in here?"

Did I say my stomach was in knots? Scratch that. It's plummeted to the damn floor.

"Yelling?" Sylvie scoffs, like the accusation is highly offensive. "We weren't *yelling*."

He snorts, hanging his coat on the hook behind the door. "Uh, yeah, you were."

Oh, fuck. *The coat.*

My head whips to the barstool, where *Logan's coat* is still hanging.

Sylvie gets an 'oh shit' look on her face as she follows my gaze. Thinking fast, she casually crosses the room and parks her ass right over the black leather.

You're stuck there for the rest of the night, my eyes tell her.

"Pfft." Sylvie waves him off. "I was *talking with purpose*. Have you met me?"

Ryan's eyes narrow, trying to figure out what the hell she meant by that.

Good luck, bruh. That's a level of chaos even I can't interpret.

"So, anyway, Rosa," Sylvie says, throwing a pointed glare at Ryan, "as I was saying before we were so *rudely* interrupted...Antonio is seeing this new guy and can't figure out if his bossy, domineering energy is sexy or just straight-up toxic. Which...fair. If this were a romance novel, it'd be a no-brainer. But in real life? It takes a *very* special kind of man—and a strong-ass partner—to make putting up with that shit worthwhile. Like with Quinn and my bosshole."

Quinn is Antonio and Sylvie's shared bestie. Hudson calls their trio *the Unholy Trinity*, but I'm pretty sure Quinn is only guilty-by-association on that front. The basshole—a.k.a. Ronan Maxwell—is Quinn's husband, but also Antonio and Sylvie's boss. From what I've heard, he's a real hardass at the office, hence the absurd nickname.

Ryan rolls his eyes and swipes the food bag from me, long since resigned to ignoring our girl talk.

"And even with those two," Sylvie continues. "It took me a while to be convinced Ronan actually deserved her. Honestly, I wasn't so sure until I saw how pathetic he was after she left his ass..."

As Ryan plates our food, Sylvie keeps blabbing about anything and everything guaranteed to make him tune out. When she asks him a direct question and he doesn't even blink, she winks, clearly pleased with herself.

Crisis averted.

Maybe.

"You good, Rosa?" Ryan asks.

Or...maybe not.

Shit.

I force a casual laugh. "Of course. Why wouldn't I be?"

He watches me closely. "You seem...jumpy."

"When is she *not* jumpy?" Sylvie snorts. "Jesus, Ry, what is up with you tonight? It's like you're new here or something."

Ryan's nose twitches as his gaze sweeps the room. "Is someone else here?"

"Do you *see* anyone else?" I ask, hoping like hell my cheeks aren't as flushed as they feel.

Stupid sexy cologne wafting through the air making me act like a Pavlovian dog.

His brown eyes flick to my bedroom door which, thankfully, is wide open. When he doesn't find whatever he's looking for, he backs off.

"Weird," he mumbles. "We eating over there?" Ryan jerks his chin toward my couch.

With no dining table, our only seating options are at the breakfast bar or in the living room.

"I'm good right here," Sylvie offers. "You two can take the couch."

God, I love her.

Ryan shrugs, a silent 'suit yourself,' and grabs a plate. I do the same and follow him over to the couch, blowing Sylvie a kiss along the way.

I exhale quietly as I take a seat, my heart still lodged in my throat.

Holy shit. That was way too close.

"So, tell me what you've been up to, Rosa." Ryan shovels some drunken noodles into his mouth.

"Just the usual," I reply casually, as if I'm not hiding a life-altering secret. "Work mostly. I'm assigned to a big image rebrand which takes up a lot of my time." I heap a big scoop of pineapple fried rice into my mouth, cutting off the impending anxiety-induced word vomit.

Less is more, Rosalie. Less. Is. More.

"That's all?" He arches a brow.

"Damn, these skewers are the shit. Where'd you get 'em, Ry?" Sylvie asks, clearly trying to distract him again.

"Royal Orchid." He barely spares her a glance. "Rosa? What'd you wind up doing on Valentine's weekend?"

Oh, not much, bro. Just, you know, banged your bestie on every available surface of our family's cabin.

"Sorry, starving." I take three more bites of rice to buy me time to think and swallow hard. "Um...just laid low mostly. Why?"

Ryan's eyes are lasered in on me. "Why were you being so weird when I wanted to hang out?"

Okay, I feel like a total jerk for playing this card, but I'm literally starting to sweat under the pressure here. I'm terrified I'm going to blurt out, "Logan and I had sex!" if we don't change the subject fast. Let's just say my impulse control isn't the best when I'm panicking.

"Why do you think, Ry? It was supposed to be my wedding day. Can't a girl wallow in peace without having to explain herself?"

His face falls. "Rosa, I didn't—"

"It's fine. Don't worry about it." I hold a hand up. "I'm over Julian, Ryan. I swear. I'm *glad* we didn't get married. I just needed to escape reality and be alone for a few days, that's all."

Not untrue.

That *was* my original intention when I went to Tahoe. It's not my fault my brother's gorgeous, sex-on-legs best friend just happened to be there, too, offering up orgasms on a silver platter. I mean, truly, I had no choice but to take him up on it. I would've been doing a disservice to all womankind if I hadn't.

I snort, earning a suspicious look from my brother.

Dammit.

This is not the time to make jokes inside your head, Rosa!

I clear my throat. "*Anyway...*enough about my shitty ex. Why were *you* free on Valentine's? No hot date?"

"Nah." He gives me a crooked grin. "But I *did* have an interesting date last weekend."

Sylvie gasps. "Interesting, as in '*I want a second date,*' or interesting as in, '*It was a complete shit show*'?"

Ryan laughs. "A little of both, actually."

Sylvie leans forward, propping her elbow on her knee, and her chin on her fist. "I'm listening..."

And just like that, the spotlight is off me.

Thank you, baby Jesus.

Ryan doesn't need much prompting from our cousin to launch into a story about his wild date with the barista and her friend.

Between bites of Thai food, he spares no details—how he and Penny really vibed, how Mercedes couldn't decide if she wanted to play the jealous ex, or if she wanted to flirt with him to make her ex jealous, and how the entire evening spiraled into super awkward passive-aggressive chaos—until he finally decided to call an Uber and get the hell out of there.

Sylvie, to absolutely no one's surprise, loves every second of it, asking for more details along the way.

I watch my brother while they dominate the conversation, remembering what Logan said about him.

"Ryan isn't afraid to settle down, Rosie."

I always assumed he'd be an eternal bachelor and love every second of it. But seeing how clearly frustrated he is that he didn't get a chance to deepen the connection he felt with Penny...I can see what Logan was talking about. Maybe Ryan's *not* some dude-bro looking for easy fun. Maybe he *does* want a real, long-term relationship with someone special.

"You know," I say, eyeing him over my plate. "I think I was wrong about you, Ry."

He freezes mid-bite, frowning in confusion. "What the hell does that mean?"

My lips quirk as I spear a piece of pineapple. "I had you pegged as the kind of guy who'd never settle down. Like, I could not picture you *ever* getting married. Or wanting kids...a house in the suburbs...the whole nine yards. But that's not true, is it?"

He's silent for a moment. "Have you been talking to Logan or something?"

My pulse spikes. "What? *No.* It was an observation I had just now."

He snorts. "Well, congrats, Rosalie. It only took your whole life to figure that out."

I roll my eyes. "God. Forget I said anything."

Sylvie laughs. "Nope. No takebacks."

I flip her off before turning back to my brother.

Ryan leans back, shaking his head. "I'm not necessarily looking for a wife. Or a white-picket-fence-epic-love-story romance. I'm a realist. I don't need my life to look like one of your books." He flicks the cover of a paperback on the table. "But...yeah, I would like to meet someone who intrigues me. Keeps me on my toes. Shares my interests." His lips curve. "And if she happened to be a bombshell with a great rack, it certainly wouldn't hurt."

"Of course not," I mumble, shaking my head.

"But seriously," he continues. "I'm not the lost cause you seemed to think I am. I just know what I want, and I have no interest in settling for second best. If I ever get married, I want *forever*, like Mom and Dad. As nauseating as they can be sometimes, I actually think it's kinda cool they're still into each other after all these years. If the right woman *is* out there somewhere, I'll find her eventually. If not, I guess it wasn't meant to be."

I absorb his words, soaking up the fact that my cocky, sarcastic brother is actually being vulnerable for a change.

And I have a bit of an epiphany.

Maybe Ryan and I aren't so different after all.

I've never given my all in a relationship before Logan. It's easy to see, in hindsight. Maybe that's because my subconscious knew who she wanted, and she refused to settle for anyone else. Ryan and I may have different methods to our madness, but the logic behind it is the same.

"Damn, you two are looking awfully broody over there," Sylvie comments, stuffing a spring roll in her mouth. "I know what will lighten things up. Hey, Ry? Have you ever made a girl squirt?"

Ryan chokes on the bite he just took. "Jesus Christ, Sylvie. I am *not* answering that."

I laugh, shaking my head. "Please don't."

"Tell me you've never made a girl squirt, without telling me you've never made a girl squirt," she sasses.

Ryan gives her a double bird.

"Okay, that's enough," I announce, setting my plate on the coffee table. "No more talk about squirting during dinner."

"You need therapy." Ryan points at Sylvie. "Or better yet, a muzzle."

"No can do. My husband would stage a riot if my mouth was out of commission." Sylvie grins. "Quite frankly, so would I. Hudson has the most lickable lollipop my tongue has ever tasted."

Ryan and I both cringe, making her laugh.

"TMI, Syl," I tell her. "T.M.I."

She snorts. "Oh, please, Rosa. Don't play coy with me. We all know nobody gets their nipples pierced unless they're a freak in the sheets. Hell, you're probably worse than I am nowadays, you dirty, dirty girl."

My eyes widen. "Sylvie!"

"Oh, for fuck's sake," Ryan grumbles. "I've lost my appetite. I'm outta here. Enjoy the Thai, you psychos."

"Oh, c'mon!" I call as he's heading toward the door. "Sit down and finish your dinner. I'll make Sylvie behave."

He looks at our cousin. "You and I both know that's

impossible, Rosa. Nobody can put a leash on that one, except maybe a small, impressionable child."

Sylvie shrugs. "He's not wrong."

He gestures to her, like *"See? She's proving my point."*

I can't dispute that, so I give him a little finger wave.

"If you need me, I'll be bleaching my brain, desperately trying to forget the last ten minutes of my life." Ryan then walks out the door, mumbling obscenities under his breath.

After the door closes, Sylvie leans back against the counter, smug as hell. "I've still got it."

I give her the stink eye. "Did you really need to mention my sex life or tell *my brother* about my piercings?"

"Who cares? I'm sure he's seen his fair share of nipple piercings."

"That's beside the point." I snort. "But thank you. I was freaking out for a minute when he started sniffing the air. You definitely saved me."

"See? Nothing to worry about. Ryan came. Ryan went. He's none the wiser about your secret relationship with his bestie, and since we chased him off, more food for us!" She fans her arms out. "You're welcome."

"You're ridiculous." I shake my head.

"You love me." She winks. "But seriously, I've got you, boo. Anytime. Anyplace."

I smile. "Ditto, babe."

After Sylvie leaves, I take a moment to reflect on the evening. I think things with Ryan went okay overall, but something tells me this won't be the last time I have to scramble to cover my tracks. I close my eyes, taking a few deep breaths, reminding myself to celebrate the little wins.

I can worry about the rest as it comes.

CHAPTER TWENTY-TWO

LOGAN

The last few weeks with Rosie have been some of the best of my life. Hard to believe it's been a month since Tahoe. We've fallen into this perfect rhythm of meeting every night after work, talking, dining, laughing, fucking until we're exhausted, and falling asleep in each other's arms. The next morning, we wake up in a mess of tangled limbs, which usually leads to slow, sleepy sex that makes it nearly impossible to leave the bed.

I'm a fucking addict. If I go more than a few hours without talking to her, I start craving her voice, her laughter, her relentless teasing. Work has been chaotic for both of us, yet that never stops us from sending flirty texts or calling each other in between meetings, or while we're driving. We used to go weeks—hell, months—without talking, and I barely thought twice about it. Rosie was always in the back of my mind, but whenever she was dating some douche who didn't deserve her—which was most of the time—I stayed in my lane.

As gratifying as it was knowing those fuckwits saw me as a threat—and trust me, there was no doubt—I didn't want to cause problems for Rosie. If anything, those dudes were just more evidence as to why she'd never be mine. After our first midnight kiss, I knew she was attracted to me. Any lingering doubts I may have had were squashed. But every guy I'd seen her with since was *nothing* like me—in looks or personality. I was convinced that Rosie was more attracted to hedge fund hot shots with small dick energy. It killed me, watching her waste time on jerks who didn't deserve her, but it wasn't my call to make. So, I shoved my feelings down, swallowed my jealousy, and acted like it didn't gut me every damn time she picked someone who wasn't me.

"Earth to Logan."

I glance down with a smile as Rosie's voice pulls me back to the present. "Sorry, spaced out for a minute. What'd you say?"

She tilts her head toward a blue and white truck. "Greek sound good? I'm craving falafel. It's a nice night. We should eat here."

I glance at the open courtyard, the clusters of people, the outdoor tables offering *zero* cover.

"You sure?" I ask, keeping my voice even.

She nods, slipping her fingers through mine like it's second nature. "Yeah."

"Works for me." I squeeze her hand, grinning like a fool.

Lately, I've watched her anxiety fade, little by little, giving me hope she's nearly ready to talk to her family. I mean, Rosie is still Rosie. Most days, the woman has enough frenetic energy running through her veins to power the whole county. But her eyes no longer dart around, searching for familiar faces whenever we step out to grab a bite. She never hesitates to hold my hand or raise up on her toes to steal a quick kiss. Granted, we're careful, sticking to a small radius in her neighborhood, but she knows there's always a risk of being seen, no matter how low it may be. Suggesting we dine outdoors in a crowded courtyard is a bold move, which only deepens my conviction.

It's a weeknight, just past seven, so thankfully, the line isn't too long. We place our order and step aside to wait as the scent of grilled meat, chopped veggies, and freshly baked pitas make my stomach growl. When it's ready, I grab the food—a falafel plate for her, chicken souvlaki wrap for me—and follow Rosie to an empty picnic table. We settle onto the same side of a bench, unwrapping our food.

She takes one look at my wrap and grimaces. "Jesus. How are you going to fit that giant thing in your mouth?"

"I guess we're about to find out." I waggle my brows suggestively. "Got any tips since you're such an expert on putting giant things in your mouth?"

Rosie chokes on her lemonade, coughing. "Oh my god, I can't believe you just went there."

I cup the back of her neck. "You walked right into that one, baby."

She laughs as I pull her closer. "Touché, Edwards."

"Don't worry, Pip." I press our lips together softly. "I'll give you a chance to redeem yourself later." She moans as I deepen the kiss, making me forget where we are for a moment.

Her cheeks are flushed as I pull back. "What was that for?"

"No reason," I say with a wink. "Just couldn't resist."

Rosie bites her lower lip as she glances down, noticing my growing erection. "First comes food, then comes sex."

I laugh. "Is that how it works?"

"Duh." She rolls her eyes. "It's like, Dating 101."

I take her hand, placing gentle kisses on each knuckle. "Is that what we're doing? Dating?"

"Are you asking me to put a label on it?" Rosie's delicate brows arch.

"What if I am?" I don't break her gaze, letting the question linger. "I don't *need* a label, but I am curious what you think."

"Honestly, I don't know what to call this, but I do think it's more than just dating. Don't you?"

I lean in, brushing my lips against hers. "Yeah, Rosie. *A lot* more."

She smiles shyly. "Good. Now that we've settled that, can we please eat? I'm freaking starving."

I chuckle. "Go to town, Pip." I tear off a big bite of my wrap, making her laugh.

"Animal," she teases.

I lick a stray drop of sauce from my thumb. "You know it, baby."

Rosie and I eat in comfortable silence for a bit, the sounds of downtown living—the distant wail of a siren, a group of people laughing, music drifting from one of the apartments above—serving as our soundtrack. As we're sitting here, a thought settles in my chest. How has it only been a month since we've been exploring this new dynamic? Being with Rosie is the most natural thing in the world. It's exhilarating and effortless, but she's also my greatest source of peace. My days before Tahoe feel like an entirely different lifetime. I didn't realize how tragically unfulfilled I was back then. But when she smiles at me like I'm her favorite fucking person, it's so substantial, I now realize the Grand Canyon had previously resided in my chest.

I never used to think about the future unless it related to my business or investments. But lately, I've envisioned all sorts of things, asking myself all kinds of questions.

Like, would Rosie ever want to trade city living for something quieter, maybe get a house together in the hills? I picture us sitting on the back deck sharing a bottle of wine, watching the city lights down below. Sharing a cup of coffee in the kitchen each morning while she's wearing nothing but my T-shirt. Then the vision sharpens, and maybe a few years later, she's standing in that same kitchen, belly round with my child. Rosie's breasts are heavy, her skin is flushed and glowing, her long, dark hair is extra shiny. Even her pouty lips have a little more natural color. I swear to god, she's never looked sexier, and I already want to give her another the second she pushes this kid out.

Whoa.

Where the hell did that come from?

And why do I want it so fucking badly?

It's not the first time I've thought about having kids with Rosie, but this *is* the first time I've ever visualized her carrying my child on such a visceral level. Instead of panicking like a sane person, my brain takes a giant fucking leap off a cliff, straight into logistics. So now I'm thinking about actually *making* the babies with her, the way she'd feel, all soft and warm, back arching as she writhed beneath me. The rising crescendo of her moans as I took her pleasure to new heights. Her breathy sighs as she begged me to plant my seed inside of her.

Fuck, that's hot.

I subtly adjust myself under the table, reminding my dick now is not the time.

Showing off your boner in public is grounds for arrest, dude.

Rosie quirks a brow. "What's that look for?"

I clear my throat. "What look?"

"Don't even." She shakes her head. "One minute you're

munching on your wrap, and the next, you look like you're ready to throw me over this table and have your wicked way with me."

She's not wrong.

I laugh. "That's how I *always* look at you, Pip."

Her eyes narrow, not buying my bullshit for one second. "Logan, what were you thinking about just now?"

Oh, nothing big. Just breeding you like a goddamn Neanderthal. Just give me a club, and I'll be all set.

"Work," I hedge. "The Olympus pitch."

Rosie snorts. "Liar, liar, pants on fire."

I reach out to tuck a piece of her dark hair behind her ear. "Eat your fried chickpeas, Rosie."

She rolls her eyes but leans into my touch, making me smile. "Worry about your own food, Edwards."

"Yes, ma'am." My lips twitch as I tack on a pithy salute.

AFTER DINNER, we head back to her place. It's a short walk, but the tension stretching between us is coiled so tightly, it might as well be miles. My skin feels too taut, my heartbeat is thudding in my chest, and don't even get me started on my dick. The city pulses all around us but all I can focus on is Rosie. The way the cool night air raises goose bumps on her arms. The way her breath hitches every time our hands brush. The intoxicating sugary, tropical scent of her skin. By the time we step into her building's lobby, I'm hanging on by a fucking thread.

I press the call button for the elevator, stealing a glance down at her as we wait. She's restless. Amped up. Wound just as tightly as I am. Her plump bottom lip is captive between her teeth, the delicate flesh already a little swollen. She shifts from one foot to another, the soft rustle of fabric against her silky skin driving me mad.

Her hands are in constant motion, spinning the ring on her index finger round and round, a tell that she's crawling out of her skin, dying to release all that pent-up energy. She does this sometimes when she's anxious, but I'd bet my Ducati tonight's is more about anticipation. Hell, if she's feeling even half of what I'm feeling, it's downright desperation for some privacy, so we can do something about it. One thing's for certain, as soon as we're behind closed doors, all bets are off.

I whisper into her ear, "You're fucking soaked right now, aren't you?"

"Wouldn't you like to know?" she replies coyly, stepping into the elevator as it arrives.

I chuckle. "It's okay, baby. I'll find out for myself in just a few."

Rosie leans against the mirrored wall opposite me, her dark eyes playfully taunting.

I take a slow step toward her.

She bites her lip.

Another step closer.

Her eyes sparkle with challenge.

Rosie loves this little battle of wills—taunting, teasing each other, to see who bends first—and I usually enjoy it, too. But tonight, I don't have the patience. I need to get my hands and mouth on her pronto.

I cage her in with my body, ignoring the few other people in this elevator. I know we're drawing attention, but I don't give one flying fuck at the moment. Her breath hitches as I take one last step, our bodies nearly flush with one another.

"You get off on teasing me, baby?" I growl into her ear.

Her lashes flutter. "What if I do?"

I trace a finger down her side and over the curve of her hip, not missing the resulting shiver. She inhales sharply, seemingly swallowing a gasp.

Ding.

I give her a wicked smile. "You're about to find out."

I take Rosie's hand as the doors open onto her floor, guiding her down the hall. I type the access code she gave me into the keypad, turning the knob when it beeps. The moment we're inside her apartment, I push her against the door, locking it.

"You wanna play, Rosie?"

"God, yes," she says on a moan.

She releases a breathless little gasp when my lips press against hers, wrapping her arms around my neck and pulling me closer. I kiss her hard, any and all of the restraint I'd been clinging to gone. Her fingers wind through my hair, pulling on the longer strands until there's a bite of pain. Fuck, I love it when she does that.

"You're not going to even ask what kind of play?" I lift her arms, peeling off her thin sweater in one go.

She groans as I palm her lace-covered breasts, licking and biting her nipples through the flimsy material. "Don't care. Do whatever you want to me."

This girl.

The trust she has in me—giving me full domain over her body—is humbling. It's a privilege I'll cherish and make damn sure I continue to earn.

I kiss along her jaw, down the graceful column of her throat, skimming my fingers just beneath the waistline of her jeans.

"These need to go," I warn, right before I pop the button and yank them down.

Rosie kicks out of her shoes while I help remove the remaining denim from her legs. Once she's down to her black bra and panties, I grab onto her hips and lift. She doesn't hesitate for a second, wrapping her shapely legs around my waist, crossing her ankles behind me.

I carry her through the apartment, our mouths never parting as we head into the bedroom. I groan as Rosie's nails score into the back of my neck, setting her down onto the mattress. As she lies there, with flushed cheeks, chest heaving, I take a moment to appreciate the view.

So fucking beautiful.

And so fucking *mine*.

"I have a surprise for you. But there are some things I need to do first."

She sits up on her elbows. "What kind of surprise? And what kinds of things?"

My lips curve into a slow, devious smile. "First, I'm going to punish you for being such a tease."

She starts abusing her poor lip again. "Go on..."

I chuckle, knowing how much she gets off my dirty words, telling her what I'm about to do to her.

I step out of my shoes, remove my socks, and pop the button on my jeans. "Then I'm going to lick your beautiful cunt until you're screaming my name."

Her lips part as her breathing gets heavier. "And then?"

I lower the zipper and push the denim over my hips. "And *then*, I'm going to fuck you hard and fast, because at that point, both of us will be begging for it." My T-shirt is next. "But that's not all."

"No?"

"Not even close." I pull my boxers down, slowly

stroking my cock. "If you're a good girl, *that's* when you can have your surprise."

Her pupils dilate as she watches my hand moving up and down. "Are you going to tell me what my surprise is, so I can have some incentive to behave?"

"Lose the bra, Rosie." I squeeze the head of my dick, willing it to relax a little.

I savor the way her tits bounce as she removes her bra. Rosie's tawny nipples are peaked, begging for my attention, but somehow, I manage to resist. I know this woman's body almost as well as my own at this point, yet I don't know if I'll ever tire of looking at her.

"Would you like me to remove my panties next, sir?"

I groan. My brain knows she's calling me that to be a brat, but my dick sure as hell didn't get the memo.

"Only if you want me to eat your pussy," I tease. "It's up to you, baby."

She flings her thong off comically fast and spreads her thighs in invitation. "You didn't answer my other question. Are you going to tell me what my incentive is for behaving?"

Oh, Rosie, let's not pretend you don't love being my good girl.

I grin. "I'd much rather *show* you."

CHAPTER TWENTY-THREE
ROSALIE

"I'd much rather *show* you."

Oh, mama.

My toes curl when Logan gets that growly tone, and the rumble from his deep timbre triggers an involuntary Kegel. I'm practically panting like a bitch in heat, and he hasn't even touched me yet. Maybe *Celeb Insider* should call him the Pussy Whisperer instead.

"That sounds like a good plan." I smile, opening my legs even wider.

He holds a finger up. "But first...I need to consult the list."

I laugh, my heart pounding with excitement as Logan's pretty eyes sparkle with mischief. My sexy to-do list has turned into a wicked little game, each new experience pulling us even closer.

He walks over to the nightstand, retrieving the notepad from the drawer. I give myself props for actually writing out a list because that baby's served me very well over the last few weeks. The air crackles with tension as Logan scans the paper, his gaze flicking back and forth as if contemplating each item carefully.

But he can't fool me.

I know he's putting on a show, delaying the big reveal. Not that I'm complaining. It's all part of the fun. One of my favorite things about this new relationship of ours is that we haven't lost our playful teasing. We've simply graduated from flirty innuendo to dirty fucking.

Sexy, filthy, *fantastic* fucking.

"Hmm," he muses, tapping a finger against his chin in mock contemplation. "Let's see what our choices are. Mutual masturbation? Nope. We've got that covered. Road head?" He looks around the room. "Highly tempting, but we'd have to leave the apartment, so that's out, too. Damn. So many options. However will I decide?"

I play along, feeding the growing need between us.

"Are there really?" I challenge. "Because last time I checked, we've already marked off quite a few."

Logan's lips pull up in the corners, and there's a playful gleam in his eyes, but he continues scanning the list. "Quiet, Pip. I'm thinking."

I mime buttoning my lips, but on the inside, I'm smiling, thinking about the other items we've crossed out so far. Sex club? Check. Twice now, in fact. Deepthroating? Yep, that too. Logan nearly lost his mind when he figured out I don't have much of a gag reflex. Waking up with him inside of me? *Way too many* checkmarks to count on that one. My pulse races as I recall his surprised—and *oh-so-enthusiastic* reaction—when I made that particular request. We both enjoyed it so much, of course I had to request an encore.

Or, you know, give him permission to wake me up like that whenever the hell he wants, because, *sweet baby Jesus,* it's hot as fuck. New kink unlocked? *Ding. Ding. Ding.* Jackpot!

Damn, with as lucky as I've been getting lately, maybe I should start playing Powerball.

Logan, meanwhile, is still dragging this out, pretending he doesn't already know how he's going to ruin me for all other men.

Ha! Like he hasn't already done that, Rosa?

He taps his chin, making a show of scanning the list, but I don't miss the way his eyes crinkle with amusement, like he's enjoying this way too much. Then, just when I'm about to demand he spit it out, his eyes flick up, dark with intent, and a cocky grin spreads across his face.

"I've got it."

I arch a brow. "Care to share with the class?"

My heart skips a beat as he sets the notepad aside and turns his full attention my way. His hand snakes out to cup my cheek, thumb tracing across my lips. Logan's pupils flare when I suck the tip of his thumb into my mouth. "You'll see. You ready for this, baby?"

I nod eagerly.

I trust that whatever he has planned will feel incredible and push us to new heights of intimacy. I am so hooked on this man, it's dizzying. But I don't just crave his touch, I crave him. The way he looks at me like I'm the only person that matters. The way my body hums in anticipation the second he walks into a room. The way his voice drops to a husky murmur when he whispers my name.

I ache for Logan when he's not around. My need for him only seems to intensify with each new moment we share. We're like magnets, drawn together by a force that defies logic. An inevitability, as if we were always meant to collide. I feel an overwhelming sense of gratitude that we've had the chance to connect like this, to explore each other in ways I never imagined. Logan isn't just my friend anymore. He's my lover. My confidant. The man who seems to get me on a level nobody ever has.

He reaches into the nightstand and pulls out a small velvety bag. One that definitely wasn't there when I left for work this morning. He unties the strings, reaches in, and pulls out a long, gleaming butt plug. I bite my lip as I notice how much bigger it is compared to the others we've played with so far. The realization of what he wants to do tonight hits me like a bolt of lightning.

Anal? Checkmark *pending*.

With Logan's very large, very girthy cock.

Yikes.

A wave of nervousness washes over me, making me gulp audibly.

Logan chuckles softly, as if he's reading my mind. "Don't worry, Pip," he assures me gently, his touch soothing as he cups my cheek again. "We'll go slow. I'd never suggest something I didn't think you can handle."

I blow out a breath, my nerves slowly dissipating. "I trust you, Logan."

He smiles, prowling toward me until I'm lying flat against the bed, and hovers over me in a plank position, careful not to squish me. He reaches out, tracing a path over my hipbone, leaving goose bumps in his wake.

"God, Pip, do you have any idea what you do to me?"

I fist my hand around his length, giving him one long stroke from the bottom up. "I have *some* idea."

Logan groans as I squeeze my fist around him.

"Later," he says, removing my hand and standing. "Face down, ass up, baby. Before we get to the main event, I need to make good on a few promises."

"Yes, please," I whimper, making him laugh again.

Logan's not the only one who's a big fan of this position, so I obey without hesitation. His warm hand presses gently on my spine, guiding me down until my head and shoulders are pinned to the mattress.

"Spread your legs, baby." God, his voice is pure sin. "As wide as you can go without dropping your hips."

I do as he says, the cool air teasing my wet, aching center. My breath hitches at the realization that I'm completely exposed, laid bare for his eyes to devour. The thought alone sends a fresh wave of desperate, aching need straight to my core, slick evidence trailing down my inner thigh. Logan still hasn't touched me, but my body's already primed. Throbbing, waiting, *aching* for him to stake his claim.

His hands land on my butt, slowly massaging the muscles. "Damn, I love your ass. You're about to make a whole lot of my filthy dreams come true with this thing."

I giggle, while at the same time, a flush blooms beneath my skin. "All talk and no action makes Logan a very boring boy."

"Smartass."

Smack!

I cry out in surprise as he spanks me, first on the right cheek, then the left. The sting is brief, but strong, leaving me gasping for air.

I moan as Logan lovingly rubs the ache away. "You want more, Rosie?"

I arch my back like a cat, wiggling my butt. "What do you think, genius?"

"I *think* you get extra feisty when I spank you because you *love it*." He reaches between my thighs, sliding his fingers through the wetness. "Your pussy seems to agree."

Backstabbing hussy.

Always selling me out.

I'm too stubborn to admit the truth so I bite my tongue.

Logan tilts my hips forward, pressing me into the soft mattress beneath us. The silky duvet is cool against my face, a stark contrast to the desire coursing through me. His breath fans across my skin as he leans in close, whispering dirty promises in my ear. Logan's fingers gently navigate my body as his lips follow, featherlike touches stoking the fire within. I'm writhing and panting beneath him. It's too much, yet not enough. He cups my breasts, rolling the barbells threaded through my nipples between his thumbs and forefingers. It sends a jolt of electricity through me, and my back arches involuntarily.

Logan chuckles deeply. "You like it when I play with your pretty tits, Rosie?"

"You know I do, Captain Obvious," I pant.

He pinches my clit, making me squirm. "Behave."

The sassy retort is on the tip of my tongue, but when Logan tips me forward again, his tongue darts out to lick me from behind, and my brain misfires. The only sounds I'm capable of are breathy little squeaks, none of which remotely resemble language. His tongue continues lapping at my core until I'm screaming and squealing and panting his name over and over again.

Just when I think I'm on the verge of collapse, he surprises me by shifting his focus. Two fingers thrust inside of me, pumping at a furious pace, right before his tongue starts drawing slow circles over my asshole.

"Oh, fuck!" I shout.

Well, okay then. I guess we're checking two things off the list tonight.

His laughter rumbles against my flesh.

Dear god, the sensation of having a tongue back there is unreal. I'd never felt comfortable enough with someone to do this before—or even *talk* about doing it, if I'm honest—but hot damn, I've been missing out. Logan's fingers continue their relentless assault on my pussy, while he uses his other hand to tease my clit.

Multi-tasking for the win!

I white-knuckle the bedding as he brings me to the edge of another orgasm, only to back off at the last second. My hips buck wildly, chasing after him, but all I find is empty air, leaving me a whimpering mess.

"Please, Logan," I gasp. "I need to come."

"Not yet, baby," he growls, pinching that little bundle of nerves again.

I can't see his face from this angle, but I'm positive there's a wicked gleam in his eyes right now.

Stupidly sexy, sadistic bastard.

He chuckles again, telling me those were not inside thoughts as I'd intended.

Oops.

Logan picks up right where he left off, bringing me to the edge once again, but then denying my body the orgasm it's earned once again.

"Dammit!" I shout. "Quit torturing me!"

"I said, *not yet*," he repeats, right before spanking me again. "The next time you come, your tight cunt will be wrapped around my cock."

My butt cheek warms from the smack, but when his lips press against the ache, followed by the gentle massage of his hand, I'm moaning and mumbling incoherently. He's reduced me to rubble, and I can't find a single fuck to give in protest.

After one more round of fingering-rimming-spanking-soothing-driving-me-crazy, Logan shifts behind me, grabbing onto my hips. And then...with one deep, possessive thrust, he's buried inside me, dragging a sharp cry from my lips as pleasure splinters through me. My body trembles, already begging for more.

"Fuck, I'll never get over how good this feels," he murmurs.

You and me both, bucko.

He starts out slow, giving me a moment to adjust to the stretch. As we find our rhythm, Logan circles each one of my wrists, binding them behind my back for leverage. His thrusts become harder and more demanding, each one sending shockwaves of pleasure through my body. In record time, I'm on the precipice, begging him not to stop this time.

Okay, maybe I throw in a few threats, too.

"So close," I whine.

With one more spank, he says, "*Now* you can let go. Squeeze me with everything you've got, Rosie."

A strangled cry rips from my throat as the orgasm crashes over me, pulling me under like a tidal wave. Pleasure blinds me, my head swimming in a hazy, euphoric fog. My walls clamp down around Logan's cock, and with a deep, guttural groan, he thrusts into me one last time, shuddering through his own release.

I collapse as he withdraws from my body, folding my arms beneath my chin. After taking a moment to catch my breath, I ask, "Tell me the truth. How red is my ass right now?"

Logan releases a bark of laughter, rubbing said ass. "Perfectly *rosy*."

I groan. "You're so freaking cheesy."

I squirm when his index finger prods my entrance.

"And *you're* so fucking sexy with my handprints on your ass and my cum dripping out of you."

I smile softly, turning my head to meet his gaze. "And apparently, you're a caveman, too."

"It's a recent development." He gives me a crooked smile as his eyes fall to the spot where his finger pushes that cum back inside of me. "And it's one hundred percent your fault."

I laugh, cringing as I feel a big glob drip out. Not missing a beat, Logan catches it, stuffing it back inside.

"You ready for round two?" Logan rubs my sore butt some more, placing soft kisses over the particularly tender spots. Pulling my hips back and my cheeks apart, his mouth descends, licking circles over the tight hole.

I moan so loudly, I'm positive my neighbors on all sides can hear. Shit, why does having your ass eaten feel so awesome?

"Plug me, baby." I give my butt a little shake for emphasis.

"Your wish is my command, sweetheart." His fingers dig into my butt cheeks as his breath ghosts over my sensitive skin. "And trust me, Pip. You're going to fucking love this."

With a sly grin, he grabs a bottle of lube from the nightstand, spreading it over his index finger with a wink. I damn near purr when he spreads it around the tight ring of muscle, before slowly pushing inside. He adds a second finger, and the slight burn makes me tense up.

"Breathe, baby," he coos. "I've got you."

My muscles loosen as I allow him the space to work his fingers in and out. Once I'm moaning, and Logan's satisfied I'm ready, he removes his fingers and reaches for the intimidating plug. He lubes it up before positioning it against my back door.

"Relax, Rosie." His voice is steadfast and calm as he presses the tip of the steel toy against me. "I promise I'm going to make this feel so fucking good."

"I know you will," I whimper, my heart racing with trepidation and excitement.

I truly have no doubt Logan will ensure this is a pleasurable experience, but my brain can't seem to wrap itself around how that supersized plug is supposed to fit in my ass.

Logan's dick is bigger than the plug, Rosa.

Damn you, inner self! Not helping.

Logan reaches under with his free hand and slowly spreads my wetness around, circling my clit. As the tension in my limbs ease, he pushes the plug gently into my ass, inch by inch, until I feel the jeweled end sitting between my cheeks.

"Good girl," he coos. "It's in."

I gasp as the plug bottoms out, trying to adjust to the fullness, but it's not uncomfortable like I'd expected. Once Logan's satisfied the plug's in place properly, he starts raining kisses all over my backside, crawling up my spine.

He lines up behind me again, his cock pressed firmly against my core, thick and ready. "This is going to be a tight fit, so don't forget to breathe, okay?"

God bless this man's rapid refractory period.

"Okay," I agree, focusing on my breaths as he pushes in.

"Christ," Logan sputters. "So fucking tight. You doing okay, baby?"

I nod the best I can in this position. "Yeah."

As Logan's dick slides into me, I can feel it rubbing against the thin barrier between him and the plug. This isn't the first time I've worn a butt plug during sex, but it's like apples and oranges with the supersized version.

Or maybe more like apples and watermelons?

We groan simultaneously once he's fully seated.

"Fuck," Logan mutters. "I need a minute, or I'm going to blow faster than Teenage Me did watching porn for the first time."

I giggle, making us both curse as the motion makes me clench, intensifying the fullness.

"Man, now I know how a double-stuffed Oreo feels," I pant.

We both laugh at that one, causing more clenching, and more swear words.

Logan glides back and forth a few times, testing it out, a subtle tugging at the base of the plug with each thrust.

"I'm so full," I pant.

Logan groans as he bottoms out again. "Good full, or bad full?"

"Good" I assure him. "Definitely good."

My nerve endings are lit up, every sensation amplified. I can feel the drag of his thick cock as he slides in and out, the flared head as he nearly pulls out entirely. My walls are hugging him so tightly, I'm not sure how he can move a single centimeter, but it feels fucking amazing so I'm not going to question it. We're a series of moans and grunts and bodies slapping as he picks up the pace, working up to an unyielding rhythm. The pleasure is almost unbearable, but there's no way in hell I'm tapping out.

"I think I'm going to come again." I fist the bedding, a garbled keening noise falling from my lips.

"Yeah, you are," Logan growls, thrusts becoming even more urgent. "And the moment you do, I'm taking your ass. I can't hold off much longer, Rosie."

"Oh god, it's so good," I whimper.

"I know, baby." *Thrust.* "And it's about to feel even better." *Thrust.*

I don't know if that's possible, I almost say, but then the most earth-shattering orgasm known to man hits, and I'm a believer. I cry out his name, blissful tears rolling down my face.

Logan's breath quickens as he fights to maintain control while I'm clenching around him. As I reach the peak, my entire body locks up, pleasure detonating through me like a live wire. He groans, his hands gripping my ass, keeping me pinned in place as he fucks me through it, making sure I feel every last aftershock. My limbs shake, breaths coming in short, desperate gasps.

Logan leans in, pressing slow, open-mouthed kisses along my spine, his breath hot against my damp skin. His cock is still nestled between my thighs, thick and pulsing, the weight of it a heavy promise. As I begin to catch my breath, I feel his fingers glide lower, followed by a gentle tug. A low moan escapes me as he slowly eases the plug out, the sensation sparking delicious tremors down my spine. Then, his fingers tighten on my hips, and suddenly, I'm weightless, flipped onto my back, spread out beneath him, my legs parted wide as he moves over me.

My head spins as he presses my knees up toward my chest, completely baring me to him. His cock drags against my over-sensitized core, the slick head teasing. I don't know when he managed to grab the bottle, but I startle as a ribbon of cold lube drips over my center. My gaze shifts to Logan, and I watch intently as he works the lubricant over his shaft. His cock is thick and powerful, glistening under the dim light with every stroke, accentuating its impressive length. The slick sound of Logan coating his shaft echoes throughout the room, building the anticipation of what's to come.

"Relax, Rosie." Logan rubs my thighs soothingly as the flared head slips inside of me. "I can't get in if you don't breathe, baby."

He slowly massages my quads, my hamstrings, and then my calves until I'm practically melting into a puddle before him. I take a deep breath, releasing it as he sinks in deeper.

As Logan stretches and fills me, I feel like I'm floating through a dream, suspended in a world where the only thing that exists is him. The euphoria consumes me, wrapping around every nerve ending like a fever I never want to break. His fingers never stop moving, circling my sensitive nub with expert precision, ratcheting up my pleasure until I'm trembling beneath him, breathless and undone.

The air is coated with the scent of us—Logan's warm spice and cedar cologne mixed with the heady aroma of sweat, musk, and our combined arousal. My skin is dewy, slick against his, as our bodies move in perfect sync. I blink up at him, dazed, captivated by the raw hunger etched across his face. His golden skin is flushed, dark blond hair hanging in messy strands over his forehead, damp with exertion, his jaw clenched as he fights for control. But his hazel eyes are what truly steal my breath. Lust-darkened, molten with need, locked onto mine like he's watching the most mesmerizing thing he's ever seen.

"Fuck, Rosie, your ass is taking me so well," he groans, his voice rough, almost desperate. "You're going to make me come so fucking hard. I need you to get there one more time, baby. Are you ready?"

I can't even form words at this point, my whole body taut with need, every nerve alight with pleasure. I nod frantically, clinging to his arms, my nails sinking into the firm, inked muscle of his biceps. "Yes! Please!"

As his thrusts grow more urgent, a familiar heat coils deep inside me, winding tighter with every movement. His words, his touch...everything about him is unraveling me. My breath hitches, a desperate sound tearing from my throat as another orgasm surges forward, teetering on the edge of release.

Logan thrusts deeper, his rhythm faltering as his breath turns ragged, the strain of restraint evident in every movement. My body clenches around him, trembling violently as wave after wave of pleasure crashes through me, stealing every coherent thought.

"This sweet ass is mine, Rosie. I'm gonna fill you up so fucking good. *Fuck.*"

He lets out a guttural moan, his grip tightening as he drives into me one last time. A shudder racks his body as he spills deep inside me, my name slipping from his lips in a low, breathless moan. He falls forward, hands fisted to the sides as he slowly withdraws from my ass. Logan flops to the side and pulls me into his warm embrace.

My heart rate slowly returns to normal as I gasp for air, completely spent.

"You okay?" he asks.

I smile softly. "More than okay."

He squeezes me tighter. "You're fucking exquisite, Rosie. You never cease to amaze me."

Heat lingers beneath my skin, the aftereffects of our passion still humming through my body. I feel completely cherished, utterly destroyed, and so perfectly taken care of all at once. A soft sigh escapes me as I press my face against his chest, inhaling the warm, familiar scent of him. I tilt my head slightly, brushing a slow, lingering kiss along his breast-bone, right over the steady thrum of his heartbeat.

"Right back atcha, Edwards."

After a much-needed shower—where Logan took his sweet time washing every inch of me with those strong, capable hands—we brushed our teeth side by side, exchanging dopey smiles in the mirror. Fresh sheets replaced the ones we thoroughly ruined, the scent of lavender detergent mixing with the lingering scent of body wash as we collapsed back into bed.

Wrapped up in each other, I drag my fingertips over his tattoos, tracing the designs just to feel him under my touch. The warmth of his skin steadies me, a calm tether to the chaos in my mind. My breath slows, my body melting into his, contentment wrapping around me like a cocoon.

Just as sleep begins to pull me under, Logan's voice rumbles low against my temple.

"You're the best thing that's ever happened to me, Pip."

A sleepy smile tugs at my lips as my mind drifts back to my reply from earlier.

Right back atcha, Edwards.

CHAPTER TWENTY-FOUR

ROSALIE

The morning after one of the best nights of my life, I walk into work feeling sore in all the right places, but in desperate need of some coffee before I get started on my workload.

"Morning, Rosalie," Trish calls as I whiz past the reception desk.

"Coffee." I point in the general direction of the break room. "Need some. I'll be back."

She laughs as I beeline it to our beloved espresso machine.

"My savior!" I walk over to the shiny black and silver monstrosity, grab a mug, and press the vanilla latte button, tapping my foot impatiently. Once I have a cup of liquid gold, I start heading back to my desk, but Avery flags me into her office as I pass by.

"Morning," I say to Avery as I step into the room.

"Morning," my boss replies. "We need to talk, Rosalie. Please close the door and have a seat."

Well, that can't be a good sign. Nothing good ever comes after, "we need to talk."

I'm racking my brain as I pull out a chair and take a seat. Is she pissed about the photoshoot? Did Thorne lodge a complaint or something?

Avery picks up the iPad that was sitting on her desk, looking at something on the screen. "Nick got an alert this morning and thought I should take a look at it."

"Nick Sullivan?" I ask.

She nods. "Yes."

Nick Sullivan is Avery and Liam's partner who runs the agency's Corporation Division in New York.

"An alert about what?"

Avery turns the tablet around, setting it on the desk in front of me. "See for yourself."

My jaw drops when I glance at the screen. "What the hell?"

Right there in full color, is a series of paparazzi photos from last night. Logan's profile is unmistakable as he leans down to kiss me, our bodies close in a way that suggests familiarity and intimacy. My facial features aren't obvious, thank god. The photos were taken from the side, and my hair hides most of my face. But anyone who knows me, and of my affiliation with Logan, could easily do the math.

Like Avery clearly has.

"Nick thought the woman in the photos looked awfully familiar and wanted my opinion on whether or not his suspicions were correct."

Like Liam and Avery, Nick isn't one to sit on the sidelines. Despite his managerial role, he stays hands-on as the publicist assigned to the BetMasters account, overseeing press releases and media strategy for Logan's company. He's in this office at least once a month for the partners' meeting, so he's well-acquainted with everyone in the Entertainment Division.

But Nick knows me a little better than the others because we met outside of work when I was at a bar celebrating my new job offer. One drink turned into some heavy flirting. That flirting turned into kissing. And the kissing... let's just say if Liam and Avery hadn't walked in, things probably would've gone in a direction we'd both regret since he wound up being one of my new bosses. I dodged a major bullet that night.

It's ancient history now—just a slightly mortifying anecdote from the past—but it's not exactly something either of us will forget since we're still sorta in each other's lives. No wonder his Spidey senses started tingling the second he saw those photos of me and Logan.

She taps the screen. "That *is* you, correct?"

I nod.

"What..." My fingers flex around my coffee mug as I process what I'm seeing. My mouth feels like it's stuffed with cotton, so I take a small sip of my latte before trying again. "How bad is it?"

Avery sighs, swiping up to show me the search results summary. "It's out there, but it's manageable."

I groan as I read through the gossip site headlines.

Mystery Woman Spotted with Logan Edwards in LA's Arts District: After a lengthy social hiatus, the billionaire CEO was spotted having dinner with an unknown brunette.

Billionaire CEO in Love? Logan Edwards, CEO of BetMasters Inc. and Flingr founder, was spotted in downtown Los Angeles canoodling with a mystery woman.

From FLINGR to RINGR? Is billionaire playboy, Logan Edwards about to put a ring on it?

The Kiss That Has Everyone Talking – Who Is She? If you know, give us the deets!

The Billionaire Bachelor May Be Off the Market and We Are NOT Okay! Flingr founder spotted in downtown LA locked in a steamy embrace.

MY PULSE POUNDS, and heat floods my face.

This is bad.

These vultures will figure out who I am in no time, and when they do, it'll be a feeding frenzy. I knew this was a possibility from the start. I don't care because Logan is worth the occasional paparazzi ambush.

But what I *do* care about is my parents or Ryan learning about my relationship with Logan from a gossip site before we have a chance to tell them. Truthfully, I was already on the verge of coming out with it. My worries about my parents have mostly faded. I can't predict the future, but Logan and I are on the same page. I can't imagine going back to being just friends now. I need to trust that.

We both want this to work—wholeheartedly—and really, that's all anyone can hope for in a relationship.

My brother, on the other hand? That's a whole different shit show. He's going to have a problem with this for multiple reasons, and I can already hear his *"Are you fucking kidding me?!"* echoing in my head. He'll no doubt be pissed that we hid this from him, especially considering Logan's his best friend and sees him at least five days a week. Logan's had *plenty* of opportunities to come clean, but instead, he kept his mouth shut at my request.

Ideally, I'd like more time to figure out the best way to approach the inevitable meltdown, but time isn't a luxury Logan and I have anymore.

Avery watches me silently, likely running through a game plan in her head like the seasoned PR professional she is.

"Rosalie, you don't owe me any details about your personal life. I want to make that clear. But in this business, you have to know your name will be out there in no time. One of the first things they'll uncover is where you work, and that Logan is one of our clients. Which means your problem has now become *my* problem.

"They're going to assume you met Logan through your job at Maxwell. And when the man in question is wealthy, attractive, and considered one of the city's most eligible bachelors? Instant tabloid fodder. Sadly, misogyny is alive and well, which means there's a high risk of unwarranted accusations coming your way. I'm sure you can imagine the colorful narrative they'll spin. As a woman, I hate to even acknowledge that bullshit, especially when it's being thrown at someone I'm fond of. But as your boss, I need to be clear. I *cannot* let this reflect poorly on the company. Do you understand what I'm getting at here, Rosalie?"

Oh, *fuck.*

The blood drains from my face as the realization slams into me like a freight train. Logan's connection to my job never even crossed my mind. I don't manage his company's socials, so I didn't consider it a conflict of interest. But that doesn't matter now because *perception* trumps reality. Tabloids thrive on sensationalism, and if they can twist the truth into something spicier, they will. The moment my name gets out, so does Maxwell & Company's. I've basically handed those bastards the scandal they were looking for on a shiny, silver platter.

Dammit. I'm so freaking screwed.

I feel like I'm going to puke. Or maybe pass out. Or maybe puke and then pass out.

The paparazzi camping outside our office isn't unheard of. If one of our clients is in deep shit, it comes with the territory. But when you have a PR firm that represents A-list celebrities suddenly caught up in a tabloid scandal of its own? The optics couldn't possibly be worse.

I take a deep breath, my stomach twisting with guilt as I meet Avery's gaze. "I'm so, so sorry, Avery. I didn't think about how this would reflect on the firm because I'm not assigned to Logan's account. If I had, I would've given you a heads-up."

"What's done is done." She swivels in her chair, steepling her perfectly manicured fingers. "What's important now is what we do moving forward. Nick will be working out of this office for the rest of the week—he's taking a redeye tonight—because Logan lives here, and it's much easier to collaborate in person. I'd like to represent you, if you're okay with that."

"Wha—" My stomach rolls. "You think *I* need representation?" I nearly drop my coffee but manage to set it on Avery's desk before spilling it everywhere. "Couldn't Nick just issue a statement on Logan's behalf while I keep my head down until this blows over?" My hands start shaking, so I drop them to my lap, tightly clasping them together.

Calm the fuck down and focus, Rosalie!

She shakes her head. "I don't think duck and cover is the right approach here. We need to be proactive, and to be frank, I'd like to control your narrative." She takes a sip of coffee. "That's what I'm damn good at, and this will go much more smoothly if we get ahead of it. Nick will handle things on Logan's end, and we'll work together on any joint statements, but *you* need somebody running interference when the media starts calling for quotes or interviews."

"I can't ask you to do that, Avery. Your workload is already insane."

She waves me off. "It won't take much if this blows over as quickly as I expect it to."

"Thank you," I say, meaning it from the bottom of my heart. "I truly appreciate this, Ave." I take a deep breath, trying to ease the tension from my shoulders. "Just tell me what you need. Whatever it takes to fix this, I'll do it."

"The usual." She takes her iPad back and grabs the digital pencil out of the clip. "Information about your current relationship and history with Logan, on anyone who might come out of the woodwork causing problems, etcetera. You've known Logan since childhood, correct?"

"Yes. Since I was eleven and he was twelve. He and my brother have been best friends since then, but Logan's been an extended part of my entire family as well."

Avery jots a few notes on her tablet. "Good. That's the angle we'll lean into, longtime friends to lovers. People eat up fairytale romances, and that's exactly how we're going to spin it." She glances up. "We'll need proof. Can you get your hands on some old photos or anything that reinforces the history between you and Logan? The more, the better. I'll sort through them and pick the strongest ones for publication."

Oh, thank God.

At least something is going my way. My parents have *tons* of pictures of us growing up together—this part will be easy.

I nod. "There should be quite a bit. I'll call my mom and see what she can dig up."

Avery's red lips curve into a soft smile. "Great. I told Trish I needed your help with a campaign, so she cleared your morning." She takes another sip of coffee before continuing. "You good if we tackle this right now?"

"Of course." I nod.

I can't believe I didn't think about the potential consequences involving work. I wouldn't blame Avery if she fired my ass, but instead, she's going above and beyond to help. I know part of that is to protect her company, but I know my boss well enough to know she's concerned about me on a personal level as well. I'm aware of how lucky I am, and I'm sure as hell not going to do anything to make this more diffi-cult for her.

"All right," she says, turning to her computer. "Let's get started."

CHAPTER TWENTY-FIVE

ROSALIE

When I finally get done with Avery, it's lunchtime, so I step out to my car for some privacy. Logan called and texted while I was meeting with my boss, but my phone was in my purse on "Do Not Disturb," so I didn't see them until a minute ago. I give his messages a quick scan before calling him back.

Logan: Do you have a minute to call me?

Logan: It's been an hour, so I'm taking that as a no.

Logan: Just got off a call with my publicist. He said your boss planned to meet with you this morning, so I'm guessing that's what you're doing now. I know this isn't ideal, but it'll be okay, Rosie. I promise whatever happens, we'll handle it together. Don't forget to breathe, and call me when you're done. Side note: those pictures are hot AF. I may have to use them for inspiration later…

I let out a quiet chuckle as I hit the call button. Only

Logan Edwards can soothe my nerves and set me on fire in the same breath.

"Are you taking deep breaths?" he asks in lieu of a greeting.

"I'm trying." I smile. "I've spent the last two hours getting grilled by Avery, so that's easier said than done. You know I love her, but the woman's *intense* when she's in crisis management mode. It's weird being on this side of things."

"I bet." Someone murmurs in the background. "Hold on a sec." There's complete silence on the other end, so I'm guessing he pressed the mute button. He's only gone for about twenty seconds before he returns. "Sorry about that." He clears his throat. "That was...uh, Ryan. He had a quick question."

"What are we gonna do, Logan?" I groan, rubbing my temples as my brother's name leaves his mouth. "We have to tell them before they see one of those headlines."

"Breathe, Pip," he reminds me. "We were going to tell them anyway. This just speeds up the timeline a little bit."

"I know." I sigh. "And I feel ready with my parents and stuff. I do. But Ryan..."

"I'll tell Ryan," Logan offers. "There's no getting around it. He's going to be upset we lied to him. I sure as hell would be, if the roles were reversed. But unless you really want to be present, I think me having a talk with him is the right thing to do. Truthfully, it's long *overdue.* I want to make sure he understands how serious this is. How I'd go out of my way to avoid hurting you. When Ryan walks away from our talk, he'll undoubtedly understand how vital you are to me."

I smile. "You're pretty vital to me too, Edwards."

"I'd better be," he jokes.

"Ass," I tease.

A notification pings on my phone, so I pull it away from my ear to see who's texting me.

> Mom: Rosa, honey, I just saw something interesting online. CALL YOUR MOTHER.

"Fuck my life," I mutter.

"What?" Logan asks.

"My mom just texted me." I breathe in, and then out. "I'm pretty sure Dr. Tate is in the know."

"Damn, that didn't take long."

"No, it did not." I pinch the bridge of my nose.

"Call her. I'm going to find Ry and see if he wants to grab drinks after work. Let me know how it goes with the good doctor."

"Oh, I will," I grumble facetiously. "I'm sure it'll be a super fun time."

He laughs. "Baby, if your mom's involved, it'll definitely be *something*."

"Don't remind me." I roll my eyes.

"I'm sure you'll be fine. Call me back when you're done if you need to."

"Okay." I sigh. "Bye, Logan."

"Bye, Pip."

I close my eyes, count to ten, and give myself a little pep talk before dialing my mom's number.

"Hello, sweetheart," she answers on the first ring. "It's nice to hear from you in the middle of the day."

"You told me to call you," I remind her. "*In shouty caps.*"

"Who knew caps lock could be so effective?" She giggles. "I should've tried that years ago. Maybe my children would visit me more often."

"Mother, we see you *all the time*," I insist. "Well, as often as we can for two adults who work a ton of hours."

"Well, it's not often enough if you ask me. Same goes for Logan. Speaking of..."

"Here we go..." I mumble to myself.

"I don't mean to pry, but... Oh, who am I kidding? Of course, I do. I've been waiting for this moment for *years*."

I squeeze my eyes shut. "Rip off the Band-Aid, Mom. What *exactly* did you see online?"

"There's no need to be so dramatic, Rosalie."

Ha! Who does she think I got it from?

"Mother, please just spit it out."

"Well, you know I don't usually pay attention to those gossip sites."

Sure you don't.

"They're so frustrating," she continues. "You can't scroll down the page to read an article without accidentally clicking on a damn ad. And sometimes, you can't close out of the ad and go back to the article. So, you don't even get to finish reading it, and it was all for nothing!"

"That's why it's called *click*bait, Mother," I inform her. "Get back to what you were saying. I feel like there was a 'but' coming. You don't normally pay attention to those gossip sites, but...?"

"*But* I happened to come across an interesting headline with Logan's name on it. Of course I had to read what it was about."

"Of course." I roll my eyes.

"And then, imagine my surprise when I see a picture of him kissing a woman who looks *exactly* like my daughter! But then I thought, there's *no way* that could be Rosalie because if she and Logan were dating, *surely* she would've told me."

"Uh-huh..."

I sigh and make a *'hurry up'* motion as she continues her guilt trip. My mom goes on and on about how we don't keep secrets in this family, pointing out how she's always raised us to be open and honest with each other, no matter how uncomfortable a conversation may be. When she starts citing examples from when she gave me *the talk,* I can't take it anymore.

"Oh, for fuck's sake. It's *me,* Mom! That's *me* kissing Logan in the picture."

She gasps. "*I knew it!* Oh, honey, that's wonderful! I'm so happy you've finally put that boy out of his misery. He's had it *bad* for you since you were kids. He was so heart-broken when you and Julian got engaged."

"*What the hell?* Was I the only person who didn't see it?"

"Oh, come on, Rosa. You'd have to be blind to miss it. I'm shocked it's taken you this long to come together. Logan's not the only one who's been carrying a torch all these years. In high school, you *both* constantly watched each other. Your bodies would naturally gravitate toward one another whenever you were in the same room. Hell, you *still* do both of those things.

"You two have gotten better at schooling your facial expressions, but back then, you smiled at him like he hung the moon, and he gazed at you like you were a living fantasy. Do you think I didn't know about all those nights you two spent getting frisky up in the treehouse? I never understood why you started dating that quarterback, but I figured you had to make your own mistakes in life to learn from them, so I kept my lips sealed."

I blink rapidly, processing everything she just told me. "I... Wha... How... We were just *talking* in the treehouse."

"Well, that's disappointing." She chuckles. "I knew you weren't having sex. I would've put you on birth control a lot sooner if I suspected it. But I thought for sure there was at least some kissing involved."

"Nope." I shake my head, even though she can't see me. "No kissing."

"Hmm. That's too bad. But anyway, I'm happy for you, Rosalie. You deserve someone who sees the real you and loves you for exactly who you are. So does Logan."

Warmth spreads through my chest, filling me with a quiet reassurance.

"Thanks, Mom."

Her voice softens. "*Does* he make you happy? Genuinely happy?"

It's the easiest question I've ever had to answer.

"Happier than I've ever been in my life. More than I thought possible."

"Then that's all that matters." I can tell she's smiling.

For a brief moment, I allow myself to find comfort in her words. I take a few deep breaths, feeling my muscles relax through each exhale.

"Well, the sex matters, too," she adds, "but based on those photos, I'm assuming you have no trouble in that department. Is he keeping you sexually satisfied, sweetheart? Does he pay attention to multiple erogenous zones like any self-respecting man should? Because if not, we *will* be having words. How many orgasms does he deliver on average before seeking his own?"

My jaw drops. "Mother!"

"What? They're valid questions. When did the sex part first happen, by the way? Ooh, I'm sure my listeners would love to hear all about how you two finally got together."

"I am *not* discussing my sex life on your podcast, Mom. *Ever.* In fact, I'm not discussing my sex life with you *at all*, so get that idea out of your head right now."

"Fine," she huffs. "Just give me a rating. Would you say you're highly satisfied, satisfied, somewhat satisfied, somewhat *unsatisfied*, or unsatisfied?"

What does she think this is? A customer service survey?

"Boundaries, Mother. We've discussed this. Many, *many* times. You *must* respect them."

"I didn't hear a rating," she singsongs.

Christ on a cracker, I'm going to scream.

"I'm hanging up now, Mom. You can tell Dad, but no one else until we tell Ryan. Good—"

"Wait, one last thing!"

I bang the back of my head against the headrest. "What?"

"What's your favorite position together?"

"Oh my god. Mother, *stop.*"

"Any compatible kinks? What's the freakiest thing you two have done so far?"

Is it possible to divorce your parents at age twenty-seven? If so, I want in.

"Mom, staaaaahhhhp," I groan. "Please."

"Okay, okay. I swear this is the last question. Does he have the *equipment* to keep you satisfied? Because I could tell Julian wasn't up to par, honey. I have a sixth sense about these things, and I don't want that for you. People can say size doesn't matter all they want, but who are they kidding? Of course, it matters! Thankfully, I've never had to worry about that with your father. If anything, his size may have been a bit intimidating at first..."

I slam my hand on the wheel, accidentally making the horn blare. "*STOP.*"

"Oh, Rosalie, grow up," Mom scoffs. "If you'd let me finish, all I was trying to say was, if your brother takes after your dad, which I suspect he does based on their similar builds, he's going to make some woman *very* happy one day."

This woman is straight-up unhinged. Unhinged, I tell you!

"MOM! Logan is *like* a son to you, and Ryan is your *actual* son. And I understand Dad is your husband, but he's *my dad!* Their penises should never, *ever* be a topic of discussion between us!"

She laughs. "Rosalie, how many times do I have to say this? Consensual sex is a *beautiful* part of life, and the more open we are to receiving it, the more fulfilled our lives will be. There is *nothing* shameful about it. If you're not exploring all there is to offer with an open mind, you're robbing yourself of *great satisfaction.*

"Besides, this is what I *do for a living,* and I've had great success with it. Sex—*and sexual organs*—are perfectly natural. It's not like I was asking for pictures or measurements. Believe it or not, I *do* understand where the line is. But if we're just talking? Very few topics are off-limits."

"Well, this is one of them," I argue. "*This* topic is off-limits!"

She sighs dramatically. "Fine. But you're only hurting yourself if you're not willing to open up, Rosa."

"I'll take that risk." I scrub a hand down my face. "Can I hang up now?"

"One last thing. I promise it's not a question."

I clench my teeth. "What."

"Tell Logan he has my blessing, and I'm sure your

father will feel the same. I know he doesn't *need* our approval, but I wanted to share."

Despite the insanity of this conversation, I smile. "I'll tell him."

"Oh! And I'll put together one of my special boxes for you two. I just got in a delightful new vibrating cock ring I think you'll like."

Dear. God.

One of my mother's favorite perks of being a well-known sex therapist is the free samples. Sex toy companies from across the globe are constantly sending her new products to try, hoping she'll give them a marketing plug on-air. If she really likes something, she buys it in bulk and adds it to her *special boxes*. My mom still offers therapy outside of her podcast, and every new client receives a box as a welcome to her practice. It's sort of like a "welcome to the neighborhood" basket, but with dildos and flavored lube. According to her, they're a *big* hit.

Sylvie is never, *ever* going to let me live this down.

"That's really not necessary, Mother," I grumble.

"Oh, *nonsense*. I insist. You know what I always say... *your pleasure is my pleasure*."

Awesome. She's officially figured out a way to include her branding tagline into everyday conversation.

Kill me now.

We say our goodbyes, and after hanging up, I think about what she said about how Logan and I acted around each other in high school. Were we really that obvious? If so, why couldn't we ever see it in each other? And did my engagement truly break his heart? Ugh, my chest hurts just thinking about it. I'm quite familiar with that feeling because a little part of me felt it every time I saw him with a beautiful new woman on his arm.

God, all those wasted years.

I take a deep breath, resolving to make the most of every moment we have now. Logan's going to tell my brother about us tonight, and then we'll be free to be together publicly. The tabloid assholes may have tossed a wrench in our plan, but I'm confident in Avery and Nick's ability to counteract them.

Whatever life throws at us, Logan and I are going to tackle it together.

CHAPTER TWENTY-SIX
LOGAN

"Did you even hear what I said, Logan?!" Rosie throws her hands up in exasperation. "She's curating one of her *special boxes* for us! My *mother* is giving us a bunch of *'Dr. Tate Approved'* sex toys!" Her face falls into her hands as she groans.

I shrug, kicking my feet up on the coffee table. "I heard you just fine. I just don't see the problem. Why look a gift horse in the mouth?" I poke her thigh. "If they're *'Dr. Tate Approved,'* they're probably top tier."

She spreads her fingers, glaring at me through the gap. "Do *not* feed the monster."

I pull her hand away from her face. "C'mon, Pip. It's not a big deal. She'll hand the box over, you'll take the box, and that'll be the end of it as far as she's concerned."

"Have you *met* my mother?" Rosie deadpans.

"Okay, that's fair." I laugh.

She flops onto the couch with a dramatic sigh, her head landing in my lap, legs stretched across the cushions. I take the opportunity to run my fingers through her silky hair.

She sighs and closes her eyes. "I love that you're here, but I hate that Ryan couldn't go out with you tonight. I want to get this over with, so we can stop worrying."

"I know." I trail my fingers down her bare arm, watching as goose bumps rise in my wake. "But Ry seemed really excited the coffee girl said yes to another date. He promised to call if their night ended early, but I wouldn't count on it."

Rosie moans as I start massaging her scalp. "You're the best boyfriend ever."

I smile. "That's the first time you've called me that."

She opens one eye, looking up at me. "No, it's not."

"Uh, *yeah*, it is. Trust me, I would've remembered."

Her lips press together as she thinks. Then she opens the other eye and says, "Huh. Well, I've said it inside my head a bunch."

"Is that so?" I arch a brow. "Does that mean you want to officially be my girlfriend?"

Rosie twists her body until she's sitting up beside me. "Do *you* want to officially be my boyfriend?"

"Hmm." I stroke my beard in mock contemplation. "Jury's still out."

"Dick." She smacks my arm, making me laugh.

I catch her wrist before she can pull away and yank her onto my lap.

I cradle her jaw and press our foreheads together. "I don't know if those titles feel quite right."

"Me neither." Her nose scrunches. "But what else is there?"

I remind myself now is not the time to impulsively propose marriage just because I'd much rather be her husband.

"Ooh!" She holds up a finger. "You could be my lover-boy. Or maybe boytoy. Wait...I know! We could be each other's *luv-ahs*." Rosie grins, as if she's so proud of her smartassery.

I playfully bite the tip of her pointed finger. "Uh, no. I'm gonna veto all of those options."

She sticks her tongue out. "Lame."

"Significant other? Partner?" My lips twitch. "What about bae?"

"Ew." She makes a face. "You're really freaking bad at this, Logan. Like, terrible."

"Christ, tell me how you really feel," I joke, tickling her side. "I think what I came up with is a lot better than *boytoy*, thank you very much."

"Yeah, to *you*," she mutters.

I smile, unable to resist the urge to lean in for a quick kiss. "Rosie, if you want to call me your boyfriend, I'm fine with that. But if it doesn't feel right, why do we need a label for somebody else's benefit? I know you're the only person I want to be with, and vice versa. I say we skip 'em and just be...*together*. What do you think?"

Rosie wriggles her butt, smiling when she feels my body responding to hers. "I'd be okay with that."

"Well, then we'll run with it." I wrap my hands around her hips. "Are you sure you're doing okay with this whole photo leak situation? I'm sorry I kissed you out in public like that. I know better, but it's been so long since they've published a photo of me, and we've been a little more relaxed about being out together...I guess it slipped to the back of my mind."

"Logan, I *really* don't care," she assures me, beautiful brown eyes unwavering. "I've always known it was a possibility, and you have no reason to apologize. Sure, the timing sucks, and I'm not exactly thrilled they've resurrected the *billionaire bachelor."* I chuckle when Rosie rolls her eyes and frames those last two words with a set of air quotes.

"But I know how the cycle goes," she continues. "The gossipmongers will get bored soon enough. If there's no interest in gossip, there's no demand for photos. If there's no demand for photos, the paps aren't going to waste their time. I'm a big girl, Logan. I can handle a few dickheads toting cameras, or keyboard warriors talking shit about someone they've never met. *We* know the truth, and that's what matters to me."

Just when I think she couldn't possibly be more perfect for me, she proves me wrong.

Most of the women I've dated since my name started making headlines were all about the photo ops. I even discovered a few of them were tipping off the paps themselves. I already knew Rosie wasn't that type of person, but it's still nice to hear because I've always fucking hated the attention. I was more worried about her taking offense to something the internet assholes might say, but I should've known she'd brush it off without a second thought. Rosie gets paid to manage and shape a celebrity's public image. She knows how this stuff works much better than I ever will.

I frame her face with my hands. "Rosalie Elena Morales, you're fucking spectacular, you know that?"

Her pink lips curve into a crooked grin as she mirrors my pose. "Logan I-Don't-Have-A-Middle-Name-Even-Though-That's-Totally-Weird Edwards, you're pretty fucking amazing yourself. But you know you've already got me, right? You can back off on the swoon a bit. Save some for later, so you don't have to blow your whole load all at once. Ya know?"

"*Back off on the swoon?*" I laugh. "You know, I'd like to

think I'm fairly fluent in Rosie-speak, but I'm a little stumped on this one."

"Oh, please." She rolls her eyes as she sits back. "You know damn well what you do to me by being all sweet, and smolder-y, and sexy, one hundred percent of the time. Isn't that exhausting?"

"Smolder-y?" I echo, amused.

"Shut up." Rosie whacks me in the chest. "You know what I mean."

"No, I *don't* know what you mean," I insist, pulling her closer. "I'm just being me. I'm the same guy you've always known, but now that I get to do filthy-as-fuck things to you, I don't have to hold back on the parts I used to keep in check."

She blushes. "See!" Rosie points to her pinkened cheeks. "I'm blushing like a virgin in a strip club! *I'm not a virgin, Logan!*"

I hold my hands up in a placating gesture. "I'm perfectly aware, Pip, considering *my dick's been inside of you many times.*"

I fight a grin when her flush deepens. "*This is not normal for me!* I do *not* easily blush! But ever since the cabin, I swear I've done it more than I ever have in my entire life combined. It's all your fault, Logan! You and your goddamn swoon factor! You've got that baby cranked up to eleventy thousand, like twenty-four, seven!"

I try not to laugh. I swear I do. But Rosie's like a feral kitten caught in a hurricane—tiny, fierce, and ready to claw her way out by any means necessary. A whirlwind of flailing limbs and sharp, sassy quips, but fuck if it isn't the hottest thing I've ever seen. The drama, the passion, the chaos, the sheer *Rosie-ness* of it all, wrecks me in the best possible way. This beautifully flustered woman makes me so goddamn happy, my laughter just spills out.

And when it finally dies down, and she's glaring at me like she's about to cut off my balls, I only have one thought on my mind.

"God, I love you."

She gasps.

A heartbeat of silence stretches between us.

Oh, fuck.

Did I say that out loud?

"You *love* me?" Rosie questions.

Yep, I sure did.

Welp, it's not exactly the way I planned on doing this, but what the hell?

"Yeah, Rosie. I do." I grin.

"Wait." Her brows crinkle. "You love me like, in a *found family* kind of way, or you *luuuuurve me?*"

"Both, you nut." I laugh, smacking a kiss on her forehead. "But mostly in a '*it hurts to breathe whenever I think about never being able to kiss you again*' kind of way."

"Swoony bastard," she mumbles under her breath.

I cup a hand over my ear. "What's that? I didn't quite hear you."

She rolls her eyes, but then she smiles the prettiest smile I've ever seen. "I love you in both ways too, Logan."

"Yeah?"

Her eyes are glassy as she nods. "Yeah."

I take her mouth in a slow kiss, but like always, it doesn't stay that way for long. I could easily lose myself in her all night, but we really need to finish talking first. With a groan, I force myself to pull back and lift her off my lap.

"I really need to talk to Ry."

"Yeah, you really do." Rosie sighs. "I'd hate to say this, but maybe you should stay at your place tonight. That way, if Ry's date *does* end early, you'll be right there. But if not, you can catch him in the morning before my mom's party."

I groan. "That would be the sensible thing to do."

I really don't want to leave, but I know she's right. If I stay at my place, I'll be there when he gets home. When I bought the building, I converted the top floor into two penthouses. I took the west-facing unit, and Ryan was quick to rent out the east-facing one, a fact Rosie wasted no time giving us shit for, cracking all sorts of codependency jokes.

It's been hella convenient until recently because we spent so much time together, but not so much when I can't bring Rosie back to my place without risking an awkward run-in with her brother.

"Well, you could do it at my mom's birthday party, but half my family is going to be there, so maybe it's not the best option."

Jesus. That would be a shit show of epic proportions. I love the Morales family. Hell, I love Rosie's parents more than my own. But as her recent phone call with her mom proves, discretion isn't exactly their thing. *Your* business is *their* business. Great when you need backup. Not so great when you need to have a conversation that might end in some choice words and a right hook to the face. Probably best to keep the witnesses out of it.

"I'll pass on that one."

She points at me. "Smart move."

I give her one more kiss before reluctantly getting up to grab my keys off the counter. She joins me at the door as I'm sliding my jacket on.

"Text me to let me know you got home safely on that death trap."

Here we go again.

Rosie *hates* my Ducati. She hates *all* motorcycles, really, but I think that's more out of a fear of the unknown. She's never even been on a motorcycle before. I'm on a not-so-covert mission to get her on the back of my bike someday, at least once, so she can see what she's missing.

I chuckle. "That *death trap* is a masterpiece in Italian engineering and one of only five hundred worldwide. Plus, it makes it *way* easier to find parking."

"Uh-huh," she replies. "You're still never getting me on the back of that thing."

I wind my arm behind her back, pulling her closer. "I'll break you down one of these days." I trail kisses down the slope of her neck. "Think about it. We could take a ride out to Big Bear this summer, two hours with all those horses rumbling between your thighs..." I ghost my hand over her breast, barely skimming the erect nipple poking out of her T-shirt. "Stay in a secluded cabin, since those have been so good to us." I palm her ass as our lips meet again, kissing Rosie until she's breathless. "You'd look so fucking hot spread out over my bike, taking my cock." I grin as she whimpers. "Would you like that, baby?" She releases a throaty moan as my hand slides between her legs, feeling the wetness through her leggings. "Oh, I think you'd like that very much." Just as she grips my forearm, trying to trap my hand, I step back and open the door. "Think about that tonight when you're getting off. If you're a good girl and record it for me, I might return the favor."

I pick my helmet off the floor and step into the hallway.

"Night, Pip. Make a real good mess of those sheets when you're thinking about me later." I wink.

Rosie pins me with the mother of all glares, flips me off, and slams the door in my face.

I grin. "That's the spirit! Except maybe add another finger."

I walk away, laughing as she cusses me out through the door.

God, I love that woman.

CHAPTER TWENTY-SEVEN
ROSALIE

It seems like I'm one of the last to arrive as I step into the backyard where my mom's party is being held. The smell of grilled meat fills the air as my dad mans the barbecue, flipping burgers with one hand, while holding a bottle of beer in the other. He's with my uncle Brian—my mom's brother—probably arguing over the best angle for perfect grill marks. My mom is sitting at the patio table gesticulating wildly while talking to my aunt Teresa, while Teresa, who's Sylvie's mom, is hugging baby Olivia to her chest. I haven't spotted Logan yet, but I can *feel* his presence. My skin prickles with awareness, knowing he's somewhere nearby, throwing his sexy pheromones in my direction.

"Pumpkin!" my dad calls. "Get over here."

"Hey, Dad," I say as I join him at the grill.

"Excuse me, Rosalie." Uncle Brian scoots me out of the way. "Nature calls."

My dad swings an arm around my neck, pulling me closer. He waits until my uncle is inside the house and then says, "I hear you have some news, kiddo."

My eyes scan the yard, looking for my brother. "We still need to talk to Ry, so it's not public yet."

My dad smiles. "Logan mentioned that."

He lifts his chin, directing my gaze over to the giant palm shading the back corner of the yard. Logan's standing next to Sylvie's husband, half-listening as he slowly undresses me with his eyes. My nipples instantly tighten, and I pray the lining in my bra is doing the trick to hide the evidence.

Chill out, you horny bitches. The whole family doesn't need to know how badly you want Logan's lips to wrap around you right now.

"Don't worry," my dad continues, saving my nipples from further scolding. "Your brother's not here yet. Sounds like he's been a slippery little weasel the last two days."

"I'm sure he's slipping into *something*," I grumble. "Or some*one*."

I'm glad my brother got another chance with Penny, especially after our last talk, but I may be a bit salty that Logan left my apartment for nothing last night. It turns out, Ryan's date went so well, he stayed the night at Penny's. And since she's off work today, he was continuing their *date* this morning.

In other words, my brother wanted to get laid again before taking off.

My dad barks in laughter. "Good for him. Nothing wrong with starting your day with a little Morning Glory, if you catch my drift." He wags his dark, bushy eyebrows.

I gag. "People in Tokyo are catching your drift, Dad."

My dad is nowhere near as bad as my mom, but the man has a shocking number of euphemisms at the ready.

"Well, mum's the word, sweetheart, but like I told Logan, I'm happy for you guys. It's about damn time."

"Thanks, Da—"

"Daddy, save me!" A loud squeal follows the lilting voice.

A second later, Hudson's oldest daughter Lily races by, with two of my younger cousins in hot pursuit. Lily's golden pigtails bounce with each step, her sparkly pink princess dress billowing behind her.

Hudson scoops her up, saving the damsel in distress, but then he takes her to the ground and starts tickling. The other two kids dogpile on Hudson's back, trying to rescue their princess from the dastardly Tickle Monster—aka Hudson—as they all dissolve into a fit of giggles.

My ovaries swoon, and I finally get what Sylvie's been saying all these months. She swears watching Hudson be a dad is one of her biggest turn-ons. According to her, anyone can be a father, but it takes a real man to be a great *daddy*. Hence, why she's always mauling him after the girls go to bed.

I smile as I take a moment to soak in the pandemonium of a Morales-O'Hare family gathering. It's oddly comforting, the dependable chaos is reassuring, like a warm hug.

You know, if warm hugs felt like swimming in a washing machine during the spin cycle.

I make my way over to my mom, setting a wrapped gift on the table beside her and kissing her cheek. "Happy birthday, Mom."

Logan's deep, rumbly laugh rolls through me from somewhere behind us, and I have to resist the urge to turn around like a lovesick fool as a shiver rakes down my spine.

My mom's eyes light up as she pats my hand. "Thank you, sweetheart."

Sylvie sidles up to me, tucking her arm into the crook of my elbow. "Hey, you."

"Hey."

Olivia stretches a chubby arm toward her mama, so Sylvie bends down to take her from my aunt. "Come here, my little lovebug." She sighs as she breathes in her daughter's sweet baby scent, placing a soft kiss on top of her dark mop of curls.

Then she tugs on my elbow with her free hand. "Excuse us, mothers. I need to harass this one for a minute."

My mom and aunt chuckle as Sylvie drags me away. Once she's deemed us out of earshot, she asks, "So, today's the day, huh?"

"Guess so." I shrug. "When the party dies down, Logan's going to take him for a drink somewhere close by."

"And once the overprotective ass knows Logan's feeding you the D, everyone else can know?"

"Yep." I smack my lips together, popping the P. "Minus the pornographic phrasing."

She shifts Olivia in her arms, the baby babbling against her ginormous chest. "Well, good luck with that."

"Yeah, thanks." I run a finger over Liv's tiny, soft hand. "How is it possible she's grown so much in just a week?"

Sylvie snorts. "Because she never gets off the teat." Olivia just happens to grab a handful of boob at that exact moment, proving her point.

I laugh. "Like father, like daughter."

Sylvie grins, looking across the yard for Hudson. He catches her eye instantly, and they exchange a smoldering look so intense it should probably come with a warning label.

"Save it for when you get home, you hussy," I tease.

She grins wickedly. "Or I'll ask Grandma to watch her for a bit while Mommy and Daddy play hide the sausage in one of the spare bedrooms. Think Dr. Tate will give us a special box too?"

I groan, shaking my head. "You're an asshole."

"I try." Sylvie pats Liv's back, still grinning. "I can't wait until everything's out in the open. I think you two make a stupidly hot couple, and the world needs to see it. Oh, wait...they already have!"

"If you didn't have a baby in your arms right now..." I bare my teeth and shake my fist in the air.

"You'd *what?*" Sylvie challenges, knowing damn well I'd never lay a finger on her. "Give me a purple nurple?"

I laugh. "Uh, no. I'm not going anywhere near your nurples. That's your husband's job."

"*What* job is this, exactly?" a deep voice rumbles behind me.

I glare at Sylvie as Hudson materializes out of thin air, smoothly scooping the baby into his arms.

I arch a brow. "You knew he was right behind me, didn't you?"

"To be fair, he just got here." Sylvie winds her arm behind Hudson's back, and I'm ninety-nine percent sure she's copping a feel.

"How've you been, Rosalie?" he asks, pale green eyes dancing with amusement.

Yep, she's definitely touching his ass.

He coughs into his fist—which was fake as hell—and honestly, I don't even want to know what she just grabbed. "Sylv's not giving you too much trouble is she?"

"No more so than usual." I shrug.

His lips curve into a smirk. "Do you mind if I steal my wife for a bit? I could use her help with something."

Sylvie pushes her tongue into her cheek, simulating a blow job. When Hudson looks down on her, she's the picture of innocence, but I'm pretty sure he caught it in his peripheral vision.

She kisses Olivia's forehead. "Wanna go see Grandma again? C'mon, sweet pea, let's go do that."

"Have fun." I give them a little finger wave as they disappear to do unholy things in my childhood home.

Please don't pick my old bedroom. My boy band posters have been through enough. Let's just say they had to witness a certain quarterback's infamous three-pump performance.

I shudder.

God, what the hell was I thinking back then?

I navigate through the commotion, greeting aunts, uncles, and cousins while sidestepping a group of kids more interested in playing tag than saying hello to a boring grownup. My aunts Camila and Tahlia, wave me over, practically vibrating with the need to spill the latest family gossip.

Oh, if only they knew.

A little while later, I toss my head back, laughing at my cousin Sofia's latest online dating disaster, when a familiar buzzing sensation sparks beneath my skin. I can feel someone watching me, and I'd bet my delicious sangria those eyes are the prettiest pair of hazels I've ever seen.

My suspicions are confirmed when my phone vibrates in my pocket.

I pull it out, angling it away from any nosy eyeballs.

Logan: You look so fucking hot in that dress. Do you know how HARD it's been keeping my distance from you? Spoiler alert: 🍆

I stifle a laugh. "I'm sorry, Sofia. I need to take this. I'll find you in a bit, and we'll finish catching up."

"Okay," she says.

I smile as I type my reply.

> Me: Logan, we agreed it has to be like this until you talk to Ry after the party. We can't risk it.

My core clenches when I read his next message.

> Logan: I'm aware. But just know, every time I see that little sundress swishing across your legs as you walk, I'm imagining ducking my head under it and eating your pretty pussy until you're soaking my face and screaming my name.

Jesus. This man and his filthy mouth.

> Me: Save those thoughts for later. AFTER you talk to my brother.

"Rosalie, could you please grab some ketchup out of the pantry?" I look up to find the source of the voice. "We could use some more barbecue-flavored chips, too."

I give my aunt Teresa a thumbs-up. "On it."

Inside the house, the terracotta tiles beneath my feet glow from the afternoon sun. There's a walk-in pantry between the large kitchen and formal dining room, so I head over there to grab what Aunt Teresa asked for.

Just as I twist the doorknob, a low voice behind me asks, "Need some help?"

I smile, licking my lips as I turn around. Since we finally have a moment alone, I make no attempt to hide my perusal and eye fuck the hell out of him. Logan's muscular arms are gripping the doorframe above us, tattoos peeking out of his fitted black tee. The worn jeans stretched over his powerful thighs are giving me all sorts of visuals of what they're capable of when he's naked. I breathe in his sexy cologne, sighing as I get a little dizzy with euphoria. I'm weighing the odds of getting caught if I pull him into the pantry for a quickie. They're not good, but if the look in Logan's eyes is any indication, he's about to risk it just like I am. My vagina's such a whore.

Sure, Rosa. It's just your vag.

What was his question again?

"I came to offer my freight services." Logan looks over his shoulder before whispering, "But now all I can think about is planting your ass next to the Cheerios, lifting up your dress, and eating you out until you're coming apart on my tongue."

Yes, please.

"That doesn't sound very sanitary," I tease. "What if someone wants cereal for breakfast?"

"I'll replace the box," he deadpans.

Logan's eyes zero in on my pert nipples. "Get in the closet, Rosie. I—"

We pull apart comically fast when the front door opens, and I do some kind of weird 'I don't know what to do with my hands' dance.

I quickly grab three bags of chips, shoving them into his arms. "Take these!" I whisper-shout.

I turn around to grab the ketchup and...

Ooh! Cheddar and sour cream Ruffles! I haven't had those in *forever*!

I grab a bag, along with some Goldfish crackers for the kids. Now that we've sufficiently covered our asses, I head out of the pantry.

Shit! Ketchup!

Doubling back and grabbing a bottle, I kick the door shut with it tucked under my arm and follow Logan toward the kitchen. We're smiling at each other like doofuses, arms loaded with snacks, when Logan halts mid-step, his throat flexing around a hard swallow.

"Hey, man," he says to my brother. "You just get here?"

My brother's dark eyes are bouncing back and forth between me and his best friend. His jaw's tight. His nostrils flare, and his fists are clenched so tightly, his knuckles are white. Ryan's madder than I've ever seen him, and I can only think of one reason for that.

He knows.

Logan seems to come to the same conclusion, because he gently nudges me to the side and steps closer to Ryan.

"Let's go for a walk, Ry."

Crack.

The sickening smack of knuckles meeting flesh splits the air. Logan jerks back, head snapping to the side. The chips fall to the floor as he presses an open palm against the wall to catch his balance.

"Why *the fuck* would I want to go anywhere with you, you lying piece of shit?!" Ryan doesn't lower his fists.

I try stepping forward, but Logan damn near clotheslines me to prevent me from getting close to the angry guy.

"I deserved that." Logan's fingers press against the quickly forming bruise on his eye. "But that's your only free shot."

My brother scoffs. "You think I'm scared of you?"

"I didn't say I *wanted* to hit you," Logan clarifies. "But I *will* take you down to the ground if I need to."

"I'd like to see you try," Ryan sneers.

"*What the hell is wrong with you?!*" I yell, stretching to the side behind Logan's back.

Ryan's furious gaze snaps to me. "I think you know *exactly* what's wrong with me, Rosa. What the fuck were you thinking?"

"Leave her out of this." Logan looks to me out of the corner of his eye. "Rosie, why don't you go—"

I dump my pantry haul on the kitchen island. "Save your breath. I'm not going anywhere while this jackass is behaving like this."

"Oh, that's rich." Ry shakes out his fists. "Take a look in a mirror, Rosa. Your judgment clearly hasn't been the best lately."

Oh, no he didn't.

Logan predicts my lunge and grabs me around the waist to stop it. "Settle down, Rosie. I am not letting you get hurt in the crossfire." He turns to Ryan. "Leave her out of this. If you're pissed, you take it out on *me*."

My brother still looks like he's ready to throw down, so I'm smart enough to withdraw. I don't feel like getting accidentally clocked in the face if these two start going at it again.

"Asshole," I mutter, leaning back against the counter, crossing my arms with a huff. "That was for you, Ryan, in case it wasn't clear."

He flips me off, so I return the gesture with both hands.

"How long?" Ryan seethes. "*How long* have you been fucking my sister behind my back?!"

Logan lifts his chin. "We've been *together* a little over a month."

Confused chatter erupts from the family members now spilling into the house. My mom and dad push their way to the front, both looking equally concerned and exasperated.

"Boys, what's going on?" my dad asks, his deep voice cutting through the noise.

Ryan doesn't take his eyes off Logan. "Didn't you know, Dad? Apparently, Logan's decided Rosa is his new plaything."

A collective gasp.

My dad's mouth falls open, as if he's shocked by his son's audacity.

Join the club, Pops.

Sylvie, standing behind my parents, grumbles, "Oh, hell no. Lemme at him." There's a bit of a tussle as Hudson holds her back, whispering in her ear.

Logan stiffens. "That's not fair, Ry, and that's certainly not true."

"Really?" Ryan scoffs. "Okay, Mr.-I-Invented-A-Hookup-App."

Logan's jaw tightens. "That has nothing to do with this. And good to know you've been judging me this whole time for it."

"That was a cheap shot, Ryan," I seethe. "And you are in *no* position to judge Logan on anything!"

Ryan steps closer, nostrils flaring. "*I told you* to stay the hell away from her. Many, *many* times! Rosalie's not someone you can just screw around with. She's my sister! And she just broke off her engagement! You're taking advantage of her vulnerability, dickhead."

"Jesus, man. Give me a little more credit than that. I am *not* taking advantage of Rosie! I'm *in love* with her, you dipshit!" Logan shouts, his voice thick with emotion.

I suck in a breath. I'm pretty sure the rest of the room is collectively holding theirs.

Well, okay then. I guess we're just throwing it all out there at once.

Logan pinches the bridge of his nose. "I've *been* in love

with her for half my life, Ry! I just didn't do anything about it until I knew she was interested."

More gasps. More murmurs. Somewhere in the back, an "Awwww" floats through the tension.

Ryan's scowl deepens, though something in his expression wavers. "You sure as hell did something about it that one New Year's Eve."

Logan rolls his eyes. "Will you get over that already? It was almost a decade ago!"

My mom's brows lift. "What is he talking about, Rosa?"

I groan, rubbing my temples. "Not now, Mom."

Ryan turns back to me. "And you? What the hell were you thinking? Of all the people in the world, you had to pick my best friend as your rebound guy? And then get photographed making out with him in public? Do you have any idea the kind of scrutiny you're subjecting yourself to, Rosa? The catty keyboard warriors are having a field day with this! Have you seen the shit they're saying about you?"

Awesome. He's clearly scrolled through the comments.

"Did you forget what I do for a living?" I glare at him. "*Of course* I know. But you know what? *I don't care,* because I don't give a shit what some stranger thinks of me, and neither does Logan. The only people's opinions who matter are the ones standing in this house watching you throw a goddamn hissy fit!"

"Hissy fit, my ass," he mutters.

I throw my hands up, exasperated. "*Read the freaking room, Ryan!* Notice how nobody else seems surprised Logan and I are together? I'd bet that's because they've seen this coming for years, just like Mom and Sylvie did."

Lots of nods from my family, backing me up.

"I *did* see it coming!" Ryan shouts. "But you know why

I kept trying to stop it? Because there's no way this can end well."

"Fuck that," Logan growls. "You don't know that."

"You wanna talk about what I *do* know?" Ryan's glare falls to Logan's hand. "The reason you got that tattoo. I knew the second I saw it, but considering she was engaged to another man at the time, I figured it was your way of making peace with it, or whatever. I'm not as clueless as you seem to fucking think."

Wait...what? The reason behind *which* tattoo?

Logan's fist flexes, the shock evident on his face.

My hand flies to my mouth as I stare at the giant *rose* inked on the top of Logan's left hand.

"Logan..." I'm all choked up. I can barely get the word out.

I think back to the first time I saw that tattoo. It was about a year ago, shortly after Julian and I got engaged. What did Ryan mean when he said he figured Logan was making peace with it? My mom told me Logan was heart-broken when he learned about my engagement. Did he get that tattoo for me?

Logan gives me a crooked smile and a shrug, like it's no big deal he branded his love for me in a spot where *the entire world* would see it every day.

Sylvie catches my eye across the room and mouths, "Damn, girl."

My brother rolls his eyes. "Can we get back to the issue at hand? Like how, oh, I don't know...my best friend and my sister have been sneaking around behind my back and lying to my face about it?"

"Gee, I wonder why," I mutter. "Clearly, you've taken the news so well."

Logan walks over to me, extending his hand. When I

take it, he pulls me in front of him, placing his hands on my shoulders. Ryan's jaw clenches right before his face falls, reading the intention behind his gesture. Logan's clearly communicating which side he'll take if Ryan forces him to choose, and it won't be my brother's.

"Ryan, if you truly believe I'd *ever* hurt her, you don't know me at all." Logan's voice has lost its power. There's a sadness in it that makes my chest ache. "Rosie's the only woman I've *ever* loved, and I think deep down, you've always known that. But the time for willful blindness is over, man, because I'm not giving her up. I *can't.*"

I sigh, briefly closing my eyes as I lean back against his solid chest. "Ryan, I love you, but Logan's right. You're just going to have to find some way to accept this because it's not going away. Logan isn't a rebound. He's *my* forever. He always has been."

Another wave of gasps and excited murmurs.

Logan's heavy arms hook around my front as he pulls me into a hug, nuzzling the spot right behind my ear.

Ryan clenches his jaw, looking around the room, realizing he has no allies in this. The entire room waits on bated breath as he decides which path to take.

Less than a minute later, he huffs, turning to our mom. "Sorry to disrupt the party, Mom. Happy birthday, but I can't deal with this shit right now. I need to get out of here."

My mom pulls Ryan into a hug, whispering something in his ear before he turns sharply on his heels and storms out the door. A beat later, the screech of truck tires echoes through the quiet street.

My parents exchange glances, then start shooing people back outside, recognizing Logan and I need some privacy.

When we're alone, Logan exhales, turning me toward him. "So, I'm your forever, huh?"

I smile, glancing down at his left hand, tracing the blooms inked into the surface. "You really got this...for me?"

He swallows with a nod. "Yeah, Rosie. I did."

"After Julian and I got engaged?" I frown. "But why?"

The gold flecks in his eyes glitter as he notices how glassy mine have become. "I guess it was my way of ensuring I'd always have a piece of you with me, even though you could never be mine."

Oh my god, you heartbreakingly romantic man.

"I love you." I trace the closely cropped hairs of his beard, never breaking our gaze. "I'm sorry it took me so long to figure my shit out, but I'm so thankful we're here now."

"Me, too, Rosie." A mischievous smile spreads across his lips. "But now that you've thrown out the whole *'forever'* thing...I'm a little concerned. That's a long-ass time to be stuck with you. I dunno if I'm up for it."

I giggle, rising on my toes and clasping my hands behind his neck. "Too bad, Edwards. No turning back now."

He pretends to think about it before smacking a hard kiss on my lips. "Okay, fine. I guess I'll learn to live with it."

I stick my tongue out. "Good. Because I'm not giving you up either."

I swear the green in his eyes just brightened. "I sorta got that with the whole 'he's my forever' thing."

I place a soft kiss on the corner of his mouth. "You know Ryan's going to come around, right? He's just hurt that we lied to him."

"I know." He catches a rogue tear with his thumb. "Are you okay after all that?"

"I'll be fine. Honestly, I think it could've been a lot worse." I carefully prod the area around his eye. "I can't believe he actually punched you. We should put some ice on that."

"Eh." Logan shrugs. "I probably would've done the same if I were in his shoes. I think he'll be more understanding once I have the chance to explain why we hid it from them."

I press my ear against his chest, listening to the steady beat of his heart. "Well...as far as relationship announcements go, that sure was a dramatic way to go about it."

His torso shakes with laughter. "Yeah, that was something all right."

I lift my chin. "But honestly? It's pretty on brand with this circus of a family. Are you sure you're ready for this?"

"Bring it on, Morales." He kisses my forehead and palms my butt with both hands. "Speaking of your family, has your mom given you the special box yet?"

I groan, burying my face in his chest. "Why are you like this?"

"You wouldn't have me any other way." He squeezes me a little tighter. "One of the many reasons why we're perfect for each other, Pip."

I smile, knowing he's right. The future may be uncertain, but the one thing that isn't? Logan and I are in this together. And I can guarantee this billionaire won't be a bachelor for much longer.

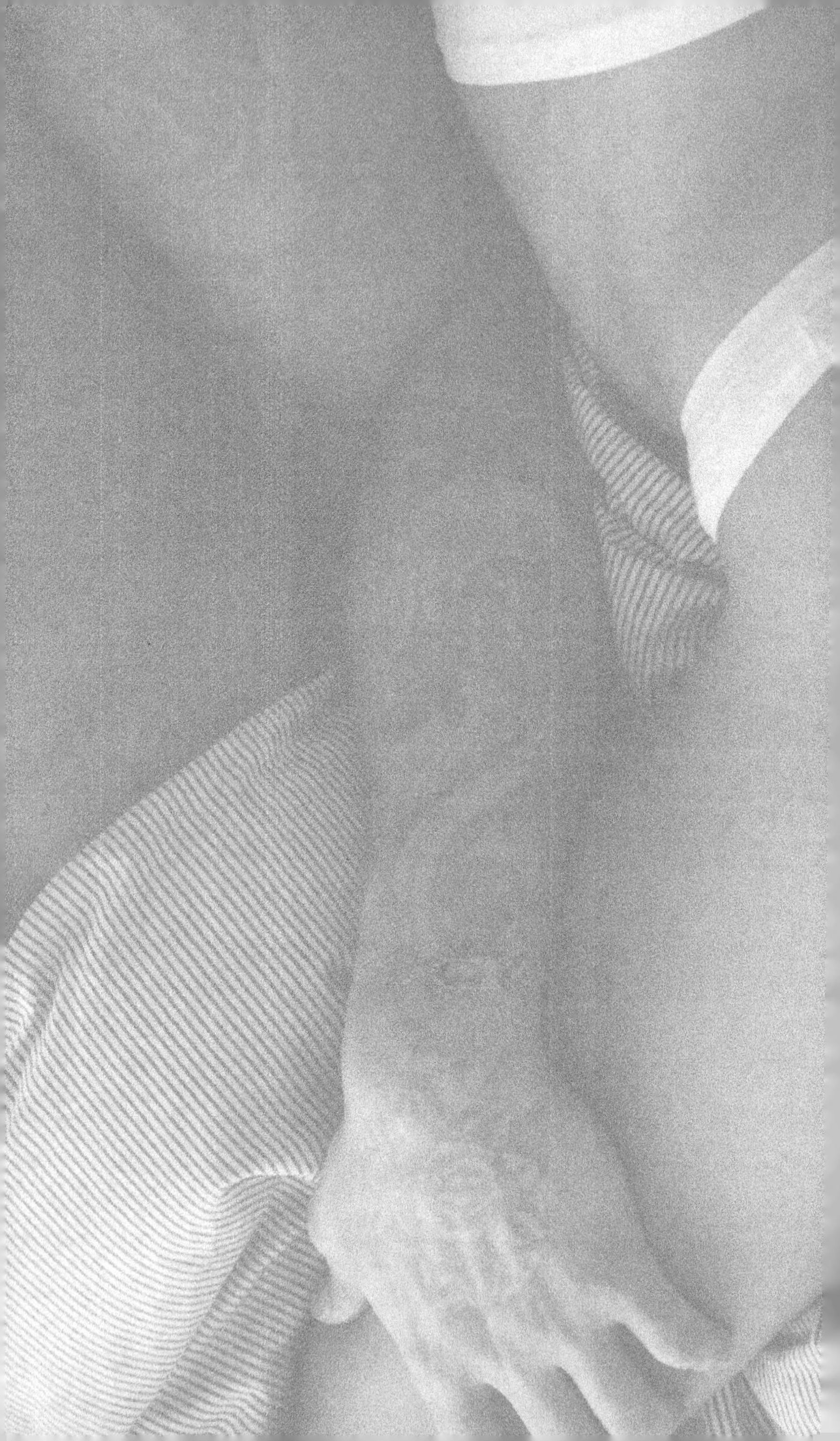

CHAPTER TWENTY-EIGHT
LOGAN

The moment I step off the elevator inside BetMasters Headquarters, all eyes are on me. More specifically the black eye I'm sporting, courtesy of our VP of Acquisitions. There's a lot of chatter, but I'm halfway to my office before anyone has the nerve to speak up.

"Damn, bossman." Pete, our CFO's assistant whistles. "That's quite the shiner."

I take a sip of my coffee. "You should see the other guy."

Sara, an intern, snickers. "A friendly disagreement over March Madness, or...?"

"Sure, that sounds plausible," I say dryly, brushing past them toward my office.

Fucking hell. I really should've listened to Rosie and iced the damn thing.

She picked up a tube of arnica for me last night, but it can only do so much at this point. I brush my employees' looks aside, knowing the state of my face is the least of my concerns right now. I have exactly two weeks to lock in the Olympus deal, and we have a lot to do between now and then.

I step into my office, setting my coffee down as I boot up my computer. Before I can settle in, my EA, Barry, walks in, clutching his tablet.

"Morning, boss. Did you hear the news? You're trending. On the interwebs and the thirtieth floor."

I groan. "Lucky me."

"Someone clearly had a go at your face. Did you ice that eye at all, or just fancy the swollen look?"

I sigh. "Why don't you ask what you really want to know, Barron?"

"Ooh, he's pulling out the legal name." He smirks, like the shit-stirring savant he is. "I daresay the gossip train's well and truly left the station. The office'll be buzzing by lunch, so go on then. What's the story behind the bruiser? Let me guess...this has to do with the woman you were seen kissing? Does she have a name?"

"Yes, she has a name," I shoot back without blinking. "Rosalie Morales."

Might as well get it out there since it's bound to be public information anytime now. Quite frankly, I'm shocked the paps didn't figure it out over the weekend.

Barry arches his brows. "As in your best mate's little sister? *That* Rosalie Morales? Bloody hell, no wonder. I'm assuming Ryan's the one who put the mark on your pretty mug?" He twirls a finger in my direction for emphasis.

Barry may be a shameless gossip, but I trust he knows when to keep his mouth shut. He understands Ryan and I had a personal relationship long before a working one, and the two do not coincide.

"Yep." I point to him. "But that stays between us."

"Like a royal vault, me." He uses his thumb and forefinger to mimic pulling a zipper across his mouth.

I shake my head, sipping my coffee. "Just run through my schedule please."

Barry chuckles, then launches into his rapid-fire breakdown of my day.

"Right then. First up, internal check-ins on the PPA integration, followed by a meeting with Gretchen's team to finalize the contingency budget. Lunch is scheduled for delivery at noon. Since your body is your temple and all that, I took the liberty of selecting a quinoa, spinach, and lentil salad topped with grilled chicken, avocado, and sweet potatoes with a lemon-tahini dressing."

"That sounds good. Thanks."

He nods. "At two, you have a call with Imani from the Vegas satellite. She only needs about ten minutes to review upcoming license renewals. Other than that, you'll be free to float around checking on each individual team's progress for the Olympus deal. I'll be sorting travel arrangements today for Vegas, so if you've any preferences for accommodation, make sure they're sent my way."

I dip my chin. "Sounds good.

"Anything else you're needing from me, then?" Barry asks, tapping his digital pen against the edge of his iPad.

"Check with Jared to ensure the dev team's data has been updated before we finalize the presentation decks."

"Already on it," Barry confirms.

"Good. And let design know I want a fresh polish on the visuals. Olympus is a luxury brand, and we need our pitch to reflect that. Their last mockup wasn't quite cutting it."

"Of course." He nods.

"Oh, and send a memo to legal. I want them to comb through every line one last time. One slip-up and the Control Board will bury our asses in red tape—something we obviously want to avoid. I expect their report on my desk by end of day Friday."

"Got it." Barry scrawls some notes on his tablet. "Anything else?"

"No, I think—"

Before I can finish my sentence, there's a single knock on my door before it swings open. Ryan steps inside, hands stuffed inside the pockets of his sharply tailored slacks.

He spots Barry and awkwardly clears his throat. "Sorry, didn't mean to interrupt."

"Morning, Ryan. Have yourself a decent weekend?" Barry's blue eyes twinkle as his gaze shifts my way. "Get up to anything...scandalous?"

Great subtly there, Bare.

Ryan frowns, looking between us. "Logan, you got a minute?"

I wave Barry off.

"And that's my cue to leave you two to verbally eviscerate each other in private. I'll just leave this door open a smidge and listen in, in case you need me for anything."

"Your husband must have the patience of a saint," I call out.

"You're not wrong," Barry singsongs.

Ryan closes the door behind my nosy assistant, shaking his head.

He exhales as he turns to face me.

I hold my palm out. "Look. If you're here to ream my ass again, save it for after business hours, will you?"

His jaw flexes as he drops into a visitor chair in front of me. "That bruise still looks pretty gnarly. Did you put an icepack on it?"

For fuck's sake. Why is everyone so obsessed with frozen water all of a sudden?

"I'll live." I shrug. "What'd you need, Ry?"

He shifts on his feet, nodding to my coffee cup. "Penny make that for you?"

Okay, half-assed small talk it is, then.

"No, the redhead did. Her name's Chloe, I think." I take another sip, watching him over the rim of the cup. "Why are you here? Because I doubt it's to discuss my black eye or the coffee shop staff."

After a beat, he decides to get to the point. "I talked to my source at Olympus this morning. Got some insight on their execs that might be helpful for the pitch."

"Such as?" I prompt.

"For starters, their VP of Strategy prefers a clean interface. Sleek, minimalistic, and intuitive is the name of the game there. Player acquisition and retention are two of their top priorities right now, so I think *we* should emphasize how this partnership supports both their short and long-term goals in that regard."

"What else?"

"Their CEO is apparently a fantasy football junkie. The dude's in no less than two dozen leagues each season. If we can showcase how our predictive analytics can boost his win ratio—or at the very least, stroke his ego—we'll have his attention. If we can make it happen, a demo on that would really sell it."

Interesting.

"So...you think we should add something along the lines of predicting which players are going to blow up based on subtle stat trends? Assist with weekly rosters or draft picks?"

Ryan nods. "Exactly. We'll be the crystal ball in his back pocket. Breakout predictions, trade optimization, weekly picks...if it boosts his bragging rights, we're going to have his buy-in."

I lean back in my chair, already picturing the UI in my mind. "Loop Development and Data Analytics into this. I want a demo that highlights how our models can optimize fantasy strategy based on league-specific formats. If they have any questions, have them come to me directly."

"Will do." Ryan nods. "Think you'll be able to resist flexing your own fantasy stats in the process?"

"Fuck my stats." I grin. "I'd give up my entire roster, including all my keepers, if we can close this deal."

He laughs. "Damn. You really want this to go through huh? I've been trying to steal your QB for years."

I sober. "It *needs* to go through, Ry. It's our game-changer."

"I know, man." He swallows. "Regardless of what's going on between us outside of this building, I'm damn good at my job. I've been here since day one, dude. I'm just as emotionally invested in this company's growth as you are. I've got your back."

"I know you do, and I appreciate it."

Neither one of us says anything for an awkward thirty seconds.

Ryan sheepishly grabs the back of his neck, shifting in his seat. "For what it's worth...it's not because I don't think you're good enough for Rosa. I may have said some shit the other day out of anger, but I didn't mean it. You're the best man I know behind my dad, Logan. But she's *my little sister,* man, and even though I'm pissed at you for lying—and I probably will be for a while—you're my bro."

I sit back, watching him carefully as he continues.

"Maybe it's selfish on my part, but if things don't work out between you and Rosa, no matter who's to blame, I can't bear the thought of there being a rift between the two of you. Having to worry about you guys being in the same place at the same time." He drags a hand down his face. "And god forbid, if you hurt her after what she just went through with Julian, I don't think I could forgive you for that. I'm just trying to protect what we all have with each other."

I take a moment to let that settle and hold his gaze.

"I meant every word when I said she's *it* for me, Ry. I know that's a tough pill to swallow, but Rosie is...it feels like I've been waiting a lifetime for the opportunity to love her like she deserves. Now that I finally have it, I won't take that for granted. I'll do whatever it takes to keep her safe. To prevent *anyone* from hurting her. When you're feeling less punchy and ready to actually listen to our reasons behind it, let me know. Maybe we can grab a beer across the street or something." I lift a shoulder. "Believe it or not, we didn't *enjoy* keeping it from you guys."

Ryan studies me for a second longer, then nods. He stands and pauses at the door. "See you later."

I exhale, the tightness in my chest feeling marginally looser.

"See ya," I murmur as the door clicks shut behind him. Well, I wouldn't exactly call that a truce, but it *was* progress.

And for now, it'll have to do.

CHAPTER TWENTY-NINE
LOGAN

After a long, grueling day, all I want to do is kick back with Rosie. But she had to work late too, so now I'm just waiting. The good news is that with everything out in the open now, she's heading over here as soon as she wraps up at the office.

I glance around my apartment, trying to see it the way Rosie will, and I'm starting to second-guess my invitation. Maybe I should've picked up some throw pillows. Or a candle. Anything to make the place feel less like a hotel and more like a home. I've never minded it before. It's modern and gets the job done. But now I'm worried she won't be comfortable here. The last thing I want is for my place to remind her of the one she shared with Julian.

Sure, the condo's functional. It has plenty of space, and everything's been professionally decorated in fifty shades of greige. But Rosie's loft is packed with character. It may be cramped, but it's also colorful and charming and always smells like the tropics or freshly baked cookies. Mine feels cavernous by comparison and smells like purified air mixed with hundred-dollar bills.

At least I've got one redeeming quality: the rooftop terrace. It's a shared space between the two penthouse units, with sprawling city views, a lap pool, and an oversized hot tub. On the other end, there's a large seating area and a gas fire pit. The roof is a great space to throw a party—something Ryan and I have definitely taken advantage of—but it's just as good when you want a quiet place to chill with someone special. Rosie's been up there before, but never as my date.

Tonight, I'm changing that.

I take the private stairwell up to the top and do one final sweep, making sure everything's set. Prosecco is chilling, the fire pit's ready to go, and the lighting is just soft enough to set the mood.

My phone buzzes with a text from Rosie.

Rosie: Just parked.

I smile as I type my reply.

Me: See you in a few.

I head back downstairs to wait. A minute later, there's a knock at my door. I open it to find my beautiful girl standing there, brown eyes scanning the space behind me before settling on my face.

"Hi," she says with a shy smile.

"Get in here, Pip." I pull her into me with more enthusiasm than I'd intended, causing her to bounce off my chest like a pinball. "Sorry. I've been waiting a long time to see you in my place. Guess I'm a little excited."

Rosie rubs the bridge of her nose. "Stupid chest muscles."

I place a soft kiss on the tip. "I seem to recall you appreciating my 'stupid chest muscles' on more than one occasion."

"Yeah, yeah," she mutters as she breezes past me, her catlike curiosity taking the lead.

I smirk, shutting the door behind her. "What do you think?"

She glances around the open floor space. "It's so... ummm."

Impersonal? Generic? Boring as shit?

I cross my arms, leaning against the counter. "Not what you were expecting?"

"Not really." Rosie shrugs. "It's not like you've ever been obnoxiously flashy, but I guess I was picturing something with *a little* more flair. For some reason I had this vision of you sitting in your secret lair with a wall of monitors and a NASA-grade control deck." She tilts her head, considering. "And some interactive holograms. Maybe some sort of robotic assembly line. A talking assistant wired into the house, perhaps?"

I shake my head, chuckling. "I think you're confusing me with Tony Stark."

"Mmm." She bites her lip. "Possibly. I do seem to have a thing for absurdly attractive tech gurus."

I grin, pushing off the counter. "Come on, goofball, let me give you the grand tour."

I take her hand and guide her into the open-concept kitchen. It's sharp, in an understated Scandinavian way. White oak cabinets, matte black finishes, and stone countertops that cost a small fortune. The pendant lights above the island are thin black rods ending in seeded glass orbs. Bougie, maybe, but I'm man enough to admit they're also sleek as hell. Like Rosie said, I'm *not* a flashy guy, but I do appreciate quality craftsmanship when I see it.

"I told the architects I wanted a chef's kitchen, but I've barely used it. Lately, I've been at your place—*obviously*—but before that, I usually worked so late I'd just grab takeout on the way home." I shrug. "Or Ryan and I would order in and watch a game."

"Bros doing bro things." Rosie snorts as she walks toward the floor-to-ceiling windows. "Okay, this view is the shit. Way better than Ry's."

"Hence, why I took the west-facing unit." I pause, giving her a minute to soak up the view before leading her down the hall. "That's the theater-slash-gaming room."

She scans the plush recliners, multiple consoles, and ridiculously large TV. "Sweet Flamin' Hot Cheetos! How big is that screen?"

"Ninety-eight inches." I duck my head, feeling a little embarrassed. "I know it's over-the-top, but with home entertainment, you kinda have to go big, or go home. Bigger screens and better speakers provide a more immersive experience."

"Well, if the online gambling thing doesn't work out, I'm sure you can get a job at Best Buy with that pitch," she jokes, making me laugh. "You know, I've always had this notion that oversized TVs were the electronics version of guys compensating for small dicks with big trucks...but apparently, you're out here rewriting the laws of science."

I give her a shameless grin. "Sorry to disprove your theory."

Her eyes fall below my belt. "Meh. I'm perfectly happy being wrong on this one."

I force myself to stay where I'm at, or we'll never make it

up to my surprise on the roof. "Stop eye-fucking me, woman. You're making me feel like a piece of meat."

"Oh, shut up." Rosie shoves me away. "Fine. Get on with the tour, you ass."

I bow dramatically, gesturing for her to walk ahead. Mostly so I don't pin her against the wall and have my way with her, but partly because at least this way, I get to enjoy the view.

Next up is the guest room. "So, this is technically the guest bedroom and bath, but it's never actually had a guest."

She peeks inside and gasps. "Holy shit! You have a portal to a Pottery Barn inside your house! I've always wanted one of these."

"Exactly why I paid top dollar and hired the best sorcerer to open one," I deadpan, earning a smile. "C'mon, smartass. Onward."

We cruise past the powder room, the laundry room, and my office. Our last stop is my bedroom. The room is extra spacious, the mattress is the most comfortable fucking thing I've ever slept on, but overall, my so-called private oasis has the personality of a software update. Necessary, sure, but nobody gets excited about a minor bug fix, no matter how you spin it.

"I know it's kinda bland," I say, rubbing the back of my neck. "But if you ever feel like bringing some of your stuff over...like pillows, candles, throw blankets, or whatever, to make you feel more at home, I'd be totally okay with that. There's plenty of room in the closet, too, if you want to stash some clothes here."

Her gaze snaps to mine, surprised. "Yeah? You really wouldn't mind?"

I step closer, brushing the hair out of her eye. "I'd actually love it, Pip. I never realized how fucking dull this place was until I started spending so much time in yours. Turns out, I'm not as into the neutral hotel aesthetic as I thought I was."

She laughs. "Well, lord knows I certainly have enough color around my apartment to spare. I could definitely bring some stuff over. But when your condo is overrun with girly shit, don't say you didn't ask for it."

"Deal." I fight a losing battle with a grin. "C'mon, I have a surprise for you up on the roof."

"A surprise, you say? Color me curious." Rosie grabs my offered hand and allows me to lead her up the staircase to the roof.

I realize I'm nervous as I push the door open. Every time she's been up here, it's been during a party. Thumping bass, people laughing and splashing in the pool, talking and drinking by the fire. It was fun, but loud and chaotic.

This is different.

This is intimate.

We step onto the rooftop, and her eyes widen at the sight in front of us. The firepit's already glowing, throwing a golden hue over the outdoor seating area. A bottle of prosecco is chilling in a bucket beside a covered tray. Beyond the low glass wall, the entire city stretches out in glittering 360-degree perfection.

"Wow." Rosie lets out a soft breath. "Logan...this is insane."

"It's a lot different when there aren't dozens of other people up here, right?" I ask, brushing my hand down her back.

"Very much so." She nods, gaze still roaming the space. "Dialing up the swoon again, Edwards." Her chin lifts, and I can't resist swooping down and taking her lips in mine.

"You know me. All swoon, all the time."

Her eyes roll. "And there you go, leveling it out once again."

Laughing, I lead her to the cushioned lounge, pouring us each a glass of sparkling wine. She toes off her shoes and settles in beside me, knees tucked beneath her. I take a moment to watch as the flames cast golden flecks in her dark irises.

"To no more hiding," I say, lifting my glass.

"No more hiding." She smiles, clinking her glass against mine. "Whatcha got under there?" Rosie gestures to the covered food tray.

"See for yourself."

She lifts the tray and gasps. "Charcuterie! If I wasn't already planning on sleeping with you tonight, this would've sealed the deal."

I laugh. "I know how much you love tiny food arranged on boards."

Since Rosie's a vegetarian, it's not the traditional deli meat and cheese spread. Instead, I went with assorted fruit, cheese, crackers, and bite-sized desserts. Her eyes light up more and more as she sees each one.

She grabs a cube of cheese, popping it into her mouth. "It just tastes so much better for some reason."

"If you say so, Morales." I throw a grape into mine. "Tastes like a grape to me."

"Whatever." She sticks her tongue out.

Rosie leans her head on my shoulder, with my arm wrapped around her as we sit in comfortable silence. We sip wine, munch on snacks, watch the lights flickering like stars below. Her fingers lazily trace circles along the back of my hand, over the petals of my tattoo.

"I still can't believe you did this."

"Why not?" I clasp our fingers together. "After all the

truths I've revealed over the last few weeks, it should be pretty self-explanatory."

"Yeah, but you chose a spot on your body where the entire world would see it all the time. What if I...God forbid, what if I married Julian? What if *you* found someone down the line you wanted to marry? Wouldn't that have been awkward?"

I pull her closer, kissing the top of her head. "It wouldn't have mattered if you married him. I mean, it would've *sucked*, but I didn't get the tattoo because I thought you'd be mine someday. I did it because there was never any doubt that I'd always be *yours*."

She pulls back just enough to meet my eyes. Hers are glassy with unshed tears. "Logan—"

I shake my head, pressing a finger over her mouth. "Rosie. Do you remember your *quinceañera*?"

"Of course I do." Her eyebrows draw together. "But why on earth are you bringing that up right now?"

I take her hand in mine. "Because that was the day I knew with absolute certainty that nobody would take my breath away like you do. Sure, we were just kids, but I will *never* forget how floored I was when you walked into that ballroom. Your pretty purple dress had these sparkles on the top that scattered light around the room, and the poofy skirt was covered in blooming fabric roses. You were the living embodiment of your favorite flower, and I had never seen anything more beautiful.

"I know your name literally means rose—or rose garden, depending which version you go with—but that was the day you became *Rosie* to me. I don't know why, but it just popped into my head the second you made your grand entrance. I wanted to call you something that felt like you... but something that was also just for *us*. Anyway...there'd always been this invisible string connecting us, but I'd never felt it more so than in that moment." I turn my wrist, facing my tattoo toward her. "This is how I chose to remember that feeling."

Rosie's lips part, but no words come out. Her eyes dart from the tattoo to my face, then back again, like her brain's trying to catch up to her heart. Slowly, she brushes her fingertips over the ink, so gently it sends a chill down my spine.

"You're such a pain in the ass," she whispers.

That catches me off guard. "*What?*"

She blinks fast, her laugh shaky. "You just had to go and say this big, beautiful thing, that makes me feel like I'm having some kind of weird out-of-body experience. And then I wonder how I could've possibly been so lucky to be sitting here with you right now, hearing you deliver all the mushy stuff that gets me all up in my feels. And then I get a little annoyed, because I have to, like, *process* all these freaking emotions, which, like, *ew*. Who the hell wants to do that? It's overwhelming, Logan. *You're* overwhelming."

I grin, utterly charmed by her adorable rambling, even though my chest aches from that last verbal punch.

"But it's not a bad thing. I swear I meant that in the best way possible." She lowers her voice. "I don't think I realized that you've been calling me Rosie since that night. Not really. But now in retrospect, I guess it did start around then. It just wasn't as obvious as the whole Pip thing we have, so I guess subconsciously, I just accepted it as another shortened version of my name. But you're the only one who's ever called me that."

I nod, not trusting myself to speak yet.

"Guess we're both a little slow on the uptake." Her

voice cracks, and she stops to swallow. "But at least we're here now."

"Right," I agree. "And that's what matters. Now that your family knows about us, there's nothing stopping us from being together. It worked out this way for a reason. I don't want to waste more time feeling bad about all the opportunities or signs we may have missed in the past. Do you?"

"No." She shakes her head. "I just want a future with you."

I smile. "Me, too, Pip."

I lean down to kiss her, slow and sweet. It's one of those kisses that makes you lose track of time, so I'm not sure how long it's been when the terrace door swings open, startling us apart.

We twist around in time to see Ryan stepping into view with a bottle of beer dangling from his fingers. He freezes when he spots us curled up together, quickly figuring out he's intruding on a romantic evening.

"Uh..." He blinks rapidly. "Sorry. Didn't realize anyone was up here."

Rosie sits up straight, grabbing her glass of wine. "Hey, Ry. You wanna join us?"

He hesitates, looking between us. "I just came up to hang for a bit. This is where I do some of my best brainstorming, but..." He fans his arm toward our setup. "Clearly I interrupted, so I'll head back down."

I clear my throat. "You don't need to do that, dude. There's plenty of snacks. Help yourself."

He shakes his head, already walking backward. "Nah. I'm good. You guys obviously have a whole...thing going on, or whatever."

"Ryan—" Rosie tries, but he's already opening the door to the stairwell.

"It's fine. Seriously, Rosa. Enjoy your night." His voice is even, but there's obvious discomfort in his expression as he turns and disappears behind the door.

Rosie sighs as the door clicks shut behind him "Well... that wasn't awkward at all."

I reach for her hand again. "He'll come around."

"I know." She leans her head against my shoulder again, but this time, it's quieter. Somber.

I tighten my arm around her, determined to keep the night from slipping into weirdness.

"He'll come around, Rosie," I repeat into her hair. "We just have to give him time."

She nods into my shoulder, her breath warm against my neck. We sit like that for a while, letting the fire crackle and the city buzz quietly below us. Even with the tension still lingering from Ryan's exit, I can't bring myself to feel anything but content. Because for the first time in a long time, I'm not chasing anything. Not running from it either. I've got the girl. I've got the vision. And even if not everything's perfect, it's real, and it's ours.

And I plan to savor every crazy beautiful moment of it.

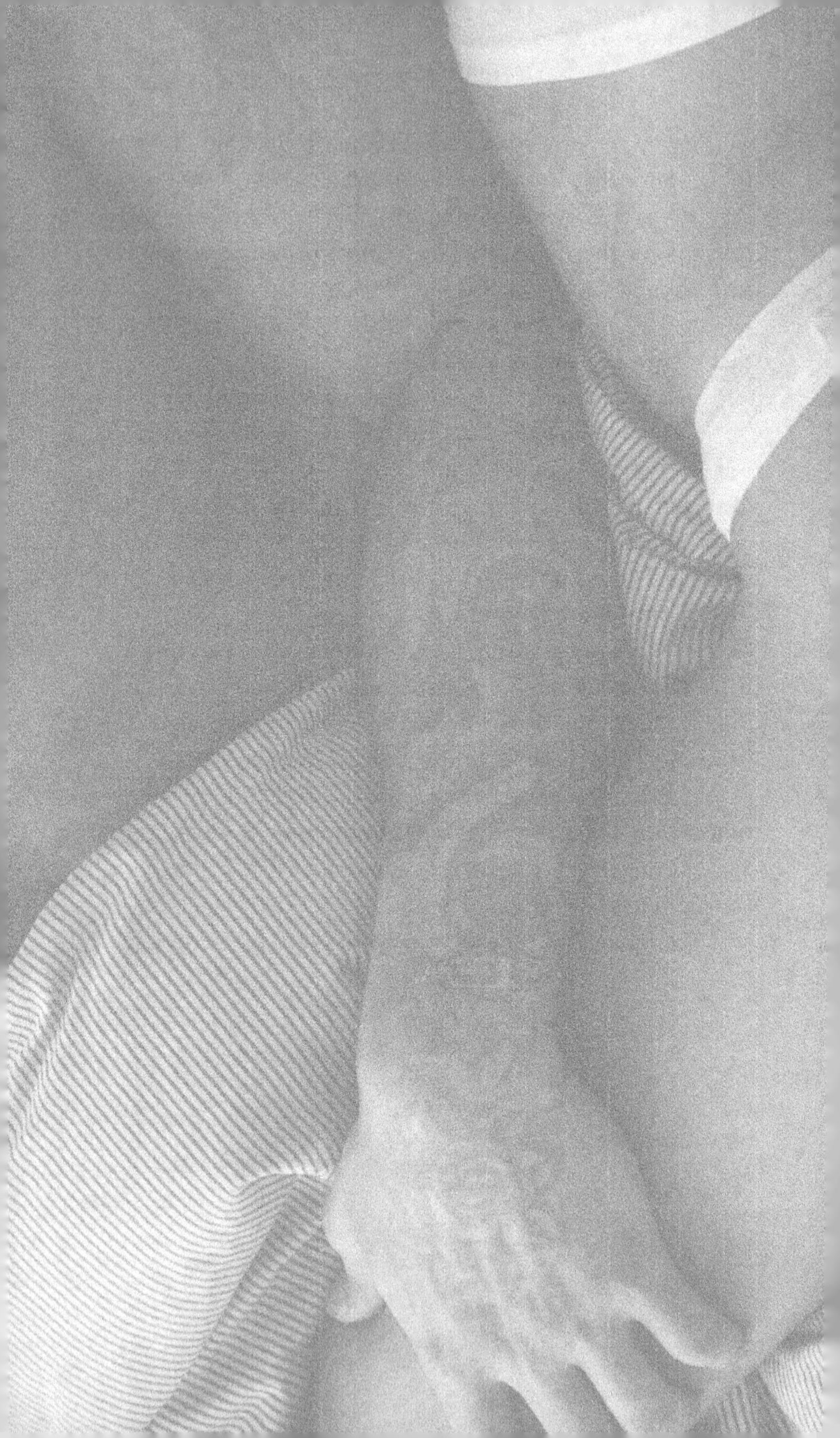

CHAPTER THIRTY

ROSALIE

I've been at work for less than an hour when shit officially hits the fan. Avery and I prepared for this, but it's still unnerving being on this side of a scandal.

"How bad is it?" I bite the tip of my thumb, waiting for my boss's reply.

Avery turns her monitor toward me. The headlines don't start out too terrible, but my stomach tightens as I get further down the list.

Billionaire's Mystery Woman Identified: Social Media Manager Rosalie Morales has officially taken this bachelor off the market.

Meet Rosalie Morales, the Woman Who Stole Logan Edwards' Heart: Sources say these two are in it to win it.

Rosalie Morales: Girlfriend or Gold-digger? Exclusive interview with Rosalie's ex, Julian Hunt.

Is the Billionaire Bachelor Being Scammed by a Beguiling Brunette? Rumor has it this PR beauty has some tricks up her sleeve.

I hold my hand up, turning away. "I've seen enough."

Avery exhales, leaning forward. "The good news is we're on top of it. We held off confirming the relationship to avoid fueling speculation, but with Julian's comments making the rounds, we need to get out in front of it, on *our* terms. We already knew they'd be working the gold-digger angle, but having your most recent ex—who happens to be a multi-millionaire—implying it's true doesn't look good."

"You think?" I arch a brow. "God, I can't believe he's trying to make me look like the bad guy when *he's* the one who cheated. Plus, I never gave a damn about Julian's trust fund, and I certainly never expected him to provide me with a lavish lifestyle. What an asshole."

"A bitter, jealous asshole, I'm guessing," Avery suggests. "But nothing we can't handle. Nick's on his way to Logan's office right now. He wants to tweak their statement to address this latest development before releasing it."

I cross my arms, trying not to let my frustration show. "Am I making a statement now, too?"

Avery shakes her head. "Not yet. If we keep you quiet,

it helps shift the narrative away from you and back onto the relationship as a whole, which is where it should be."

I know she's right. I do. But it still makes my eye twitch knowing Julian thinks he got the best of me. I have an undeniable urge to dial his number and set him straight. Preferably with lots of four-letter words and insults to his manhood.

Instead, I take a breath. "Okay. So, what exactly *is* the plan?"

Avery swivels her screen back toward herself and clicks through a few files. "We're prepping a soft rollout that reframes your image without making it look like we're playing clean up. We'll push a few lifestyle pieces through trusted outlets. Highlight your career with Maxwell, your client roster, the fact that you were already killing it before you and Logan got together. The childhood photos you provided were excellent. After we blast out your professional achievements, we're going to shift our focus to your friends-to-lovers storyline. That's where we'll really have them eating out of our hands."

"Okay," I say, knee bouncing. "What about Julian? Can we prevent him from talking to anyone else? Threaten him with a defamation suit or something?"

She sighs. "Not as long as he continues to choose his words carefully. His accusations were more *implication* than anything. Don't worry about him. Once we get our counterattack in place, Julian will look like nothing more than a bitter smarmy ex."

"Well, at least he'll be living up to his MO," I mutter.

Avery doesn't laugh, but the corner of her mouth quirks. "I'll have Tessa put together a quiet piece on your breakup timeline with Julian, just in case someone wants clarification. But overall, we're keeping it classy. I know he was a complete schmuck to you, but running a schmear campaign against him won't do us any good, so word of his adultery won't come from us." She shrugs. "But if he keeps implying shitty things, an anonymous tip might just find itself in the right hands."

I nod, breathing a little easier. Until I think about how quickly my family could get dragged into this now that I've been doxed. As if worrying about the professional implications weren't bad enough.

"Avery..." I look up at her. "If you think it's better I step away from Maxwell for a while..."

"Don't go there." She's firm, holding a hand up. "We've been through this, Rosalie. You're an asset to this firm, and we'll make damn sure everyone knows it."

"Still." I twist the rotating band on my index finger. "It's hard not to feel responsible for putting you guys in this position."

Avery leans forward, voice quieter. "Rosa. We're publicists. This is what we *do*. We don't *run* from messes; we *manage* them. If we can't protect our own people, we have no business protecting anyone else." She sits up straighter. "Now, get back to work and let me handle this. Mark my words. Within twenty-four hours, the media will be singing a different tune on Rosalie Morales."

"Thank you, Avery." I swallow the lump building in my throat. "Truly."

She nods. "That's what I'm here for."

BY THE TIME I clock out, I'm beat. I just want to go home, shower, and bury myself in Logan's arms.

And maybe consume my weight in chocolate.

But the second my heels hit the parking lot, I practically scream in frustration, knowing I have to deal with this first.

Julian fucking Hunt, aka my smarmy ex, is leaning against my car, looking down at his cell phone. His muddy brown hair is gelled back in that Wall Street bro way he thinks makes him look cool, but really, it just makes him look like a douchebag. Dressed in a designer suit that costs more than my rent, he looks exactly like the type of guy who'd drive a bright yellow Lamborghini Aventador, which of course, is parked right behind my Ford, blocking me in.

As my heels click on the pavement, Julian's dark blue eyes flick my way, and a smug smile stretches across his face. "Rosalie. Don't you look lovely?"

I come to a halt, leaving several feet between us. "What do you want, Julian?"

He holds his phone screen in my direction. On it, I can see one of the articles with a photo of me kissing Logan. "It didn't take you long to move on I see."

I snort, crossing my arms. "At least I waited until our relationship was *over* before I started sleeping with someone else."

His eyes narrow. "So you say. I always knew you had a thing for that guy. For all I know, you were so angry about me and Summer because you were projecting your own guilt about being unfaithful."

My hands curl into fists. "You don't know shit, Julian. But I'm not going to waste time trying to convince you otherwise, so believe whatever the hell you want. I don't care."

He pushes off my car, stepping closer. "I think I'm onto something here. Let's face it, Rosalie. You were never very enthusiastic in bed. Why do you think I had to look elsewhere? But maybe that's because you were so worn out from giving it up to your brother's friend?"

My blood boils. "*Or maybe*, I just wasn't that into sex with *you* because you couldn't find my clit with a goddamn GPS! You know that *little problem* I had, Julian? Well, guess what? Problem's solved! I've never been more sexually satisfied." Now *I* have a smug grin. "In fact, I never even knew it was *possible* to have as many orgasms as I've had over such a short period recently. Turns out, *I* wasn't the one suffering from a dysfunction in that scenario."

His smirk drops.

Ha! How do you like 'dem apples, you slimy bastard?

"Bitch," he sneers.

"Takes one to know one, Jules."

His jaw tightens. "He's going to get bored of you, Rosalie. And when he does, I'm going to enjoy watching you eat your words."

"Why don't you worry about your own relationship? I hear congratulations are in order? I hope you and Summer have a very happy life together." I hold a finger up. "Oh, wait. No, I don't. Get away from my car, dickhead. I have nothing else to say to you."

His expression darkens. "Think about this when you want to come crawling back to me."

I snort derisively. "Like that's ever going to happen."

Julian levels me with one final glare before sliding into his Lambo and peeling out of the lot. I watch him go, my chest rising and falling with adrenaline. My hands are shaking, frustration and anger rolling through me as I fight the urge to scream.

I yank open my car door and slide into the driver's seat, gripping the steering wheel as I take a deep breath.

"Fucking fuckhead small-dicked motherfucker," I mumble.

I desperately need to calm down before I drive anywhere, so I take a moment to call Logan.

He picks up immediately. "Hey, you."

I sigh, feeling relieved just by the sound of his voice. "Can you meet me at my place?"

Logan doesn't hesitate. "I'm already on my way. Just have to pick up dinner first. Anything specific you want?"

A small smile tugs at my lips. "Cheesy carbs of some kind?"

"You got it. Now are you going to tell me what's got you so worked up? I can tell something's off, but you seemed okay when we spoke earlier."

"I was." I lean my head against the window. "But then Julian was waiting for me after work."

The other end of the line is so quiet, I have to check to make sure our call is still connected. "Excuse me?"

I wave a dismissive hand. "I handled it."

I swear it sounded like he just growled. "Handled *what?*"

"He was trying to rattle me. Get another cheap shot in, as if his interview full of lies wasn't bad enough. I suspected it earlier when I read the article, but after seeing his face, I've no doubt there's a green-eyed monster living inside of him. I honestly don't think he'd care as much if I was seeing anyone *but* you. He tucked tail pretty quickly though, so I don't think he'll be much of a problem going forward."

"He'll be fucking sorry if he tries."

I finally crack a grin. "Don't worry, babe. I put him in his place. I told him he wouldn't know how to make a woman come if he had navigation to her clit. And then I told him you've made me come harder and more often than I ever thought possible."

"Jesus, Pip," Logan sputters.

I grin. "What? It's true."

He chuckles. "I hope I never get on your bad side."

I laugh. "Impossible."

"Well, now I'm hard *and* flattered. Remind me to thank you for the compliment later. With my tongue."

A shiver runs through me. "You can count on it, mister."

Logan clears his throat. "For real though, you're okay? Do you need me to swing by and pick you up?"

"I'm okay," I assure him, the remaining tension from the day finally draining from my body. "Hearing your voice put me back in my happy place."

"*You're* my happy place, Rosie."

I smile. "Same. I'll see you soon, okay? I love you."

"I love you, too, Pip. Always."

I close my eyes, soaking up the moment of peace.

Well, would you look at that? It turns out scandals and douchebag exes aren't so tough to weather when you've got Logan Edwards in your corner.

CHAPTER THIRTY-ONE

ROSALIE

Avery Jacobs-Maxwell is a PR genius.

Not that I had any doubt, but man, what a difference a day can make. Logan's statement has gone viral. It's *everywhere*, from gossip sites to social media feeds.

Even *Good Morning LA*, the city's top morning show, is currently discussing it on-air.

"Ladies all over LA are in mourning today because Logan Edwards, one of *Celeb Insider's* sexiest billionaire bachelors, has confirmed he is officially *off the market*. In case you've been living under a rock, the Flingr founder was recently caught locking lips in the Arts District with Social Media Manager, Rosalie Morales. But this brunette beauty is not a new fixture in his life. We've heard directly from the source, and they've known each other half their lives. She's his best friend's sister, and get this! *The woman of his dreams!* How sweet is that?"

"It's like a fairytale come to life, Krista," her co-host adds.

"Indeed," Krista replies. "I'm certainly rooting for their happily ever after."

I turn off the TV before they start speculating where we'll spend our honeymoon and how many kids we'll have.

How is this my life?

I work with celebrities every day. I've become so desensitized, I don't even get starstruck around the biggest A-listers anymore. But hearing a couple of morning talk show hosts discuss *me* like I'm one of them? That's just weird.

And as if the Google alerts flooding my inbox weren't enough, my family has been blowing up our group chat all morning. I scroll through our messages from earlier, shaking my head harder with every line.

Mom: Kudos to Logan on the statement, Rosa! It was SO romantic!

Sylvie: And 🔥

Dad: How are you doing, pumpkin?

Me: I'm fine, everyone. Logan's statement seems to be getting the job done. The vultures are backing off.

Mom: I hope you plan to reward him later… 🍆😏

Sylvie: I'm sure Rosa planned on doing that regardless. 😂

Dad: Are we talking about what I think we're talking about?

*RYAN HAS LEFT THE GROUP
*SYLVIE HAS ADDED RYAN TO THE GROUP

Sylvie: If you think we're talking about Rosa getting to the center of Logan's tootsie pop, then the answer to your question is yes.

*RYAN HAS LEFT THE GROUP
*SYLVIE HAS ADDED RYAN TO THE GROUP

Sylvie: You know I'm going to keep adding you, Ry, so don't bother leaving. Let's call it payback for being a dick the other day.

Dad: Ope. She got you there, son.

Ryan: I hate you all.

Mom: Ryan, you're 28 years old. You should be able to handle a conversation about oral sex.

Ryan: NOT WITH MY PARENTS!

Me: I'm with him on this one. We just went over this. BOUNDARIES, MOTHER!

Sylvie: What is up with these two prudes? I don't have an explanation for Ry but maybe Rosa and I were switched at birth.

Me: You're two months older than me, Sylvie. The math ain't mathing on that theory.

Sylvie: Semantics. I'd much rather talk about blow jobs anyway.

*RYAN HAS LEFT THE GROUP
*SYLVIE HAS ADDED RYAN TO THE GROUP

Dad: You kids crack me up.

Mom: Hector…this conversation has reminded me that I could use your help with something. Meet me in the bedroom, hot stuff.

Dad: Be right there, my foxy lady!

Ryan:

Me: What he said

Sylvie: Aw, Ryan and Rosa are bonding over their disgust for Mommy and Daddy's sex life. 🫣

Ryan: 👍

Me: 👍

Sylvie: There's hope for you two yet. 😊

Jesus, my family is ridiculous. But if I've learned anything this week, it's that real love, whether romantic or otherwise, isn't always picture-perfect. It's uninhibited and messy, occasionally taking the form of a raunchy group chat or my cousin's enthusiastic offers to maim my ex. Other times, it arrives via a special gift box. I suppose I should be grateful Dr. Tate didn't bring that up this morning. Though to be fair, it is still early.

I flop back onto the cushions with an exhale, staring at the ceiling as I let it all wash over me. The ground beneath my feet is a series of aftershocks, yet ironically, I've never felt more stable.

More certain of my future.

Look at me, winning at adulting before nine in the morn! Unfortunately, emotional clarity doesn't excuse me from my very grownup responsibilities, so I need to finish getting ready for work. I groan as I drag myself toward the bedroom in search of my go-to bad bitch energy outfit. First stop—lingerie drawer. Because seriously, if I'm going to face the inevitable whispers and side-eyes from random people on the street, I'll be doing it with sexy reinforcements.

I drop my robe and dig past my everyday undies, sifting through lacy cheekies and seamless thongs, until I find the duo I'm looking for. Royal purple satin bra, trimmed in inky black lace with a matching thong that sits snugly on my hips. This set is soft and seductive and superbly superfluous for the office, but that's the point. It doesn't matter if no one will see it. *I* know it's there, and that makes all the difference.

Confidence mode activated.

Next up— pants. I yank open my closet, pulling out my favorite black high-waisted wide-legged slacks. They make my vertically-challenged gams look ten miles long, and even better, they give my butt a nice lift without a flight to Brazil. I pair them with an eggplant satin blouse that drapes just low enough to be flirty but still remains professional. The jewel tone brings out the warmth in my skin, giving it an extra glow.

Now it's time for the finishing touches. I clasp a delicate gold lariat necklace around my neck, its slim drop pendant skimming just above the dip in my blouse. It's minimal, but strategic. A little sparkle, if you will, to draw the eye without being obvious. I step into my favorite strappy black heels, swipe on a touch of lip gloss, toss my beachy waves one last time, and give myself a final once-over in the mirror.

Well, hot damn.

I might feel like a trash panda disguised as a human more often than not, but on the *outside*, you'd never know it today.

I'm *that* bitch.

The one who makes you do a double take, wondering what her secret is.

God bless the power of sexy lingerie.

I adjust the drape of my blouse, grab my laptop bag, and head for the door. I blow a kiss to Frida over my shoulder as I do every morning, roll my shoulders back, lift my chin, and call to mind one motivational truth to start my day.

Rosalie Morales, you are one badass bitch. Whatever they say about you doesn't change who you are.

With a satisfied nod, I repeat the mantra in my head one more time before locking the door and striding toward the elevator. Just before the doors open, I catch my reflection on the mirrored wall and smile.

Because the woman staring back at me isn't just the sassy sidekick in a romcom anymore.

She's the damn lead.

AFTER WORK, I'm dying to pull on my comfiest pair of pjs and zone out on a documentary while I wait for Logan to get here. But when I reach my apartment, I pause. Something smells amazing, and I can swear it's drifting out from beneath the door. It's savory, and buttery, and so familiar, my chest tightens.

I unlock the door, opening it slowly. When I spy Logan standing in front of the stove, my jaw damn near unhinges. He's wearing a black T-shirt and joggers with bare feet, looking so at home in my tiny kitchen it makes me want to weep. But it's the hot pink apron he's wearing over his clothes, bedazzled with *Domestic AF* across the chest, that sends me over the edge. I want to cry in gratitude, make out with him, and have his babies, all at once.

Excuse me, sir. Could you *be* any dreamier?

Me thinks not.

"You gonna stand there looking at my ass all night, or are you actually going to come inside?" Logan teases.

Busted.

"What is happening right now?" I toe off my heels, dropping my bag by the door. "There's a muscly, tattooed guy in my kitchen cooking over a hot stove. I feel like I just walked into the opening scene of a *'Popular with Women'* porno."

He tosses a wink over his shoulder. "Play your cards right, and you just might make that a reality."

Well, slap my ass and deal me in.

There's a bottle of red wine breathing on the counter with two glasses beside it. Telling my hormones to cool it, I pour myself a little, humming as I taste subtle notes of cranberry and spice.

Curious, I pad toward the stove and peek over his shoulder. He's stirring a pan of buttery peas, but my eyes zero in on the glass pie dish on the warmer. Mashed potatoes are piped in thick swirls over some kind of filling.

Wait a damn minute...

"Is that *cottage pie?!*"

Logan quickly glances at me. "Maybe."

I gasp. "It is! Like, my nana's cottage pie! How did you pull this off?"

"The good doctor walked me through it." He grins. "I told her I wanted to do something special for you."

Aaaand my heart's officially a labradoodle with a case of the zoomies.

My nana's cottage pie is the ultimate comfort food, right up there with my *abuelita's* vegetable tamales. The matriarchs on both sides of my family have always shown their love through food. When I became a vegetarian at fourteen, I begged my grandmother to create a meatless version of her classic recipe. True to her traditional, determined Irish nature, she kept experimenting until even the carnivores in our house didn't miss the original.

God, I miss her.

"I can't believe my mom shared that recipe with you. It's one of her most closely guarded secrets."

Logan cringes.

My eyes narrow. "What was that for?"

He sets the wooden spoon down and faces me. "What was *what* for?"

"The cringe, Logan," I deadpan. "Don't even try pretending that didn't happen. What did Dr. Tate make you promise before she gave up the recipe?"

He gives me a lazy grin. "Relax, Rosie. She didn't make me promise anything."

I study him, thinking of how to rephrase my question. "Okay...so what favor did you vaguely agree to, what secret did you spill, or what awkward event do I now have to attend with you?"

Logan chuckles as he closes the distance between us, planting a kiss on my forehead and pulling me into a hug. "It's times like these where it's inconvenient we know each other so well."

I pull back, lifting my chin. "Nuh-uh. Quit trying to distract me. Tell me how my mom made you pay for that recipe because I know she didn't give up the goods for free."

Oh shit, is he blushing? That can't be a good sign.

Logan takes a step back, clearing his throat. "I may or may not have admitted we've cracked open the special box."

My eyes widen. "Logan!"

"And...that we've used some of the toys."

"Oh, hell, now she's never going to stop playing Fairy Godmother of Sex Toys," I mutter. "What were you thinking?! You know how she is!"

"At least I didn't tell her *which* toys!" he counters.

"Believe me, she tried getting that out of me, but I told her I was drawing a line. And *I was thinking* you've had a shit couple of days, and I wanted to do something that'd make you feel better. I can handle a little embarrassment with your mother, Rosie, as long as you're happy."

My mouth gapes like a fish, but I've got nothing. When he puts it that way, how can I be irritated?

Spoiler alert. I can't.

I groan. "Why do you have to be so perfect? It's annoying."

"Well, you haven't tried the food yet. For all we know, it tastes like dogshit." Logan chuckles.

"I highly doubt that."

He reaches into the overhead cabinet and removes a couple of plates. "Take a seat, Pip. I'll bring the food over in a sec."

I nab the bottle of wine and both glasses, making my way over to the couch.

A minute later, he returns with two heaping plates of veggies and legumes topped with buttery mashed potatoes and a side of peas. He sets one in front of me, presses a kiss to the top of my head, then settles in beside me.

I take my first bite, and honest-to-god, my eyes water. "Logan," I whisper, chewing slowly. "This tastes *exactly* like hers."

I close my eyes, and for a second, I can hear my nana humming over the stove and smell the juniper she always kept hanging over the door. It guts me, in the best way.

He nudges his knee against mine. "Yeah?"

"Yeah." I nod, all choked up. "Thank you."

He smiles softly. "That look on your face is all the thanks I need."

Is it possible to fall even more in love with this man? If so, I think I just did.

We eat dinner while watching Family Feud. The whole thing is so domestic and comfortable and everything I never knew I needed before now. After I take my last bite, I set my plate on the coffee table with a dramatic sigh.

"Oh, man, I think I may be carrying mashed potato twins." I pat my lower belly for emphasis.

Logan gently pokes the same spot. "Does that mean you didn't save room for dessert?"

I jolt upright. "I mean...I might have room for a bite or two. Depends what you got."

His hazel eyes sparkle, knowing damn well I'm going to take *a lot more* than a bite or two. Without answering, Logan stands and disappears into the kitchen. I hear the fridge open, some rustling, and then he returns with a small white and pink striped pastry box, tied with gold string.

My heart stutters. "Is that..."

He sets it in front of me with a grin. "One triple chocolate cheesecake from Sweet Temptations."

I open the box slowly. The glossy chocolate ganache glistens under the soft light, and I swear to all that is holy, an angel just got its wings.

"Logan," I breathe. "It's the most beautiful cheesecake in all the land." I wipe an imaginary tear from my eye.

Okay, maybe it's not so imaginary.

This is the best damn cheesecake in the world, okay?

I accept the fork he offers and dig in, taking a slow, reverent bite. The cheesecake melts on my tongue like a chocolate-drenched dream.

"Holy shit," I moan. "It's even better than I remember."

Logan leans back against the armrest, watching me with a soft smile. "Glad you like it."

I waggle my eyebrows at him playfully. "I think you just sealed your fate, Edwards."

His mouth kicks up in the corner. "How so?"

I finish chewing and lick chocolate off the corner of my lip before answering. "You're never getting rid of me now."

"I'm good with that." His voice drops to a low murmur. "Because I was never planning on letting you go, Rosie."

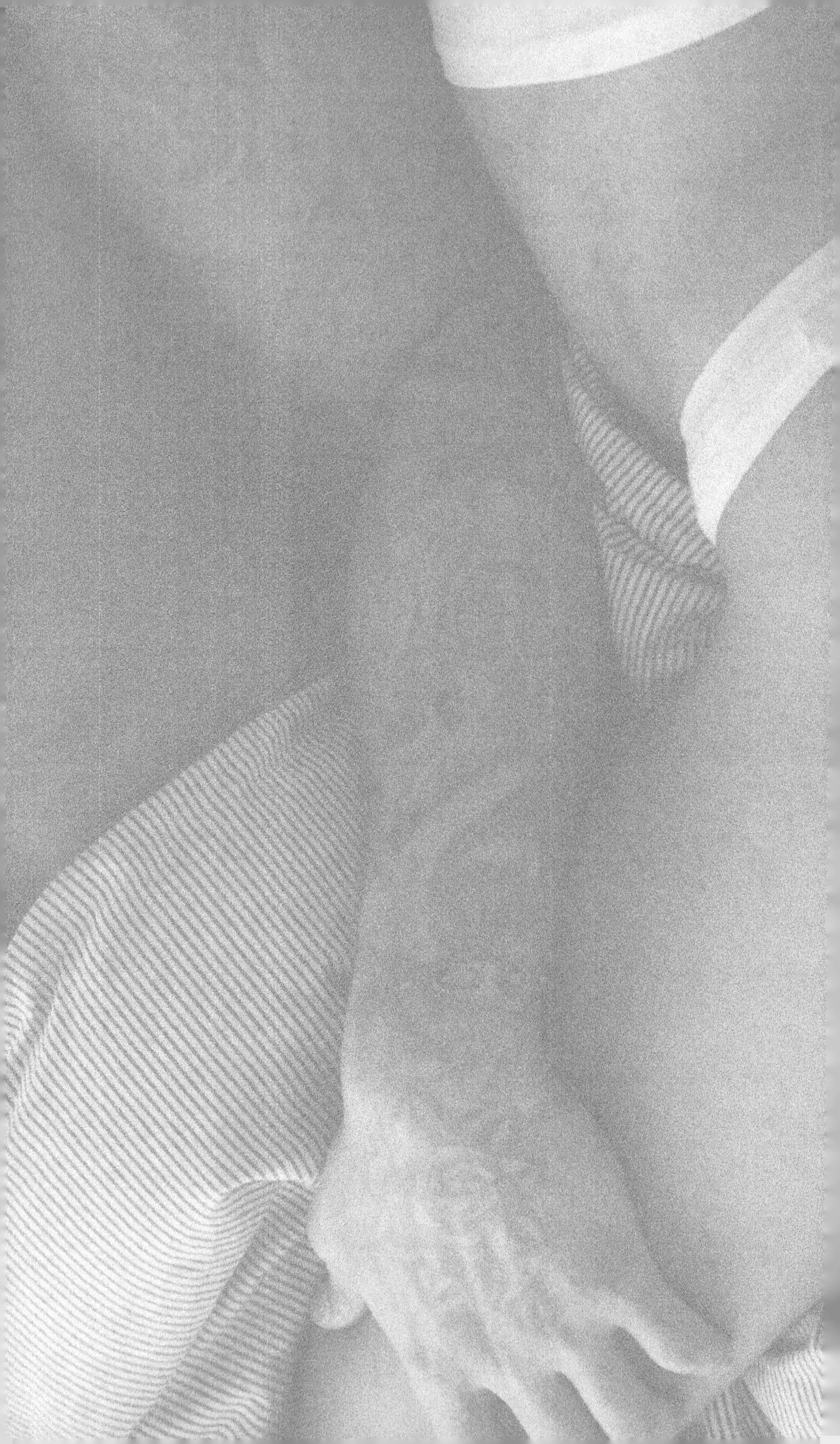

CHAPTER THIRTY-TWO
ROSALIE

The door to Brickline Coffee Works swings shut behind me, the scent of freshly brewed espresso swirling in the air. The whoosh of passing cars from early commuters blends with the rhythmic clickity-clack of my heels against the pavement. I cradle my coffee cup in both hands, inhaling the rich notes of chocolate and cinnamon before taking my first perfect sip.

"God, that's good stuff," I murmur to myself.

It's my little slice of heaven before work each day. Weirdly, coffee doesn't perk me up like it does most people —I could drink a twenty-ounce latte and still crash right after. It *is* freaking delicious, though, so I indulge on the regular. Plus, caffeine quiets the mental chaos just enough to help me focus, which is essential in my line of work.

Granted, it's dehydrating, so I'll usually chase it with some water. But plain water gets boring, so my fridge is always stocked with at least four types of flavored sparkling ones. A girl's gotta have options. Hence, the three to five beverages that usually end up crowding my desk. It's a whole system, really. Hydrate, caffeinate, repeat. Hydrate, caffeinate, re—

My cell buzzes inside my purse, and I dig through my patent leather crossbody to find a message from my client, Jett. I giggle to myself when I read his contact name. My phone has an excellent firewall, but all of my clients have fake names in my contact list, just in case. It's sort of an unspoken system we have in Hollywood that comes in handy when you're trying to protect your privacy. Sometimes—okay, *most* of the time—we have fun with it and use the most ridiculous names we can come up with. For some reason, the names I make up always seem to sound like seventies porn stars.

Weird, right?

> Randy Hardwood: Would these work?

> Randy Hardwood: 5 attached photos

"Holy abs, Batman," I mutter as I flip through the pictures he sent.

I asked Jett to get a few poolside shots with his newly adopted pit bull, and yeah...he definitely delivered. The camera's focus is on his adorable doggo's face, but since said dog is lying on Jett's lap, and Jett happens to be shirtless, his six-pack just happens to be in the shot as well. His fans are going to eat these up.

I fumble with my coffee cup, trying to walk and type at the same time.

> Me: They're perfect! I'll get these posted later today.

My heel snags on a crack and—bam—I'm suddenly airborne. Coffee flies. Arms flail. And then I hit the ground.

"Son of a bitch!" I cry out as my left wrist takes the brunt of it.

I land hard on my ass, breath knocked out of me, clutching my wrist as pain pulses up my arm. Thank god I wore pants today. At least the people who just witnessed me falling on my ass won't get a peek at my undies. But when I spot my coffee staining the concrete instead of delighting my taste buds like it should be, I let out a pitiful whimper.

"Rosie!" a familiar voice bellows.

My six-foot-three knight in black leather cuts through the crowd, jaw locked tight.

Damn, why is that so hot?

Logan drops to his knees beside me, eyes scanning my face. "Rosie, baby, are you hurt? What happened?"

"I tripped." I flex my fingers and immediately regret it, wincing as a sharp pain shoots up the side of my forearm. "My wrist slammed into the ground when I tried to catch myself. I think it just needs some ice. Maybe an ACE bandage. And there will probably be whining involved at some point."

The next thing I know, I'm being scooped off the ground, cradled against Logan's chest in a full-on bridal carry. He turns toward my building's entrance like a man on a mission.

"Logan," I hiss, cheeks burning as I realize how much attention we're drawing. "Put me down. My legs are fine."

"Not a fucking chance," he growls, eyes locked ahead.

I twist slightly in his arms, trying not to jostle my wrist. "This is a little overkill, don't you think?"

"No, I don't," he snaps, then softens just enough to add, "Please, Pip. Just let me help."

He muscles through the doors of my building, and

when they close behind us, he lets me down, gently, like I could shatter into pieces at any moment. As soon as my feet hit the marble, I wobble a bit, my injured wrist tucked against me.

"Are you hurt anywhere else?" His hazel eyes are laced with worry as they rake over me.

I shake my head. "No. Just...give me a second."

With one hand at the small of my back, Logan guides me toward the seating area. His other hand clenches, knuckles white. He crouches down in front of me, gently reaching for my wrist. His hands are warm and steady, making me realize how much mine are shaking.

"Rosie, we should get this X-rayed. It's swelling already."

I wince as his fingertips prod an especially tender spot. "Nothing some ice and an ACE bandage can't fix."

He lifts a brow. "Did I miss all the years you went to med school?"

I roll my eyes. "Logan, you know damn well this isn't the first time I've tripped over my own two feet." I rotate my wrist, testing it. It's sore and stiff, but I definitely have full range of motion. "I've learned by now what does and does not warrant a visit to the doctor. The last thing I want to do is spend the next eight hours in an ER waiting room just to be told I have a mild sprain. I'd much rather go upstairs, ice it for a bit, pop some ibuprofen, and wrap it. If it's still bothering me tomorrow—or gets worse—I can make an appointment with my regular doctor."

His jaw tics as he studies my face, clearly having some sort of internal debate. Finally, he releases a harsh exhale. "Fine. But I'm going to be watching you carefully. If you seem to be in any more pain, we're going in."

I nod. "Deal."

Without another word, he rises and extends his hand. I take it, letting him pull me to my feet. We reach the elevator, and he presses the call button, pulling me into his chest as we wait. I sigh, breathing in his woodsy cologne, grateful for the quiet reprieve.

"What are you doing here anyway?" I tilt my chin up, meeting his gaze. "I thought you had a full day."

Logan didn't stay over last night because he had to be in the office extra early for an important meeting. We both knew he wouldn't get the sleep he needed if we were together.

"I do," he says, tucking a piece of hair behind my ear. "But I had to swing by my place for a thumb drive I left in my laptop bag, so I figured I'd surprise you with your favorite coffee on the way back."

He ushers me into the elevator and hits the button for my floor.

"Didn't make it in time for the surprise," he adds with a small smile, "but I'm glad I got here when I did."

"Me too," I admit. "I mean, I could've handled myself if you weren't there, but it's a nice surprise."

The elevator glides to a stop on my floor with a soft ding. Logan keeps his arm around me as the doors part, not saying a word as we step into the hallway. I use my good hand to punch in the code to unlock my door, and Logan turns the knob to push it open.

Once we're inside, I kick off my shoes and head straight for the couch, collapsing with a sigh. Now that the adrenaline is wearing off, I'm left feeling sore, rattled, and extra cranky because I still really want that coffee.

Logan hangs his jacket on the hook behind my front door, and steps into the kitchen. A few seconds later, I hear the freezer drawer open, followed by some shuffling and the drawer being closed. He joins me on the couch with an ice pack wrapped in a dish towel, guiding my hand to the arm of the couch and carefully positioning it over my wrist.

"Try to keep it elevated."

He sets my phone on the coffee table. Huh. I didn't even realize I'd dropped it, but now that I think about it, it definitely wasn't in my hand.

"Yes, Dr. Edwards," I sass.

His mouth kicks up in the corner. "Save the role play for later, Pip. I'll be more than happy to play doctor with you when you're not *actually* injured."

"I'm holding you to that." I chuckle. "Don't you need to get back to work?"

His eyes flick to mine. "It can wait."

"Logan, don't be dumb. Your presentation is tomorrow. We both know you should not be here right now. I appreciate your help down there, but I promise you, I'll be fine. I'll even work from home today if that makes you feel better."

"It would actually make me feel *a lot* better. And you have to promise to call me if your wrist gets worse, or you need anything. DoorDash whatever you want or need using my account." He pulls his phone out of his pocket and starts typing something on the screen. "I'm sending you my login info now."

My phone vibrates with a text alert.

I smile, channeling my inner cartoon villain as I say, "Oh, you're going to regret giving me that kind of power. I'm already planning my meals for the next month."

He laughs and kisses me softly before standing. "Go to town, baby. Now where's your First Aid kit?"

"Under the bathroom sink."

While he's off doing that, I grab my phone to text my

boss. Easier said than done one-handed, so I use voice-to-text and pray Autocorrect isn't in a mood.

I mean, seriously. Who the hell ever wants to actually type the word duck?

> Me: I had a little mishap this morning, so I'll need to work from home today. I'll be fine, but I'll call you in a bit to explain.

She responds instantly. I swear the woman has her phone surgically attached to her hand.

> Avery: I can't wait to hear this one.

A minute or so later, Logan returns with an ACE bandage, a bottle of water, and some Advil. After wrapping my wrist like a pro and ensuring I take the pills like a good little patient, he gives me one last kiss before slipping his jacket back on.

"I love you," I tell him.

He freezes in the doorway and grins. "Damn, I'll never get sick of hearing that."

"Are you still planning on coming over after you're done?" I bite my lip, not missing the way his gaze zooms in on the action. "I need to experience some of your *bedside manner*, Dr. Edwards. Especially if you'll be out of town for the whole next day and night. Besides, we can't have you getting on that plane all stressed out, can we? I hear orgasms are great for anxiety relief. We should at least try it, in the name of science. Don't you think?"

"Oh, definitely. I'm a big fan of supporting scientific research." His eyes darken as his knuckles whiten around the doorknob. "Fuck. I need to get out of here before I talk myself out of leaving." He points to me. "Quit being so damn irresistible, woman." He quickly steps over the threshold and closes the door as he adds, "Love you, Pip."

"Looking forward to seeing you tonight! Sorry not sorry if I get started without you!" I shout through the door.

Pretty sure I hear him groan on the other side. Excellent.

I shift on the couch, squirming. Welp. That backfired spectacularly.

Now I'm way too worked up to focus. Guess I'll have to take the edge off before I can even pretend to be productive. Good thing I only need one hand for a little *ménage à moi*. Logan's too busy to be distracted today, but that doesn't mean I can't record a sexy little video for him to watch later.

I mean...it's only fair. He keeps me fed, I supply him with spank bank material. We'll call it mutual satisfaction. Or...perhaps foreplay with a side of DoorDash?

Who knew relationships could be so freaking awesome?

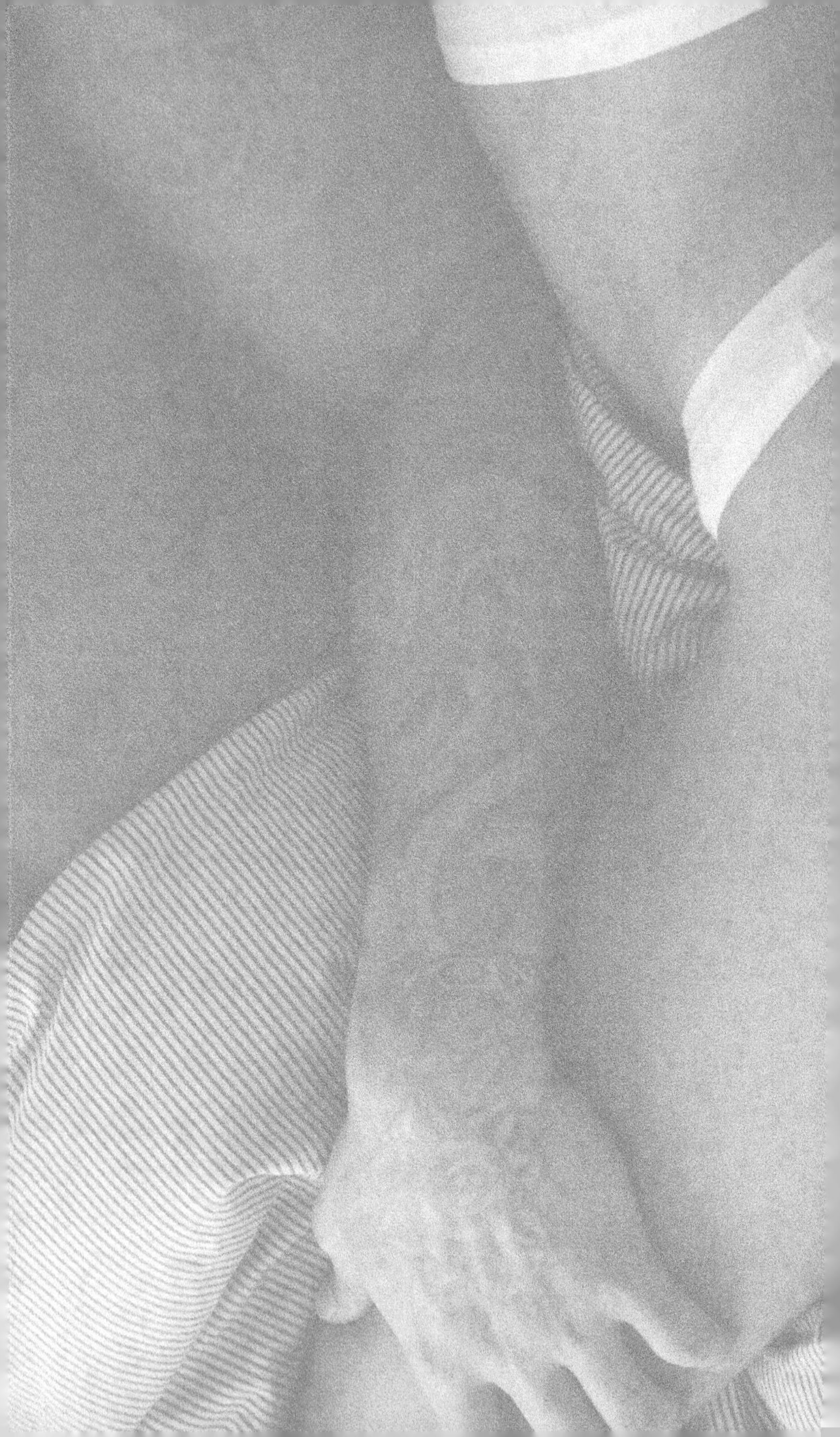

CHAPTER THIRTY-THREE
LOGAN

After months of prep, late-night test runs, and back-to-back strategy sessions, pitch day is finally here. As we soar above the Mojave on our short flight, in the comfort of a chartered jet, the weight of this deal settles firmly on my shoulders. If this meeting goes as planned, Olympus Resorts & Gaming will sign an exclusive five-year partnership with us. I've been calling this deal a game-changer, but honestly, that sells it short. Securing this contract could be *legacy-defining*.

Ryan sits across the table, flipping through the final version of our presentation deck on his laptop. Jared's across the aisle, scrolling through notes, lips moving as he mentally runs through the demo for probably the hundredth time.

It took the whole team to get us here, but the three of us will be the ones in that room. Showing up with a full entourage might look more like posturing than a partnership, and we want to project confidence, not overwhelm them.

Ryan closes his laptop. "You nervous?"

I nod. "Of course I am. There's so much on the line."

"Well, lucky for you, I'm awesome under pressure, so the Olympus team will likely never even notice you have the jitters." He grins.

Cocky little shit.

I scrub a hand down my face, not-so-accidentally flipping him off. "I'll be fine. Just worry about your part."

Ryan 'scratches' the bridge of his nose using his middle finger. "Don't worry, sweetheart. I've got it covered."

My lips twitch, fighting a smile at the familiar ribbing. Ryan might not be ready to talk yet, but he keeps showing me in subtle ways he's not planning to throw our friendship away. I'm not sure if he realizes he's doing it—and I'm sure as shit not going to point it out—but it's reassuring nonetheless. I can breathe easier knowing I haven't lost my best friend simply because I fell in love with his sister.

After less than an hour in the air, the tires squeal softly against the runway, and in the distance, the skyline shimmers in the late morning sun, glass towers flashing like polished mirrors. My pulse kicks up as it always does when I land in this city.

Day or night, Vegas never fails to hit different for me.

Every time I'm here, there's extra energy buzzing beneath my skin. It's the same feeling I had when I first decided to launch BetMasters, and it hasn't faded no matter how often I'm in town. Our executive offices are in Los Angeles because that'll always be home to me, but we're incorporated in Nevada for the favorable tax laws and business regulations. Since California still hasn't legalized sports betting or online casinos, it made sense to establish a satellite office in Vegas, as it's one of the biggest gambling hubs in the world.

I've always believed knowledge is power, which is why Ryan and I fly out here regularly to keep tabs on what the major players in the casino business are up to. Like his cousin Sylvie, Ryan graduated from UNLV, so he's got roots here—connections that occasionally work to our advantage.

After taxiing toward the private hangers, I sling my laptop bag over my shoulder just as the cabin door opens and the dry desert heat spills inside. Imani—Barry's Vegas counterpart and the glue holding our satellite office together —is already waiting on the tarmac, tablet in hand and a smile that could outshine the damn sun. Her braids are pulled into a sleek bun, diamond stud earrings glinting in the sunlight.

"Welcome back to Vegas, gentlemen," she says, handing each of us a hotel key card before turning back to me. "You're all checked in at the Olympus Grand in adjacent suites. The town car behind me will take you directly to the hotel so you can freshen up before your meeting. You'll meet with Mr. Takahashi and his team in the same hotel. Their executive offices are located on the top floor of the Zeus tower." She hands me another card, but this one is slim without any hotel branding on it. "This keycard will give you access to that floor through the tower's elevator." She hands me a business card. "Your usual driver is unavailable this week, so Kyle will be her replacement. Here's his contact information. He'll be on call whenever you need him. Just text him at that number."

"Thanks, Imani. Appreciate you handling everything," I say. "You're on top of it, as always."

"Remember that when it's time for my annual bonus." She smiles.

No wonder Barry calls her his evil twin.

I smirk. "I swear, I'm knee-deep in smartasses these days."

Her sculpted brows lift. "Sounds like *you're* the

common denominator in that scenario, bossman. Maybe you need to look inward to figure out why that is."

I laugh. "Touché."

Imani tucks her stylus behind her ear. "You have just over two hours before the meeting begins. When you get to your suites, you should each find a light snack platter—per Barry's specifications—along with hard copies of each presentation deck, just in case. The concierge is on standby if you need anything pressed."

"Thank you," Ryan, Jared, and I all say at relatively the same time.

"Is there anything else you need?"

I look to the guys as they shake their heads. "No. I think we're good for now. I'll touch base with you after the meeting."

She nods. "Sounds good. I'm heading back to the office, so you know where to find me. Good luck, gentlemen."

"Thank you," we repeat.

Imani gives a final nod and turns toward the private hangar, her heels clicking with purpose as she disappears inside.

We pivot toward the waiting car just in time to see our driver—a tall, broad-shouldered man dressed in a crisp black uniform—closing the trunk after loading our bags. He steps forward and opens the back door for us with a practiced smile.

"Good morning, gentlemen. I'm Kyle, and I'll be your dedicated chauffeur while you're in town. I know I've got some big shoes to fill, but I can assure you that you're in good hands. There's a minibar inside the vehicle. Help yourself to anything you'd like, and I'll have you at the Olympus Grand in under twenty."

"Appreciate it," I reply, climbing in behind Jared and Ryan.

As the car pulls away from the tarmac, I lean my head back against the seat, watching the skyline blur past the window. In two hours, it's go time. And our next move, the next era of BetMasters, rides on what happens in that conference room. It's one meeting. A mere moment in time. But for me, it's the culmination of every risk, every sleepless night, every damn reason I built this company in the first place.

It's the proof that every gamble I ever made was worth it.

THE CONFERENCE ROOM at Olympus screams power, but in that kind of understated flex only serious money can pull off. Black-and-white marble floors. Chrome accents. Floor-to-ceiling windows that turn the Strip into a centerpiece. The twelve-person table looks like something out of a billionaire boardroom fantasy. Sculpted, glossy, and flanked by leather chairs that say *you can sit here, but only if you can afford it.*

Jared clocks the projector setup right away and heads over to hook in his laptop like he owns the place. After a quick systems check, he gives me a subtle nod.

Showtime.

I take one last look out the window, ground myself with a breath, then turn back to the table.

A moment later, the glass door glides open, and the Olympus team steps in. Greg Takahashi, Olympus's CEO, leads the pack with a firm handshake and a measured smile, followed by a handful of well-dressed executives.

"Gentlemen." He grips each of our hands in turn as his team claims their seats. "We appreciate you flying out for this."

I flash a smooth, controlled grin. "Our pleasure. We appreciate the opportunity."

Greg runs through introductions on his side, then takes the seat at the head of the table. "I'm excited to see what you've got. Shall we?"

I nod, keeping my tone smooth but confident. "Absolutely. Before we dive in, let me briefly introduce my team."

I gesture to my left. "This is Ryan Morales, our VP of Acquisitions. He's been with BetMasters since the beginning and played a major role in structuring the proposal we'll walk you through today."

Then I motion to my right. "And this is Jared Chen, our Head of Product and Innovation. He's leading the integration of our predictive analytics engine, the backbone of what we're proposing with this partnership."

Greg nods, interest flickering behind his glasses. "Good to meet you both."

Ryan and Jared echo the sentiment.

I cue the first slide. "Okay, ladies and gentlemen. I know your time is valuable, so let's dive in."

Since Ryan could charm the granny panties off a nun, we decided he'd be the one to kick things off, and, as expected, he doesn't disappoint. His warm-up is so smooth, it could practically be its own TED Talk.

"This isn't just about enhancing the customer experience," he says, voice steady, confident. "It's about redefining what's possible in sports betting. It's the kind of advantage that will give Olympus Gaming & Resorts a lead your competitors can't touch, no matter how hard they try…"

As Ryan wraps, Jared steps forward, offers a quick nod to the room, and advances the slide.

"What we're proposing isn't hypothetical. Our model is sharp enough to adjust odds mid-game with near-flawless accuracy. It's passed every stress test we've thrown at it, and integration is ready to go the moment you give us the green light."

He clicks to a clean, minimal slide showing key milestones.

"You'll see the rollout phases here, but the bottom line is this: we're delivering predictive accuracy that holds up under pressure. It's fast, stable, and scalable, no matter how many users are on the platform. It's the kind of edge that keeps players engaged and your competitors scrambling."

Then he steps back, letting the data speak for itself.

All eyes shift to me as I rise and grab the clicker, advancing to the next slide. On the screen is a mockup of a personalized fantasy dashboard with charts, player stats, win projections, and the like. It's the stuff that makes a fantasy junkie feel like a goddamn Wall Street analyst.

"You've seen what our predictive model can do for your existing players, now let me show you how it'll help you gain new ones."

Every Olympus executive sits up taller, leaning closer, showing me I've got their undivided attention.

Ryan and I share a look, mentally high-fiving one another.

"Odds are, at least three people in this room are in more than one fantasy football league each season." I raise my hand. "I'm one of them. Anyone else?"

I quickly glance at Greg, whose sheepish grin and raised

index finger confirms the intel Ryan had is dead-on. Ryan, along with three more Olympus execs, also raise their hands, prompting a round of quiet chuckles throughout the room.

"Well, I suspect you'll be especially interested in this next part, both personally and professionally."

I click to the next slide, where our fantasy league simulation begins its flow—player performance forecasts, weekly matchup insights, live stat shifts, all tailored in real time.

"This model pulls from actual league data and overlays our predictive engine to generate customized recommendations: draft picks, trade suggestions, weekly starters, sleeper alerts. At the start of each season, users input their league's structure and scoring rules. Whether it's PPR, dynasty, standard, or something entirely custom, our tool adapts. It automatically tailors predictions, player rankings, and trade advice to fit."

I pause for dramatic effect, then grin.

"And it updates every second."

Click.

The final slide appears—a projection graph showing player growth and retention over time.

"But this isn't about tossing more features at users. It's about building smarter systems that meet them where they already are...then pulling them deeper into the ecosystem. Give a player a win, and they'll come back. Give them an edge, and you've got them for life."

I take a beat.

"Fantasy is the gateway, if you will, where casual fans become loyal users, and where untapped demographics enter the sports betting world for the first time. For Olympus, that means player growth and retention, two of your core objectives."

I step back, remote still in hand, the final graph glowing behind me.

"If our model can do that for fantasy football—something people obsess over for free—imagine what it can do across your entire gaming platform. Partnering with BetMasters doesn't just raise the ceiling. It revolutionizes it."

A few beats of silence follow while the Olympus team processes everything we just laid out. My pulse is jacked, nervous energy buzzing so hard, I feel like Rosie. I have to consciously remind myself not to pace.

After what feels like an hour—but is probably less than a minute—Takahashi leans forward, fingers steepled, eyes fixed on the graph behind me.

"This," he says slowly, "is exactly what we were hoping for."

Beside him, Olympus's CFO—a sharp-eyed woman with a no-nonsense bob—taps her pen once against her legal pad. "Let's talk terms."

I don't let my grin show. Not yet. But when I glance at Ryan, he's already looking at me with that spark in his eye.

The one that says: *We did it, brother.*

He gives me the smallest of nods.

I return it.

Yeah. We fucking did.

CHAPTER THIRTY-FOUR

LOGAN

It took longer than anticipated, as their legal team insisted on combing through every line item one by one, but the deal is officially closed. Together, BetMasters and Olympus are about to change the game. Once players see what we're offering, they won't want to place their bets anywhere else.

Despite the late hour, Jared was on his way back to the airport the moment we wrapped. His wife is due to deliver their first child next week, so he didn't feel comfortable staying the night. I don't blame him one bit—if Rosie were about to have our baby, I would be glued to her side—so I had our chartered jet staff on standby, waiting to take him home. Ryan and I have some loose ends to tie up at our satellite office in the morning, so we'll fly back tomorrow afternoon.

"C'mon, man, let's hit the tables." Ryan slaps me on the back. "Whoever walks away with the highest winnings buys dinner."

"Blackjack?"

"Is that a real question?" He raises his brows, and the

gesture combined with the sarcasm is so similar to something his sister would do, I laugh to myself.

Kyle drives us to a newly refurbished casino we've been meaning to check out, and we find the nearest high-stakes blackjack table. Ryan's in the zone, doubling down like it's a reflex, his stack of chips growing taller with every smug win.

Lady Luck must've clocked out after our Olympus pitch, because I might as well be lighting hundred-dollar bills on fire.

"Dude," I mutter after my sixth busted hand in a row. "This is painful. I'm sitting the next few out. I'm sick of embarrassing myself."

Ryan sips his whiskey and grins. "A little humility's good for you, Edwards."

"Have you looked in a mirror lately, Morales?" I deadpan.

He just laughs and taps the felt, signaling for another card. "Maybe it's karma. You date my sister behind my back, you lose your ass in Vegas while I rake in the dough."

"Blackjack for the gentleman to my left," the dealer announces, gesturing to Ryan like he's the king of the damn table.

The dealer flips his hole card. It's only a five, bringing his total to sixteen, so he hits again and pulls a king of spades.

The dealer busts.

Ryan snorts as a fresh stack of chips is pushed toward him. "And that, my friend, is what we call sweet, sweet justice."

"Son of a bitch," I grumble, slumping back in my seat.

He swings an arm around my shoulder. "Aw, don't be grumpy, sweet pea. C'mon, let's take a break at that piano bar we passed on the way in. Maybe your luck will reset after a few drinks."

"Fine, but you're buying."

We gather our chips, head to the cashier's cage to exchange them, and then make our way to the Encore Lounge, a piano bar tucked into the corner of the resort.

Inside, the lighting is low, the drinks are served in fine crystal, and a tuxedo-clad pianist glides his fingers across a glossy black Steinway with impossible grace. It's the kind of place designed to seduce with subtlety. You won't find a boisterous crowd singing along to "Sweet Caroline" here.

While that kind of schtick can be fun—especially after a few drinks—I'm hoping the chill, upscale vibe will give me and Ryan a chance to talk. Hanging out tonight has felt like old times for the most part, but the stilted energy between us isn't fully going away until we hash things out. And honestly, I'd rather get it over with than keep pretending nothing's off.

We slide into a curved booth, and not even two seconds later, a waitress approaches and takes our drink orders. I ask for a bourbon, Ryan orders a gin-ginger beer concoction. Ryan leans back, arms stretched along the top of the leather.

There's an awkward silence between us. He's acknowledging the elephant in the room, but he's letting me stew in it for a bit, which is fair, I suppose.

"So...you and Rosa." His tone may seem casual, but anyone who knows him as well as I do could hear the resentment buried in his voice. "She's the reason you wouldn't go out with Penny's friend?"

"Yep." I nod. "And I know you're pissed, but if you're willing to listen, I'd like to explain why we kept our relationship under wraps at first."

Our drinks arrive, so we hold off a sec until the waitress leaves.

Ryan takes a sip of his gin. "I have some questions first."

"Okay..." I swallow the sudden lump in my throat. "Shoot."

"At my mom's party...you said you'd been dating for about a month. Well, when I thought about it, that would've been around the same time you were in Lake Tahoe, so it's not adding up."

"Yeah, about that..." I chug half my bourbon, relishing the burn. "Rosie showed up at the cabin the weekend she was supposed to get married. It was a freak coincidence. She had no idea I was there, and I had no idea she was coming. But for three nights of my vacation, we were at the cabin together."

"But there's only one bed, and you're too tall to sleep on that small-ass couch." A deep crease forms between his brows. "Did Rosa bunk in the living room?"

Oh, Christ. Is he really going there?

What's the right thing to say in this situation? "No, dude, she did *not* sleep on the couch, but I did give her at least six orgasms on it. Does that count?" Yeah...probably shouldn't go that route unless I'm in the mood to get punched again.

Shit.

I look him straight in the eye. "Ryan, I will answer that question if you really want me to, but trust me, *you don't*."

"Fucking hell," he mutters. "So, you're saying your relationship with my sister started because *you hooked up with her on a weekend when she was incredibly vulnerable?* Nice. Real standup move there, Logan."

He looks like he's about to throw down, but I probably do too after that bullshit accusation.

"Fuck you, Ry." I pinch the bridge of my nose and take a deep breath. "My relationship with Rosie didn't start in Tahoe. It started on *the day we met*. When I look back, there were so many defining moments between us. If I hadn't been such a chickenshit, we'd probably be married by now. Maybe even have a kid or two."

I look up, my voice steady. "Yeah, I've dated other women, but Rosie's the only one I've ever loved. I've been in love with her since we were kids, and I never stopped. How many times do I have to tell you that before you believe me? So, when she gave me the green light to take things to the next level? You're damn right I took it. And I'm not gonna apologize for that or let anyone accuse me of taking advantage of her—which, by the way, this is the second time you've done that now. Rosie is *everything* to me. She has been for a long fucking time."

Ryan exhales through his nose, clenching his jaw. Then he picks up his drink, downs it in one long gulp, and mutters, "Motherfucker."

I scratch the side of my head. "Motherfucker...*I don't know what to say to that without looking like a complete asshole?*"

"Exactly." He scrubs a hand down his face.

I give him a minute to see if he wants to elaborate.

He sighs, setting his glass on the table. "I know you love her, Logan, and that you'd never take advantage of her. I don't know why I keep saying stupid shit when I'm pissed. I guess..." Ryan gestures between us. "Maybe it's because I can't stop asking myself why you couldn't trust me with the truth? I understand why you'd want to keep your relationship private from the general public, but we're *family*, man. I wouldn't have gotten so fired up if you'd just talked to me."

"Seriously? History does not agree with you there, bud."

I arch a brow. "Ryan, I literally cannot tell you how many times I've tried talking to you over the years about pursuing Rosie. Every single time I even *hinted* at the subject you shot me down. And I know I don't need to remind you about how you reacted when you saw me kissing her on New Year's Eve. Clearly, you're still holding onto some feelings about that, considering you recently threw it in my face."

"I wouldn't exactly call them *feelings*," he mutters.

"Well..." I wave him off. "That night, my teenage dream of making Rosie mine went up in smoke, but not because I didn't want her. After seeing how strongly you reacted when I finally did make a move, I backed off. Then with me being away at Stanford and the whole Flingr whirlwind...by the time things started settling down, your sister was swimming in the deep end of the dating pool." I shrug, as if it was no big deal, but it really fucking bothered me. "I kept waiting for the timing to be right, but the odds of that happening kept getting worse. And then she got engaged, so..."

Ryan doesn't say anything at first. Just sits there, tracing his finger along the rim of his glass.

"I didn't know that," he says eventually. "After everything took off..." His lips curve into a crooked smile. "You were partying, traveling, always had a gorgeous fucking woman on your arm. Hell, I was there for a lot of it, and it definitely seemed like you were living the dream, man."

I huff out a humorless laugh. "Not everything is as it seems, Ry."

He searches my eyes. "I'm your best friend. If you were so miserable, why didn't you tell me?"

"What would be the point?" I shrug. "I didn't want to bring everyone around me down. I knew what my problem was. I was *pining*. But the one person I wanted wasn't available, so I kept chugging along, going out, and pretending everything was great. It just got to the point where I couldn't fake the social shit anymore, which is why I defaulted back to my high-school-hermit setting."

"Shit, you really were the biggest fucking hermit in high school," he teases.

"Oh, fuck off." I flip him off. "But just so you know, I wasn't miserable. I love work, the people at the office, hanging with you, your family. I had plenty of joy in my life before Rosie and I got together. But now that I have her... she's everything I've been missing, man."

He nods once, and for the first time since our rift began, the heaviness in his eyes fades a bit.

"I've been a dick," he says.

"Yep," I agree because the man did say he wanted honesty, right?

Ryan smirks. "But you get where I'm coming from, don't you?"

"Yeah." I nod. "I do."

There's a pregnant pause before Ryan lifts his glass in a toast.

"I really am happy for you, Logan. For both of you. Just...promise me you'll take care of Rosa, okay?"

I clink my glass against his. "Of course."

We slip into a comfortable silence, nursing our drinks, listening to the pianist play moody covers. Right when I'm about to excuse myself to go check in with Rosie, Ryan straightens in his seat, suddenly alert.

"What's going on?" I ask.

"Corner barstool. Blonde in the red dress."

I follow his gaze and spot a woman at the bar who fits the description. I'm a little surprised she's the one who's caught his eye, to be honest. Don't get me wrong...she's a total smoke show. Curves in all the right places, an air of effortless sophistication, and enough confidence to command an empire.

But Ryan usually goes for the chill, boho-beachy types. This one looks like she could eat him for breakfast without smudging her bright red lipstick, then run a Fortune 500 board meeting right after.

"You gonna go for it? What happened to Penny?"

"Penny went back to her ex." His shoulders lift, eyes never leaving the beautiful blonde. "God, she's fucking stunning. You think I should go talk to her?"

"Why the hell not? We're in Vegas. Shoot your shot, Casanova. I'm going to head back to my room and call Rosie anyway. I'll just order some room service for dinner."

Ryan grins, finishes his drink, and stands. "Wish me luck, buddy."

"Good luck," I say, already pulling out my phone. "Don't do anything stupid like get married."

He flips me off over his shoulder as he makes his way over to the blonde. I laugh, watching his approach as I head toward the exit. Ryan is in full flirt mode, which she seems to appreciate if I'm reading her body language correctly.

I have a feeling Ry's about to have himself a real wild night.

CHAPTER THIRTY-FIVE
ROSALIE

My phone lights up with an incoming FaceTime call, and I grab it so quickly, I accidentally press the red button, denying the call.

"Dammit!"

I've been waiting for Logan to call me all night to tell me how his meeting went. I dial him back, and he answers right away.

"Accidentally hang up on me again?" he asks.

"Yes," I grumble, sitting up in bed.

Logan's warm chuckle rumbles through the line. "Ah, Pip, you never fail to make me smile."

Now I'm smiling.

His hazel eyes are twinkly, his tie is hanging loosely around his neck, and his hair is mussed, like he's been running his hands through it. I can tell he's had a long day, but he still looks so freaking good, it's unfair.

"God, I wish I was in that bed with you," he says.

"Me too. If you were here, I could be showing you how proud and happy I am for you. With my mouth." I poke my cheek with my tongue to demonstrate.

He groans. "Don't say things like that. I have to drop in at the satellite office in the morning. I'm so fucking tempted to charter another jet to fly me back there tonight and bring me back in the morning."

I snort. "Logan, that is an egregious waste of money. I have no idea how much a chartered jet costs, but I know it's not cheap. I mean, I know I've got skills, but I don't think they're 'paying for a private jet' kind of skills."

His lips quirk up in the corner. "Baby, I disagree. Your blowjobs are fucking priceless."

I roll my eyes. "I'll make you a deal. You tell me all about how your presentation went, and when you're done…" I slide the hoodie I'm wearing—which just happens to be his—off my shoulder, to show him what I'm wearing underneath. "We can have some FaceTime sex."

"You're killing me, Pip." Logan bites his knuckles. "Show me what else you're wearing."

"Can't," I say simply. "Not wearing anything else."

"Jesus," he mutters, removing his tie and unbuttoning his shirt.

"Presentation, Logan," I remind him, lowering the zipper slightly to entice him. "The sooner you give me all the details on how awesome you guys were, the sooner we can get to the orgasms."

Logan sent me a quick text after they finished their meeting, but he was heading out to celebrate with my brother, so I haven't had a chance to talk with him until now. I am so freaking proud of him, and I want to hear how it went before we get too distracted by the sexy stuff.

"You always know just what to say to get me to bend to your will, Rosie."

I chuckle, listening intently as he tells me about how smoothly my brother opened the meeting. How

Jared took over the middle, and how Logan came in at the end to close the deal. As if that didn't already make this day the best ever, Logan and my brother finally had their little heart-to-heart afterward. Their bestie status is officially reinstated, which is a huge relief for both of us.

"I'm so proud of you," I tell him with a smile. "And not just because you closed this deal. You deserve every success you've had and every bit of good fortune. I mean it, Logan. I've never known someone who's more driven or dedicated than you are. At work. In life.

"On top of that, you somehow balance it all in a way that doesn't compromise who you are or prevent you from spending quality time with the people who matter to you. Do you know how rare that is? I seriously don't know how you manage it, but I'm so, so lucky to be a part of it."

I dab at my watery eyes. "God, look at me. I promised you phone sex, but I'm over here giving a lecture on emotional intimacy. Why do you always make me emote? There's another one of your special talents. Not just anyone can do that, you know."

I let out a shaky laugh.

"Rosie, look at me."

Logan's voice is trembling, and when I lift my gaze, I see why. His eyes are glassy, the green in them more vivid than ever.

I nibble my lower lip, waiting for him to continue.

"*I'm* the lucky one," he insists. "I didn't think it was possible to love you more, but you just proved me wrong. I really fucking wish we were having this conversation in person right now so I could show you how much." His gaze drops to my lips. "Jesus, Pip. The things I want to do to that mouth."

"Aaaaannnnd we've just turned the corner from sappy to horny, ladies and gentlemen."

Yes, we have, my clenching vagina agrees.

Logan laughs. "Oh yeah? Prove it."

"Why, sir! However would I do that?" My voice is overly dramatic and slightly scandalized because I'm ridiculous like that.

He shakes his head. "Set the phone on your nightstand, facing the bed. I want to see all of you."

Ooh, he's bringing out the bossy tone that make my nipples take notice.

I set my phone on the magnetic charging stand, positioning it just right so the camera can see most of my bed. While I was doing that, Logan lost his shirt and tie, putting his glorious chest and abs on display for my viewing pleasure.

"Now what?"

"Scoot back, take off the hoodie, and spread your legs. I want to see how wet you are already, from thinking about getting off with me."

"Oh, god," I whisper.

Logan groans as I pull the zipper down and his hoodie falls off my shoulders revealing my breasts. There's an awkward moment where the sleeve gets stuck on my ACE bandage, but he doesn't seem to notice because as I'm pulling it off, he seems hypnotized by the bouncing of my boobs. I prop myself up with some pillows, lying diagonally across the mattress so he can see me better.

"Show me how much you want this, Pip. Spread your legs and dip two fingers inside. I want to see how wet and shiny they are when they come out."

Damn, he's so dirty.

I spread my legs, moaning as I glide two fingers inside as

he instructed. When I pull them out and hold them up to the camera, they glisten under the lighting, coated with my arousal.

"Fuck, that's so hot." His voice is gravelly now, like he barely has a leash on his control. "I want to watch you rub that pretty little clit, like you're getting yourself ready to take my cock. But do it nice and slow. Tease yourself, baby."

I moan as I begin a slow rotation. "I love your filthy mouth so, so much."

"I'm just getting started, baby."

I glance at the screen, seeing his eyes darken, locked on my every move. "I want to see you, Logan. I need to watch you, too."

His lips curve into a grin as he adjusts his screen. The angle isn't perfect, but I can now see him from his head down to mid-thigh, which gives me all the good stuff. Logan unbuckles his belt, lowers his slacks and boxers, pushing them down his legs until they're out of sight. His thick cock is fully erect as he wraps his fist around it, groaning as he slides down from root to tip.

"Is this what you wanted, Rosie?"

"God, yes!" I shout as I rub myself faster, lost in the moment.

"Ease up, Rosie," he commands. "Nice and slow, remember." When I do as he says, he adds, "Good girl."

Why is that so hot? I used to think it was condescending to say that to a grown woman, but with Logan, man, it just does it for me.

"Logan, I need more." I'm panting, lifting my hips slightly. "Please."

"Grab the silicone dildo. The thick one. And the bullet."

Yaaasss, girl, my vagina cheers.

I scramble to grab my new favorite toy out of the night-stand drawer, along with the mini vibe, and resume my position. I'm so wet, no lube is necessary. Since my left hand is mostly out of commission, I carefully use it to hold the mini vibrator over my clit and switch it on to a lightly pulsing beat, while my right hand works the dildo inside of me.

"Rosie, you are my every fantasy come true, you know that? Look at you. You're a fucking goddess."

"Oh, god, Logan, it's not you, but it's such a good substitute." My eyes roll back as pleasure zings down my spine.

"That's it, baby. Keep fucking yourself, just the way you like it."

The muscles on his arm flex as he strokes himself, and his breath shudders every time he reaches the head, twisting his fist before working it back down again.

"Fuck, I wish I could taste you. My tongue would be all over that pretty pussy, licking and sucking until you were screaming my name. And then I would kiss you, so you could see how fucking incredible you taste, and so I could keep tasting you as my cock reminds you who's going to be railing you for the rest of your life."

"Logan, I'm so close," I pant. "I want you to come with me. Can you get there?"

"Yeah, baby, I can get there." He strokes faster. "When I get home, I want you to be waiting for me in my apartment. Do you think you can do that?"

"I can do that," I agree, moaning like a porn star as I pick up the pace.

"First, I want you on your knees, and I'm going to fuck that sassy mouth of yours until I come down your throat."

I whimper and my toes curl. "I'm good with that."

"Then I'm going to bend you over my kitchen counter, eat your delicious cunt from behind, and then fuck you like an animal until you can't walk before I come all over your perfect ass."

"Holy hell..." My back arches as the first sign of my orgasm builds.

"Then I'm going to clean you up and make love to you in the bedroom until we can't stay awake any longer. The following morning, you're going to sit on my face so I can eat *you* for breakfast, and then I'm going to cook you whatever food you're in the mood for."

"You know I won't say no to food." I gasp. "Or face-sitting for that matter. Almost there... God, Logan."

"I'm right there with you, baby. Let it go."

My body tenses, my legs shake, and I scream Logan's name as a wildly intense orgasm rips through me. At the same time, he groans my name like a prayer as long jets of cum shoot onto his stomach. I switch off the vibe, letting it roll to the side, and gently remove the dildo from my body. We both lie there panting, catching our breath as we watch each other through the screen.

"Jesus, Pip." Logan's lips curve into a dopey smile as he wipes himself off with his discarded shirt. "I'm fucking wrecked."

"Same." I laugh, turning to my side. "We should probably get some sleep, huh?"

"Yeah, you're probably right." His smile softens. "I love you, Rosie. Always."

"Love you." I yawn as my eyes flutter shut. "Stay with me, okay?"

He shifts in bed until he's lying down like I am. "I'm not going anywhere. Sweet dreams, baby."

The last thing I see before drifting off is his sleepy face, watching me through the screen. We might be hundreds of miles apart, but in this moment, with his voice in my ear and that look in his eyes, I've never felt closer to him.

CHAPTER THIRTY-SIX
LOGAN

It's been almost two months since we closed the Olympus deal and life has been good. Not because of the money or the positive press—although that *has* been nice—but mostly because of how content I've been. Happy.

Really fucking happy.

Settled in a way I never knew was possible.

And I owe it all to the woman who's been snoring on my couch for the last few hours, although she'd totally deny the snoring part if I ever called her on it.

I glance toward the living room, where Rosie is napping, one bare leg exposed from beneath the fuzzy blanket that's draped over her. She came over straight from visiting her cousin, unzipped her shorts, did some Houdini thing where she removed her bra without taking off her top, dropped them both right where she was standing, and crawled onto the couch. Her lingerie and shorts are now neatly folded on my dresser, while a barely-dressed Rosie snoozes away.

I smile as I watch her, taking in the rare sight of Rosalie Morales at rest in the middle of the day. She's always moving, buzzing around with her signature energy. I don't think she knows what to do with herself if she's not juggling twenty different things at once. It's just how she rolls. Some people might think it's chaotic—and if I'm being real, Rosie *is* chaotic—but the way her brain processes so much stimuli at once is fucking beautiful to me. It's kind of like a super-power. I know she's had her challenges over the years, but the more educated the world becomes on neurodivergence, the more space there is for her to be herself. If you ask me, it takes someone truly special to thrive in an environment where you're constantly jumping over hurdles.

The scent of tomatoes and garlic mingles with the light breeze drifting in through the open windows. I stir the sauce and glance toward the hallway, my nerves kicking in about the surprise waiting in the bedroom. I'm not sure why. I'm confident in Rosie's commitment to me. I'm almost positive she'll say yes. But the slim probability that she'll say no is nagging at me because it'd crush me. I'd understand if she thought it was too soon, but it'd still hurt.

Rosie groans, drawing my eyes back to her as she stretches, arms overhead and spine arching off the couch. Her top rides up, exposing the smooth curve of her stomach and two very erect nipples pressing against the fabric.

Christ.

"How long have I been asleep?" she mumbles.

My brain stalls because I'm staring at her chest like a teenage idiot.

"Logan?"

"Hmm?"

"How long was I sleeping?" Rosie sits up, looking around. "And where are my shorts?"

Shit.

I never thought my tidiness would work against me, but here we are.

"Uh...they're in the bedroom. I'll grab 'em."

"I can get—"

I'm already in the hallway before she can finish her sentence. "Nope. I'm good."

I grab the shorts and hustle back to the living room. She gives me her *What the hell is wrong with you?* look so I take a breath and casually toss her shorts on the couch and make my way back to the kitchen.

"Thanks," Rosie mutters.

There's some shuffling as she slips them on before padding barefoot—still braless—over to the kitchen to join me.

"That smells amazing." Rosie comes up beside me, leaning against the counter. "Whatcha making?"

"Keeping it simple. Spaghetti, garlic bread, salad." My eyes dart down to her nipples again.

Why the fuck am I acting like I've never seen a pair of breasts before?

She follows my gaze, smirking when she sees what I'm looking at. "Perv."

I shrug. "In my defense, you're braless and wearing a thin-as-fuck white T-shirt with pierced nipples. My eyes are going to naturally be drawn to them. Plus, you have a really great rack, and I never claimed to be a saint."

She laughs. "Oh, I'm *well aware* you're not a saint. For which I am quite grateful. Also...my rack thanks you for the compliment."

I grab her by the hip, pulling her in for a quick kiss. "Your rack can thank me more thoroughly later if you're up for it. But first...you're on salad duty." I give her a little nudge and a light smack on the ass. "Get to it, woman."

She pulls open the fridge, making a show out of bending forward as she digs through the crisper.

I damn near drop the spoon as I'm taste-testing the sauce.

"We need music." She scrolls through her phone, selecting a playlist before connecting it to the apartment's built-in sound system. "Look at us playing house."

Damn, if she only knew how close she is to the mark.

"You know I'm game for a little role play, baby. All you need to do is ask."

Say yes, and we won't be *playing* anymore.

Rosie bumps her hip into mine as she reaches over to grab a cutting board. "Always making it dirty."

I set the sauce on the warmer, grab a large pot, and fill it with water.

"Which you just admitted you love," I remind her.

Her full lips curve into a knowing grin. "Yes, I did."

We fall into an easy rhythm after that, Rosie putting together a garden salad while I boil the pasta, trying—and mostly failing—to not get distracted by the way her hips sway instinctively to the beat.

We eat on the terrace, like we have been every Saturday lately, talking, laughing...kissing. When the kissing becomes heated, I know I need to hit the brakes before I get distracted and ruin my surprise.

"Hey," I say, pulling back slightly and brushing my thumb along her jaw, "there's something I want to show you."

She raises an eyebrow. "Does it start with a D and end with a K?"

I chuckle, pressing a kiss to the corner of her mouth. "No. But I can show you that later." I stand and tug her up with me, interlacing our fingers. "Come back downstairs with me."

Rosie's still half-smiling as we head inside, probably

from whatever smartass remark she's holding on to, but there's curiosity in her eyes now.

When we reach the bedroom door, I pause.

"Okay, close your eyes." My hand tightens around hers.

"You'd better not let me trip over anything."

I place my hands on her shoulders. "I've got you, Pip."

She sighs dramatically but closes her eyes anyway.

I push the door open and guide her inside, careful to leave a wide gap away from any hazards.

"Okay," I say softly. "You can look now."

She blinks her eyes open. "Um...what am I looking at? I mean, besides your bedroom."

I step beside her, nodding toward the new chaise lounge. "That."

Rosie's gaze sweeps over the curved tufted chair in the corner of the room. It's teal velvet, the boldest piece in the room, so it sticks out like a sore thumb. If I have my way, there will be more color in here soon enough to offset it though.

"It's pretty." Rosie steps forward, trailing her finger over the top edge. "This is what you wanted to show me? A new piece of furniture?"

"Yeah." I nod. "Because I got it for you."

Her brows knit together in confusion. "For me? Why?"

Here goes...

I clear my throat. "Well...I figured it'd hold quite a bit of laundry. You know...if you weren't in the mood to put it away after pulling it out of the dryer?" I rub the back of my neck. "I'd say you've got room for at least three or four loads on there, maybe more."

She stares at the chaise for a moment, then to me, then back at the chair, then back to me. "You bought me a laundry chair?"

"Yeah. I did."

"Because..." she prompts.

I exhale. "Because I want you to move in with me, Rosie."

Her eyes widen.

"I know it's fast," I continue. "And if you're not ready, that's okay. But we're together practically every night, and we both have our stuff at each other's places. I figured why keep doing the back and forth when I know I want you in my bed *every* night, and I want to wake up with you every morning? I know change is hard for you, but—"

"Change isn't *that* hard for me," she argues.

"Rosie, you enjoy change about as much as a housecat," I deadpan. "But this is you and me we're talking about. Is changing your address really that big of a shake up?"

"Ooh! Can we get a cat?" she asks. "I haven't had a kitty since Mr. Meowgi moved onto greener pastures."

I grin, remembering the striped cat she had growing up. That little guy hissed at Ryan all the time, but he adored Rosie and followed her everywhere.

"Rosie, if you move in with me, we can get ten cats for all I care."

"Well that's a bit excessive." She rolls her eyes. "But I'm good with one or two."

"So...is that a yes?"

She launches herself at me, arms around my neck. "Of course it is. I can't believe you even thought there was a chance I'd say no."

I hold her tight, burying my face in her hair. "You have no idea how happy that makes me."

"I think I have *some* idea," she murmurs against my neck. "I mean, you have a *really* great showerhead. Plus, having your dick on demand isn't so bad either."

I lift her off the ground, laughing. "What's mine is yours, baby."

She grins, eyes sparkling. "Flying to Tahoe that weekend is the second-best decision I've ever made."

I lift a brow. "What's the first?"

Rosie smiles. "Taking a chance on us."

And as I kiss her again, the twinkling Los Angeles skyline serving as our backdrop, I echo the sentiment in my mind. It may have taken us fifteen years to get here, but with the way everything's worked out, I wouldn't have changed a thing. What matters most is the incredible woman in my arms is right where she belongs.

With me.

Forever.

EPILOGUE
ROSALIE

Fat snowflakes fall from the night sky, coating the deck in a fresh layer of powder as Logan and I step outside. The cold air nips at my skin, but I'm too distracted by the incredible view before me to care. The moon is full, reflecting on the still water below. In the distance, fireworks launch into the sky from one of the ski resorts, exploding in an array of colors as Lake Tahoe rings in the new year.

Logan wraps his arms around me, pulling me into his warmth as we watch the show. "Happy New Year, Rosie."

I sigh. "Happy New Year."

"Big things on the horizon. You ready to take on the new job when we get back?"

"I am." I nod against his chest. "I'm excited to get started."

Jett Ashford's rebranding campaign went better than any of us expected. After that, Avery started pulling me into meetings with other clients who were struggling with their image. A few weeks ago, she told me Maxwell & Company was opening a new Brand Strategist position and asked if I'd be interested in filling it.

"I'm proud of you," Logan murmurs, rubbing slow circles on my back. "You just keep kicking ass and taking names."

I smile. "Damn right I do."

He pulls back just enough to meet my eyes. "Hey, do you know what today is?"

I frown. "Is that a trick question?"

He chuckles, pressing a kiss to my forehead. "No. Obviously, you know the date on the calendar. But there's another reason this particular day is special."

I think about it for a moment, completely stumped.

"I've got nothin'."

Logan's lips quirk. "Exactly ten years ago today, at almost this exact time, I finally had the nerve to kiss the girl of my dreams for the first time. It was a kiss I'll never forget."

I grin, thinking about that night. I hadn't made the connection until now that it's sort of an anniversary of ours.

"Is it because that's the first time you felt my boobs?"

"Well, yes, that too." He laughs. "But more so because before your brother interrupted us, I remember thinking to myself that I'd be perfectly happy kissing your lips for the rest of my life. And now..." He lowers himself to one knee.

My breath catches as my brain pieces everything together. "Logan..."

He gives me a crooked smile as he opens his palm, revealing a ring box with a delicate oval-cut solitaire set in a thin gold band that catches the moonlight.

"Rosalie Elena Morales, I have loved you for so long, I honestly don't remember what it feels like to not love you. But over the last ten months, that love has grown into something so monumental, most days, it feels like my chest is going to burst because you make my heart so full. You are my best friend, my living dream, my *entire world*. And if you'll do me the honor, I will spend the rest of my life proving it to you."

He takes his gloves off, pulls the ring out of the box and holds it up toward me. "Marry me, Pip."

My cheeks hurt from smiling so hard as a tear rolls down my face. "Was there a question mark at the end of that, or...? Cause I've gotta be honest, I'm a little unclear."

Logan's chest rumbles with silent laughter as he shakes his head. "Only you, Rosie. Only you."

I peel off my gloves and decide to stop torturing the poor man. "Of course I'll marry you. Gimme the ring."

His eyes sparkle with amusement as he slides the ring on my finger.

As cool as I'm trying to play it, my hand trembles as he does it, which does not go unnoticed. Logan sees me like no one else ever has. He knows I hate drawing attention when I'm anxious, so he just gives my hand a reassuring squeeze, which instantly soothes my nerves.

The second the ring is in place, I tackle him, taking us both to the ground. We're only wearing parkas, so we probably shouldn't be rolling around in the snow, but neither one of us cares as we make out under the glow of the moon.

Logan pulls back just enough to cup my face, brushing his nose against mine. "I love you, Pip."

I grin, leaning into the bunny kisses. "I love you. Now take me inside before we get frostbite. And we should probably have some kind of dirty celebration since you put a ring on it."

I belt out a surprised laugh as Logan abruptly stands with me in his arms, running toward the cabin. "Baby, we've got a lifetime of dirty celebrations ahead of us."

I smile.
Bring it on, Edwards.

If you'd like to be one of the first to know about new releases or sales, scan the QR code below to sign up for Laura's newsletter:

ABOUT THE AUTHOR

Laura Lee is the *USA Today* bestselling author of sexy and seductive romances, best known for the Windsor Academy and Bedding the Billionaire series.

She won her first writing contest at the ripe old age of nine, earning a trip to the state capital to showcase her manuscript. Thankfully, those early works are locked away where they belong—never to see the light of day again. These days, Laura lives in the Pacific Northwest with her wonderfully tolerant husband, two beautiful children, and a crew of ridiculously spoiled cats.

When she's not chauffeuring kids, writing, or binge-watching HGTV, you'll likely find her with her nose in a spicy romance and an iced matcha by her side. Always on the hunt for her next book boyfriend, Laura loves connecting with fellow romance lovers.

For more information about the author, check out her website at: www.LauraLeeBooks.com

You can also find her "working" on social media quite frequently.

Facebook: @LauraLeeBooks1
Instagram: @LauraLeeBooks
Reader's Group: @Laura Lee's Lounge
TikTok: @AuthorLauraLee

ACKNOWLEDGMENTS

It's been a hot minute since I've made it all the way to the end of a book and had to write these, so bear with me. I've been pretty open about struggling to find my muse after battling one of the toughest things I've ever gone through in my personal life. I had six unfinished books sitting on my computer (yes, SIX) before someone I've known in the book world for years approached me, asking me to join a promotion she was hosting with several other authors.

Rosie and Logan's story was originally supposed to be a quick and easy novella. The deadline was far enough away that the pressure was minimal, so I figured—what better way to challenge myself? My personal life was finally stabilizing a bit, and I was determined to find my writing mojo again. So I joined the promotion and immediately started plotting *Billionaire Bachelor*. Little did I know how deeply I would fall for these characters—how much more story I had to tell. The words wouldn't stop flowing, and before I knew it, a 20,000-word novella that ended on a "happy for now" note became the 93,000-word novel you just finished reading.

So, first and foremost, thank you to Tracey for inviting me to that promo. I'm not sure this book would've ever made it into the world without you.

To my "hot mess sister from another mister," Michaela: There are not enough thank-yous in existence for everything you've done for me, but for this book, I'll specifically thank you for allowing me to blend your neurodivergent quirks with mine and plant them into Rosie's character. She wouldn't be the same without you—and neither would I.

To my chat gals: Cora, Holly, Julia, Alley, Sara, Penelope, Greer, Ranch, Amanda, and Rachel — thank you for being my sounding board, my cheerleaders, and my unwavering support when I needed you. This business can be hard and lonely at times, but knowing we'll always have each other's backs—both personally and professionally— makes the hard days a little easier and the good days even better.

To my sensitivity reader, Ari: Thanks for making me snort-laugh continuously, nearly spit out my drink on numerous occasions, and smile so hard I had tears in my eyes. Your special brand of feedback is officially my new favorite.

To my Chaotic Creatives ladies: Britt, Ari, and Suzanne — thanks for ensuring my socials don't fade into oblivion. We all know they would've done so a long time ago if I were still in charge.

To my editor, Ellie: Thank you for once again squeezing me into your busy schedule and getting the finished product back to me on ridiculously short notice.

To my husband and kiddos: Thank you for understanding why I needed to lock myself away in my office day and night—and for not running away when I'd occasionally surface looking like a zombie.

To the best writing buddy I could've ever asked for, Maverick: Every fictional cat I've ever written has been in your image. I even gave one of them your name. You were there from the beginning, and since this is the last book we will have ever written together, I'd be remiss not to thank you for the last thirteen amazing years. Writing will never be the same without you by my side. You were truly one of a kind and will forever own a piece of my heart.

Last but never least, to my readers: Whether this is the first book of mine you've picked up or you've been with me since the beginning, thank you for taking the time to read my words. You're the reason I get to do what I love for a living, and I am eternally grateful. If you've been with me for a while, thank you for your patience and understanding while I was struggling. I hope Rosie and Logan's story was worth the wait. 🤍

www.ingramcontent.com/pod-product-compliance
Lightning Source LLC
Chambersburg PA
CBHW070234200726
48293CB00005B/1607